ONCE UPON A TIME IN THE
TWENTY-FIRST CENTURY

ONCE UPON A TIME IN THE TWENTY-FIRST CENTURY

UNEXPECTED EXERCISES IN CREATIVE WRITING

Edited by Robin Behn

THE UNIVERSITY OF ALABAMA PRESS
Tuscaloosa

IN ASSOCIATION WITH
GEORGE F. THOMPSON PUBLISHING

The University of Alabama Press
Tuscaloosa, Alabama 35487-0380
uapress.ua.edu

Inquiries about reproducing material from this work should be addressed to the University of Alabama Press.

Typeface: Scala Pro / Scala Sans Pro
Cover design: David Nees

Cataloging-in-Publication data is available from the Library of Congress.
ISBN: 978-0-8173-5942-3
E-ISBN: 978-0-8173-9232-1

In memory of Robert Behn, English teacher extraordinaire.

CONTENTS

Quick Found-Language Sonnets

Recycle language into fourteen-line poems.
Molly Goldman, Kenny Kruse, and Sally Rodgers

Social Network Haiku

Update the haiku form by writing away messages and Facebook haiku.
Chapin Gray and Kirk Pinho

Rhymes Real Cool: Studies in Rap Lyrics

Tap some rhymes to use in rap.
Christopher McCarter

Oral Poetry: The Physical Landscape of Your Poetic Voice

Tones, tempos, and timbres—shape your poem with your voice.
Curtis Rutherford

Collaborative Ghazal

Explore this mesmerizing Arabic form and write one with a group or on your own.
Chapin Gray and Kirk Pinho

Collaborative Abecedarian (For Up to Twenty-Six Writers)

Fall in love with the alphabet all over again and use it to organize and inspire a poem.
Sally Rodgers

The Triolet

A French poetic form full of rhymes and repetition.
Pia Simone Garber

Oh, Ode!

Swoon! Celebrate! Write an ode and then try an Exquisite Corpse ode as a group.
Leia Wilson

Sestinas: Six Words, Obsessed!

Learn the basic sestina form, "cheat" your way to an abridged sestina, write a giant sestina, and take the Ode-Sestina Challenge.
Chapin Gray, Jenny Gropp, and Kirk Pinho

Nonce, Not Nonsense: Poetry Meets the Future

Work with the "Century" and the "Portion," and then create your own unique poetry form.
Jenny Gropp and Emma Sovich

ACKNOWLEDGMENTS

HEARTFELT THANKS TO THE MFA students who have taught in the Creative Writing Club at the University of Alabama over the years. Your originality, your daring, your collaborative spirit, your zaniness, your dedication, your insight, your generosity, your hard work—it's all captured here in these exercises. And an equally heartfelt thanks to all the young writers who have been part of the Creative Writing Club. You made us want to do this. You constantly wowed us with your writing. You were nonstop fun every single week. Thanks, too, to the teachers, chairs, librarians, staff, and principals who helped us spread the word.

This book would not have come together without a lot of help. Jenny Gropp's long-term dedication to this project is worth special mention. Each stage of this project benefitted from her keen insight, positive energy, and editorial excellence. In addition, Kit Emslie handled complex details with perseverance and utter professionalism; Luke Percy carried out correspondence with aplomb; and Nabila Lovelace completed the formatting with agility. To each of them, abiding thanks!

The Creative Writing Club began with the support of Dean Robert F. Olin of the College of Arts and Sciences, and he continues to be our champion. The publication of this volume would not have been possible without his support and that of the College of Arts and Sciences at the University of Alabama. The English Department and Program in Creative Writing have been steadfast supporters. George Thompson of George F. Thompson Publishing has been the wisest of advisors at every stage of the process—this book is much better for his influence. Finally, all hail the University of Alabama Press! It has been a privilege and a pleasure to work with Daniel Waterman, editor extraordinaire, who believed in this project from the beginning, and Claire Lewis Evans and Kristen Hop, who have offered expert insight and attention to detail.

Introduction

THIS BOOK IS A COLLECTION of ways to get started, or to keep going, in the art of creative writing. The twenty-six letters of the alphabet, at this very moment as you are reading, are arranging themselves into this invitation to you. The letters have been a little lonely waiting for you to read them here. Thank you for releasing them with your shimmering reader's brain!

Now that they have your attention, they would like to tell you a little something about what they have in store for you and how you can use them. They know you have met before. The letters are indeed honored to have been everywhere from your first-grade primer, your recipe collection, and your online news (but, ah, they do miss the feel of the columns and the actual pulp of the newspaper!), to your Facebook page, your texts, and your Tweets. They have even flowed or stuttered from your pen onto essay exams and been strewn through job applications and the Internal Revenue Code. But, today, they have in mind something even more wild for themselves. To start with, they would like to tell you how this book happened to them.

It all started some years ago in Tuscaloosa, Alabama. The letters think it is quite amazing that they come from where all the vowels are *As*—A-l-a-b-a-m-a—like someone put a tongue depressor on them and said, "*Say 'Aaaaaa . . .',*" and they did.

And then someone said, "Ok, make a word out of that."

And they said, "We need a few consonants for a word."

And someone said, "Ok, you can have just *three* consonants."

And then the letters said, "*Alabama!*"

And someone said, "You did it!"

And the letters said, "Of course we did, for we were both the *someone talking* and *the words who answered*, because the whole entire thing is made out of *us*."

And someone said, "That is a very long, ungrammatical sentence, you know."

And the letters said, "Why thank you! We enjoyed it very much. And we are going to keep acting however we please, especially if it pleases a reader, too. And we are going to tell you a story about letters and words and Alabama and this book, so how about if we start with 'once upon a time'? Okay?"

And someone said, "Okay!"

Once upon a time, there were about a hundred students at a school in Tuscaloosa called the Capitol School. The teachers there cared very much about letters and words, and the students were learning to read and do-ing "school writing"—that is, writing sentences and paragraphs, descrip-tions and reports, summaries and essays. Lots of attention was being paid to punctuation and grammar, spelling tests and book reports—well, you get the idea. Then some parents who happened to be graduate stu-dents and a faculty member in the Creative Writing Program at the Uni-versity of Alabama, which was just down the block, got together to see what they could do to make writing at the school a little wilder. Happily, the school said, "Sure, come on over." So the writer-parents came over to try out some new creative writing adventures. It was a lot of fun for both the teachers and the students. After that, the writer-parents came over for a whole semester in which they "took over" the whole school, with ev-ery class writing to every other class as if they were different characters and towns in a giant county. So that was a great start to letting the letters A–Z have their own way and words become art. In our case, it began hap-pening in Alabama because that is our home state, but anyone can let the letters loose, and they can become art in any state or country, any "real" or virtual place.

Now, Alabama is a land of catfish and hushpuppies. A land of sacred football and secret footfalls through moonlit loblolly pines. It's a state of great beauty and geological diversity. It is also a land of religion, fried ice cream, mascara, engines swinging from trees, and more species of fresh-water fish than anywhere else in the USA. Why should't writing be just as diverse? The writer-parents wanted to offer a creative writing program to kids and young adults to make writing come alive, to make the alpha-bet fun again, to give everybody a chance to get up close and personal with language and fall in love with it and feel its joy and wield its power.

In 2004, the group of MFA writers who had been working at the Capi-tol School held a meeting in the Department of English at the University of Alabama to see who else might be interested in working on some sort of project with young people on behalf of letters. The meeting was held in a third-floor room that feels like a giant living room, with broken-down couches and not very comfortable chairs that can be moved around. The writers all drew the chairs into a circle. In those days there was a blackboard in the front; nowadays there is a whiteboard, a screen, and a computer that projects information from the Internet. But back then it was chalk. The writer-parent volunteers from the Capitol School told the MFA in creative writing graduate students about their project and got a conversation going about what to do next. Words flew around the room, and some of the words alighted on the blackboard. Then a vote was held, and this is what was talked about and what was decided.

It had been the experience of many of the graduate students in the room that writing was quite fun, at least some of the time, up until high school. They had some memories of the feel of the pencil in their hand, the thrill of figuring out how to write in cursive, the excitement of knowing the "haiku lady" was coming to visit the class, the mystique of writing letters from camp sealed with secret crushes and sealing wax, the creation of posters with fluorescent markers, the perfecting of one's signature, the time they got to write a story in response to a story in the class reader; but when they got to high school and then college, there was this tiny, insidious, silk-on-silk sound of a necktie being tied too tight around the throat from which the writing voice is trying to come out. Writing stopped being fluent. It stopped being creative. It stopped being fun. Instead, it became crucial, impossible, sometimes scary. Writing got all structured and serious—the thesis statement, the paragraph structure, the lab report, the term paper, the application essay, the standardized writing test. Writing became a matter of figuring out exactly what the teacher *wanted* you to write, in the way the teacher *wanted* you to write it, and in response to the exact assignment that the teacher or the textbook *wanted* you to complete. And, while you were at it, there had better be some complex, compound, confounding, confuddling types of sentences in the mix. And some commas where there are supposed to be commas, and no commas where there are not supposed to be commas. And certain things must go inside the parentheses, and certain things must be left out in the cold (outside the hug of the parentheses). And you had better cite your sources or else, or else #.#.#.# . . . Writing got exhausting. Writing, by the time of high school and college and beyond, became about trying to do it right. Writing was about using this proper voice, doing this proper thing in this proper way. And all of this was necessary, absolutely necessary, to graduate from high school and succeed in college, and graduate from college and go into the world of work where you would have to keep on writing exactly right. Writing was a hard job and you had to work hard at it and try never to make a mistake. Yes, the MFA students all said, in high school writing started to feel like that.

"I almost fell out of love with language," one of them said.

"I did fall out of love," another one said.

"But . . ." they all said. But I had my secret writing I did in my journal. But I loved to read sci-fi with a flashlight. But I wrote fanfiction about Harry Potter. But I had one teacher who asked me to show her my poems and she encouraged me to keep writing them. But I came across Allen Ginsberg in the public library. But when we read *Native Son* in class I wanted to write like Richard Wright. But I came across a poem by Edna St. Vincent Millay that made me weep. But I read something by Don DeLillo that rearranged the molecules of my brain, and I wanted to do to a reader what he had done to me.

These graduate students realized how lucky they were, and they shared the crucial experiences that had turned them on to the *art* and fun of writing, that made them want to engage with language as creative writers and as flexible, discerning, excited readers. They decided to create a group for young writers called the Creative Writing Club, a free weekly meeting after school when anyone could come to that very same living-room-sort-of-room they were sitting in and hang out with other young people who also were curious about writing. The idea was to mix together the graduate students in creative writing with slightly younger writers and make a place where writing could be fun, exploratory, and wild again—or for the first time. And the Creative Writing Club has been meeting on Wednesdays after school in the English Department at the University of Alabama ever since. We welcome any young writer who wants to come, and we have so much fun that we want to share our club with you. The letters insisted that we do this!

We start each meeting with a few ten-minute talks by local writers who tell us a bit about how they started out writing and read to us a little of their poetry, fiction, nonfiction, or whatever it is they are up to. And so, almost immediately, if you are in the Creative Writing Club, the CWC as we call it, you become aware that there are real, live, breathing human beings who are doing creative writing right now, in all sorts of various and unexpected ways, and you are invited to become one of these letter-creatures yourself. Then, we get down to writing or up to writing or across to writing or . . .

The graduate students and I looked around to find some good exercises and activities in creative writing to do during the Wednesday club. We knew there were a few books of creative writing exercises out there at the time, but all of them seemed to commit the sin that I once heard the poet William Matthews describe in conversation by saying, "Creative writing is not criticism in reverse!" In other words, according to Matthews, when we write creatively, we don't do "backward reading" or reverse construction of the thinking you might do in an English class when you are asked to analyze a story or a poem. In such a class, you might be asked to identify the theme of the poem or describe the character traits of the protagonist and show how they grow throughout the story or explain to your teacher the main point of an essay. But when we write creatively, we do not first decide what the theme, character traits, or "point" will be and then just plug those in, thinking like a critic or analyzer in reverse. The writer/teachers in the CWC all knew that. When they were writing creatively, their imaginations were working in much more exploratory, playful, and even chaotic ways. It felt like the letters were pulling them along, rather than the writers pushing the letters. And in the backs of the writers' minds, instead of a bunch of questions on a test, there were a host of contemporary and historical literary influences and models and a sense of belonging to a culture, right now, where the private and the public, the local and the global, the literary and the pop, and everything else were all whispering in their ears at the same time as they wrote.

So we set about inventing new creative writing exercises and adventures that encourage writers' imaginations to move the way writers' imaginations really move, while also introducing a host of literary influences that have fueled the development of the art form for many centuries and continue to do so right up to the present moment. We wanted to share what we, as writers, were excited about and what the writing process is really like. We didn't want to "dumb it down" to a few basics. We didn't want to suggest that creative writing is "criticism in reverse." We couldn't find any collections of exercises that were like that. And so, over the years, we made up our own exercises based on the myriad of passions and obsessions and approaches of the writers teaching in the CWC.

We use these exercises in the Creative Writing Club, and they result in awesome poems, plays, stories, paragraphs, lists, sketches, and other kinds of writing from everyone. These exercises work well for anyone of any age wanting to try creative writing, whether in a class, in some other group setting, or for individuals. The CWC holds a public reading and self-publishes an anthology of participants' creative writing at the end of each semester. At the reading we get all the adults and younger kids in the audience to do some of these exercises, and they all enjoy themselves. Our CWC teachers take these exercises into college-level creative writing classes at the University of Alabama, and their student-writers eat them up. These exercises are just too fun, effective, and enlightening to stay a secret any longer. And so we figured it was time to make them available to a larger audience through this book.

We took the very best of these exercises and wrote them down—we included the "how to" steps along with a discussion of how to approach the activity, what to keep in mind, and what it feels like to do the exercise. You'll find the voice of a particular creative writer talking to you in each of these exercises, sharing something that they are really interested in and showing you how to try it, too. We hope you will find a lot of invitations to letting the letters have their way with you. If you want to know whether you are "doing it right," the answer is always *yes*! We don't believe in labeling writing as "good" or "bad." What we do believe in is the act of writing—of letting yourself try something you haven't tried before. Sometimes someone asks us, "Am I a writer?" Our answer is: "A writer is someone who is writing." We hope these exercises will lead you to "write like a writer." It takes many different kinds of writing to make a world of writing, and we think you will find a huge variety of invitations here that lead you into that big world.

These are writing adventures, and like any true adventure, you can't know how it is going to turn out before you start. The letters don't know, either. So don't make a plan in advance. Just follow the steps and prompts, and see where they take you. You can do each exercise in order, working through the whole book. You can jump around and pick the exercises that appeal to you. Or, you can pick an exercise you like and do it over and over again, making different pieces of writing from the same activity, for as long as you like. You can get together with others in a class or set up your own writing club or group. Think of this book as a whole bunch of choices—candy store, dictionary, web links, field of wildflowers—you can pick whatever you like, whenever you want.

If you happen to be a teacher or just one of those people who likes doing things in an organized sort of way (the letters experience this thrillingly organized feeling sometimes when they line up in a very long word like LLANFAIRPWLLGWYNGYLLGOGERYCHWYRNDROBWLLL-LANTYSILIOGOGOGOCH, the name of a town in North Wales that means, roughly, "St. Mary's Church in the hollow of the white hazel near the rapid whirlpool of Llantysilio of the red cave"), you might want to go straight through this book from the beginning to the end. The book is organized into three parts. The first part, "Genres and Forms Galore," gives you a starting place for your writing: many choices of "forms." We touch on some types of writing you may have heard of, such as stories, sonnets, and haiku, and show you some very new ways to approach them. We add to that some already-invented literary forms you may not have come across yet, such as ghazals (when the letters say the word *ghazal*, they feel like they are all clearing their throats, all at once, which gets everyone's attention!), abecedarians, and odes, and provide intriguing and specific approaches to them. Finally, we show how you can adapt or invent structures for writing from unlikely places—job applications, recipes, travel guides, comics, flyers, alibis—and put these forms to work in unexpected ways for new purposes. You'll get a sense of how forms aren't something writers "fill in" because they have to, but rather, forms are energy-giving and ever-changing for writers, inviting participation in a long and growing literary tradition.

In the second part of the book, "Ye Olde Language Lets Loose," we offer lots of exercises that introduce you to starting places for your imagination, ranging from popular songs, unreadable foreign languages, and other writers' beginnings to truffles, "the horse in motion," and sheer sound. We also take you through new methods for developing and expanding your writing—swapping, erasing, splicing, combining, gleaning, obsessing, chasing hyperlinks, collaborating, interviewing, flipping, revamping, and more. You'll see what writers start with and how they keep on going.

Finally, in the third part of the book, "Slews of Styles and Subjects," we explore the many subjects that writers write about and the huge range of literary styles they employ. We draw from a host of master writers and writing movements—the Beats, Italo Calvino, Robert Frost, Franz Kafka, Jamaica Kincaid, Flannery O'Connor, Harryette Mullen (the letters love that she wrote a whole book called *Sleeping with the Dictionary*!), the Oulipo movement (the letters love "N+7," one of their dictionary games!), realism and non-realism, Gertrude Stein (she makes the letters feel hypnotized, which they like!), and Wallace Stevens, to name a few. We also touch on lots of subjects—love, death, inanimate objects, superheroes, animals, zombies, political rants, love songs, and many others.

We hope these exercises keep you warm on a cold night and cool on a hot night. We trust they'll keep you company and keep you writing. Go for it!

Sincerely,

abcdefghijklmnopqrstuvwxyz

"The gang of 26"

For the Creative Writing Club

p.s. Don't forget about us!!

!@#$%^&*()_+?><":{}|/,.

I

Genres and Forms Galore

This section offers a selection of ways to get started and develop your writing by using a broad array of genres and forms.

You might already be familiar with the idea of *genre*. You may have noticed that literature is often organized, studied, or anthologized in basic categories, such as poetry, fiction, creative nonfiction, and drama. Similarly, you may be familiar with some commonly practiced *forms* that writing takes within these genres, such as the sonnet as a form of poetry, the short story as a form of fiction, the lyric essay as a form of creative nonfiction, and the one-act play as a form of drama.

Our exercises are designed to explore, expand, and *explode* your sense of what is possible in genres and forms by giving you new writerly moves to make. We want you to experience what it is like for a writer to be "led on" by their approach to genres and forms—to have the sense that the type of writing you are choosing to do is itself leading you to put together words you wouldn't have thought to put together before. But don't worry! We won't tell you to just "go write a sonnet," or "go write a one-act play" and come back in ten minutes. We couldn't do that, either. The letters are curling up and blurring—or is that cursive writing?— thinking about how hard that would be. So, instead of just pushing you off in a general direction, we will give you very particular steps to take within each exercise.

Our *genres* go beyond what you might expect. We have some familiar genres such as poetry, stories, and novels, but we take each one in unexpected directions such as a Facebook haiku or a quick found-language sonnet, a short story mini tragedy, or a *Pillow Book*–inspired list to spur nonfiction. We also show you how modes of writing from rather nonliterary parts of life can be enlisted for creative purposes: spells, instruction manuals, postcards, legal documents, comics, guidebooks, recipes, job applications, and flyers can all become "creative writing" when led astray by our prompts.

And when it comes to *forms*—the patterns and methods employed within these genres—we have a host of ways of proceeding to delight and surprise you, to give you a way of moving forward. We hope these forms will be an engine for your writing, whether on your own or with a part- ner or a group. Expect the unexpected: a form for a recipe that doesn't include food, an interview method that leads to the absurd, a way to ex- change postcards that leaves an exotic story in its wake, a travel guide that journeys to the interior of *you*.

I'll Put a Spell on You

Pia Simone Garber, A. B. Gorham, Megan Paonessa, and Betsy Seymour

The art of spell writing, using repetition, and chanting.

IT'S TIME TO GET WHAT you want. Let's say you've paid your dues, and now you need to write out a wish list of all the things you want to happen. Have an urge to hear your favorite song? Why turn on the stereo when you can summon the live band to your front lawn? You may already be writing to record strange and beautiful moments or to create towns full of the weirdest people you've ever met, but how often does this writing result in something really *happening*? Never? It's because you haven't yet learned to write spells.

A spell is a piece of writing that expresses what you want to happen. Not only can you call forth the spirits to grow a jungle in your living room, but you can write a spell:

- to never have to go to bed, ever.
- to grow a lamp out of the ground when walking on a dark street.
- to make vegetables taste like ice cream.
- to make that poster in your room come alive and tell you who has been snooping around.

Wouldn't that be the cat's pajamas? Think of all the things you could make *happen*.

Some spells, like this one from *Technicians of the Sacred*, a book edited by Jerome Rothenberg, use anaphora, the repetition of a word or phrase at the beginning of a line, to create a sound of insisting, over and over.

A LIST OF BAD DREAMS CHANTED AS A CAUSE & CURE FOR MISSING SOULS

To dream that one's hair is falling out.
To dream that all one's teeth are falling out.
To dream that one is being saved.
To dream that one is being nursed.

To dream that one is very dirty.

To dream that one is dissolving.

To dream that one is in mourning, as shown by the hair.

To dream that one is being beaten, beaten on the neck,

up to the ears, and all about the face.

This spell is both a cause and a cure for the missing souls, which means that the spell is written about and to those souls; the spell wants to explain the reason why the souls are missing and "cure" them by releasing them from their former duties on Earth. The anaphora of "To dream that" makes the spell list-like, invoking scenarios in the dream in order to keep them from happening in reality. *One* is repeated again and again until it seems to morph into other beings, making the singular appear multiple. The spell addresses both details of the physical body as well as potential scary, intense, or happy moments that you may live through. Check out the different verbs and the way the actions define the person being described. By calling these actions forth, the moments are blown up like a balloon in order that they may float away.

This excerpt from the Aztec spell "Offering Flowers," also in Jerome Rothenberg's book, uses repetition to gain control over things:

I offer flowers. I sow flower seeds. I plant flowers . . .

. . .

I make a flower necklace, a flower garland, a paper of flowers, a bouquet, a flower shield, hand flowers. I thread them. I string them. I provide them with grass. I provide them with leaves. I make a pendant of them. I smell something. I smell them. I cause one to smell something. I cause him to smell. I offer flowers to one. I offer him flowers. I provide him with flowers. I provide one with flowers . . .

. . .

I destroy one with flowers; I destroy him with flowers; I injure one with flowers: with drink, with food, with flowers, with tobacco, with capes, with gold . . .

The purpose of this spell is destructive in nature, but before the speaker can destroy anything, they must first gain power over the flowers. The speaker invokes the spirit of the flowers by repeating their name and imagining herself manipulating the flowers. Eventually, the speaker gains power over the man by getting power over the flowers. The flowers become a character in the spell and their name is repeated again and again until they too seem to morph into other beings, making the singular appear multiple. Not only does the speaker have the ability to injure "him" with flowers, but also with other materials, precious and simple alike.

It's one thing to write a spell, but to *say* or *chant* the spell is what allows you to manipulate the atmosphere around you in order to make things *happen*. Think of this as gaining power over your world by conjuring up new possibilities. What do you wish was available to you that isn't?

Now it's time to write your own spell. Pay attention to how it will sound out loud. Use lots of repetition, and try anaphora. A good way to begin writing a spell is to brainstorm unusual circumstances. Here are some categories to get you started, but feel free to think beyond these:

1. A spell to conjure your lost rain jacket from third grade or a banana you once ate or a pet turtle you once had. What or who else would you like to bring back? What havoc could they wreak on the most boring of days?
2. A spell to destroy all cell phones (then radio towers then telephone wires then . . .).
3. A spell to shrink distance or make time obsolete: For example, your bathroom door opens to Hawaii, your boring class speeds up.

You write a spell because something is driving you crazy, or you believe that the world would be better if all the trees would bow to you, or to guarantee that your hair grows long enough to throw around a giant dragonfly and pull yourself up to ride it.

In order to keep your spell going, you must summon many parts of the world around you. When describing the world you are trying to manipulate, think of the cardinal directions: north, south, east, and west. What is happening above you? Below you? To your left? To your right? Be specific. Tell the scene what to do!

Give yourself twenty minutes to write the spell. Use anaphora and repetition to bring out the music in your spell. Write the spell so that someone reading it can understand the circumstances that caused you to write the spell. What can the reader figure out from reading your spell?

If you have extra time, write a result of your spell. Did it work? What happened?

Bake a Cake in an Earthquake

How-To Guides and Process Descriptions

Pia Simone Garber, A. B. Gorham, Megan Paonessa, and Betsy Seymour

Let a story emerge from your instructions.

EVER HAVE A MOMENT WHEN you think to yourself, "My life is soooo ordinary?" or "When did everything get so boring?" When times like that come up, the only cure is to take charge and rewrite your world the way you think it should be! Even the most mundane activities can be crazy awesome when you take control. Writing can reshape the world around you. One way to do that is to *describe a process* for how to make, remake, or change something in the world.

How-To You Do?
Have you ever had to give a demonstration speech or explain to someone how a game is played, or have you ever read an instruction manual? *Boooorrring.* Right? Wrong. Let's make these forms work for us. Check out the following excerpt from a poem by Thomas James, "Mummy of a Lady Named Jemutesonekh"—this is a process that will catch your attention. It is written from the point of view of a mummy—the "character" who was mummified.

MUMMY OF A LADY NAMED JEMUTESONEKH

XXI Dynasty
My brain was next. A pointed instrument
Hooked it through my nostrils, strand by strand.
A voice swayed over me. I paid no notice.
For weeks my body swam in sweet perfume.
I came out scoured. I was skin and bone.
They lifted me into the sun again
And packed my empty skull with cinnamon.

They slit my toes; a razor gashed my fingertips.
Stitched shut at last, my limbs were chaste and valuable,

Stuffed with paste of cloves and wild honey.
My eyes were empty, so they filled them up,
Inserting little nuggets of obsidian.
A basalt scarab wedged between my breasts
Replaced the tinny music of my heart.

Hands touched my sutures. I was so important!
They oiled my pores, rubbing a fragrance in.
An amber gum oozed down to soothe my temples.
I wanted to sit up. My skin was luminous,
Frail as the shadow of an emerald.
Before I learned to love myself too much,
My body wound itself in spools of linen.

The author is instructing us on a process—the process of mummification—but the poem is about more than that.

The poem is about an ancient Egyptian woman's embalming, about the physicality of the process, the taking out of brains, the replacing of the eyeballs, and the preserving of the body according the traditions described in *The Book of the Dead*. Through this process the woman becomes godlike, everlasting in her "painted box." She declares, "I was so important!" as though her mummification was a final act of love, as though the way her skin was sewn and rubbed with oils was a way of adoring her. So there is much more here than a poem about the process of mummification. The poem invites us to think about what makes someone feel important.

There are works of short fiction that do the same thing this poem does, that talk about one thing while evoking another, that use the "process" of something—like a cookbook's instructions for baking a cake or a five-step manual on how to build a house of cards—as a device within a larger story. In the example below, Lorrie Moore describes the process of adopting a cat. As you read, pick out what else you see happening.

FROM "AMAHL AND THE NIGHT VISITORS: A GUIDE TO THE TENOR OF LOVE"

11/30. Understand that your cat is a whore and can't help you. She takes on love with the whiskery adjustments of gold-digger. She is a gorgeous nomad, an unfriend. Recall how just last month when you got her from Bob downstairs, after Bob had become suddenly allergic, she leaped into your lap and purred, guttural as a German chanteuse, familiar and furry as a mold. And Bob, visibly heartbroken, still in the room, sneezing and giving instructions, hoping for one last cat nuzzle, descended to his hands and knees and jiggled his fingers in the shag. The cat only blinked. For you, however, she smiled, gave a fish-breath peep, and settled.

"Oh, well," said Bob, getting up off the floor. "Now I'm just a thing of her kittenish past."

That's the way with Bob. He'll say to the cat, "You be a good girl now, honey," and then just shrug, go back downstairs to his apartment, play jagged, creepy jazz, drink wine, stare out at the wintry scalp of the mountain.

12/1. Moss Watson, the man you truly love like no other, is singing December 23 in the Owonta Opera production of *Amahl and the Night Visitors*. He's playing Kaspar, the partially deaf Wise Man. Wisdom, says Moss, arrives in all forms. And you think, Yes, sometimes as a king and sometimes as a hesitant phone call that says the king'll be late at rehearsal don't wait up, and then when you call back to tell him to be careful not to let the cat out when he comes home, you discover there's been no rehearsal there at all.

At three o'clock in the morning you hear his car in the driveway, the thud of the front door. When he comes into the bedroom, you see his huge height framed for a minute in the doorway, his hair lit bright as curry. When he stoops to take off his shoes, it is as if some small piece of his back has given way, allowing him this one slow bend. He is quiet. When he gets into bed he kisses one of your shoulders, then pulls the covers up to his chin. He knows you're awake. "I'm tired," he announces softly, to ward you off when you roll toward him. Say: "You didn't let the cat out, did you?"

He says no, but he probably should have. "You're turning into a cat mom. Cats, Trudy, are the worst sorts of surrogates."

Tell him you've always wanted to run off and join the surrogates.

Tell him you love him.

Tell him you know he didn't have rehearsal tonight.

. . .

12/2. Your cat is growing, eats huge and sloppy as a racehorse. Bob named her Stardust Sweetheart, a bit much even for Bob, so you and Moss think up other names for her: Pudge, Pudge-muffin, Pooch, Poop-ster, Secretariat, Stephanie, Emily. Call her all of them. "She has to learn to deal with confusion," says Moss. "And we've gotta start letting her outside."

Say: "No. She's still too little. Something could happen." Pick her up and away from Moss. Bring her into the bathroom with you. Hold her up to the mirror. Say: "Whossat? Whossat pretty kitty?" Wonder if you could turn into Bob.

"Amahl and the Night Visitors: A Guide to the Tenor of Love" has a main character who is about to adopt a cat, and Moore presents the process step by step. This technique makes her readers a part of the process; she commands and directs us on how to behave. She writes, "**Understand** that your cat . . ." and "Moss Watson, the man **you** truly love like no other . . ." and "**Tell** him you love him." These are all guidelines Moore wants her characters to follow, and she writes them like instructions, but is this like any manual you've ever read?

Moore's story isn't just about a cat. It's about divorce, adultery, fear, abandonment, emotional baggage, the list goes on. . . . So, let's think about how Moore is using the cat adoption process to tell the story of her character's marriage. What other information has she inserted into the process of adopting and owning a cat in order to create the story? There's a setting here. We are in an apartment building. There are neighbors, and the neighbors have personalities. We are in rooms, the rooms have furniture and host meals, and there are interactions and discussions and even arguments that take place in these rooms. Moore is doing what writers call "exploding the moment." For every ounce of cat we get, we also get a few more ounces of story, plot, emotion, and setting.

So now it's your turn. The first thing you have to decide on is the framework. If you're creating a how-to guide or a process description, then you'll need to figure out something to explain before you go about figuring out what else is happening. So, here are some ideas below that you can grab and get going with, but maybe you have a few ideas to fill in yourself.

1. How to Enter a Child's Dream
2. How to Put Your Brother in a Full Nelson
3. The Steps to Playing Blackjack
4. How to Drive a Car at the Speed of Light
5. How to _____
6. How to _____
7. How to _____

Once you've got a couple of ideas to start with, then you can begin picturing how you might "explode the moment." Remember, one idea doesn't have to have anything to do with the other. Thomas James can talk about what makes someone feel important while also explaining how to mummify someone, and Lorrie Moore can adopt a cat and explore a marriage at the same time. You too can do something extraordinary with your process. Here's another chart to fill in. What are some ideas you could be writing about at the same time you're telling us "how to" do whatever it is you thought of up above?

1. The polar ice caps are melting.
2. I moved to a new city two years ago.
3. I have a secret.
4. Someone is mad at someone else.
5. _____
6. _____
7. _____
8. _____

Now go. Get writing.

Start with your process idea. What's the first step to completing your process description? This is where you begin. But after you introduce your first step, make sure to incorporate your other story line. For the next twenty minutes, write a story where your steps twist and turn around the thoughts, places, and conversations of characters you create. If you finish too soon, go back and "explode the moment" by thinking about what else you could insert between the lines of your process description.

Guidebooks Galore!

CHART UNCHARTED PLACES

Pia Simone Garber, A. B. Gorham, Megan Paonessa, and Betsy Seymour

Create a guide to your room, cell phone, refrigerator, and more.

G UIDEBOOKS HELP US TRAVERSE THE unknown. It's a common idea. Say you're heading somewhere new: You're planning a trip to Costa Rica and you need to know which beach has the best sand. Or you've never been to Boise, and you can't find the bakery, and there you are standing on the streets of downtown, and you look to your right and you see it: the bookstore. The bookstore in all of its glory with its guidebook section nestled there in the back corner. These books will show you where to go. They will guide you in the best direction and you will find your bread, and when you go home later, you will say, "I have found the best bread in all of Idaho with help from this guidebook here!" The words on the pages in a guidebook help you pinpoint your next move. These words help you wind your way through the unknown. These words are an eight-dollar tour guide you don't have to pay by the hour and they are waiting to show you the way. And these guidebooks, they are everywhere, and boy, are they *boooooooring*.

But they don't have to be. Take, for instance, this piece by Jonathan Stern in which he plays with the form of a guidebook:

THE LONELY PLANET GUIDE TO MY APARTMENT

ORIENTATION

My Apartment's vast expanse of unfurnished space can be daunting at first, and its population of one difficult to communicate with. After going through customs, you'll see a large area with a couch to the left. Much of My Apartment's "television viewing" occurs here, as does the very occasional *making out with a girl* (see "Festivals"). To the north is the *food district*, with its colorful cereal boxes and *antojitos*, or "little whims."

WHAT TO BRING

A good rule of thumb is "If it's something you'll want, you have to bring it in yourself." This applies to water, as well as to toilet paper and English-language periodicals. Most important, come with plenty of cash, as there's sure to be someone with his hand out. In My Apartment, it's axiomatic that you have to grease the wheels to make the engine run.

WHEN TO GO

The best time to travel to My Apartment is typically after most people in their twenties are already showered and dressed and at a job. Visits on Saturdays and Sundays before 2 P.M. are highly discouraged, and can result in lengthy delays at the border (see "Getting There and Away").

LOCAL CUSTOMS

The population of My Apartment has a daily ritual of *bitching*, which occurs at the end of the workday and prior to ordering in food. Usually, meals are taken during reruns of "Stargate Atlantis." Don't be put off by impulsive sobbing or unprovoked rages. These traits have been passed down through generations and are part of the colorful heritage of My Apartment's people. The annual *Birthday Meltdown* (see "Festivals") is a tour de force of recrimination and self-loathing, highlighted by fanciful stilt-walkers and dancers wearing hand-sewn headdresses.

Other headings used are: Dangers and Annoyances, Things to See and Do, Places to Eat, Night Life, Mule Rentals and Wildlife.

It's funny, right? But, what makes it so? Jonathan Stern, after all, didn't do much beyond just writing a basic guidebook. But because he takes a form that is usually so dry, so humorless, so textbooky, and winds it around something personal and new, he produces fresh writing.

So, brainstorm your list of guidebook topics. Like Jonathan Stern, what's something you can write about in order to produce your own guidebook? For instance, a guidebook to your favorite family vacation or to your bedroom. Or on a smaller level, your MP3 player or cell phone contact list. Or on a less physical level, a guidebook to your memory or to an imaginary place. The options are endless, but list five:

1. _____
2. _____
3. _____
4. _____
5. _____

Let's take a look at a section from Gertrude Stein's *Tender Buttons* in which she catalogues the contents of her refrigerator:

MILK.

A white egg and a colored pan and a cabbage showing settlement, a constant increase.

A cold in a nose, a single cold nose makes an excuse. Two are more necessary.

All the goods are stolen, all the blisters are in the cup.

Cooking, cooking is the recognition between sudden and nearly sudden very little and all large holes.

A real pint, one that is open and closed and in the middle is so bad.

Tender colds, seen eye holders, all work, the best of change, the meaning, the dark red, all this and bitten, really bitten.

Guessing again and golfing again and the best men, the very best men.

MILK.

Climb up in sight climb in the whole utter needles and a guess a whole guess is hanging. Hanging hanging.

EGGS.

Kind height, kind in the right stomach with a little sudden mill.

Cunning shawl, cunning shawl to be steady.

In white in white handkerchiefs with little dots in a white belt all shadows are singular they are singular and procured and relieved.

No that is not the cows shame and a precocious sound, it is a bite.

Cut up alone the paved way which is harm. Harm is old boat and a likely dash.

What's different from Stern to Stein? From the apartment to the refrigerator? They are both writing about something physical. They are both cataloging the contents of a place. But while Stern uses straight language, so that we can "see" the real objects from his descriptions, Stein is more poetic. She gives us an *impression* of the objects she describes. While Stern uses each heading once, Stein repeats.

Now it's time to choose your topic. Pick one and try to brainstorm some subject headings. For instance, if you choose your cell phone contact list, what are five headings you could come up with? Would each name be a heading or would you pick and choose, leaving out those you don't talk to anymore? Would you categorize the contacts into their own headings with "Uncle Fred" and "Aunt Mimi" as separate headings or would you categorize all of your uncles and aunts under one heading that would read, "People Who Give Me Money on Christmas"? How would the choice of these headings change what would be included underneath?

Now go. Guide us. Show us things we've never seen before. And if you get stuck, just ask yourself, what's another heading I could add? And then keep writing.

Postcard Stories

Zachary Doss, Meredith Noseworthy, and Bethany Startin

Two characters have an exotic exchange through postcards.

H AVE YOU EVER RECEIVED A postcard? Or sent one? My aunt used to travel all over the United States, and she would send my brothers and me postcards from wherever she ended up. They always had pictures of the places she saw: cacti and sunsets from "Sunny Arizona," trees and beaches encouraging me to "Visit Hawaii," or fishing boats sitting in a harbor offering me "Greetings from Maine." They all said the same things: "Wish you were here" and "Thinking of you."

A postcard has a sense of place. When you send a postcard, you are sending a part of the place you are visiting. You are offering a loved one a glimpse of something you are seeing or experiencing. You are letting them know that you are thinking of them and you wish they were there with you, but since they can't be, you're sending a little bit of yourself back through the mail for them.

We're going to write postcards to and from imaginary people. Maybe you've heard of *epistolary novels*, which are novels told using letters. You can use postcards to do that same thing, except instead of letters, we're going to use postcards. Unlike letters, postcards require you to write short bits. There's not much room back there! Postcards have the benefit of including multiple layers of information; there is the image on the front, the note on the back, and even the stamp. All of these things tell a story. You can use real postcards, or you can use note cards to do the same thing—they even have the benefit of allowing you to draw, paint, or collage your own image on the back.

Griffin and Sabine: An Extraordinary Correspondence, by Nick Bantock, is one of my favorite epistolary novels. The two characters—a stamp-making woman, Sabine, living in the South Pacific, and a postcard artist, Griffin, in London—have a strange connection. Let's take a look at some of their early exchanges. So far Sabine has sent a postcard to Griffin asking him to send her one of his postcard-artworks and commenting on some changes he had made to it when drafting. Griffin obliges and confesses that he doesn't remember ever meeting a woman named Sabine. She responds that he doesn't know her, but that she's been "watching" his art for a long time. He replies:

> *Ms. Strohem*
> *What's going on? How in the world could you know I darkened the sky behind the kangaroo? It was only a light cobalt for about half an hour. And what do you mean by "phenomenon" and "tangible"?*
> *Ok. If getting me intrigued is what you're after, you've succeeded, but you can hardly expect me to spill my life story to a stranger.*
> *Why are you being so ruddy mysterious?*
> *Griffin Moss*
> *P.S. Your postcards are handmade—did you do them yourself?*
>
> *Griffin—you're right. I am being mysterious, but I assure you it's for good reason. What I have to say will be disturbing, and I wish you no distress.*
> *I share your sight. When you draw and paint, I see what you're doing while you do it. I know your work almost as well as I know my own. Of course I do not expect you to believe this without proof: Last week while working on a head in chalk, you paused and lightly sketched a bird in the bottom corner of the paper. You then erased it, and obliterated all trace with heavy black. Don't be alarmed—I only wish you well.*
> *Sabine*
> *Yes the pictures on the cards are mine.*

One of the neat things about the postcard format is that because there isn't much space, every detail in the language matters. There's an abruptness and urgency to the exchanges between Griffin and Sabine—he really needs to know what the secret is! And even though there's not too much space, when Sabine confesses, she still hedges her answer, understanding that Griffin may not take the news well. The different styles of writing also allow for Griffin and Sabine to develop entirely distinct voices. There's a neat kind of suspense in the postcard form, because the readers only get what's in the text, even as the characters reference life events that occurred elsewhere, at another time.

Another aspect of writing that you can show in postcard stories is the active editing process. Take a look at this:

Sabine,

　. . .

Send me something from the islands. Some~~thing~~ magic that will heal my
ailing soul.
How can I miss you this badly when we've never met?
Love, Griffin

Toward the end of this postcard (which is situated right before the sto-
ry's climactic moment), Griffin crosses out part of the word "something"
so that it will read to Sabine as "some magic." This gives us a neat win-
dow into his mind as he was writing the postcard to Sabine. You can use
this technique in your own postcard stories to show your readers a little
bit more of your characters. Are they bad spellers? Do they change their
mind often as they are writing? Or are they very careful and deliberate,
never needing to cross out their words?

Instructions

You need:

Two sets of index cards in a variety of colors

One set of larger, white, index cards

Pens

Paperclips

Friends/collaborators (This is a great collaborative exercise to do with
lots of people, but you can also do it with just one or two others.)

Step 1. To prepare for your postcard-writing adventures, you need to
create characters. Each of the participants should take two index cards in
the same color. Spend up to five minutes creating a character on each in-
dex card—here are some example details you might want to include (you
can come up with some more categories if you like):

Name: _____

Age: _____

Job: _____

Hobbies: _____

Quirks: _____

Pet peeves: _____

You can go all-out and create a supervillain character who goes salsa dancing on weekends, or you can think up someone more "ordinary"—like a college student who has a phobia of frogs. Anything goes! At the end of five minutes, each writer will have created lists of traits for two characters. (Make sure these two characters are described on the same color index card.)

Step 2. Next up, you and your collaborators should each take a single index card of another color. You're going to use this to create a setting. Again, give yourselves about five minutes. Here are some ideas for details about the setting:

Geographic location: _____

Type of lodging: _____

Weather: _____

Tourist attractions: _____

What the locals are like (friendly, horrible, noisy . . .): _____

_____

Traveling companion: _____

Again, think up more categories if you like. Consider picking a setting that's completely different from the typical vacation destination—like camping in the Amazon rainforest or prison.

Step 3 (optional). Collaboratively come up with some reasons why people might write postcards. Rather than the typical "Weather lovely, wish you were here" postcards that we tend to send when we go on real vacations, think of some out-of-the-box or even surreal reasons. What if one character wanted to tell another to leave him alone? Or what if someone wanted to complain about how horrible her holiday is and how annoying her traveling companion is being?

You can write these ideas down on a list that everyone can see, or you can just keep them in your heads.

Step 4. Now, put all the colored index cards facedown in the center of your group. Make one pile of character cards and one pile of setting cards. Mix up each pile. Then, each writer should take one of the large white index cards, two premade "character" cards, and one "setting" card. These are the tools you're going to use to build your postcard.

On one side of your white index card, start writing a postcard from one of the characters to the other (you get to pick which is which), sent from the setting you've picked. This can make for some fantastic combinations—when we did this in our class, one of our students wrote a poetic love letter from the middle of the Antarctic, all crammed into a single index card. You can include an address and stamp on this side, and you also have the option of drawing your own artwork on the back. Even stick figures can be awesome additions, so get artistic!

Step 5. This is where the real collaboration comes in. Once you've finished your first white postcard, place it face down in the center of the group, and pick up someone else's finished white postcard, along with another blank white index card. Now, you're going to compose a response to their original postcard, using what they've written as a springboard, along with your own imagination. They might have given you a bit of info about the characters and the setting, but the rest is yours to fill in—maybe they've told you that one character is summering in the south of France, but only you can give that character a dancing bear as a traveling companion.

Once you've completed your response postcard, paper-clip it behind the first one, and put them both face down together in the center. Next, pick up another set of postcards that others have been working on, along with another blank white index card, and compose a new addition to that paper-clipped set. As I'm sure you can imagine, this game can get pretty frantic and exciting, especially if you have lots of people all working on postcards together. When you have a bunch of writers all crafting a story like this, imaginations tend to run wild, and some awesomely intriguing plot twists emerge.

COMMENTARY

One of the neatest things about this game is the way it uses all the elements of storytelling to create a fun, developed narrative. You need to come up with characters and a setting at the beginning, as well as an impetus for writing—as you've seen, there are plenty of reasons that are more exciting than just "Missing you!" or "Wish you were here!"—and then you need to follow that up with a constant stream of action and reaction. (This is also how a lot of great novelists developed their plots, so when you're playing this game, you're following in some really impressive footsteps.)

On top of that, the collaborative element of this exercise works really well, especially because all the postcards are effectively anonymous. You don't know which of your friends/collaborators you might be responding to, and this creates a freeing, no-holds-barred atmosphere where you can take the story and characters in unexpected directions. Plus, when doing this, you're creating characters and plot with very little time or information—this means you need to plumb the depths of your mind to come up with ideas, and that's where real creativity springs to life.

STUDENT EXAMPLES

Here are a few student examples (since these were collaborative projects, we don't know for certain who is responsible for which parts of the writing, but the Creative Writing Club at the University of Alabama wrote these one Wednesday afternoon).

This first example shows how much character development you can produce between the exchanges of two characters who know each other well. Here's the text from the original colored index cards that the first writer used for inspiration:

Character #1

  Name: George
  Job: Diplomat from a nonexistent country
  Travel method: Bicycle
  Personality: Forgetful
  Pet: Iguana
  Secret: Looking for a country to take over

Character #2

  Name: Honey
  Job: Roller-skating waitress
          She hates cats, books, and anywhere without a mall
  Personality trait: Overly excited
  Ambition: To open her own nail salon

Setting

  Location: Florida beaches
  Weather: Sunny with freak blizzards

Lodgings: A youth hostel

Tourist attractions: Nothing for miles except sand

As you can see from the postcards below, some of the above details didn't make it into the postcards. That's fine. The colored index cards are just to give you a jumping-off point, and you can invent things anew instead of using the premade settings and characters.

Postcard 1a:

Dear Honey,

> *I continue my quest, looking for the country so I can rule it, but am having bike trouble. Again. LOL. Would not have happened if you had agreed to join me, all your fault, not. LOL. The room, when I got back there, had disappeared. Spent first night in snow, second night in sand. Going granular, my dear. You'd like the detail. You'd hate the way the sky rewrites itself. A work in progress, moi. Send the dog, if he ever materializes. Could use some company for when I get my minions. Wish you were here. George*

Postcard 1b (paper-clipped to Postcard 1a):

Dearest George,

> *Oh, I was so heartbroken to receive your missive! We are so close to our perpetual communion, and yet so far. It is just like in that one Taylor Swift song.*
>
> *My darling, I have made my decision. Ours is a love star-crossed but real. I am setting out to find you, with only my pet squid Algernon to protect me. (Algernon is a rather useless bodyguard.) It may take many nights, but we are destiny.*
>
> *Yours, Honey*

In this last example, one of the characters draws attention to the fact that the postcard is a public space—anyone who sees it can read everything that was written on it:

Dearest Frankie,

> *I am writing to inform you of your incredible boringness as a human being. I will be surprised if you even manage a tan, you loaf of Wonder Bread. I hope a group of turtles storms onto the beach and buries you*

there for all time, so that you can be a constant reminder of how sur-
vival of the fittest has clearly failed.
Also, you forgot your parrot. I have mailed it separately. I even gave it
an airhole.
—Susan

Address: Susan Snut, 5555 Stacey Lane, Akron, Ohio, 02341
This is Frankie here, writing you to tell you I'm thinking of you. On this
beach it is so sunny! But I am alone and wishing you were here. Visit soon.

Dear Frankie,
You don't get it. Did you get the parrot? The hotel said it never arrived
and you are not listed as a guest so I am trying the post office. I have
news about our youngest but not the sort you can write on a postcard. I
bet you can't afford a stamp.
—S

Frankie,
I wrote you a week ago; where are my glasses? And my shoes? Call me
back at . . . never mind, people will find out my number. But write back
or I'll come get you. And YOU KNOW WHY!

When your group has finished writing the postcards, try reading them
aloud. Have two people read back and forth, bringing the postcard "con-
versation" to life. If you are part of a class or even a public poetry reading,
these "characters" can stand up in the audience and voice their postcard
messages from various places in the room. The audience will have fun
"overhearing" the private correspondence.

Creative Nonfiction

Kenny Kruse

Twenty little memoir projects, plus a squirrel.

WHEN YOU THINK ABOUT WRITING nonfiction, you probably think *school* and *encyclopedia*, *textbook*, and *newspaper*. Well, nonfiction can be way more exciting than the essays you have to write for history class, the lab reports you do in chemistry, and the descriptions of cell reproduction in your biology textbook.

Nonfiction can be creative, an artistic representation of your experience. If you were in a room with five of your classmates and an *asteroid* (of all things!) came through the ceiling, what would you tell people about it? You might tell your parents first that the asteroid had destroyed your textbooks so they wouldn't make you do your homework. You might tell your best friend about how the person you have a crush on acted when they heard the noise. You might tell your older sibling how brave you were when you cleared the wreckage to check for survivors. You might have been thinking about snowboarding—you love snowboarding; you are an expert!—when the asteroid hit, so maybe you would include that. Maybe you were thinking about the time you fell off the monkey bars at recess in second grade, so maybe you include a little playground gravel in the wreckage, too. Maybe you know that an asteroid hit a classroom in Saudi Arabia at that exact moment, so you include parts of a news story you found about that, too.

But would your other classmates in the room tell the same stories? They might tell their best friends about the people they had crushes on. They might have noticed something that you didn't, either because you didn't see it, because you were focusing on something else, or because you had your eyes closed—whatever! The point is that every single one of these stories would be *true*! They would all be classified as nonfiction, but none of them would be the same. They might overlap in some ways, but everyone's experience is different, so everyone will describe the thing that has happened in distinctive ways. In fact, a single writer might describe the same event in varying ways, depending on what audience they are writing for. Everyone's account of an event will be different because everyone is different—different things matter to everyone, and everyone's memory works differently. Creative nonfiction understands this! In fact, the word *essay* is from the French word *essayer*, which means "to try." This means that you might not feel like your writing is perfect, and that is okay!

So first, I want you to close your eyes, clear your head, and get ready to write. I want you to write the story of what has happened while you were reading this chapter so far. You can include anything—what is happening on planet Mars, what is happening in the carpet fibers beneath your feet, what is happening on the other side of the wall or the country or the world, or what is happening in your mind or your kidney. Go as big or as small as you want. Write for about five minutes.

Now you are a creative nonfiction writer. Do you think anyone else could have written that? Did you surprise yourself? Here is my own example. Notice how I think about the story of rescuing a baby squirrel, while also giving directions, reminiscing about childhood, imagining life "off the grid," and citing researched squirrel facts.

HOW TO CARE FOR A BABY SQUIRREL

When you first learn to handle baby squirrels they will be lethargic. They will, inevitably, have been abandoned and will, therefore, exhibit intense separation anxiety. They will hug the muzzle of the bottle as if it is their last link to life because, quite frankly, it is.

When you care for a baby squirrel, you have to remind yourself that our objects are more than they seem. A Tupperware is not a Tupperware. It is a plastic box. Not even a box, a shape. It has become Tupperware because we are accustomed to it in that role. When caring for a baby squirrel, *Tupperware* can become *nest*, can become *cage, coffin, playground, world.*

When you start caring for a baby squirrel, you will remember that you care. You will find an ocean of caring inside of your rib cage for this squirrel, and it doesn't make sense, no, how you can dive three miles down into the ocean of your caring for a squirrel, but you can't muster even a single tear when your grandfather dies.

Caring for baby squirrels will become moot by the year 2100, as the population of the earth will have grown to sixteen billion souls, and food will be scarce. *Caring* for baby squirrels will become *frying, grilling, baking*, and *roasting*.

Carol, the squirrel rehabilitator with whom we eventually entrusted Snacks, our baby squirrel, is the only wildlife rehabilitator who specialized in squirrels in the whole state of Michigan. She is not crazy like a cat lady. She is not like that woman who died in a trailer full of guinea pigs and guinea pig poop. She is not that kind of obsessive. I can promise you that.

There were no baby squirrels in Utah, because there were no squirrels. A squirrel-less childhood, that's what I had. There were no squirrels to lose, to hit with cars, or to care for until they sputtered out, the rancid mold of dead squirrel on a highway, the tarty paste of squirrel meat in porridge.

In fact, not only were squirrels not eaten in Utah, they were not around to destroy houses and crops. The natural lifespan of a squirrel is five years, but only 1 percent of squirrels survive that long in the contemporary United States. Most squirrels die within their first year, victims of cars, cats, coyotes, lonely old men who abandon society for an off-the-grid life, scraping their teeth against the bones of squirrels, blowing their noses on pine cones.

If I were to live off-the-grid, my mouth wouldn't be coffee-bitter right now. I wouldn't have to board a plane in the morning and return to the place where I lived with Snacks, surely dead by now, even though she lived with the only squirrel-specializing rehabilitator in the state of Michigan.

My parents dressed me as a squirrel until I was thirteen years old. They made me sleep in a tree, and they drugged me for the winter to simulate hibernation. When I woke up every March, they would give me a different name. My current name is my fourteenth name after which the state of Utah passed a new law—the Squirrel-Impersonating Child-Abuse Law—for my special case, and I was entered into an all-too-human state-run foster care system.

For this next exercise I want you to think of something you are an expert on, the way I was an expert on squirrel rescue. Come on! Everyone's an expert at something. You probably know a lot about something, whether it is playing lacrosse, painting with watercolors, baking carrot cake, raising baby turtles, or playing the cello. You *are* an expert at some-thing! Still nothing? You are an expert at tying shoelaces. You are an ex-pert at zipping your backpack. Everyone is an expert at something.

Now, we are going to do a variation on Jim Simmerman's "Twenty Lit-tle Poetry Projects," from *The Practice of Poetry*. We are going to write Twenty Little Memoir Projects. For each of these prompts, write just three sentences, and keep in mind the thing that you are an expert on. The finished product will be a single nonfiction piece. Don't be afraid of going wherever your mind takes you, though, because our minds take in-teresting leaps while we are thinking, and your writing will do the same thing. Here is an exercise to help you make leaps and let your mind move around while thinking about what you are an expert on. Remember, write three sentences for each step.

TWENTY LITTLE MEMOIR PROJECTS

1. Write down three facts about the thing you are an expert on.
2. Describe three important physical objects having to do with this topic.
3. Write about your first time at the ocean or, if you have never been the ocean, remember your first time going somewhere else.
4. Write about the thing you are an expert on in the future tense.
5. Use the proper name of a person and the proper name of a place and say some things about them.
6. Describe a scene from your childhood that relates in some way to this story, but don't tell us the whole story. Use smell and taste in the scene.
7. Change direction and digress from the last thing you said.
8. Write down the thing you are thinking at this exact moment.
9. Now write something specific but ridiculous and obviously untrue.
10. Connect an unrelated physical object to something you have written so far.
11. Write about something you think may have happened but are not too sure about.
12. Use a metaphor to describe your favorite person in the world.
13. Write something from someone else's perspective.
14. Write about something you saw yesterday and don't connect it to any-thing you have written so far.
15. Write down what you would do if you had to move to a different state tomorrow.

16. Use something you overheard or made up that is still believable, for dialogue.

17. Use an example of false cause-and-effect logic that you wish were true.

18. Write about something else that was going on in your life when you became an expert in the thing you are an expert in.

19. Make an if/then statement about something you wish were true.

20. Write about something with a strong sense of smell that seems completely unrelated to what you have written so far.

Okay. You're done. Wow, that was fun, right? Read over what you wrote. Does it surprise you? Is it true? Here is another example I wrote:

THE ART OF THE SHOELACE

If you think that the tying of shoelaces is a simple task, imagine the ugliest tie-job you have ever seen. The way the bows are small and knobby, the way the extra lace drags through the mud. Imagine the crusted mess of double-knotted laces that never comes undone.

The art of tying shoelaces is all in the fingers, and the extent to which the fingers are nimble depends entirely on whether or not they have been pushed through rigorous morning finger yoga. We're talking piano playing; we're talking secretary-style typing.

A finely-tied pair of shoelaces is as infinite as the ocean, the sea salt crust around your nose and the sunburn on your shoulders and the wind whipping through your hair and you close your eyes and imagine that you are a sea turtle.

The great philosophers and mathematicians of our age have all foreseen the downfall of the shoelace. They predict that by the year 2050, shoelaces will be obsolete in a shocking 78 percent of the inhabited square miles on earth. There will be no need for shoelaces when we while away our existences in fish tanks.

The shoelace was not invented in Madagascar in the second century by a woman named Mary Beth Adawama. She did not tire of caring for her children while waiting for the chickens to lay their eggs, and she did not tire of carrying out chemical tests in her laboratory. She did not mind walking barefoot each day—no, she did not.

My nanny taught me to tie my shoes on my first day of kindergarten. My mother had begun working again. My nanny asked me, as I pulled the bunny through the hole, "You love me better than your mommy, right?"

The bunny never goes through the hole, not really, because after all it is simply a question of a piece of string, pulled through our fingers in different ways, falling in on itself, a mess of false courage and electrons.

Outside the air is a swamp. I never want to leave the air-conditioning again. I've been wearing sandals now for eleven days and counting.

If I were to rank the five things that are most important to me in the world, they would be:

1. The art of shoelace tying.
2. Good Thai, Japanese, Mexican, Peruvian, and Indian food.
3. The color of shoelaces at dawn and at dusk.
4. A carefully crafted fruit smoothie of which passion fruit is an integral component.
5. World peace, especially regarding footwear.

What could have happened the first time I tripped over my shoelace is something like this. I get a bathroom pass from Mrs. Allen, my recently married fourth-grade teacher. There is Kristy Tompkins by the door, crying because her parents have just gotten divorced. Now, years later, her mother has just died from breast cancer. I trip over my lace before the door has fully closed, and no one in the classroom notices.

A tied shoelace is like a fingerprint, a snowflake, the hollow brown outline of removed roadkill on the freeway. Everything in this whole world is unique. It will only happen this way once.

In an MTV interview just weeks before she died, R&B artist Aaliyah is quoted as saying, "I knew I would be a singer and a dancer the first time I tied my shoelaces myself. The pattern in the laces taught me how to dance. The way the tips hung against my soles taught me how to harmonize."

Yesterday I was sitting on a cemetery wall waiting for a friend to meet me. An elderly man walked along the graves, gathering the flowers of the week. At first I was offended when he trashed them against the fence, but no one wants to see that rot.

I don't know how to tie my shoes in other countries, in other languages, in other climates.

What did you notice was the difference, she asks her daughter, *when you asked nicely and when you demanded?* I take a bite of my sandwich. The small girl unties her shoe, starts again.

Well, now that you have learned, my mother said, sipping red wine from a white mug, *to tie your shoe, let's move on.* I scratched my head and then my cat's head. *I think "piano" can be your new "shoe."*

If you don't tie your shoe correctly, this man will be executed in China. If you don't tie your shoe correctly, this butterfly will flutter-crumble to the ground, a heap of wing and yellow. If you don't tie your shoe correctly, you won't make it there in time.

The smell of old shoes and the smell of old shoelaces are not necessarily related. Have you ever removed the laces from an old leather boot you found in the corner of a barn? Well? Have you done it? Brushed your hands against the fibers, wondered what historical fingers wove them? Wondered whose life it was that is only marked by this dingy mess of matter in the corner of a darkening barn, here, a place that no one even thinks about, not even in dreams?

If you are interested in other things you might do with creative non-fiction, you should go read "Girl" by Jamaica Kincaid. Some other things you might want to read are "The Fourth State of Matter" by Jo Ann Beard, *Refuge* by Terry Tempest Williams, or *About a Mountain* by John D'Agata.

Tropes Unlimited

GENRE FICTION

Kristin Aardsma and Brian Oliu

Explore the habits of genre fiction (fantasy, horror, sci-fi, mystery, etc.) and put them to use.

EVER SAVE THE WORLD FROM a race of alien space vampires that have come to earth during the San Francisco Gold Rush in hopes of finding romance, preferably in the form of a damsel locked in a tower by an evil wizard? Me neither! But hey, what's stopping you from writing about it? We're going to take a close look at genre fiction and all of its wildness. Genre fiction, such as sci-fi or romance, uses expected traits of that genre in order to appeal to its fans. A stuffy definition, definitely, but it brings up a good point: a reader of genre fiction expects certain things from the author. For example, if you tell your friends you just wrote a horror story "Midnight in the Death Doom Decay Blood Room of Evil" and it's about a visit to your grandmother's house and she made you perfectly (not poisoned or filled with the teeth of zombies) delicious cupcakes, then you're going to let your reader down. So, what's your favorite genre? Horror? Sci-Fi? Fantasy? Romance? Western? Suspense? All of the above? What do you find cool about it?

Got a genre in mind? Sweet. Now, brainstorm a list of things that are found in that genre. For example, you wouldn't have a sci-fi story that didn't involve aliens, the future, or space, would ya? Write them down. Having trouble? Think of your favorite book written in that genre. Let's say my genre is fantasy. Here's a list of things that popped into my head:

FANTASY
- Kings/Queens (feudal society)
- Main character is a prince or princess
- Dragons
- Magic (often a complicated learning process or rite of passage)
- Armed combat (jousting)

- Modern children either traveling back in time or to another world where they play an important role in history
- Welsh legends and landscape
- Complicated imaginary geography (often there's a map at the beginning of the book)
- A journey or mission
- Set in the distant past or future
- King Arthur
- Struggle between good and evil
- Uses ideas from religion and folklore
- Talking animals
- Climax overlaps with a storm

All of these elements came from fantasy books that I've read (mostly young adult fantasy, like the *Narnia* books or the *Dark Is Rising* series)— you might come up with other ideas for the same genre based on your own reading. The list can have both general ideas ("monumental struggle between good and evil") and smaller details ("talking animals"). Just try to list as many commonly recurring themes, ideas, and images as possible. Take a while to do this—the longer your list is, and the more specific, the more fun the writing will be.

Now that you have your list, your task is to use ALL of these tropes, conventions, and clichés in a piece of writing. Make it as over-the-top as possible! Think ridiculous blockbuster film! You can go about it in two ways: either a how-to about writing in that genre (see James Pinkerton's "How to Write Suspense") or a super-short story à la Neil Gaiman's "Forbidden Brides of the Faceless Slaves in the Nameless House of the Night of Dread Desire" (Best. Title. Ever.). Remember, it's supposed to be overblown and absolutely wild. If the people want horror, GIVE THEM HORROR! Need a jumping off point? How about this: "Amanda returns from the grocery store and realizes her wallet is missing." You fill in the blanks (and by blanks I mean alien invasions). Refer to your list for things to include.

Where Frankenstein Meets Frodo, Part One

CREATING A CHARACTER FOR GENRE FICTION BY CREATING THEIR FACEBOOK PAGE

Kristin Aardsma and Brian Oliu

Like Frankenstein's creator, build a character bit by bit until it's ready to come to life in your own genre fiction.

THESE DAYS, MANY PEOPLE SHOW who they are and discover more about who celebrities and their friends are by making and reading Facebook pages. Let's use Facebook to create a character who can be in a genre fiction piece. First, choose a type of genre fiction. Now choose a type of character that goes with your genre.

Here are some examples:

Genre	Character
Fantasy	Princess, evil stepmother
Suspense	Detective, fugitive
Horror	Murderer, victim, zombie
Sci-Fi	Robot, space pioneer
Etc.	Etc.

Now choose one character type, such as a space pioneer in a sci-fi story, and get ready to learn more about that character by creating a mock Facebook page.

Get out a sheet of paper and a pen, and somewhere on the page draw a small portrait of your new character. This is going to be your character's Facebook photo.

Now that you have a Facebook "photo" for your character, answer the following questions about your character on your sheet of paper. If you wish, format your writing so it looks like a real Facebook homepage.

- What is their favorite quote?
- Where did/do they go to school?

- Favorite activities/interests?
- Movies?
- Books/Authors?
- TV Shows?
- Who are their heroes?
- What is your character's age, location, gender, occupation?
- What other categories are important for this character? Princess points earned? Places where their victims are buried?

Start thinking about lots of details, like who the character would like to meet, who their heroes are, what their favorite movies are, etcetera, which is why making a mock Facebook page is so useful. That way, if you ever have questions as to how your character might act if they met a stranger next to a dumpster in New Jersey who quotes Murakami, you can refer back to this sheet to jog your memory. You will see that, yes, your character's favorite book is *Hard-Boiled Wonderland and the End of the World* by Haruki Murakami and this stranger may play a significant role later in your story.

Now let's develop this character further by letting a few images guide us.

1. *Hat*: Imagine that your character is standing outside and it's a little chilly, so they are wearing a hat. Describe that hat. Is it giant and floppy? What kind of animal could you compare this hat to? What color is it? What fabric? How and when do they wear it?
2. *Garbage can*: What kind of things are in your character's garbage? Go through your character's living quarters and describe what each garbage or trash can is filled with. Are there any items that are particularly strange? Normal? Interesting? Telling? Keep in mind that whatever is in those cans is going to reveal a detail about your character in a way that will allow you to not overtly explain it.
3. You provide an image and then expand on it, asking yourself questions to reveal your character through the image:

_____

_____

_____

To continue this writing, think of a few different ways you can reveal nuances of your character without directly explaining them. What other items (like *hat* and *garbage*) and what other questions or categories could you expand upon? Go for it. Continue to build your character in this way and in "Where Frankenstein Meets Frodo, Part Two" (see p. 44) you'll have the opportunity to work on setting the scene!

Where Frankenstein Meets Frodo, Part Two

Our Hero's Hundred-Story Hotel and Other Settings for Your Genre Fiction Character

Kristin Aardsma and Brian Oliu

Give your main character a room (or rooms) of their own.

IF YOU'VE DONE THE EXERCISE "Where Frankenstein Meets Frodo, Part One" (see p. 41), you've got the hero (or anti-hero!) of your genre story. Nice work! You can call it a day. Just kidding; there's more to genre fiction than having a super-swanky character. What about putting them someplace? Heck, maybe they'll actually *do* something!

We're going to do what we did with the character again, but this time we'll be describing the room that your character is currently in. Make a list of the following things about the room.

- What pictures are on the wall?
- What does the floor or ground look like?
- How many doors are there? What do they look like? Where do they lead?
- What kind of building is this room in? An office building? A hotel? A home?
- Does the building have one, two, eight, twenty stories?
- What part of the world is the room in? The building?

Now that you've crafted your torture chamber/antebellum mansion/ kitchen/board room, it's time to place your character from "Where Frankenstein Meets Frodo, Part One" in that room. Some things to jot down:

- How many times has this person been in this room?
- Why is this person there?
- Why does or doesn't your character want to be there?
- Does your character touch or pick up anything from a table? Who goes there?

That's a pretty sweet looking room you have going on there. I like what you've done with the place. Aha, but what's that over there? On that table that you just imagined? A letter, huh? What does it say?

Try writing this scene two ways: once from the point of view of the character (first person); then from the point of view of someone who is watching the character (third person). When you write in first person, think about how your character might describe their surroundings. Would the character be likely to speak clearly, in a muddled way, tersely, with colorful metaphors? Does your character cackle maniacally? How would you show this? If they were going to compare the room or something in it to something else they've seen, how would they do so? Is your character alone in this room?

Now, try writing about the character in this room or place from a different point of view. This time, observe your familiar character (#1), referring to the character in third person as them, from the point of view of *another* character—let's call them character #2—who narrates the story. So, the story's "I"—character #2—will tell the reader about character #1. Think about who your narrator is. Do they have a relationship of some sort with character #1? If so, what is it—are they enemies, relatives, business partners, best friends, conjoined twins? Does character #2 know any of character #1's secrets? Does character #1 know that character #2 can see them? Keep the writing focused on character #1—and realize that you'll let us know something about character #2 by how they describes character #1.

Writing doesn't have to be this super-secret thing; it can be collaborative! You can do this exercise with another writer, too. Have them create a character and a room and trade off with them: put your character in their room and vice versa. Maybe they're the person who wrote the mysterious letter? Who knows?

What's Your Alibi?

Jessie Bailey, Jesse Delong, A. B. Gorham, and Lisa Tallin

How will your character explain their way out of this one?

OH NO! WHILE WALKING TO class this morning, you pass an open gate creaking in the wind, and near the gate you notice a dog's leash. On the leash's red fabric, a row of snow-bright diamonds spells the name Maximilian Reginald III. Never having seen a more stunning leash in your life, you pick it up, tilting the diamonds in the sun. Just then an old woman walks out of the front door of a house behind the gate. "Where is my Maximilian," she says, pressing a hand to her forehead. "Whatever have you done with my Maximilian?" She looks at you as you fumble to hide the leash behind your back. As you are about to say something, anything, to prove your innocence, you realize you are unable to speak. If only you had a moment to sit down, calm yourself, and write out your *alibi*.

Scenes like this happen all the time in literature. Your challenge as a writer is not only to imagine these scenes, but also to imagine the thousands of different ways a character would react to them.

Before you can write an alibi, though, you need a character. Since you don't want a normal, boring, everyday character, give the character some quirky traits. Consider the characteristics you will need, like an odd physical trait, an unusual occupation, and something else peculiar they do.

Here are three categories of "character traits" with examples:

An Odd Physical Trait	An Unusual Occupation	Another Thing He/She Does
Has two different colored eyes	Reads minds	Sketches people at the bus station
Has hair down to their ankles	Plucks feathers from chickens	Braids rope from fallen tree bark
One arm is shorter than the other	Designs superhero costumes	Invented a special kind of birdseed for kiwis
_____	_____	_____
_____	_____	_____
_____	_____	_____

The traits given in the columns are just examples. Try to create a couple more for each category. Once you've created additional character traits, choose one from each column on the list. The ones you choose will be the characteristics of your imagined person.

Now that you have an odd character, see what kind of trouble this costume-designing, tree-bark-braiding, ankle-long-hair-wearing person can be blamed for. Choose one of the following scenarios, put your character into it, and write your character's alibi.

Scenario 1

The police call you to the station. You are not worried, however, since earlier that morning you saw a bunch of cop cars around the neighborhood. *This must be routine questioning,* you think. But while there, the police accuse you of murder. "Murder?" you say. "Who could I have possibly murdered?" A large sergeant with a handlebar mustache tosses you a newspaper article. On the paper, you read:

> The local health inspector found Mayor Snickelfritz in a giant tub of chocolate pudding at a local Hershey factory during a routine inspection. In his pockets police found a goldfish, a silver dollar coin, and a matchbook from his sister's fourth wedding to her astronaut husband.

To be fair, the police allow you twenty minutes to write your alibi down on a piece of paper. You must tell them how you knew the victim, where you were during the crime, and why you couldn't have done it. Remember to consider your character's qualities while writing the story. For example, maybe your character could not have lifted Mayor Snickelfritz because one arm is shorter than the other. Any quirky characteristic could tie in.

Scenario 2

Last week for Mrs. Edelman's science class, you wrote a report on the banana slug. As detailed in your report, the banana slug is the mascot of your neighboring town's high school, Willow High. Coincidently, three days after you gave your report, the school's beloved banana slug went missing from its terrarium in the Willow High School biology lab. The police, however, don't think this thievery is coincidental, and after school the sergeant waits outside for you and takes you down to the station. There, he says the Willow High night janitor picked your face out of a lineup. The sergeant gives you twenty minutes to write your alibi.

SCENARIO 3

Two nights ago, you received an email claiming the Allusive Order of the Banana Slugs (a secret, members-only society that has resided in your town for the last hundred years) found an ancient scroll in their library predicting aliens will come to your town and retrieve an object they left behind years ago. Thinking the email to be spam, you delete it and decide to go to bed. Before you go to bed, you look for your red hat since every night you lay all your clothes out for the next morning. Surprisingly, you can't find your hat. After an hour, you give up searching and go to sleep.

The next morning, while walking to school, you notice the sundial is missing from in front of town hall. Only a square of dead grass marks the sundial's place. Before class starts, all the kids are talking about the missing sundial, and in the beginning of first period, the principle calls you into his office where the sergeant is waiting for you. He's swinging your red hat in his hands. Once again, he gives you twenty minutes to write your alibi.

EXTRA SCENARIO

Just for fun, after you are done writing the alibi, consider writing your confession. Maybe, ten years later, you feel so guilty about the crime(s), you decide to write a letter to the police. What would your confession look like?

Interviews

For Groups Large and Small

Jenny Gropp and Stephen Hess

"I feel that I am as necessary as my face": conduct an absurdist interview.

A N INTERVIEW IS A PROCESS of questioning that usually takes place between two people, an interviewer and interviewee. These roles are strict and, in an interview, it is uncommon for the interviewee to ask questions, while it is also uncommon for the interviewer to themself personally in any way. The interview is, almost always, intended for a larger audience: a famous person is interviewed for a magazine article; someone whose home was destroyed by a tornado is interviewed for the news. The interview is not only practical, but in writing—as the poet Loren Goodman is about to show us—the interview is a viable form of its own, one that can elicit surprising results.

Check out part one from Goodman's poem "Interviews":

INTERVIEWS

(1)

A: What disturbs you?

B: The fact that I have a skeleton inside.

A: May your anxiety be applicable to other forms of art?

B: First, it should be noted that anxiety itself is a form of art, and that I am not concerned with forms.

A: You have developed a reputation in your interviews for becoming evasive—how do you respond?

B: Would you rather I become a vase? Or jump in a pond? I feel that I am as necessary as my face.

A: What are your thoughts on control and merit?

B: Merit has it badges, while control is another form of emptiness.

A: What do you think of the weak?

B: Five days is never enough—five teeth cannot fill a
  mouth—lets us have 20–28 day weeks.

Clearly this interviewer/interviewee relationship is comically skewed, to say the least. But how, exactly? There are a couple of things to consider when analyzing the comic effect of this piece. First, look at the way that Goodman toes the line between reality and absurdity. He uses the doctor-patient relationship as the basis for the interaction, but you learn from the first answer on that this is no ordinary patient—his answers are absurdly candid. So one good strategy when writing an interview of your own is to take a stereotypical relationship, such as the doctor-patient one, the policeman-citizen one, or something stranger, like foreigner-native or disaster victim–reporter, and use it as a framework for a rather shocking interaction.

Another thing to keep in mind is the way Goodman uses the interview format to create humor. When the "doctor" asks a question, the "patient" doesn't seem to answer it directly. The answers are surprising:

A: You have developed a reputation in your interviews for
  becoming evasive—how do you respond?

B: Would you rather I become a vase? Or jump in a pond? I
  feel that I am as necessary as my face.

And then the doctor continues with a nearly non sequitur question:

A: What are your thoughts on control and merit?

By infusing the interaction with a sense of near randomness, Goodman fuels the absurdist part of the interview; the reader is continually waiting to see what the next turn will be.

Finally, look at the way Goodman uses tricks of language to create humor:

A: What do you think of the weak?

B: Five days is never enough—five teeth cannot fill a
  mouth—let us have 20–28 day weeks.

He uses *homophones*—two words that are pronounced the same way but differ in meaning or spelling or both (e.g., *bare* and *bear*)—to prompt a response from the patient. You might try this tactic, or one like it, as well.

Now that we're armed with a couple of Goodman's interview writing tactics, let's write some of our own interviews, adding a twist of our own to the mix. Before we start writing, let's consider some possible, specific interviewer/interviewee relationships like the ones we discussed above.

- journalist/disaster victim
- reporter/famous person
- police officer/citizen
- employer/potential employee
- person conducting a poll or survey/person willing to participate
- _____
- _____
- _____
- _____

Now that we have a list of possible roles, let's mix them up. Imagining what funny, odd, and interesting encounters can arise: a journalist-employer–police officer who also wants to ask occasional questions about the survey he has been designing at home is interviewing a famous person who survived an earthquake (just minutes ago) and needs a new job but is not willing to participate in the survey.

Now, let's take this good absurdist energy into our own writing with this quick, fill-in-the-blank assignment using section two from Goodman's *Interviews*.

(2)

Q: _____

A: I dunno. Maybe I go somewhere else.

Q: _____

A: Puerto Rico—you know—it's been twenty years. Twenty years, never been there.

Q: _____

A: Lot a stuff.

Q: _____

A: Mac and cheese. Potato. Spinach. Chicken. Rolls.

Q: _____

A: Julio said he's hungry. He calls on the phone. Mike said
fix him up too. So hey, I said Julio fix me up too.

. . . .

Q: _____

A: No, I don't do that.

. . . .

Q: _____

A: No way, no.

When you're finished, compare your interviewer's questions and comments with Goodman's:

(2)

Q: What would you do if you got $10,000?

A: I dunno. Maybe I go somewhere else.

Q: Where?

A: Puerto Rico—you know—it's been twenty years. Twenty
years, never been there.

Q: What is that you're eating?

A: Lot a stuff.

Q: Yeah, but what?

A: Mac and cheese. Potato. Spinach. Chicken. Rolls.

Q: Where'd you get it?

A: Julio said he's hungry. He calls on the phone. Mike said
fix him up too. So hey, I said Julio fix me up too.

Q: They fixed you up, huh.

A: Yeah (smiles).

Q: Would you do that (bunji jumping)?

A: No-o-o-o.

Q: No? Why not? Would you do it for money?

A: (Pause) Yeah.

Q: How much?

A: I dunno . . . a hundred, two hundred dollars.

Q: What about an airplane, how much to jump out of an airplane?

A: No, I don't do that.

Q: Not for a thousand?

A: Huh-uh.

Q: Ten-thousand?

A: No way, no.

Finally, now that you've taken part in a written interview with one of Goodman's interviewees and your own odd hybrid interviewer, and compared your results to Goodman's, write your own whole interview. Write at least ten questions, and be sure to leave space for answers.

When you're finished with your questions, trade papers with another writer. Take ten minutes or so and answer their questions, keeping in mind all of the strategies above.

For your grand finale, write a whole interview poem, where you alone create both the questions and the answers. Pick a fresh situation and interviewer/interviewee pair with new personalities.

Once Upon a Time in the Twenty-First Century

Retelling Fairy Tales

Pia Simone Garber

Why was Little Red Riding Hood so readily tricked by the Big Bad Wolf and what would you have done in her place?

WHEN I WAS GROWING UP, fairy tales were a feast for my imagination. I would pretend for hours, imagining I was a mermaid, a witch, a hero, and sometimes even a giant or ogre. I read every fairy tale I could find. From huge, dusty books passed down to me by my mother, I learned how to trick a monster out of its treasure, and I learned that a wicked spell can be broken with a kiss. In my mind I placed myself in those stories, daydreaming about how I would fare on a voyage East o' the Sun, West o' the Moon or whether I would have climbed that beanstalk.

As I got older, my love of fairy tales remained strong, but I began to question the old tales. Why was Little Red Riding Hood so readily tricked by the Big Bad Wolf, and what would I have done in her place? I discovered retellings of the classic tales by Francesca Lia Block and Jane Yolen that set my beloved stories in the modern era, in places like Los Angeles and New York City. The characters in these "new" stories behaved more like people I knew and recognized. I began once again to imagine myself in the tales, only this time they were taking place in my own world.

The retelling of old tales is a way to explore elements of your life and to find the magic that exists in your own world. It is also a way to examine what these stories mean and the ways in which they have shaped your culture. I will show you some elements of storytelling in three parts. First we will examine characters and learn to write through a persona. Then we will drop our characters into a modern setting and imagine how they might respond. Finally, we will create our own tales, imagining magical explanations for common, everyday things.

GETTING STARTED

Most fairy tales originated as folk traditions told aloud all over the world.

Every culture has its own stories. Think of tales from Africa, such as stories about Anansi the spider-god, or Native American stories featuring Coyote. Think of North American folk legends like Paul Bunyan and British tales such as "Jack the Giant Killer." Think of well-known tales, too, such as those retold by Disney: *Cinderella, Sleeping Beauty, The Little Mermaid.*

Start your writing by making a list of all the fairy tales you can think of. Beside the name of the tale write down anything you think is connected to the story, such as characters, places, objects, or activities. For example:

1. *Snow White: wicked queen, poisoned apple, enchanted sleep, seven dwarfs, prince*
2. *Hansel and Gretel: witch, forest, gingerbread house, oven, escape*

Keep going until you have at least five stories and at least five elements of each story. These will be your base of inspiration from which you will pull ideas for each of the following writings.

MINOR CHARACTERS GET THEIR SAY!

Stories change with each retelling, and because these tales were told long before anyone thought to write them down, there are many different versions. If you read and compare, for example, "Donkeyskin" by Charles Perrault and "Cinderella" by the Brothers Grimm, you will find that both versions tell the story of a wealthy girl forced by unhappy circumstances to work as a servant. Both girls are motherless, both have magical help, and each marries a prince who rescues her from poverty. The aspects of the story that differ, however, are far more striking. When you read the Grimm's version, do you miss the fairy godmother? Or when reading the Perrault tale, do you wonder where the stepsisters are? What is it that the cast of supporting characters contributes to the story?

Supporting characters, such as the stepsister or the fairy godmother in "Cinderella," or the woodcutter and grandmother in "Little Red Riding Hood," represent the untold side of the tale. Although we don't explicitly hear them say it, we understand that if they had their way, their version of the story would look much different. Reading the following excerpt from Denise Duhamel's poem "The Ugly Stepsister," can you hear how the stepsister is eager for an audience?

You don't know what it was like.

My mother marries this bum who takes off on us,

after only a few months, leaving his little Cinderella

behind. Oh yes, Cindy will try to tell you

that her father died. She's like that, she's a martyr.

But between you and me, he took up

with a dame close to Cindy's age.

My mother never got a cent out of him

for child support. So that explains

why sometimes the old lady was gruff.

The stepsister feels the need to explain herself, to tell the "true" version of the story. She defends her family while also recharacterizing Cinderella as a liar whose father abandoned her.

Now It's Your Turn:

From any tale you choose, pick a character whose viewpoint is not the focus of the original story. Create a profile for your character, as if you were filling out a social networking website, using the following prompts. Your character can be anyone mentioned in the story, a silent witness to the events that take place, or even an object from the story, like the spinning wheel from "Sleeping Beauty." Think about why this character or object might need their story told as you flesh out their "personality."

Character's Name: _____

Nickname: _____

Looks Like: _____

Favorite School Subject: _____

Who I'd Like to Meet: _____

Interests and Hobbies: _____

Favorite Food: _____

Favorite Hangout Spot: _____

Never Leaves Home Without: _____

Weakness: _____

Worst Habit: _____

Worst Enemy: _____

Magical Abilities: _____

Special Talent: _____

The word **persona** comes from the Latin word for *mask*. In literature it refers to writing in which the author has assumed the role and personality of a character who is distinct from the writer's own personality. The writer wears this literary "mask" and speaks in first person, as "I," in the voice of the character. Writing in a persona is telling a story from the character's perspective. Now that you have created your profile, put on the "mask" of your character and retell the tale, speaking in their voice. Create excuses and explanations for your character or object's behavior, imagining how they saw the story unfold. Write a poem or several paragraphs from this fresh point of view, using your "profile" for inspiration.

Here is a student example written by Shira Pollio. In it, the wicked fairy from "Beauty and the Beast" explains herself.

I'm always the evil fairy, somehow. They want me to be an angel (which I'm *not*) or they say I'm evil. "Oh, poor Beast," everyone always sighs, "How awful of that fairy to curse him so." Well, I'm sick of it. Let me tell you what really happened.

To start with you should have seen how the people were living in his kingdom. All the wealthy were living in his castle while his people were starving on the street. It was winter and you know what that means. People were freezing to death every night. I spent the summer in what I guess you could call love, though it was a very clumsy courtship. He was smart, kind, funny but not given the good fortune to be born wealthy. I know what they say. "It must have been his fault. There must be some laziness or oversight that made him so." Is it some flaw to have bad luck? Is it laziness to not be born a noble? And his eyes . . . They were the warmest eyes I had ever seen. It was as if they were lit from within by a candle flame, small but strong. I had been called away on business during the fall. It was a small matter, annoying but unavoidable. When I came to our cottage in the winter, I saw that that warm light had been put out forever. He had died in the cold.

I believe the punishment should fit the crime. What else is a ruler who would let his people live and die like this—while he lives in splendor—but a monster?

Adapting to a Modern Setting

Now it's time to bring classic tales into the modern world and imagine modern parallels for major elements of a classic fairy tale. Anne Sexton does this in the following stanzas from her poem, "Cinderella." This poem comes from Sexton's *Transformations*, a whole book of modern retellings:

> You always read about it:
> the plumber with twelve children
> who wins the Irish Sweepstakes.
> From toilets to riches.
> That story.
>
> . . .
>
> Or a milkman who serves the wealthy,
> eggs, cream, butter, yogurt, milk,
> the white truck like an ambulance
> who goes into real estate
> and makes a pile.
> From homogenized to martinis at lunch.
>
> Or the charwoman
> who is on the bus when it cracks up
> and collects enough from the insurance.
> From mops to Bonwit Teller.
> That story.

Sexton re-creates Cinderella over and over again, placing her as a modern service worker and giving her an updated way to get rich.

It is important when modernizing a story that you pay attention to the details of your setting and to how your character interacts with it. Is your character from another world and stuck in our world by accident, such as occurs in the movie *Enchanted* directed by Kevin Lima, or is your character from this modern world? In the story "Bones" by Francesca Lia Block, a modern retelling of "Bluebeard," the main character is a modern adolescent girl and Bluebeard has become a young rock star named Derrick Blue. In this excerpt, the girl has realized that her life is in danger and is trying to escape from Derrick's mansion to her car outside.

> I will rewrite the story of Bluebeard. The girl's brothers don't come
> to save her on horses, baring swords, full of power and at exactly the

right moment. There are no brothers. There is no sister to call out a warning. There is only a slightly feral one-hundred-pound girl with choppy black hair, kohl-smeared eyes, torn jeans, and a pair of boots with steel toes. This girl has a little knife to slash with, a little pocket knife, and she can run. That is one thing about her—she has always been able to run. Fast. Not because she is strong or is running toward something but because she has learned to run away.

I pounded through the house, staggering down the hallways, falling down the steps. It was a hot streaky dawn full of insecticides, exhaust, flowers that could make you sick or fall in love. My battered Impala was still parked there on the side of the road and I opened it and collapsed inside. I wanted to lie down on the shredded seats and sleep and sleep.

Notice how Block describes her character's modern clothing and uses such details as the girl's car and insecticides to place her in a modern time.

Your Turn

Make a list of modern situations and places. Think of local places or perhaps public places. For example:

1. My school
2. The movie theater
3. A nail salon
4. The soccer field
5. The White House
6. _____
7. _____
8. _____
9. _____
10. _____

From this list, pick your favorite and imagine this setting in as much detail as you can. What would a person see around them? What would they hear and smell? Make another list, this time describing details that are clearly modern and are particular to the place you have chosen. For example:

In my school . . .

> 1. *The walls are painted pale yellow. They are dirty and smudged from students touching them.*
> 2. *As I walk between classes I hear buzzing coming from people's headphones, and I hear cell phones chiming.*

Take the fairy-tale character of your choosing and imagine them in the setting you have just described. Is it a new world for your character? Think of what aspects of your character's personality might come to light in this situation. How might their story play out in this setting? Write several paragraphs describing your storybook character doing something in this modern setting that is similar to what they do in their fairy tale (for instance, Sleeping Beauty might sleep through class). What is happening around them? How do they react? What do they have to say?

Inventing Your Own Origin Tale Using a Modern "Fairy Tale" Element

Now that you have retold fairy tales from different perspectives and in different settings, you can invent your own tale. Many authors of fairy tales have used elements common in folk and fairy tales as inspiration for their own original works. For example, Hans Christian Andersen's stories contain such elements as wicked queens, witches casting spells, and tricksters. More recently, J. K. Rowling used classic fairy-tale models to create her own *The Tales of Beedle the Bard*, written as a complement to her Harry Potter series, and set in the same wizarding world. Her story "The Warlock's Hairy Heart" involves a chilling scenario of a young bride-to-be discovering a frightening side of her betrothed, which is reminiscent of the tale of Bluebeard. Like these authors, you will reuse classic fairy-tale elements.

An **origin tale** is a story that tells us how something or someone came into existence or why things are the way they are. This type of story is found in cultures all over the world. Some examples are *Just So Stories* by Rudyard Kipling (in which he explains such things as why the camel has a hump and why elephants' trunks are so long), the Choctaw legend "How Poison Came into the World," and the West African tale "Why Turtles Live in Water." Origin stories might involve talking animals, monsters, or other supernatural beings. The origin being described is often the result of a problem or accident that needs solving. The result is a complex explanation of something rather ordinary. In the Tlingit folk legend, "How Mosquitoes Came to Be," mosquitoes are created from the ashes of a giant who kills humans and drinks their blood. Even after his death, he vows to continue preying on humans.

> Yet the giant still spoke: "Though I'm dead, though you killed me, I'm going to keep on eating you and all the other humans in the world forever!"
>
> "That's what you think!" said the man. "I'm about to make sure that you can never eat anyone again." He cut the giant's body into pieces and burned each one in the fire. Then he took the ashes and threw them into the air for the winds to scatter.
>
> Instantly each of the particles turned into a mosquito. The cloud of ashes became a cloud of mosquitoes, and from the midst the man heard the giant's voice laughing, saying, "Yes, I'll eat you people until the end of time."

Notice that the mosquito, an often-irritating little monster of an insect, came about as a result of a man's attempt to rid the world of a monster. In origin stories one thing is often transformed into another while still retaining some distinct characteristic of its previous form.

YOUR TURN

To begin writing your own origin tale, create a list of ten fairy-tale elements and their modern counterparts. Fairy-tale elements include characters, settings, and objects. These elements will become the characters and places in your story.

Now make another list. This time write down modern objects or ideas, such as computers or presidential elections or skyscrapers. Choose one of these to be the subject of your own origin tale.

Fairy Tale Element	Modern Counterpart(s)
Prince	*Football Player, Movie Star*
Castle	*Mansion, Mall*
Magic Mirror	*Magic Cell Phone*
_____	_____
_____	_____

Combining what you have learned about persona and setting, write several paragraphs inventing the origin of the modern object you chose. Was it created out of something else? Why was it created? Did it originally have another purpose or look different? Use the list you have just created for inspiration.

Here's a student example, in which Beth Lindly explains to us how the iPod Touch was created.

Once upon a time there was a magical lake that held all the people of the kingdom's needs. You simply had to touch the surface and it would bring a menu of all the things that you wanted and a lot of things that you didn't. One day a genius named Steve Jobs visited the lake. "I will harness this power," he thought to himself. So he scooped up all the water and put it in a little box. He used all of the lake and the people got really mad and chased him away. He dropped his box and an apple got embedded in the back of it. Then he marketed it to millions.

"Is He for Real?"

CHARACTER-BASED FLASH FICTION, PART ONE: DEFINING A CHARACTER THROUGH ACTION AND DIALOGUE

Katie Berger, Laura Kochman, and Brandi Wells

Conjure up a living, breathing character in as few words as possible.

H AVE YOU EVER READ A story where the characters just seem to come alive right on the page? Does a character sometimes feel so cool you want to be their best friend, so annoying you want to scream at the story? Writers love to create realistic characters who could easily be people in our lives.

In flash fiction, a writer creates a character who's living, breathing, and real while using as few words as possible. Maybe your character's blue eyes don't have much to do with her personality, but maybe the scar on her cheek does. Maybe your character's clothes don't have much to do with who he really is, but maybe they do. As you paint your character with a small amount of words, sometimes what to leave out becomes just as important as what to leave in

Sometimes what characters *do* can define their personalities better than anything else about them. In the flash fiction piece "Salvador Late or Early," Sandra Cisneros describes an average day in the life of her character:

> Salvador, late or early, sooner or later arrives with the string of younger brothers ready. Helps his mama, who is busy with the business of the baby. Tugs the arms of Cecilio, Arturito, makes them hurry, because today, like yesterday, Arturito has dropped the cigar box of crayons, has let go the hundred little fingers of red, green, yellow, blue, and nub of black sticks that tumble and spill over and beyond the asphalt puddles until the crossing-guard lady holds back the blur of traffic for Salvador to collect them again.

Do you see how his actions (helping his brothers, collecting the spilled crayons) show us what Salvador is like?

Characters always have plenty to say, and you can include their voices in particular places within your flash fiction, too. In "My Children Explain the Big Issues," a series of short nonfiction pieces, Will Baker uses dialogue at the end of several pieces to create a defining moment for the young character.

FATE

I first explained to Cole that there was no advantage in dumping the sand from his sandbox onto the patio. He would have more fun bulldozing and trucking inside the two-by-twelve frame. Heavy-equipment guys stayed within the boundaries, part of their job, and the sand would be no good scattered abroad, would get mixed with dead beetles and cat poop.

Next I warned him firmly not to shovel out his patrimony, warned him twice. The third time I physically removed him from the box and underscored my point very emphatically. At this stage, he was in danger of losing important privileges. Reasonable tolerance had already been shown him and there was no further room for negotiation. There was a line in the sand. Did he understand the gravity of the situation? Between whimpers, he nodded.

The last time I lifted him by his ear, held his contorted face close to mine, and posed a furious question to him: "Why? Why are you doing this?"

Shaking all over with sobs of deep grief, he tried to answer. "Eyeadhoo."

"What?"

"Eyeadhoo, eyeadhoo!"

One more second, grinding my teeth, and the translation came to me. I had to. I had to.

. . .

EAST AND WEST

My other daughter, Willa, is a Tibetan Buddhist nun on retreat. For three years I cannot see her. She writes me to explain subtle points of the doctrine of emptiness, or the merit in abandoning ego, serving others unselfishly.

I will write back to remind her of a party I took her to in 1970.

The apartment was painted entirely in black, and candles were burning. There was loud music and a smell of incense and skunky weed. It was very crowded, some dancing and others talking and laughing. People were wearing ornaments of turquoise, bone, feather, and stained glass.

I glimpsed my six-year-old daughter, at midnight, sitting cross-legged on the floor opposite a young man with very long blond hair. He had no shoes and his shirt was only a painted rag. They were in very deep conversation, eyes locked. I did not hear what the young man had just said, but I overheard my daughter very clearly, her voice definite and assured.

"But," she was saying, "you and I are not the same person."

Now let's write a character-based flash fiction for ourselves. Think of your best friend or favorite family member. Make a list of everything that makes up who they are. Next, circle which elements of that person you think really define their personality. Here is a list one writer made about her brother, with the things she believed best defined his personality in bold:

- Blond hair
- Blue eyes
- Tall
- **Wears skateboarding T-shirts**
- Wears glasses
- **Enlisted in the Air Force**
- Loves Mountain Dew
- Collects international flags
- **Has a loud voice**
- **Collects vintage video games**

The things you circled in your own list can make wonderful material for your short piece. See if you can write about your special person using less than two hundred words or using one side of an index card. You can describe what they do every day (like Sandra Cisneros does with Salvador), create some dialogue for them (like Will Baker does), or use a combination of the two. Write about your character using the details that are most important.

"Is He for Real?"

CHARACTER-BASED FLASH FICTION, PART TWO: DEFINING A CHARACTER THROUGH AN UNEXPECTED SETTING

Katie Berger, Laura Kochman, and Brandi Wells

"The mermaid sitting in my tree was drenched . . ."

NOW THAT WE'VE IMAGINED CHARACTERS in situations that define who they are in "'Is He for Real': Character-Based Flash Fiction, Part One" (see p. 63), let's move them into new, unlikely situations. In creative writing, the term *apocryphilia* means putting a character somewhere he doesn't belong, or giving her characteristics that she doesn't normally have: Abraham Lincoln in space. Smokey the Bear starting forest fires. Barbie as a feminist. Consider the following example. How does Darby Larson's story, "Your Narrator and the Mermaid," work with the idea of apocryphilia? The story begins with a mermaid, located outside her normal setting, but it doesn't stop there. The writer uses apocryphilia as a jumping off point for his story and expands it into something larger and more meaningful:

> The mermaid sitting in my tree was drenched.
>
> I didn't ask her where she had been, why she was here, why she was dripping, sitting in my tree, looking curiously at me.
>
> I climbed the tree and sat next to her. We looked at things together from the branch where we were sitting.
>
> And it wasn't long until the gravity of Earth reversed. And the mermaid and me and my tree and my house fell into the air.
>
> I had hung on to my tree which was floating on the sea, the sea that flowed high above the surface of the world like a river, like a ring.
>
> I sat on my branch looking curiously down at the water, at the mermaid, at a hundred mermaids.

For our own flash fiction apocryphilia, let's make a list of famous stock characters. Here are some characters to get you started:

1. Betty Crocker
2. G.I. Joe
3. Batman
4. The Cowardly Lion
5. Macbeth
6. Cat Woman
7. Big Bird
8. _____
9. _____
10. _____
11. _____
12. _____
13. _____
14. _____
15. _____

List as many characters as you can think of, then write up a flash fiction that places one of the characters you listed in the most unlikely setting you can think of. Perhaps G.I. Joe is volunteering at an animal shelter, petting kittens. Or maybe Big Bird is having dinner at KFC. Stretch your mind to come up with as many outlandish scenarios as possible. Then expand one of these scenarios into a flash fiction.

Here are some suggestions for further reading:

Brouwer, Joel. "Diagnosis." *Centuries*. New York: Four Way Books, 2003.

Dumanis, Michael, and Cate Marvin, eds. *Legitimate Dangers: American Poets of the New Century*. Louisville, KY: Sarabande Books, 2006.

Hume, Christine. "Explanation." In Dumanis and Marvin, *Legitimate Dangers*, 171–72.

Blanco, Richard. "Perfect City Code." Dumanis and Marvin, *Legitimate Dangers*, 46–74.

McGrath, Campbell. "The Prose Poem." In *No Boundaries: Prose Poems by 24 American Poets*, edited by Ray Gonzalez. North Adams, MA: Tupelo Press, 2003.

Mullen, Harryette. "Black Nikes." *Santa Monica Review*. Fall 1997.

Waldrop, Rosmarie. "Nouns." *Alligatorzine 71* (2009), http://www.alligatorzine.be/pages/051/zine71.html.

Collaboration with Fly

Learning from Lydia Davis

Stephen Hess

Be inspired by this flash fiction master's work to write your own flash fiction.

THIS ASSIGNMENT IS SIMPLE. The titles of several stories by Lydia Davis are listed below. Your task is to write new flash fictions for her titles. Give yourself twenty minutes. For the first fifteen minutes, write three stories, one every five minutes. For the final five minutes, look back to your favorite of the three and continue to work on it.

- "A Man from Her Past"
- "Collaboration with Fly"
- "The Walk"
- "Lonely"
- "Varieties of Disturbance"
- "Burning Family Members"
- "For Sixty Cents"
- "How She Could Not Drive"
- "Special Chair"
- "New Year's Resolution"
- "Letter to a Funeral Parlor"
- "Thyroid Diary"
- "In a Northern Country"
- "Her Damage"
- "Selfish"
- "Old Mother and the Grouch"

All titles come from:

Davis, Lydia. *Varieties of Disturbance.* New York: Farrar, Straus and Giroux, 2007.

The Relationship between Truth and Fiction

Ashley Chambers, Annie Hartnett, and Christopher McCarter

How can "truth" inspire a writer of fiction?

WHAT EXACTLY IS TRUTH? AND WHAT ABOUT FICTION?

WHAT IS TRUTH? WE OFTEN think about "truth" as *Truth* with a capital *T*, that peculiar thing that stands above all others, towering in height, hovering over everything else that isn't "truth," casting non-truths in the shadow of what is true. It might be helpful to think about "truth" as being defined by its opposites—those things that *aren't* true. What, then, is "fiction"? Is "fiction" the opposite of "truth"? As writers, I believe it's our job to uncapitalize that giant *T*, and teach "truth" how it's maybe not so different from "fiction."

But let's first back up for a minute. Regardless of how we define "truth" and "fiction"—both sticky terms, to say the least—the more important question here is: How can we use what we individually understand to be "truth" to help us in our own writing? How can "truth" (the events of our day-to-day lives, however mundane they may be) inspire us as writers of fiction? And to that point, as writers, language artists, and story magicians, when exactly does "truth" become "fiction," and when does "fiction" become "truth"? Are writers creators or destroyers (or both) of "truth"? Can we create our own "truth(s)" in and through our writing? Most importantly, how can thinking about all of this help inspire future stories?

And while we're on the topic, let's push these ideas even further. What do you think the difference is between an author and their narrators, speakers, and characters? One reason I love being a writer is that I'm allowed to do whatever I want once I'm living in the world of my stories. As it turns out, there aren't any real rules in writing. I can bend, manipulate, and rearrange "truths" from my personal life however I see fit for the world of my characters, however the story I'm writing demands that they exist in that created world. In fact, as soon as I call something fiction, *It is!* There's real magic in writing because I can say something is so and then, *Poof! It is!*

Thinking about all of this, then, how can we use our notions of what "truth" is to help us as writers?

REAL LIFE EXAMPLES OF TRANSFORMING "TRUTH" INTO "FICTION"
Consider this condensed excerpt from a story I wrote after I moved to Tuscaloosa, Alabama, a few months ago. After you read it, I'm going to explain how I used "truths" from my personal life to help me come up with a new story.

ADAPTED FROM "THE DIVING BOARD"

BY ASHLEY CHAMBERS

Home again for the second time today, the woman regards her apartment's flawed roof from the interior hallway. She plans the height of her future ladder and the length of her future board, cautious to avoid stepping on any of the dozens of disoriented three-legged lizards scurrying in confused circles away from the cat's food bowl. A handful of lizards are floating in the apartment's standing rainwater, some headless, some enlarged from water retention.

The woman's construction techniques are efficient and to the point, and she envisions the partially digested fourth legs of the lizards as synchronized swimmers in her cat's stomach, making eternity stand still while reaching out toward one another in a sort of desperate effort to collect, coalesce, and cocreate a new, single, stronger, more resilient lizard, one who bites back and withstands the cat's fourth-leg-swallowing antics.

The woman doesn't play music while she works.

Instead, she inhales, exhales, and erects, and she sweats, clenching bolts between her trembling teeth, a screwdriver under her arm, mapping out the structure of the diving stand and ladder. She'll need a stand and a ladder, that's for sure, which are both suddenly flourishing before her in towering height. Her apartment palpitates in the style of a cardiaccongenital defect, or are there actually two hearts? Her apartment beats like a heart with a second heart beating inside of it.

"Wait, what?" the woman asks her cat, "I've already assembled them? I was just preparing to secure the base."

But the cat and her limitless stomach are asleep now, too.

In fact, the cat can't bear to say goodbye.

The woman's on her own, the humidity in her apartment intensifying, the cat's tail twitching left and right, tormenting the barely audible murmurings of those lizards in the apartment who have thus far succeeded in maintaining the integrity of all four legs, and when the woman focuses, she understands with tremendous clarity that the cat's stomach is also cavernous, wide, and available beneath her like a swimming pool, and then she remembers she still requires a board! Definitely some buoyancy!

Yes, of course, she recalls, materializing her fulcrum.

After reading this, what do you think is true? Similarly, what do you think is fictional? Do you think I really constructed an imaginary diving board in my living room? Let me tell you a couple of things before you decide.

I moved from Oregon to Alabama to attend graduate school. I had never visited or lived in the South before this move. It was quite a shock when I arrived here to find out that my apartment (which I'd already signed a lease on) had a faulty roof, and that my elderly fluffy cat (who also accompanied me in my trek across the country) would develop a new (and slightly disgusting) habit of lizard hunting. My kitchen and living room ceiling collapsed during my first experience with a severe southern rainstorm two months after I arrived, and my landlords weren't especially professional or responsive, so I had to live with a fair amount of rainwater in my house for a few days. This was a difficult time for me, so rather than feel sorry for myself, I tried to use the events of my day-to-day life to help me create a new story, one with a magical ending, a magical ending that did not actually occur in my real life.

In my real life, I sadly did not construct a diving board to solve my problems. Eventually roofers came and patched up the faulty rafters and molding drywall. I can't say for sure whether or not the partially digested fourth lizard legs of my cat's lizard prey really floated like synchronized swimmers in *her* stomach (notice how the cat in my story is a *he*), but that's how I imagined them, especially because at any given time I had to deal with *real* three-legged lizards scurrying in *real* confused circles in my apartment. What matters here is that I chose to turn a hard situation into a fictional, magical situation through the process of writing. In a way, turning what we perceive to be "truth" into "fiction" can be pretty therapeutic. In writing fiction, we can create new, better, and improved "truths" for ourselves. That is what I try to do.

Consider this second example, a short story by a friend of mine. Christopher also recently moved to Alabama for graduate school. Before Alabama, he lived in San Jose, California, where he worked at a fancy pizza restaurant. While reading this story, try to identify which details are true and which details he *might* have fabricated in the name of "fiction."

SHORT-DISTANCE

BY CHRISTOPHER MCCARTER

He said the Nero d'Avola is a good way to start. You ordered that glass of wine. You ordered bottled water. He said alright. You pushed your menu to the edge of the table and he came back. You ordered the Caesar salad, but just a half order. You ordered the fingerling potato pizza and laughed when he said that is redundant, no? He poured you more bottled water and said you were in for a real treat. You put your napkin in your lap at this and folded your arms over the table. You smelled him leaving (damp wood, grapefruit pith).

He came with your Caesar, just the half order. You said this dressing is remarkable when he came back to check on you. Someone took your plate away but he brought you a new one with new flatware. He did not look at you when he did this. So you said politely you don't need to bother. You said you really don't mind. But he insisted. He pretended not to hear. He offered you another glass of wine. You ordered again the glass he thought was best (this time, Brunello). You thought about how long he's been working this job.

He came with your new glass of wine. He came with a dark look on his face. Then he came with your potato pizza. You said I need nothing else, I can die happy. He chuckled as if to insinuate is that all it takes, wow. He took some time but came back to see how everything was. You said it was redundant in the best way possible, but my personal trainer is going to murder me. He smiled lightly at this and asked is there anything else you need right now. You shook your head no, chewing very politely.

After your last bite, someone took your plate away. You felt full and warm. He came back, this time with hair in his face. You somehow felt sad, too, but then he asked can I interest you in any dessert. He sounded like a Midwestern mother, encouraging by being persuasive. But you are from Toronto, so what do you know about that. He poured you more water. You said you would think about it.

He came back with a red mouth and now his hair was wet. You said you decided on dessert and laughed about giving in. He asked could you really refuse. You ordered the hazelnut budino because he said before it was luxuriating like silk. He poured you more bottled water. He leaned in very close, but without touching, to wipe down your table. He caught your eyes and for too long you stared. Then he said your boots are so dope.

He came with a clean spoon. He came with your boot on his face. He came with your dessert. He poured more bottled water over you. He asked would you like anything else in your life or was that it. You ordered three sons and another glass of wine. You asked him his name. He said my name is Temple. And he said there is only one son to give you because I'm not a mother, I'm a liminal man.

What's true in this story? Well, as we know, Christopher *did* used to work at an upscale pizza restaurant, so he used all of the names of the wine he could remember from the wine list. The restaurant *did* have an amazing Caesar salad and a potato truffle pizza. When he worked at the restaurant, he *did* wear vetiver and bergamot essential oils. "Vetiver," says Christopher, "has a very earthy, woody scent and bergamot is often mistaken for citrus, like grapefruit." When Christopher wrote this story, he *did* have a particular customer in mind, someone he had waited on a couple of times. This customer *did* wear very nice boots on one occasion. Everything else, however, was entirely fabricated in the name of "fiction."

BRAINSTORMING
Now think of a "true" event, memory, or family story from your own childhood. This "truth" can be anything you want it to be, as long as it is "true" in the way we've talked about "truth" thus far.

My Truth: _____

EXERCISE I: LIST MAKING
Now write as many "truths" as you possibly can about the "true" event

you've chosen. Try to come up with a list of at least twenty "truths." If I were just starting to work on my diving board story, some of my truths might have been:

1. I had to wait three days before the roofer came to patch up my roof;
2. I called my landlord five times in two days before she called me back;
3. The air conditioner broke during this fiasco and I thought I was going to die of heat stroke.

These don't need to be complete sentences, just words or phrases that you understand to signify "true" details related to your event.

Twenty "Truths"

1. _____
2. _____
3. _____
4. _____
5. _____
6. _____
7. _____
8. _____
9. _____
10. _____
11. _____
12. _____
13. _____
14. _____
15. _____
16. _____
17. _____
18. _____
19. _____
20. _____

Now, in a separate list, *imagine* at least five "truths" that you might like to include in a fictional story about this event. These should be fictional, in that they did not occur in real life during the event you've chosen from your childhood. These are "truths" for the story you're going to write, but are not "truths" for the event as it occurred in your real life.

Five Fictional "Truths"

1. _____
2. _____
3. _____
4. _____
5. _____

Now write a story that includes four "truths." Two must be real, from your first list, and two must be imagined, from your second list. You are allowed to include other real and/or imagined "truths," but they can't be from the lists you've already created. Push yourself to remember and also to invent details as you are writing. Write for about twenty minutes without stopping.

Little Novels

Jessie Bailey and Pia Simone Garber

Condense classic novels and movies into tiny pieces.

WHAT DO A CHESHIRE CAT, a little girl in a blue dress, and white roses painted red have in common? *Alice's Adventures in Wonderland*, of course! Okay, okay. Where do you encounter Hogwarts School of Witchcraft and Wizardry? We know, we know, it's too easy: Harry Potter! These aren't difficult at all. But can you imagine writing puzzles that are a little harder, a little more creative, a little bit odd?

Read the passages below from Denise Duhamel and Maureen Seaton's book of poetry, *Little Novels*. The book is a collection of collaborative poems based on classic novels. See if you can guess which classic novel is the title of each passage.

> Alice asked herself the question any
> Maid in a muddle of wickets might ask:
> "Which of you china chimps dances burlesque?"
> The anarchy of arithmetic spelled
> Nothing but nonsense: sleight of tongue, bells-bells,
> Chaos' Law practiced at tea parties.
> The norm was six fingers and marmalade
> Gloves that left orange sticky fingerprints.
> Alice saved the Knave of Hearts from the wince
> Of beheading—Royal Flush, what a girl!
> Alice, whether giraffe-necked or minuscule,
> Loved rabbit holes and salty mushroom stew.
> She hated rapid growth and shrinkage—her new
> Jurassic view or brow wide as a penny.

> Jack Merridew was born to villainy,
> You could tell by his fire-red hair, his
> Sunburn and scowl. Jack wasn't the type to miss
> Home, except mashed potatoes and radio.

He couldn't kill his first hog, but the slow
Seething of his submachine-gun brain cells
Made his second a breeze. He knew about hell
And yellow fire, but glamorous murder
Near blood-warm lagoons and witchy birds
Won out. Even Simon, levitating,
Light as angel food cake, felt a stirring
Of madness, his hair spiked like a fright wig.
Even the smallest boy, fed ferns and figs,
Imagined himself bloated with victory.

Do you know them? Were they easy to tell, or did they surprise you, confuse you, throw you into a topsy-turvy world where you recognize what you're looking at, but find it different, weirder, somehow new?

Now it's time to write your own condensed version of a novel or movie that you've seen. Don't just give plot summary. Don't just tell us what you saw or who the main characters are. Instead, think of how Duhamel and Seaton twist the famous works into something a little bit demented. Focus on the minute details in a book, those that only you would be drawn to and plunk them in amid more concrete details. The key is to mix the concrete with the abstract, the obvious with the fresh.

Obvious Details

Cheshire Cat, white roses painted red, a blue dress, and a white apron

Fresh Details

Her mother may have enjoyed hip hop, were she alive now.
The blue dress was actually cerulean, and 73 percent polyester.
The Cheshire cat loved getting splinters in his front paw.

WRITING A RIDDLE

Choose a book or movie you know well and that you think others will know well enough to guess. You want this riddle to be fun to solve, but you don't want to choose a topic so obscure that your audience will never get the answer.

In ten lines or ten sentences, describe the book or movie that you chose without naming the title. Avoid naming the major characters or any other aspect that will be too easy for your audience to guess. You can include names of supporting characters, setting, etc.

Use these guidelines for what you should include in your description. They can be in any order or manner you choose. Remember, you want to describe the story a little bit sideways to make the riddle more fun for guessing:

- 2–3 lines describing characters (physical, historical, or emotional descriptions)
- 1 line of setting
- 1–2 lines of plot
- 1 line of dialogue
- 1 line of rising action/climax
- 1 line of protagonist's thoughts

Fill up the rest of your ten lines as you see fit. Now see who can guess your riddle!

It Is By Chance That We Meet

Writing a One-Act Play through Collaboration

Alex Czaja, Romy Feder, and Stephen Thomas

Here, you and three others will write a one-act play.

"THE MAGIC OF THE THEATER" is a phrase you'll sometimes hear from people who've just returned from seeing a play. Aside from some people's annoying habits of repeating clichés they've heard others say, what is this about? Like most clichés, there's a kernel of truth buried in the schlock. When the lights go down in a darkened theater, the audience members all around you fall quiet, the lights go up on the scene, and the first words of the script ring out—it's true that there's something there that transcends other forms of storytelling, including the comparative inertness of prerecorded movies and TV.

It should come as no surprise, then, that actors saying lines a writer wrote on a stage is one of the oldest ways of telling a story. Originating in festivals celebrating the god of wine and fertility (Dionysus) in ancient Greece, theater in its earliest manifestations had a highly predictable structure. Indeed, Sophocles's addition of a third actor to the traditional two-actor stage was considered a major innovation in the fifth century BCE!

Today, however, we don't have to follow any old rules, and playwrights around the world have taken live theater in some pretty crazy directions, from using no actors at all (Samuel Beckett), to nonactors (Young Jean Lee), to using a military fort as the stage (SNAFU Dance Theater). Indeed, the trend in the twentieth century was to diverge as sharply from your predecessors as your imagination could take you.

But all that randomness can get out of hand, and "innovation" can sometimes become sloppy and nonsensical. Sometimes rules are good! The virtuosity of athletes necessitates the rules of sport; the breakthroughs of science are built on the backs of the hard-won empirical truths of the thinkers who came before them. Likewise, in art, it's often when we strictly limit ourselves to a highly defined set of rules that we can become most productive and unexpectedly unique.

Here, then, is our activity: you and three others will write a one-act play. In part one, you and one other partner will create your own characters, setting, and dialogue, and write a scene that'll end up as either scene 1 or scene 2. In part two, you and your partner will team up with another pair of writers to combine your scenes and, all together, write scene three.

PART ONE

Step 1: Create a Character. Every great playwright knows that an interesting character makes for an interesting story. In order to create a complex character, it is important to know their personality intimately before you write the first line of your play. Knowing your character's history, their greatest fears and desires, their tics and habits, will inform how your character responds to other characters and a range of situations. Below you will fill out a questionnaire that will take you deep into the mind of your character as you flesh out your character's backstory and discover their inner motivations and limitations.

Name: _____

Age: _____

Status (e.g., human, ghost, inanimate object):_____

Occupation (or lack thereof): _____

Hobbies: _____

Relationship status: _____

Hometown: _____

What are they most embarrassed about and why (e.g., forgetting their anniversary, wetting the bed)? _____

_____

_____

_____

What do they dream about (e.g., retirement, swimming in a pool of chocolate)?_____

_____

_____

_____

What was the proudest day of their life (e.g., the birth of their first child, winning Monopoly)?_____

_____

_____

_____

What is the meanest thing they have ever done (e.g., putting gum under their desk, plucking the wings off a fly, shaving their neighbor's cat)? ___

_____

_____

_____

What are they looking forward to (e.g., first kiss, performing a rock 'n' roll show)? _____

_____

_____

_____

What are they most stressed about (e.g., losing their job, the apocalypse)?

_____

_____

_____

Step 2: Create a Setting for Your Play! The setting of a play often simply describes the scene design: how do you imagine your play would look on the stage? Is the space spare or is it cluttered with objects that indicate the period in which the play is set? Do you want your actors to do the work in terms of creating the mood of the time period, or do you want the furniture, signage, and lighting to establish the place?

A playwright can choose to give as many or as few cues to their readers, actors, and directors. In *The Red Letter Plays*, Suzan-Lori Parks writes: "Place: Here/Time: Now . . ." These directions leave a ton of room for the director and set designer to create whatever kind of environment they feel is authentic to the play. Decide whether you want your setting to be super specific or deliberately vague.

Settings often indicate the tone of the beginning of the play. Are the actors on the stage as soon as the curtain lifts? Is there a podcast playing? Can the audience hear exterior sounds: cars honking, sirens, laughter, crying, doors slamming, a teapot whistling? Are the actors already in the middle of an activity? In *Reasons to Be Pretty*, Neil LaBute establishes that the actors are "already deep in the middle of it. A nice little fight." You can choose to set up the first scenario within your setting description.

Playwrights also often indicate the socio-economic circumstances of the characters or time period whentheir play is set. If your play takes place during any particular historical time period, you can write details that give the reader a sense of how this affects the lives of your characters.

Read the following setting descriptions to help you develop your own setting:

Neil LaBute, Reasons to Be Pretty

Setting: The outlying suburbs, not very long ago. Lights burst on. At home. Two people in their bedroom, already deep in the middle of it. A nice little fight. Wham!

Suzan-Lori Parks, The Red Letter Plays

Place: Here

Time: Now

Author's Note: The setting should be spare, to reflect the poverty of the world of the play.

Tennessee Williams, The Glass Menagerie

Setting: The Wingfield apartment is in the rear of the building, one of those vast hive-like conglomerations of cellular living-units that flower as warty growths in overcrowded urban centers of lower middle-class population and are symptomatic of the impulse of this largest and fundamentally en-slaved section of American society to avoid fluidity and differentiation and to exist and function as one interfused mass of automatism . . .

Sarah Ruhl, The Clean House

Place: A metaphysical Connecticut. Or, a house that is not far from the sea and not far from the city.

Set: A white living room. White couch, white vase, white lamp, white rug. A balcony.

Note: The living room needn't be full of living room detail, though it should feel human. The space should transform and surprise. The balcony should feel high but also intimate—a close-up shot.

Select a setting from the list below, or write your own.

Setting Bank

On the set of a game show, museum, post office, airplane, battlefield, tiled corner of a public restroom, football game (hot dog stand), principal's office, sewer, zoo, cemetery, haunted house, the woods, movie theatre, a line at the supermarket, telephone booth, on a ladder, a roof,

International Space Station, Camelot, on the surface of Mars, at sea, Atlantis (and/or underwater), the White House, desert, skydiving or falling from the sky or in mid-air, Olde England.

Setting: _____

_____

_____

_____

_____

Step 3: Write a scene. Congrats! You now have a character and setting. Now you will join forces with another playwright (someone who has also completed steps 1 and 2). Together, you and your partner will write the first scene of your play! To start, each playwright should select a mood for their character. How do you want your character to feel? What mood will make for interesting writing?

Mood Bank

frustrated, elated, stressed, wacky, careless, confused, lost, heartbroken, desperate, cocky, jealous, insecure, aggressive, critical, exhausted, flirty, hungry, anxious, shy, overconfident, brave.

Step 4: Chose a setting. In step 2 you and your partner created settings. Now, you and your partner will pick one of the settings you created for your play. GO!

Step 5: Start your dialogue. Select a first line for Character 1 from the First Line Bank below. Character 2 will respond to this line. You and your partner will continue this conversation between your characters, passing the paper back and forth, exchanging lines of dialogue. Remember, how will your character's mood impact what they say? How will the setting influence this meeting?

Character 1 Selects a First Line.

First Line Bank

"How did you get here?"

"How dare you!"

"Can you help me?"

"I need to tell you . . ."

Now write your scene below. (Each character should have at least ten lines of dialogue but feel free to write more):

Example

Scene is in a cemetery. Character 1 is a gravedigger named Bo who is feeling lost. Character 2 is a ghost named Dara who is angry.

> BO: How did you get here?
>
> DARA: I was murdered!

Step 6: Now, an event will occur in your play.

Choose from the Event Bank below.

Event Bank

Phone call with sudden news; one of the characters tries/fails to kiss the other character; character punches the other; character reveals a secret; character starts crying; character is trying to hide from someone chasing them (a bandit on the loose, etc.); character remembers something they forgot to do; something previously said upset your character and they bring it up.

The event will change your character's mood. Choose a new mood for your character from the Mood Bank on the previous page and continue writing your scene below.

Example

> EVENT: Character (Dara) decides to reveal a secret
>
> DARA: There's something I never told my dear lover boy Bo. I wasn't killed by your boss like everyone told you, sweetie baby. (*Bo looks confused, starts shoveling dirt at Dara. The dirt flies through Dara and lands against the headstone of a dog named Bobo. Bo looks even more confused.*) Baby, I meant to tell you earlier but you never listened, you big he-man gravedigger you.
>
> BO: Sweety, I'm confused. That doggy has my same name. But, like, double my name. (*Bo starts saying his name and the dog's name.*) BOBOBOBO. It's like a doggy name that is double better than one Bo. Wait (*Bo looks less confused*), who killed you?

Part Two

Welcome! You and your partner have now joined forces with another pair. You are now a group of four. Your task in part two is to combine the scenes you've already written, and write a third scene together.

Step 1: Introduce your character to the group. First, read your character description aloud to your new group members. Next, read your scenes aloud to each other. (You will read your character's lines.)

Step 2: As a group, select what will be scene 1 and scene 2. Will the first scene be the scene you wrote with your partner? Or will it be the other pair's scene? What's a more natural transition, the end of your scene to the beginning of the other one, or vice versa? Which would make more sense? Which would be funnier?

Scene 1: _____

Scene 2: _____

Step 3: As a group of four, pick a new setting. You may use one of the settings descriptions that didn't get selected during part one or you may use the Setting Bank to create a new setting.

Write a few sentences describing your new setting here. Remember to be specific!

New setting: _____

_____

_____

_____

Step 4: Pick a final fate. What will happen to your character by the very end of the play? Select a final fate for your character from the Fate Bank below.

Fate Bank

Your character has a revelation; dies at the end of scene; falls in love with two characters and can't decide which person they love more; has an emotional breakdown; tries to turn one character against another character; reveals a secret; starts a blog about the other characters.

Step 5: Write your final scene. It's now time to write your final scene, which will involve all four characters. Assign each playwright numbers one through four. Roll a die to determine who speaks next. If your number is rolled, it is your character's turn to speak. Roll a five? Write a stage direction (as you saw in the Bo and Dara scene above). Roll a six, and as a group you'll decide who speaks next.

Continue rolling the dice and bring your characters to their final fate!

Quick Found-Language Sonnets

Molly Goldman, Kenny Kruse, and Sally Rodgers

Recycle language into fourteen-line poems.

THIS EXERCISE IS A TWO parter and requires you to start looking at and collecting language from your everyday life, which you will form into several fourteen-line poems called sonnets.

It's easy to ignore all the words floating around in the world—they come out of the mouths of friends, family, and teachers; from the TV, radio, and movies; in newspapers, magazines, and textbooks; and they're on the walls at school—language is really everywhere. Surprisingly, a lot of that language is beautiful or stirring, even though it may not come from a poem or novel. Poet Louis Zukofsky once said he considers overheard language and language in books "raw material" waiting to be mined for his own use. If you start looking at the language around you as raw material, you'll have a never-ending supply of words and ideas at your fingertips.

For example, here is a ten-line poem a group wrote together using only the language we found on items in the recycling bin:

> "We're here to eavesdrop
> and intervene with edge,"
> the Colossus in Clay speaks.
> "All hail linguistics in textbooks,
> as its paper is mechanically flawless!"
> exclaims Bob Smallwood.
> They immediately notice the absence
> of the airline's bump, which was suspected
> of having eye problems. No problem!
> Better prices soon to drop.

This fun and funny poem, a combination of our favorite words and phrases from the recycling bin, only took us about ten minutes to write.

Once you start noticing the language around you, you can figure out why you are attracted to certain words and sentences and why you find others boring. My teacher Kristi Maxwell called this "reading (or listening) for texture." Every word, every letter has a texture made up of the way it sounds, the way it feels on your tongue, what you see in your mind when you hear the word and what other words the word might make you think of. The following exercise is adapted from Maxwell.

Your job is to find twenty ten-syllable lines from as many different sources as possible, and then use those lines to write several sonnets. For our purposes here, we will call a "sonnet" a poem that is fourteen lines long with each line made up of around ten syllables. I found my lines over a couple of days and recommend you do the same. Don't rush it. You want to be thoughtful in your choices.

Here is a list of the twenty "lines," each made up of ten syllables, from a language hunt, as well as their sources:

1. A raw, gray light breaking over the hills
Cormac McCarthy, *No Country for Old Men*
2. Only a ridge which divides the waters
Mark Mazower, *The Balkans*
3. Out in the pasture under a cork tree
Munro Leaf, *The Story of Ferdinand*
4. If you were a bumble bee and a bull
Munro Leaf, *The Story of Ferdinand*
5. by a yellow flame, humming all the time
Tony Johnston, *The Quilt Story*
6. Sinking roots into dirt just seems to work
Arizona Daily Star
7. I have serious reason to believe
Antoine de Saint-Exupéry, *The Little Prince*
8. Try to be happy . . . Let the glass globe be
Antoine de Saint-Exupéry, *The Little Prince*
9. "I am unlucky," said the lamplighter
Antoine de Saint-Exupéry, *The Little Prince*
10. I stare at the snake. The snake stares at me
Edward Abbey, *Down the River*
11. a shot pops across the canyons raking
Charles Bowden, *Frog Mountain Blues*

12. You're a stranger in Transylvania

Lenny Bruce, *The Essential Lenny Bruce*

13. That's the joystick, moves the wings, the rudder

Lenny Bruce, *The Essential Lenny Bruce*

14. A salami is a really big wave.

Scarlett, a three-year-old from the preschool class I teach, said this at school

15. She wrapped it round her in the quiet dark

Quilt Story

16. New house. New Horse. New Bed. Everything smelled

Quilt Story

17. tree has a hollow that collects water

Arizona Daily Star

18. You can afford the beautiful smile

Arizona Daily Star

19. small pockets of short-lived fires cannot

Fire-safety pamphlet

20. You are here: the Gorge, Mt. Hood, Pacific

A food box

Some Things to Notice about Found Language

The incomplete sentences or sentence fragments—when looking for language, I didn't limit myself to complete sentences. Sometimes the ten syllables I liked the most were only a small part of a larger sentence (for example, "small pockets of short-lived fires cannot"), and other times, the ten syllables make up a complete thought ("'I am unlucky,' said the lamplighter").

The variety of my sources—*The Story of Ferdinand* and *The Quilt Story* are children's books, and I also found a line from an article as well as one from an advertisement in the *Arizona Daily Star,* the local newspaper in Tucson. One of my lines comes from a food box and another from a fire-safety pamphlet. A wide range of sources usually makes for interesting poetic results.

When searching for your lines, you might want to think about characters and setting. My lines provided me with the poem's title character (the Lamplighter) as well as a setting (the Gorge, Mt. Hood, and the Pacific Ocean are all in Oregon, which is where my food box came from). Don't stress out about this, though. If you get lines from a variety of sources, characters, settings, and a theme will usually emerge.

Below is the poem I created with these found lines. The only rule I followed when writing the poem was to never use the lines in the same order twice. I wrote these in about an hour and went back later and fixed up the ones I liked. It was easy to write these poems quickly because I already had most of the language I needed right in front of me!

LIFE OF LAMPLIGHTER

You're a stranger in Transylvania—
a raw, gray light breaking over the hills.
If you were a bumble bee, a bull or
small pockets of short-lived fires you could
use the joystick, move the wings, the rudders.
I have serious reason to believe
sinking roots into dirt will always work.
By a yellow flame, humming the whole time,
I stare at the snake, the snake stares at me.
A shot across the canyons cracking
only a ridge which divides the waters.
Out in the pasture, under a cork tree.
"I am unlucky," said the lamplighter.
Try to be happy . . . let the glass globe be.

I have serious reason to believe
you're a stranger in Transylvania.
Out in the pasture, humming all the time,
by a yellow flame under a cork tree.
Sinking your roots into dirt never works.
You're the joystick, move the wings, the rudder.
Shoot a pop across the canyons, rake those
small pockets of short-lived fires into
a ridge that only divides the waters.
Then stare at the snake and let it stare back.
We are here: the Gorge, Mt. Hood, Pacific.
If only you were a bumble bee, a bull.
If only you were lucky, light the lamp.
A raw, gray light breaking over the hills.

New house. New horse. New bed. Everything smells

unlucky. You are the last lamplighter,
and I break raw gray light over the hills.
My pockets are full of short-lived fires,
and you're a stranger in Transylvania,
sinking your teeth into the working dirt.
You can afford the beautiful smile,
to wrap it round us in the quiet dark.
You can afford the yellow flame, humming
like a tree hollow collecting water.
You can afford to let the glass glove be
here: the Gorge, Mt. Hood, Pacific Ocean.
The ridge dividing the waters divides
you at the joystick. Moves wings. Moves rudders.

We are unlucky, says the lamplighter.
Our throats are hollow and collect water.
Gorge ogre, mouth organ, Pacific o
Even the yellow flame hums all the time.
Stills the small pockets of short-lived fires.
Still, it wraps round us in the quiet dark.
Still, a raw gray light breaks over the hills.
Is happy to leave the glass globe alone.
Are happy to grow fatter in the warm.
Worm our roots into dirt. Our workers' hands,
our forest, the ridge. Divide the weather
into strangers who transfuse cold water.
If we were a bumblebee and a bull,
if we were a snake staring at itself.

It is dark. Wrap the yellow flame and hum,
It is dark. Drop quiet in the water
hallow, the winter smile. The waters
divide the sinking roots, the dirt, the roots.
Someone believes in bumblebees and globes.
Someone believes in Transylvania.
But who is estranged, who is raw and hums?
Broken light, grey light, who is unlucky?
Who lights lamps, who breaks light, the glass, the hills
the glass? Try to be the newest canyon,

sinkhole. Then try to be the newest tooth,
dirty tooth. Try to be the lamplighter.
Here are the fires we could not put out.
Here is the ocean, o happy pasture.

Notice that in the first two sonnets, I basically just moved around the lines without changing much or writing between them. By the third sonnet, I started to get comfortable with the language and freely changed lines and made connections between lines in ways I didn't in the first two. Later, I decided to keep only the last three sonnets and "threw out" the first two.

Okay, so now that you've read the examples, here are some ideas to get you started in your own language hunt. Remember, try to keep the lines to around ten syllables each, but if you have trouble counting syllables, make sure the "line" you write down is about sentence length—no single word lines or paragraphs here!

1. Write down one thing from a billboard.
2. Write down something from TV or a movie.
3. Write down one song lyric.
4. Write down something your teacher says in class.
5. Write down a line from a textbook.
6. Write down a line from a novel.
7. Write down a line from a children's book.
8. Write down a line from a nonfiction book.
9. Write down two things you overhear.
10. Write down something from a label/box in your kitchen.
11. Write down something from a bathroom stall.
12. Write down a Facebook status (not your own).
13. Write down something from a magazine.
14. Write down something from a newspaper.
15. Write down something from an advertisement.
16. Open the dictionary to a random page and write down a sentence you like.
17–20. Write down words, sentences, images—anything you want from anywhere you see/read/hear it!

Now that you have your lines, spend about an hour arranging them and writing them into as many sonnets (fourteen-line poems) as you can. Three to five sonnets is a good goal. You may end up with five poems you like, or you may end up with one poem you really love. The point is, the more you write, the more likely you are to end up with poems that make you happy! And one last thing, don't worry too much about making sense at first. After playing with the language for a while, you will see that poems create their own logic, which is likely to be different than the logic you encounter elsewhere in life.

Social Network Haiku

Chapin Gray and Kirk Pinho

Update the haiku form by writing away messages and Facebook haiku.

BEFORE SHAKESPEAREAN SONNETS, AND VICTORIAN and Elizabethan odes, there were haikus. You might say they are the granddaddy of all forms, sitting in their reclining chair, always doing something, but waiting for us—their grandkids—to pay attention to them. So let's go visit grandpa and have a nice discussion with him!

Traditionally haikus have three lines: the first line has five syllables, the second line has seven, and the third line has five. Using amazing mathematical skills, we conclude that they contain a total of . . . drumroll! . . . seventeen syllables! And though haikus are generally thought of as being quiet musings on nature—trees, frogs, lakes—they can be about virtually anything.

The only real requirement is that they have a turn somewhere in the poem. What do we mean by "turn"? Surprise the reader! Give them a reason to say, "WOW! I wasn't expecting that!" Consider this one we crafted in just about five minutes:

> Maybe a willow
> caught my shadow in its teeth,
> pulled it to the dirt.

Where do you think the turn is? Where is the surprising moment in this haiku? Everyone will have different ideas, but that's part of the beauty of these little beauties. So let's put our haiku skills to the test using as a backdrop something that certainly wasn't around when haikus were first written centuries ago in Japan.

AWAY MESSAGE HAIKUS

Your online friend, HaikuRiter54285, is kind of a weird little fellow. On top of not having any idea what the five digits in his screen name mean, you never know where he is when he puts an away message up.

He constructs a haiku for everyone, keeps them vague, and makes sure that they are interesting. So, you're going to copy his little strategy and write your own.

What did you do yesterday? What do you wish you were doing yesterday? These are all questions you can ask yourself when you are writing these haiku. For example, I was in class yesterday but I really wanted to be shooting hoops. But, these being away messages, I didn't want to tell people that I was in COM240 in Bob Smith Hall on the campus of Frog Leg University in Laramie, Wyoming from two to two fifty. So I wrote this instead:

> The netting snapping
> back like a breeze, idle,
> glory of muscle.

So, consider this and write some haikus for all occasions: when you're in school, when you're hanging with your friends, when you're at practice, when you're doing homework, when you're eating dinner, when you're being goofy, when you're cleaning out the litter box, etc. So get to it. Make us ROFL and LOL; make us OMG and 4REALZ?

Profile Haikus

Who doesn't have a Facebook page these days? Maybe you have an online journal. Or maybe you're a social butterfly and you have both. But since no one uses Friendster anymore, you probably don't have one of those. One of the things that most social networking thingamajigs have in common is that they ask you about yourself, your interests, your life, so you get more friend requests! So, with haikus, tell us about what you do, your hometown, your hero, your relationship status. *But* don't forget to have the surprising moment in your little three-line ditty. For example, I like to play guitar (believe me, not well!), so for one of my "interests" haikus, I wrote this:

> Fantastic guitar!
> Someone says through sweat, dark,
> breaks it on the ground.

Maybe, when you're done with these, and if they are interesting enough, we will add each other as Facebook friends. You can read our bulletins, surveys, and look at all the cool graphics on our pages. But be wary: our profile songs change on a daily basis.

Rhymes Real Cool

STUDIES IN RAP LYRICS

Christopher McCarter

Tap some rhymes to use in rap.

As far back as Sugarhill Gang's unmistakable 1979 classic, "Rapper's Delight," rap music has made rhyming a mainstay of the genre. The best way to hear these rhymes is to listen to the lyrics being performed. But before things get too *bumpin'*, let's start by looking at just a handful of rhymes. This way, we will begin to see exactly how rappers across the decades have brought language together into rhymes.

Probably the most common and easiest to identify is the **perfect rhyme**. Words that have a perfect rhyme generally have the same number of syllables and the same vowel sounds.

For example:

> brightest / tightest

or:

> flame / game

There is also the **slant rhyme**, which is much more flexible and mysterious. The slant rhyme is sometimes known as a near rhyme or *imperfect* rhyme because it is very close to a perfect rhyme, but not as exact. Slant rhymes usually contain an assonant rhyme (i.e., words whose vowel sounds rhyme) or a consonant rhymes (i.e., words whose consonant sounds rhyme). This is what makes the slant rhyme more flexible. It can move lyrics into new territory without too much interruption of your *flow*.

For example:

> ready / heavy
> (long -*ea* sound: assonant rhyme)

or:

> Rockefeller / a capella
> (hard -*ck* and -*ll* sound: consonant rhyme)

Eye rhyme is a rhyme that relies less on the sound of the rhyme and more on how the words look on the page. Eye rhymes reflect how our pronunciation of similar looking words can vary.

For example:

> prove / love

or:

> cough / bough

The last and maybe most challenging rhyme is the **scarce rhyme**. What makes a good scarce rhyme is the surprise of the rhyme. This usually means rhyming words that are multi-syllabic and which have limited rhyming potential. The benefit of this rhyme, though, is that it shows how you, the rapper, are able to really flex your rhyming muscle.

For example:

> bodyguards / two big cars

This rhyme combines a word and a phrase that both have three syllables and end with the same vowel sound. Thus, their combination is rare, or scare.

Or:

> divorcé / Lee Dorsey

Again, this rhyme combines a word and a proper noun with the same number of syllables and the same vowel sounds: -o and -ey.

The way words sound together is not the only relationship that makes rhyming possible. Where the words are within the lyric can also affect the outcome of your rap.

For example, we often expect rhymes to fall at the end of the line. This is known as a **terminal rhyme** and usually indicates where a line ends or where the line terminates.

For example:

> Well it's the *Taking of Pelham One Two Three*
> If you want a doo-doo rhyme then come see <u>me</u>

But rhymes can really happen anywhere in the line. Sometimes they fall at the very beginning of a line, which is called a **head rhyme**. Head rhyme can be thought of as a kind of *alliteration*, where the line begins with some variation of two or more rhyming words.

For example:

> Fast and exciting, my passion is frightening
> Now let me put some more vocab in your I.V.

In this lyric, "fast and exciting," the head rhyme, initiates the *-a*, *-i*, and *-ing* sounds. These sounds return in "passion is frightening" and partially in "vocab in your I.V."

Sometimes rhymes can even happen in the middle of the line, which is known as **internal rhyme**. This placement of the rhyme can strengthen the lyric, giving it force and power by building up certain rhyming sounds close together.

For example:

> Now I'ma get the mozzarella like a Rockefeller, still be
> in the Church of Lalibela, singing hymns a capella

Now, to show how these different rhymes can bring specific qualities to lyrics, I will analyze a verse from Sugarhill Gang's "Rapper's Delight."

> Check it out—I'm the C-A-S-A, the N-O-V-A and
> The rest is F-L-Y[1]
> You see,[2] I go by the code of the Doctor of the Mix
> And these reason I'll tell you why[1]
> You see,[2] I'm six-foot-one[3] and tons[3] of fun[3]
> And I dress to a tee[4]
> You see,[2] and I got more clothes than Muhammad Ali[4]
> And I dress so viciously[4]
> I got bodyguards,[5] I got two big cars[5]
> I definitely ain't the wack[6]
> I got a Lincoln Continental and
> A sun-roofed Cadillac[6]

[1] Perfect rhyme: "Y" and "why" are perfect end rhymes. They have the same number of syllables and the same vowel sounds.

[2] Perfect rhyme: "see," "see," and "see" all rhyme perfectly. They are also head rhymes. They do not mark the end of the line, but instead, start the line in the repeated phrase "You see."

[3] Slant rhyme/assonant rhyme: "one," "tons," "fun" are not completely perfect rhymes, considering the *s* on tons, but they all have the same vowel sound. Therefore, they all have the same assonance and can be considered imperfect or slant rhymes. They also start internally and then make up the end rhyme, which allows for a build up across the line. I like to call this "priming," where the internal rhyme prepares (or primes) your audience for the terminal rhyme. When you finally strike that terminal rhyme, the iron is red hot!

[4] Perfect rhyme: "tee," "see" are perfect rhymes, but "tee" starts a new end rhyme with the second syllable in "Ali." It also rhymes with the following "see," which is an internal rhyme. In this relationship, you can see how the terminal rhyme "tee" and the internal rhyme "see" create a super smooth transition between lines. That's so fresh! "Ali" and "viciously" have a different number of syllables, but their end consonant sounds -*li* and -*ly* rhyme. These words have some of the same consonance. They also fall as end rhymes, originally started by their imperfect rhyme with "tee." I really enjoy how Sugarhill Gang is able to layer their rhyming techniques here.

[5] Scarce rhyme: "bodyguards," "two big cars" are multisyllabic with few rhyming opportunities. However, in this case, the lyricist coupled "bodyguards" with a short phrase that rhymes with its ending vowel sound, -*uar* and -*ar*. This is surprising because it is a scarce rhyme, but also because "bodyguards" foreshadows the new end rhyme "two big cars." Now that's what I call $wagger!

[6] Slant rhyme/consonance: "Wack" and "Cadillac" have different numbers of syllables but end with the same hard -*ck* sound. The end rhymes give their consonant sounds more emphasis, closing out the verse so that the next rapper can pick it up. The repetition of a hard -*ck* consonant sound also feels like a nice ending or close to a rhyme.

Before you start writing your own rap, you might want to practice analyzing a couple rap verses. Check out the *Anthology of Rap* for an array of lyrics from contemporary rappers and artists that came long before them.

Once you have some lyrics to look at, follow the model outlined above. Start your analysis by highlighting or underlining all the words that seem to rhyme, either by sound or visually. Then go back over them and try to make their relationship more specific. Determine if they are perfect, slant, scarce, or eye rhymes. Then figure out their position in the line, if they are end rhymes, head rhymes, or internal rhymes. Once you've done all of this, you might notice how certain rhymes or word relationships reoccur, and how these rhymes give specific style to the rap.

Now you are ready to write your own rap lyrics. To get started in the right direction, first decide what you want to write about. Rap lyrics can be about anything, but a lot of the time they deal with certain themes. Here are just a few of those themes that might inspire your lyrical genius:

1. Design your ideal life. Do you have a house? Is it made out of diamonds? Do you have a car? Or do you skateboard everywhere? Do you brag and boast about everything and anything? Or, to play it down, is your ideal life a modest one?

2. Delve into your deepest feelings. Look back at an emotional past experience. Maybe you got your heart broken. Tell what happened. Maybe you lost a loved one. Say why that was hard. Be expressive, heartfelt, and sincere. You might learn something new about yourself.

3. Just be silly and fun and see where it takes. Challenge yourself by making the most outrageous rhymes possible. Start with a word you think couldn't rhyme with anything, like orange or meerkat.

Now that you have a topic in mind, make a word bank. Write down all the words that come to mind that are related to your topic. But don't spend too much time thinking about what words you choose. Focus on generating a fat bank of words first. Then go back over them and see which ones rhyme or which ones stand out to you. Once you have a few rhymes in mind, you are ready to start rapping. If you get stuck, look back at your word bank for inspiration. Your task is to write ten lines using at least three of the four different kinds of rhymes (perfect, slant, scarce, and eye). Remember to vary where your rhymes fall in the line (terminal, head, and internal) to make smooth or unexpected transitions. Be relaxed and have fun.

Now you are part of a long line of some of the coolest and most talented writers!

Oral Poetry

THE PHYSICAL LANDSCAPE OF YOUR POETIC VOICE

Curtis Rutherford

Tones, tempos, and timbres—shape your poem with your voice.

WHAT IS ORAL POETRY? It's poetry that's created not just for you to read, but hear as well. Maybe you thought that poetry was strictly words that you experience on the page? Keep in mind that poetry existed hundreds of years before written literature ever did. Oral traditions in poetry have been floating around in many different cultures for centuries. So there is a smorgasbord of unwritten ancestral traditions to take in. These traditions are connected to many societies and customs, such as those of the indigenous people of Mexico and the Caribbean, shamans, spiritualists, enslaved African Americans, and Native Americans. These oral poetries were used in celebrations and for medicinal purposes, work-related activities, social gatherings, and worship services. For the most part (but not entirely), these amazing oral traditions and influences have been submerged in our culture. But never fear, there is a reemergence of familiar oral poetics in art forms such as hip hop, rap, and slam poetry.

When thinking about oral poetry consider how the poet uses their voice as a poetic tool. You must think about the landscape of your voice. What do I mean by the *landscape* of your voice? Oral poets use their tones, tempo, and the timbre of their words (sometimes they use physical gestures and music, too) to give the poem its full body and to convey meaning for the audience. Think of it this way—with your physical voice, alone, you can: create any mood/atmosphere you want, emphasize certain words or themes, get away with using many refrains/lists without a reader skipping over repeated lines, and really highlight wordplay. Just imagine all this being at your fingertips! Well, let me rephrase . . . it's all at the tip of your tongue!

You have the ability to use your voice to contour your poem, through your words, or through nonsense syllables, as you use syllabic strategies and pauses in your written poems to achieve the same goals. Think of it as building a landscape with what you say out loud, with shouts, whispers, and moments where you speed up or slow down. You can sound sweet, or you can sound sinister and mean. Use your voice's topography to make your poem's argument(s). Sure, your written poem can be read aloud, but the examples I'll present to you will show you a new world of possibilities.

Now, we have the poet (that's you), and we have the words of your poem. The sense of voice on the written page is up to interpretation. The reader has to decode your diction, syntax, and subject matter to deduce the poem's personality. But in oral poetry, this is all up to your performance; you have much more control and more tools at your disposal.

Think of yourself as not just being the benevolent ruler of your words hoping that your audience understands the atmosphere you are trying to build, as you would in written poetry. Rather, see yourself as a part of the circle of words and voice that create the work. You'll be adding another layer of the act of poem building and get to physically be a part of your poem.

Let's take a look at the musician/poet, Tom Waits. His piece "Frank's Wild Years" from the *Swordfishtrombones* album (1984) is a great example of how the intonations of voice help build a character. In some excerpts from this piece, we hear a funny, yet disturbing narrative of a fellow named Frank told in the third person. I'll mark the modulation of Waits' voice so you can see how he does it. The syllables in **bold** are emphasized by Waits. The underlined words are spoken quickly together as a unit. By looking at Waits' speech patterns we can see which elements he is showing as important, using vocal cues.

> **Frank** settled down out in the **valley**
> And he hung his **wild years** on a nail
> That he **drove** through
> his wife's **forehead**.

The bolded words make it clear that Frank is the main character, and begin to give a sense of his energy, his brash way of being. Compare that to a passage about his wife, where the quickly spoken words blur together the details about her and her dog, making it sound like she is less important:

His **wife** was a spent piece of used **jet trash**
<u>Made good Bloody Marys</u>
<u>Kept her mouth shut most of the time</u>
<u>Had a little Chihuahua named Carlos</u>
<u>That had some kind of skin disease</u>
<u>And was totally blind</u>
(Clears throat)

Every element of this poem is intentional: the light, jazzy music on the track, the clearing of the throat, speeding past boring details that highlight the tragedy of Frank's submission to the "American Middle-Class Dream." And his attitude toward his wife. Waits's quick tempo on certain phrases has a unique effect. Phrases like "down San Fernando Road, assumed a thirty-thousand-dollar loan at fifteen and a quarter percent and put a down payment on a little two bedroom place" add a level of hilarity, as the tempo seems to illustrate the irony of Frank's plight, and later, his victory at liberating himself: "Never could stand that dog."

Let's take a look at the words that Waits is emphasizing:

- Frank
- Valley
- Wild years
- Drove
- Forehead
- Wife
- Jet trash

The words that are pushed forward, the words that ring in the listener's ear through Waits's emphasis are constructing the ambiance the poet wants to achieve. Tom Waits is known for his character-building skills within his songs and oral poetry. A stalking, streetwise layer is added, with the emphasized words: *wild years* and *jet trash*. All of these layers of meaning and nuance mixed with the intentional timbre, tone, and tempo of Waits's voice make the poem more than just Waits reading words on paper; he is showing us how a poet can enter into the circle with his words and voice. This is the crux of oral poetry—being able to occupy poetic space with your poem in order for the poem to be fully experienced.

Let's look at another poet who uses words and staging in her work for emotional impact. María Sabina, a Mazteca shaman from Oaxaca, Mexico, used an invocation style, and spouted nonsense syllables in an attempt to build atmosphere. The words from *The Midnight Velada* seem to hypnotize in their repetition, and the staging notes for a second performer show how we can use physical gestures and other players, too. Here is an excerpt from *The Midnight Velada*:

> Hmmm hmmm hmmm
> Sap woman
> Dew woman
> [The man urges her on. "Work, work," he says.]
> She is a book woman
> Ah Jesusi
> Hmmm hmmm hmmm
> Hmmm hmmm hmmm
> So so so
> Lord clown woman

The invocative spirit of her performance allows for a wide range of possibilities in this poem. By taking on accompaniment in *The Midnight Velada*, getting another player/poet to cheer her on and shout at choreographed moments, she is building an atmosphere of mystery and anticipation. The poetic words mixed with nonsense syllables and made-up words allow her to use her poetic voice at a wider range than simply reciting words on the page. In many ways Sabina's poem is closer to older oral traditions. Her poem does more than wow with language. The poet is actually *entering* into the poem and occupying artistic space with her voice and the ambiance it shapes. She is building a poem through the landscape of her voice.

Now write your own oral poem to be presented aloud. For your form, you can use one of the examples just discussed here or come up with a form of your own. For the subject of your poem, choose one of the following topics, or invent your own.

1. Zombies come to your campus.
2. Your first day of school.

3. The exact moment you realized you wanted to write poetry/fiction/
   nonfiction.

4. How your favorite song makes you feel.

5. The time your pet gave you relationship advice.

Collaborative Ghazal

Chapin Gray and Kirk Pinho

*Explore this mesmerizing Arabic form and write one with a group
or on your own.*

D ERIVED MORE THAN ONE THOUSAND years before we were born,
ghazals (pronounced HU-zzle) are an ancient Persian form of po-
etry that essentially allows people to meditate about anything over the
course of one poem—whether that poem be about a squirrel you saw get
run over, a game your baseball team lost, or the part you weren't able to
snag in the school's performance of *My Fair Lady*.

Essentially, ghazals are made of a couple different components. First,
you pick an ending sequence for each couplet—a two-line stanza—and
also a word that contains the same rhyming pattern. Consider the first
few lines of this bombastic ghazal written by Peggy O'Brien:

> My mother's standing pointing at the sky in a dream,
> "Can you see it, there?" I hear her cry in a dream.
>
> My head is in the clouds like yours. I know it now:
> But you're the one to blame. I'm in a quandary, in a dream.
>
> Give me the blank banked tall with vague immensities—
> I too am racing, drifting, floating high in a dream.

The first couplet of a ghazal—as showcased above—has the same words
ending the first two lines ("in a dream," as above). This awesome end-
ing to each line also has a word proceeding it which rhymes throughout
the poem. In the case of the first three couplets shown above, the long *I*
sound is something that is repeated—*sky, cry, quandary* (a slant rhyme!),
high, etc. That pattern is repeated until the last couplet—there can be as
many couplets as you want!

Therefore, the first couplet has the two lines that end in "to a dream,"
for example, but the first line of the couplets after that doesn't have a re-
peating phrase.

Here is a ghazal written collaboratively by students one afternoon:

I begged you to leave that day in the fog
but then I saw you outside; you had stayed, in the fog.

Emerging out of the dark ocean,
just trying to find your way in the fog.

The blossom stuck to the arch of your foot.
Look: it's the only song that played in the fog.

I tend to find an open house
with two cats astray in the fog.

A soft touch of light comes forth from the bay
but ends up drifting along the waves in the fog.

She sat in the way.
There was nothing she could say in the fog.

The coup d'etat, like an umbrella, frayed in the fog.
As we swayed to some lickable refrain in the fog.

Notice how "in the fog" is the line that's repeated, and all the students did their darndest to make sure to repeat the long *A* sound at least once in every couplet. You should do that, too.

Now you try it. Get together some of your buddies, put on some tunes, and go to town (not literally, of course). As a group, pick a phrase (much like "in the fog") that can be repeated several times without it becoming mundane. With that as your backdrop, choose a sound that can also be repeated over and over, a sound that occurs in lots of words (much like the long *A* sound in the collaborative ghazal that we wrote). This sound will recur in the position just before the repeated phrase in the second line of every couplet.

Then, once you've done that, you should each come up with your own couplets to contribute to your communal ghazal. One of the awesome things about ghazals is that they allow each couplet to stand on its own. Therefore, if I write about roller coasters, you can write about dolphins, and it will all go together to create a whole-ghazal mood.

Or, if you're a loner, do this exercise by yourself. To do so, write a couplet a day for your ghazal, being sure to follow the rules. When you return each day to write a new couplet, you will have something different on your mind, so you can create a series of couplets that are loosely linked by their ending phrases, while each couplet stands like an island on its own.

Collaborative Abecedarian
(For Up to Twenty-Six Writers)

Sally Rodgers

Fall in love with the alphabet all over again and use it to organize and inspire a poem.

WHEN WE THINK OF THE alphabet, most of us probably think about kindergarten and learning to sing our *ABC*s. We might think of the grades assigned in school, with A being the best and F being the letter we all dread, or using the alphabet to organize things (think "alphabetical order," like in the phone book). But really, the alphabet is so much more than that! Almost everything we want to say can be said using the alphabet (what would we do without it?!?), and did you realize that using alphabetical organization can be creative, too? An **abecedarian** is a form of poetry that uses the alphabet to order its lines. In its simplest form, the poem begins with a line that starts with an *A*. The poem should be twenty-six lines total, each beginning with the next letter in the alphabet. Not only has this form has been around since ancient times, but its name is really fun to say (the first syllable rhymes with "lab," the next two syllables are the "b" sound followed by an "s" sound, and the end rhymes with "librarian")!

I think it's important that *abecedarian* is so much fun to say because the end result should be fun to read and to hear. We sometimes forget, but when it comes down to it, each letter is just a sound that can be detached from all denotative meaning (such as a dictionary definition). Like musical notes or keys on a piano, if you get letters down to their pure sound form, they should each bring their own type of joy to both the speaker and the listener.

Two examples of abecedarians written recently are *Alphabet*, a book-length poem by Inger Christensen, and "Jinglejangle" by Harryette Mullen from her alphabet-organized book *Sleeping with the Dictionary*.

Here are the first five "chapters" of Christensen's book:

1

apricot trees exist, apricot trees exist

2

bracken exists; and blackberries, blackberries;
bromine exists; and hydrogen, hydrogen

3

cicadas exist; chicory, chromium,
citrus trees; cicadas exist;
cicadas, cedars, cypresses, the cerebellum

4

doves exist, dreamers, and dolls;
killers exist, and doves, and doves;
haze, dioxin, and days; days
exist, days and death; and poems
exist; poems, days, death

5

early fall exists; aftertaste, afterthought;
seclusion and angels exist;
widows and elk exist; every
detail exists; memory, memory's light;
afterglow exists; oaks, elms,
junipers, sameness, loneliness exist;
eider ducks, spiders, and vinegar
exist, and the future, the future

In Christensen's poem, she brings order and sense to the world around her by naming the things that exist. The book is divided into fourteen sections, one for each letter of the alphabet *A* through *N*. The number of lines in each section increases as it moves through the alphabet, so the first section contains only one line, but the fourteenth section is fourteen pages long. One tactic that dominates these poems is the use of several kinds of repetition. The most obvious is repeating a sound at the beginning of words (as in the *s* sound starting "cicadas, cedars, cypresses, the cerebellum"). This is called *alliteration*. Christensen makes use of this kind of repetition throughout her poem, but she also repeats whole words again and again. In section four, *doves* is the first word as well as the ninth and eleventh word. The "apricot trees" of the first section come back several times throughout the poem. You can see them here in the last three lines of section six: "apricot trees exist, apricot trees exist/in countries whose warmth will call forth the exact/colour of apricots in the flesh." This, to borrow a term from stand-up comedy, is known as a *call back*. In stand-up, it's a way the comic can remind the audience of a joke they made earlier in their set. If it goes over well, the audience will laugh without the comedian having to repeat the entire joke. Here, Christensen repeats the entirety of that beautiful and sparse first line, reminding readers of the earlier section and giving them a moment to glance back over what they have already read.

Now let's look at the abecedarian poem in Harryette Mullen's *Sleeping with the Dictionary*. Here are the *L* and *M* sections. Try reading them out loud!

> Laffy Taffy lame brain large & in charge late great later gator Lazy
>> Daisy
> Lean Cuisine lean & mean mean machine legal eagle Leggo my
>> Eggo
>>> Licken' Chicken licking stick Liddle Kiddle li-
>> quor's quicker
> lit crit liver quiver lizard's gizzard local yokel long dong Loony
>> Toons Loopy Doopy
> loose screws loosey-goosey lovie-dovie low blow lucky duck lump
>> sum lunch bunch
> lust in the dust Lynyrd Skynyrd
>
> Mac Attack mad dad made in the shade Magilla Gorilla main-
>> frame maitai Mango Tango
> Manila Thriller Mantan Mars bars master blaster Maui Bowie
>> May Day Meal Deal
> Meals on Wheels mean green meet & greet mellow yellow Messy
>> Bessy
> Micmac might makes right Mighty Aphrodite miles of smiles
>> Milli Vanilli
> Mingus Among Us mishmash Missy-Prissy mock croc Mod
>> Squad mojo moldy oldie
> Money Honey moose on the loose mop top Mork from Ork motor
>> voter muckamuck
> muck chuck mukluk multi-culti mumbo jumbo mu shu mushy-
>> gushy my guy

Harryette Mullen makes use of alliteration, too, but she also uses *asso-nance* (the repetition of vowel sounds), *consonance* (the repetition of con-sonant sounds), and *rhyme*. She uses these devices so heavily that her poem becomes happily dominated by sound, almost reminiscent of a Dr. Seuss story (she even name-drops *The Cat in the Hat* in the *C* sec-tion). Mullen's poem expands the type of language that we generally think of as "poetic." While Christensen's poem contains plenty of sur-prises, her diction (types of words) remains constant throughout. Mul-len, on the other hand, borrows heavily from both high and low culture, sticking product names (like Choco Taco and Best Western) in proximity to the names of celebrities and popular musicians (Milli Vanilli) as well as highly revered jazz musicians (Mingus Among Us references bassist Charles Mingus). Mullen's rule throughout is to use compound words that rhyme. This sometimes results in "noise" words, or *onomatopoeia*.

Now that we've read the examples, let's get to writing. First, write the alphabet on a series of twenty-six note cards, one letter per card. Then di-vide the note cards as evenly as possible among you and other writers. Make sure no one has two letters in a row. This will ensure that jumps in voice happen consistently between each letter, creating uniform variety in a poem authored by up to twenty-six people. It will also allow for the types of "callbacks" that Christensen employs. If you get stuck, try refer-encing something you said earlier!

Take a few minutes per note card (try not to spend more than ten minutes on any one letter). Aim for a variety of lengths and techniques. Some letters can be just one sentence (or sentence fragment) long, while for others you may want to fill every last square inch of both sides with words. For some letters you might want to copy Christensen's style (nam-ing what exists in the world) while on other letters you might borrow from Mullen (a concentration on sound, rhyme, popular culture, and compound words and phrases). You can even try to combine the different techniques in one card.

After everyone finishes their letters, take turns reading each one out loud in alphabetical order. Hearing these puppies read aloud is a big part of enjoying them, so don't skimp on the drama—stand up, pull your shoulders back, take a deep breath, and project your voice!

The Triolet

Pia Simone Garber

A French poetic form full of rhymes and repetition.

A TRIOLET IS A FRENCH FORM that relies heavily on rhymes and a *refrain* (a phrase that recurs at intervals in a poem or song, often at the end of or between stanzas of verses, like a chorus). The rhyme scheme of a triolet is:

A (1st refrain)
B (2nd refrain)
a (rhymes with 1st refrain)
A (repeat 1st refrain)
a (rhymes with 1st refrain)
b (rhymes with 2nd refrain)
A (1st refrain)
B (2nd refrain)

So, each triolet has two sets of rhymes. Rhyme Aa consists of a refrain and two rhyming lines, and rhyme Bb consists of a second refrain and one rhyming line. This kind of repetition results in poems with very interesting sound repetition, like this one, "If You Were Lady Beatrice," by Sara Teasdale:

> If you were Lady Beatrice
> And I the Florentine,
> I'd never waste my time like this—
> If you were Lady Beatrice
> I'd woo and then demand a kiss,
> Nor weep like Dante here, I ween,
> If you were Lady Beatrice
> And I the Florentine.

In another example of a triolet, by Molly Peacock, the refrain is not the entire line, but only the second half of the line.

FOOD FOR TALK

The bird delights in human food,
claw clamped to the lip of the cup,
and I delight in human good
the way the bird delights in food,
soft and foreign to its beak, wooed
by something not its own abrupt
crack of the seed. So human good
is soft law to the sharp lip's cup.

There is also some variation between refrains: "human food" becomes "human good" and "the lip of the cup" becomes "the sharp lip's cup." Ultimately, the "perfectness" of your repetition and rhyme is up to you. As long as the refrain is a recognizable repetition, the cyclical and musical nature of the triolet will come through.

So, now you know the formula for a triolet, but are you ready to write one of your own? Try working it out, step by step:

1. Pick your two refrain rhymes. One way to do this is to simply write two lines of poetry that you really like and make those your A and B refrain lines, building your triolet around rhyming with those lines. Or, you can start by picking two words with different rhyming sounds and write your refrain lines around those words.

2. Get out a piece of scrap paper and list as many rhymes for your A and B refrain words as you possibly can. If you have access to a rhyming dictionary, that will help, or if you have access to the Internet, use RhymeZone.com. Otherwise, just brainstorm for a few minutes, keeping in mind the different types of rhymes that you can make.

3. Use these rhymes to generate the rest of your triolet. Do you want it to be silly? Serious? Spooky? The words you choose will change your poem's tone and meaning. Try out different rhyme words and don't be afraid to tweak your triolet as you write it.

Oh, Ode!

Leia Wilson

Swoon! Celebrate! Write an ode and then try an Exquisite Corpse ode as a group.

ARE YOU READY TO WRITE an ode? While there is no set definition for what an ode is, or what it should be, it is generally understood to be a somewhat lengthy meditation on an object, place, person, or event. Modern odes don't have specific rhyme schemes or a certain number of stanzas—you can just let your imagination run until you've said all you have to say. Typically, odes directly address their subject and are reflective. William Wordsworth's "Imitations of Immortality," Percy Shelley's "Ode to the West Wind," and Keats's "Ode to a Nightingale" are famous examples of odes. Odes usually take on a serious or contemplative disposition; however, it is not uncommon for modern odes to be sarcastic, humorous, or ironic. Or any combination of feelings! An ode can be written to anything, or for anything.

Here is Shelley's "Ode to the West Wind":

> O wild West Wind, thou breath of Autumn's being,
> Thou, from whose unseen presence the leaves dead
> Are driven, like ghosts from an enchanter fleeing,
>
> Yellow, and black, and pale, and hectic red,
> Pestilence-stricken multitudes: O thou,
> Who chariotest to their dark wintry bed
>
> The wingèd seeds, where they lie cold and low,
> Each like a corpse within its grave, until
> Thine azure sister of the Spring shall blow
>
> Her clarion o'er the dreaming earth, and fill
> (Driving sweet buds like flocks to feed in air)
> With living hues and odours plain and hill:
>
> Wild Spirit, which art moving everywhere;
> Destroyer and Preserver; hear, oh hear!

Shelley's ode is an example of a Horatian Ode. It is a more classical approach to writing an ode. Like many poets before him, and after, Shelley is using the poet as a voice of revolution and change. Unlike most modern odes, Shelley's ode is highly controlled and formal. It is composed of five stanzas (four three lined stanzas and a couplet, all in iambic pentameter). The speaker of the poem invokes the West Wind by using an apostrophe—"O wild West Wind." He describes the power of the wind as both "destroyer and preserver" and asks the West Wind to sweep him out of his torpor. He is linking nature and art by using powerful imagery—"driving sweet buds like flocks to feed in air." We see that the season of spring itself is a metaphor for a "spring" of imagination and morality. He uses the season as a metaphor for what he hopes his art will bring to human consciousness—truth, beauty, authentic experience.

However, not all odes have to be about the social or ethical role of the poet. We would all be exhausted if this were the case, poets included! Look up a modern ode by Pablo Neruda, "Ode to Tomatoes." It is clear that Neruda is having fun with his ode. It's almost as if we are being warned of the dangers of tomatoes ("the tomato invades the kitchen")—an absurd danger. He springboards from halving the tomato to talking about its juice in the streets and how all-encompassing its presence can be. He follows the tangent through until the end. Every line and simile in this poem never strays far from its original subject—that's very important for an ode. Everything in this poem is about tomatoes.

Now look up "Ode to the Dictionary," another example from Neruda. This time the poem isn't all laughs. He uses the end of the poem to comment on language, on how alive language can be if you're willing to make it so.

EXERCISE 1: WRITING AN ODE

Okay, now that you've seen a couple of examples, it's time to try writing an ode. Remember: you can write an ode about *anything*—a pet, the neighbor's dog, the bird outside your window that sings at five in the morning, school, food, an inanimate object—you can even write an ode to yourself. If there's a topic that's really important to you, write about that! Once you've got your subject, it helps to pretend that you are painting a still life of your topic, except you're going to be using words to compose your painting. The more detail the better. Go ahead and get sidetracked, or start following an image that isn't (at first glance!) directly related to your original subject. Then try to wind your way back to your initial topic. You might produce some interesting comparisons.

EXERCISE 2: EXQUISITE CORPSE ODE

Now that you've written an ode, you can expand your horizons and try something collaborative! This is especially fun to do if you pick a topic that everybody will be sure to have a different opinion about, like food. Writing by yourself is fun in itself, but sometimes bringing other people into the equation can give your writing a new energy it didn't have before and really push you to think about things in a new way.

The Exquisite Corpse. Here's how it works: you need two or more people (friends, family, classmates) and some paper. As a group, choose a subject for your ode. You write one line. You pass the paper to your friend, who writes the second line. This part is important: before your friend passes the paper, they should fold the paper so only the second line is showing. Once they've securely hidden the first line, they pass their paper to the next person. Remember to have each person fold the paper back each time before the paper is passed so that only the previous line is showing.

This exercise works best if you don't think about the other lines already written. Focus only on the line that is in front of you—hone in on a detail, a great word, something the line triggered for you personally. Really push yourself—often times the lines will be chaotic, but sometimes chaos is surprising. It's okay if the Exquisite Corpse doesn't make sense. The fact that it is associative is the greatest thing about it. And, in the case of the Exquisite Corpse Ode, there will be the one unifying factor— the topic you and your friends choose at the beginning.

Sestinas

SIX WORDS, OBSESSED!

Chapin Gray, Jenny Gropp, and Kirk Pinho

Learn the basic sestina form, "cheat" your way to an abridged sestina, write a giant sestina, and take the Ode-Sestina Challenge.

TAKE A LOOK AT THIS poem—it's a sestina—and see if you can figure out what makes a sestina a sestina.

DEATH METAL NUMBER ONE

BY ERNEST HILBERT

For Eric Bohnenstiel
For hours in flames going the speed of darkness,
Hard wall of black noise whited out with light,
Ecstasy, whiskey, coarse thrum of it all,
Gloom was your hymn, your argument, undead
Majesty. In an age of irony,
You were too serious, my monster, and died.

It's hard to feel sorry for you. You died
Like a jammed chainsaw, howling Hessian god, darkness
Your only friend, what squalid irony,
No one rushed to your aid when you became light
Fare, a joke for the hip, those you wished dead
With silver tonnage on their cortex, after all.

They told you to grow up, get a job and all,
Leave the hell and graves to those who have died,
So you hid in fjord and swamp. Brain-dead
Ex-con, history was unkind when your darkness
And pure grime were mislaid in pop-star light.
It felt good in the days before irony,

To go so fast, yes, when that chic irony
Couldn't snuff your Viking growls, soaked with blood all
Night, smoky barbarian sweat, subpoena, light-
Ning you rode until dawn, until you died
On stage, Ben Gay for the neck, and darkness
Whirling back toward you again like the dead.

Concrete thud, mouthful of windshield, the dead
Of night luring you along with the sad irony
Of a botched tattoo, cool skeleton darkness
Your home, a moveable blood feast for all,
Threw chains into the wood-chipper, what died
Down your throat, what ruptured bulb of lost light?

Cold beer in winter lot, last of daylight
On your humming Chevette, you will raise the dead,
Every inch of you a new scar. We died
When you first hit the lights, before irony
Took it all away, harsh glory and hot rush, all
The things we left to you in slow darkness.

So don't laugh, make light, pour slick irony
Over the dissonant dead, those who fought for us all,
Whose darkness will still sting ears after we've died.

(If you want to take a gander at another sestina, we recommend looking up John Ashbery's "Farm Implements and Rutabagas in a Landscape.")

Did you guess that the sestina's secret lies at the end of each line? The sestina uses the same six words over and over again until you have six stanzas of six lines each. A good way to scan a sestina is to mark the end words with the letters *A, B, C, D, E,* and *F,* like this:

For hours in flames going the speed of **darkness, (A)**
Hard wall of black noise whited out with **light, (B)**
Ecstasy, whiskey, coarse thrum of it **all, (C)**
Gloom was your hymn, your argument, **undead (D)**
Majesty. In an age of **irony, (E)**
You were too serious, my monster, and **died. (F)**

If you begin with the first stanza, you'll find that all sestinas follow the same pattern of end words for six stanzas:

1. ABCDEF
2. AEBDC
3. CFDABE
4. ECBFAD
5. DEACFB
6. BDFECA

But what about the final stanza, the tercet? What's different there? You'll notice that Hilbert and Ashbery's endings are a little different in terms of patterning:

Hilbert:
So don't laugh, make light (B), pour slick irony (E)
Over the dissonant dead (D), those who fought for us all, (C)
Whose darkness (A) will still sting ears after we've died. (F)
Ashbery:
Soon filled the apartment (B). It was domestic thunder, (A)
The color of spinach (F). Popeye chuckled and scratched (C)
His balls: it sure was pleasant (D) to spend a day in the country. (E)

The final tercet is known as the **envoi**, and its pattern can change, as long as it includes all six words used as end words in the stanzas above. Typically, the envoi ends with E, C, A or A, C, E, and incorporates B, D, and F somewhere in the lines, but as you can see, Hilbert changed that—he ended with E, C, and F, and incorporated B, D, and A into the lines. With today's sestinas, this kind of changing is more and more common. It's up to you if you want to write a traditional envoi, like Ashbery, or a rogue envoi, like Hilbert—just don't change the pattern of those first six stanzas.

So, overall, here's your sestina form (thirty-nine lines total):

1. ABCDEF
2. FAEBDC
3. CFDABE
4. ECBFAD

    5. DEACFB

    6. BDFECA

    7. (envoi) ECA or ACE (incorporate BDF within lines), or go *ROGUE!*

Check out this awesome sestina written by Christopher Louvet, "Sestina with Clementines, Beer, and Guitar." It makes a lot of allusions to a famous sestina by Elizabeth Bishop called, simply, "Sestina." Look up Bishop's poem and take note of the similarities.

December settles on the beach supermarket.
In the marvelously artificial light, a man
stands in the fruit section near a woman.
Looking at the pineapples and clementines,
he wonders what they would play on a guitar,
though he intends to buy only beer.

He thinks that his desire for beer
and the warm sea winds outside the supermarket
could both be explained by a guitar
though misunderstood too easily by a man.
Bruises and early harvesting mar the clementines.
He picks up a lime, imagines saying to the woman,

Most fruits prefer flamenco; but the woman
is selecting oranges. She seems as interested in a beer
as the shelves must be in the clementines.
The athletic winds hurdle the supermarket.
Half-resolved, rejecting the lime, the man
ridicules the idea of fruit playing guitar

as holiday classics, articulated on three guitars,
discourage him from speaking to the woman.
The songs' elevator sophistication mocks the man
like a morning kiss spoiled by an aftertaste of beer;
in the conditioned cool of the supermarket,
he feels like an overripe clementine.

We are what we are, say the clementines.
Hark! The herald angels sing, offer the guitars.

After collecting her oranges in the supermarket
with careful consideration, the woman
wants artichokes, more stoic than bottles of beer;
when she walks past him she doesn't see the man.

But, agile and ardent as the winds, while the man
abandons his equation with the clementine
and forsakes the fruits to search for tonight's beer,
the oranges in her basket take up a guitar
and play a sly, endearing legato for the woman.
She hums along in the aisles of the supermarket.

Among the beer, trying to ignore the holiday guitar,
the man agrees with the inscrutable clementines.
The woman waits in the supermarket's checkout line.

Now that you know what a sestina's form is, try to write one. There
are two decent ways to begin drafting a sestina. One is to write a six-line
stanza and then force yourself to use the end words you come up with
that way. A second and perhaps better way is to think of your six words
first. Make sure to choose a good selection of words—a nice cache of flex-
ible verbs, nouns, and adjectives will be sure to help your poem along its
way to excellence. To start you on your way to becoming a six-word ex-
pert, we suggest you write a six-word sestina. Lloyd Schwartz is one guy
who's done this:

SIX WORDS

yes
no
maybe
sometimes
always
never

Never?
Yes.
Always?
No.

Sometimes?
Maybe—

maybe
never
sometimes.
Yes—
no
always:

always
maybe.
No—
never
yes.
Sometimes,

sometimes
(always)
yes.
Maybe
Never . . .
No,

no—
sometimes.
Never.
Always?
Maybe.
Yes—

yes no
maybe sometimes
always never.

Lloyd's a clever guy—he was able to make a whole conversation, al-
most philosophically so, out of six common, conflicting words. Here is
another six-word sestina by Peter Pereira:

VALENTINE SESTINA

So
I
love
always.
Will
you?

You
so
will
I
always
love.

Love
you
always,
so
I
will.

Will
love
I
you
so
always?

Always
will
so
love
you
I.

I

always
you
will
love
so.

I will
always love
you so.

And here is a shorter version of the same idea, a four-word "quatrina" by a student, Lura Tiller:

RAVEN SESTINA

Flying
raven
above
fields

fields
flying
above
raven

above
raven
fields
flying

raven
flying
above
fields

Think about what six words you can choose that will be in good dialogue with one another, and write your own six-word sestina. Remember, a good selection of verbs, nouns, and adjectives can only help.

When you're finished, write a whole sestina with longer lines. Look back at the word order chart, and get ready to choose six words that have a lot of variety and flexibility. What will you write about? You could write a long, meandering *ode* (refer to "Oh, Ode!" on page 116 for ideas) in sestina form—we call this the **Ode-Sestina Challenge**—or you could write about one of your obsessions.

Give yourself plenty of time to write your sestina. Get obsessed!

Nonce, Not Nonsense

POETRY MEETS THE FUTURE

Jenny Gropp and Emma Sovich

Work with the "Century" and the "Portion," and then create your own unique poetry form.

MANY POEMS ARE WRITTEN IN patterns invented by the poet, which are called nonce forms. The adjective is derived by misdivision from the medieval phrase "for then anes," meaning "for then once" or "for the one time." By the Renaissance this had become "for the nonce," or a nonce form. All the traditional patterns of poetry started out as nonce forms.

Take the sonnet, for example. As you might know, a sonnet is a fourteen-line poem in iambic pentameter with a carefully patterned rhyme scheme. But do you know how many different appearances the form has taken on over the centuries? The first known sonnet form, the Petrarchan sonnet was introduced in the fourteenth century by Italian poet Petrarch. Then, in the early sixteenth century, Sir Thomas Wyatt introduced the Petrarchan sonnet into English poetry. Later in the sixteenth century, Shakespeare was dissatisfied with the way the Petrarchan sonnet fit into relatively rhyme-poor English and decided to bend the form to better accommodate the English language. Then, even later in the sixteenth century, Edmund Spenser introduced his own take on the Shakespearean sonnet, the Spenserian sonnet. Each of these forms was once a nonce form, and each now stands as its own poetry-form giant. So somewhere inside of their poetry-making heads, Petrarch, Shakespeare, and Spenser were able to conjure up poem "containers" that other writers have deemed important to the craft.

Writers today are still conjuring up nonce forms that are being noticed in the poetry community. Take poet Joel Brouwer, who wrote a book full of one-hundred-word prose poems, aptly titled *Centuries*. Brouwer uses the one-hundred-word constraint to consider broad topics in an abbreviated space; his poems have titles like "History," "Century," and "N" (the letter). Take his poem "Aesthetics" as an example of treating a general topic in a short but powerful moment:

AESTHETICS

Your brother has leukemia. Carve marble. The elections were rigged.
Write a villanelle. A girl shivers in streetlight, takes off her mittens,
pulls a silver yo-yo from her pocket. Dogs bark behind a fence. Use oil
on wood. Consider pace and breath while choreographing your divorce;
you will have to move through it forever. Two men in green fatigues
tie a woman flat to a table. One has a rubber hose, the other a pliers.
A third man arrives with sandwiches and a Thermos. A body has soft
and hard parts, like a piano. Music comes from where they meet.

Hank Lazer created a nonce form: he wrote a book called *Portions* where all the poems are exactly fifty-four words long and in tercets of three words per line. Lazer wrote in the form for five years and became a master of his own idea. But how did he come up with his form? In the Jewish tradition, fifty-four portions of the Torah are read each year; each portion is named for its initial key word. "My form for each poem became $3 \times 18 = 54$ words, the building block of 18 being a mystical Jewish number," Lazer writes in an afterword. The book's three sections include eighteen, thirty-six, and eighteen poems respectively. So every take on a number in the book directly relates to Jewish tradition.

Take a look at one of Lazer's poems, "Humid":

HUMID

humid blanket thick
air wrap this
body awkward walking

as in dream
as with tongue
thickly coated &

speech a dream
babble wanting to
but not able

to say proper
words of blessing
superfluous i suppose

to bless what
is much more
than too specific

us begin baruch
& soon hit
scripted mystic unpronounceables

Now that you're familiar with Brouwer and Lazer's nonce forms, it's your turn. Write your poem following the form of *Centuries* or *Portions*— either a one-hundred-word paragraph or fifty-four-word poem in three-line stanzas, each containing three words per line. Or make up your own counting rules and create your own nonce form.

Poetry from Math

THE FIB AND BEYOND

Jenny Gropp and Emma Sovich

Learn a poetic form based on the Fibonacci sequence, and then head further into the realm of poetry and equations.

THE FIB

WE CREATIVE WRITERS SPEND so much time with words that we might not always pay attention to the really cool things that can be found in the world of math and science. But here is a poetry form that combines words and math and science—it's called the Fib, and it's based on the Fibonacci sequence, considered by many to be one of the foundations of art, science, and life.

The Fibonacci sequence is a series of numbers starting from 0 or 1 where the next number in the sequence is the sum of the previous two numbers. 0+1 = 1 and 1+1 = 2 and so on. Simple math, right? The number sequence looks like this: 1, 1, 2, 3, 5, 8, 13, 21, 34, 55 and on and on . . . This sequence of number appears in all kinds of places in nature, including in the pattern of branch growth on trees and the seeds on a raspberry! It has influenced art and architecture throughout history, including ancient temples in Egypt with rooms added on in spatial proportions based on the sequence. The obvious next step is, of course, a poem.

The Fib was invented in 2006 by Gregory K. Pincus and it was popularized on the geek-favorite technology news site Slashdot.org. The rules are very simple: each line of the Fib poem contains only as many syllables as the corresponding number in the Fibonacci sequence.

Here's an example by Pincus himself, with my notations on the side indicating the number of syllables in each line:

(1) One

(1) Small,

(2) Precise,

(3) Poetic,

(5) Spiraling mixture:

(8) Math plus poetry yields the Fib.

Very simple, right? The Fib can go on for as many lines as you want it
to, and can cover any topic you choose. Let's look at some more Fibs. Here
is the first portion of A. E. Stallings's "Four Fibs." Note that the lines in
this Fib rhyme, which adds another dimension of sound to the form.

1.
Did
Eve
Believe
or grapple
over the apple?
Eavesdropping Adam heard her say
To the snake-oil salesman she was not born yesterday.

The Fib can contain more than one stanza, where each stanza starts a
new sequence, like in this poem by Tony Leuzzi:

DEER SIGHTING

It
had—
as I
remember—
just finished raining
when I saw them in a meadow
nosing the wet, saw-toothed leaves of purple coneflowers.

Six
or
seven
of them tread
the stippled path light
dipping their brown, velveted heads
to green, abrasive tongues that cupped the fallen water.

And
I—
tense as
the unplucked

string on some guitar—
marveled at their movement, which was
clear and fluid, a graceful pouring forth, like water . . .

What do you notice about these poems? How does the form affect the speed that you read, the pace of the poem and the way the words and ideas slowly build up? You can do some very interesting things with Fibs.

Start with a topic to write about. Think of the way the form of the Fib starts out small and expands and gets endlessly larger. What kinds of things start out small or simple and grow and grow? Maybe your Fib is a snake that gets larger and longer the more it eats, or maybe your Fib is a rubber band ball that needs more and more pieces added to it until it becomes huge. Or maybe your Fib is about something more abstract, like the steps a baby takes when first learning to walk, tiny at first, then more complicated until the child is running relay races. Choose a topic that you think can grow with the lines of your Fib, and then write a six-line Fib.

More Poetry Based on Numbers

Now think about other numbers, sequences of numbers, or equations that are important to you. These can be as simple or complex as you like. Start by listing as many of these as you can in the space below:

Zip code of your birthplace or favorite place: _____

Phone numbers: _____

Number of steps from one room to another: _____

_____

_____

_____

OK, so, as an example, let's take a zip code for Tuscaloosa, Alabama: 35487. A nonce form for this zip code could be a five-line poem, one for each number in the zip code, with each number in the zip code being the number of words in each line. So:

line 1: 3 words
line 2: 5 words
line 3: 4 words

line 4: 8 words
line 5: 7 words

You can even link zip codes, writing poems about the places you've lived and the places you want to visit. But now, take one of the numbers *you* came up with and do the same mental legwork. How can you turn your number (or sequence of numbers or equation) into a poem form?

To really bend your brain, you could puzzle over this: $A^2 + B^2 = C^2$. It's the Pythagorean Theorem, a geometry formula that goes back to ancient Greece (er, yeah, most of them do). The letters could represent stanzas, or they could represent rhyme, or practically anything. How might you "square" a rhyme? How might your form show an adding up to, an equal sign?

Pillow Book Lists

OBSERVING EXPERIENCE FOR CREATIVE NONFICTION

Katie Berger and Pia Simone Garber

*Get started with autobiographical writing by making expressive lists
and snatching up the details right by your side.*

BUT I HAVE NOTHING INTERESTING TO SAY!

CREATIVE NONFICTION CAN BE FRUSTRATING to write, especially if you feel like you haven't experienced anything exciting in your life. But nonfiction writer Claire Dederer points out that the content of your experience, what you actually did, is less important than the transformation you felt as you experienced it. So if you've driven to Mexico City in a hot pink limousine to see heavy metal rock band KISS perform live on April Fool's Day, and the experience completely changed your views of the world, that's great. Write about that. But if you walked around the local park today and thought of some new ideas, that's also great. Write about that, too. While some creative nonfiction writers do extraordinary things, see extraordinary sights, and then write about them, other creative nonfiction writers tackle their own backyards or neighborhoods or schools. No one's a better expert on your life than you.

OBSERVING EXPERIENCE: EXPRESSIVE LISTS

One of the easiest ways to start exploring your own experiences in nonfiction writing is to take some time to carefully observe the world around you. Think about it—how often do you pay attention to all the sights you see as you go about your day? What kinds of things happen all around you during your regular old routine? Maybe there's a park or an empty lot or even a busy store that you walk by every day. Or maybe you hear other people's conversations over the hum of your headphones. Anything you see or hear is something to write about.

During the late tenth century in Japan, Sei Shonagon, a lady-in-waiting to the Empress Sadako, kept a *Pillow Book*, an observational diary tucked inside the writer's pillow to write in before bed. In her pillow book, she made lists of observations, overheard gossip, and personal thoughts based on the world around her. Some of the titles of her lists include, "Elegant Things," "Different Ways of Speaking," and "Things That Belong in a House." Here is the text of another of her lists, "Things That Cannot Be Compared":

> Summer and winter. Night and day. Rain and sunshine. Youth and age. A person's laughter and his anger. Black and white. Love and hatred. The little indigo plant and the philodendron. Rain and mist.
>
> When one has stopped loving somebody, one feels that he has become someone else, even though he is still the same person.
>
> In a garden full of evergreens the crows are all asleep. Then, towards the middle of the night, the crows in one of the trees suddenly wake up in a great flurry and start flapping about. Their unrest spreads to the other trees, and soon all the birds have been startled from their sleep and are cawing in alarm. How different from the same crows in daytime!

Notice how the items in this list vary from simple, short ideas to a single, complex moment about crows described in detail. At first Shonagon's list is an assortment of paired ideas that cannot be compared because they are opposites, or very different from each other. But she concludes with detailed observations that are incomparable to anything else because they are so unique and because of the effect they have on the observer.

A more contemporary approach to this type of list is this one, by Gretchen Legler, titled "Things That Seem Ugly or Troubling but Upon Closer Inspection are Beautiful":

> A river in winter with ice floes jammed violently against one another; you can see dark water in between the white and gray floes, sparkling in the sunshine.
>
> Abandoned barns, their huge roofs sagging like the backs of tired horses.
>
> The slick, black body of a baby goat, stillborn, lying in the hay between its confused mother's hooves.
>
> A limp newly hatched baby bird that has fallen onto the grass from a nest in the pine tree and has died with part of its bright blue eggshell still attached to its damp feathers.

The angry red fists of rhubarb when they first appear in the dark soil of the spring garden.

Legler describes moments she has observed, using her words to express the kinds of emotions they instilled in her. The winter river is fierce and terrifying, the abandoned barns seem sad and old, the newly grown rhubarb is upsettingly vivid. Compare these experiences to Legler's descriptions of the baby bird and baby goat. Those depictions are sad but Legler finds a kind of beauty in the emotion and in the image-heavy description.

EXERCISE

Create your own list of observations, paying attention to detail and using your description to imply the emotions these observations set off. Start by choosing some items that you have in your bag. Think of items that you see so often you almost forget they're there. Move onto other things you see indoors and outdoors. Some items will be short phrases, and some will become longer sentences.

Now describe some of these objects in as much detail as you can muster. Even if those objects seem totally mundane at first, think about ways that you can write about them that bring them to life in an unexpected way. Finally, try to come up with an inventive title for your list that implies something about these objects that is more than meets the eye.

A Travel Guide of the Self

Katie Berger and Pia Simone Garber

*Take yourself on a tour of you through travel writing and second-
person point of view.*

Have you ever thumbed through a travel magazine or guide-
book? A must-have for vacationers who want to know something
about a place before they visit, this handy literature is addressed to a
"you." "If you visit Chicago, be sure to check out Navy Pier." "You might
want to avoid the Statue of Liberty on Memorial Day because of the
crowds." Using this guidebook voice, writer Jennifer Henderson wrote a
creative nonfiction piece called "Displacement":

> This is the Oz Museum in Wamego, Kansas. Here you can see the
> giant Tin Man just inside the front door, rosy cheeks, a smile straight
> as piano keys. It's only the top half of him lounging on the floor, the
> part with a heart stuck like a prize to his left chest. You can pose with
> him, smiling awkwardly as the woman selling sheets of cloth printed
> with yellow bricks and ruby red slippers tells you to smile and say, "Fly-
> ing monkeys!" You say it and the camera catches your grin, off centered.
> Forced. You'll look at this photograph later, when you've left Kansas for
> good.

But wait! Henderson is writing about so much more than the Oz Mu-
seum. Did you notice that she's also writing about herself when she says
"You'll look at this photograph later, when you've left Kansas for good."
Of course, you as a reader probably haven't left Kansas, but Henderson is
writing about herself, telling her own story, using the guidebook form.
You'll find more of it in this piece:

> "Over there, behind that door," the guide tells you, "is the one of the
> largest collections of Oz memorabilia." Her red hair is thin under the
> bright lights. You walk past showcases filled with L. Frank Baum's first
> books and hundreds of children's toys—dolls, kites, mobiles, stuffed

animals, everything you feel now you might have longed for once. There are photographs of Dorothy and Toto during casting, an evolution of Dorothy's pigtails and blue checkered gingham dress. She looks like you, your dad once said. You wore your hair in braids for weeks.

With those last two sentences, Henderson gives us an insight into her personal life, through her desire to please her father.

EXERCISE

Think of a cool place you've visited, or if you want, think of one of your favorite local hangouts. This place can be as exotic as a tropical island or as simple as where you get your hair cut. If you were writing a guidebook about this place, what would you include?

Name of place: _____

Details *anyone* would see in this place:

_____

_____

_____

Now think about how, through talking about this place, you can also talk about yourself. What might a traveler experiencing this place *as you* feel or think or remember?

Things *you* notice, feel, remember, wonder, or think about in this place:

_____

_____

_____

Not sure what to write? If you go back to the example, you'll see that Henderson wrote about leaving Kansas, the way she remembers wearing her hair when she was a little girl, and how she forces a smile for the camera. So how will you, the writer of this guidebook, react to your place? Try it out! Using both the details *anyone* would notice and the details only *you* would notice or remember, write a travel guide to your chosen place, addressing the reader as "you" and giving away hints about yourself as you do so.

Expert Experience

THE ART OF THE UNLIKELY, OPINIONATED REVIEW

Katie Berger and Pia Simone Garber

Creative nonfiction meets the review when you write your own brief, detailed—and unexpected—review of something you know a lot about.

WHAT DO YOU THINK OF when you think of a "review"? Do you think of a review of a book? Of a restaurant? Of the newest Lady Gaga album? To review something is to dissect your experience of that thing. What emotions did that book bring up for you? How delicious and fragrant was your risotto with mushrooms at that new Italian place? Which tracks on that new album are the best for dancing to? The reviewer breaks down the experience, defining and describing it for an audience who wasn't there.

So what does a review have to do with *creative nonfiction*? It's all in what you choose to review, and how! The blog *300 Reviews*, which was around from 2009 to 2012, showcased three-hundred-word reviews of things and experiences that you might not ever think would warrant a review, like missing the train or shopping for cologne. Here's an excerpt from Casie Wexler's review of soup. Not any specific soup, but the larger concept of soup as a whole.

#25—SOUP

Soup is a fixture on most menus. This hot, cold, or, unfortunately, lukewarm liquid meal is comforting even in its most bastardized forms. Still, though it might be difficult, we must make distinctions. It is a painful fact for soup lovers to accept, but the truth is, not all soups are created equally.

Consider soup to be a system of European feudalism from the middle ages. A soup such as French Onion would be considered a lord, whereas a canned, viscous, over-salted can of chicken noodle soup would be a serf.

Lordly soups reign over the epicurean feudal manor, making lowly soups look even more pitiful and peasant-like than ever before. . . .

A mid-grade soup of some quality, like a good tomato soup, is a fine example of a vassal soup. It is not a meal on its own, yet it is an essential complement to a grilled cheese sandwich, a Monte Cristo, or goldfish crackers. . . .

Serf soups are the kind of things that are used when an appropriate meal or soup cannot be prepared, usually due to illness. When the taste buds are coated and the throat is shellacked in mucus, few things are as comforting as an easy to prepare can of serf-soup. All soup castes, from lords to serfs, are needed to run a successful gastronomic fiefdom. However, take heed because soup cannot revolt, but consumers of soup can and will.

Notice that in this review, though the author discusses soup as a larger concept, she also describes different kinds of soup in detail and rates them on the strange scale of "European Feudalism." The common experience of eating soup is rendered strange and interesting through this classification, but at the same time potentially familiar experiences are described, such as the pairing of tomato soup with grilled cheese or goldfish crackers.

EXERCISE

What are you an "expert" in? Think: what do I experience frequently, or in my daily life, that I have developed a writable opinion about? Make a list of at least five possibilities.

Now choose one thing from this list that you really want to review. Write a review of something you are an expert in that is both brief (one hundred to three hundred words) and also as detailed as possible. Remember to include both familiar and unfamiliar or new ways of looking at whatever you are reviewing, and try bringing a new approach to talking about this subject, the way Wexler used Feudalism to review soup.

II

Ye Olde Language Lets Loose

Imagine yourself on a blah sort of day, sitting down in front of a blank page or the blinking cursor on the computer screen, hoping to write something. Tick, tock. Tick, tock. Sometimes it is hard to figure out how to begin. You could write your whole life story or the story of the history of the earth or a poem about the most important dream you ever had that you cannot quite remember, but all those choices seem a little too daunting this afternoon. It's too hard to figure out how to start those things, and you don't really know what you would say, anyway, if you *could* find a way to begin. It's easy to get discouraged if you have a huge, swamping idea, or no idea at all, when you sit down to try to write. You stare and stare at the screen or the page, until finally a word emerges. It is, not surprisingly, a four-letter word. The word is *help.*

Immediately, the letters spring into action. "Much obliged," they say. "Glad to. It's our specialty!"

The letters have been in this tough situation many times before, not knowing how to get going or how to keep creating words on a page. Sometimes the problem is that the writer doesn't have an initial energy, impulse, task, mission, interest, hook—a dive-off-the-diving-board *umph* to start into the writing. In school, usually, this starting energy is already created for us—it is called the assignment. The way of keeping on going is often created for us, too—a five paragraph essay or short answer to complete, a proof to prove, or an argument to make. In creative writing, however, it helps to be able to give yourself a way to get started and a way to keep going. In the first section of this book, we sampled lots of genres and forms that help writers move forward. In this section, we will explore lots of *sources* for writing that you can partake of like drinking water from a natural source where it flows out of a rock before you set off on your word hike. We will give you lots of ways to initiate the writing process. Then, once you have begun putting words together, we will show you lots of unexpected *methods* to keep developing that first urge until it turns into a piece of writing you hadn't planned to make. The poet Robert Frost wrote, "No surprise for the writer, no surprise for the reader." He meant that writers don't know in advance all that they will do during the writing process. Frost talked about how a poem (or any piece of writing, really), is a "piece of ice that rides on its own melting." You have to be willing to let the process of writing unfold in ways you didn't anticipate. Your writing will create a life of its own as it goes along. In that spirit, we offer in this section some sources to draw upon and some methods to help that "melting" happen.

The sources in this section include a range of authors as disparate as Paul Bowles, Beckian Fritz Goldberg, John Milton, Charles Baudelaire, Harryette Mullen, H.D., Lou Reed, Anne Carson, Matsuo Basho, and James Joyce. The sources we suggest include existing literary works such as poems and novels, literature written in foreign languages you might not know how to read, pop songs and children's songs, found phrases, studies in motion, board games, comic strips, obsessions, obituaries, classifieds, crazy headlines, animals' thoughts, secrets, paintings, photos, and online plot generators, just to name a few. We will show you how to find these beginning places (have you noticed you *don't* need to have your own grand idea in order to begin?), and then we will show you some *methods* creative writers use to take these beginnings for a ride. We will alter texts, slipping our own words into others' words; erase texts to reveal their hidden inner-texts; translate according to sounds and shapes of unfamiliar languages; turn sounds, music, and fast-forward gibberish into new words; write under the influences of songs' sounds and stories; invent a town and its inhabitants and dramas on Facebook; mash images together into new images and stories; get totally, utterly obsessed with our obsessions; chase tabloid headlines representing overlooked points of view; genetically modify, zoom in on, or explode our own previous drafts of poems; and write collaboratively with others, all while "making it new" as Ezra Pound famously said. We will tune our ears to avoid clichés with fresh plots and metaphors while engaging in these new sources and methods. We promise you'll write something you wouldn't have written before. We promise you'll surprise yourself as the letters surprise you. We promise the letters will have a grand time, riding on their own ride.

TNT Prose

Explodable, Expandable Text

Jenny Gropp and Kirsten Jorgenson

Use your own words as dynamite to blow out the words of an existing text, revealing a new piece of writing when the dust clears.

I T COULD BE ANY TEXT, set to pop at any time, in any imaginable way. The book you love the most, the book you hate the most, the newspaper, a fashion magazine, or even a cereal box are all explodable texts, just waiting for you to ignite the TNT, blow them apart, and then put them back together again as your very own.

By inserting your own words between the words of the source text of your choice, you make *your* words dynamite. We can look to an avant-garde, punk-rock writer like Kathy Acker for some inspiration. Acker was famous for sampling from other people's work.

Another possibility for exploding and expanding texts is to write between the lines of an existing text. For instance, I wrote a short fiction, called "Small Magic," in collaboration with Davis Schneiderman. We chose a series of paragraphs from some of our very favorite texts. Our method was as follows:

- Choose three passages from a book you enjoy.
- Send those three passages to the other person.
- Write between the lines of those passages.
- Return the altered passages plus three more new passages to the person who sent them to you.
- Repeat for as long as you feel is necessary.

The idea was that we would create a piece of fiction that would be radically different from the texts we used as sources by expanding and exploding the space between words and sentences in their original form.

Here's an example of how we began with a sentence from Paul Bowles's *The Sheltering Sky* and then inserted words into Bowles's sentence, writing entirely new sentences and creating new characters to inhabit the words we received from Bowles.

Paul Bowles wrote:

> Death is always on the way, but the fact that you don't know when it will arrive seems to take away from the finiteness of life.

We wrote:

> But, David Adams, death from a plane crash is always on the way, Bede replies, through your mouth now, back to me.
>
> Death is a husband puttering in the basement, a body whose place you hold beside yours in bed, a body without which you are unable to rest peacefully, not fully so, not while you speculate about each shuffling footstep. Is it now? Is it now? Will he come now? Always one eye open, arranging your limbs about you in a manner you imagine he might find pleasing upon his inevitable—certain—arrival.
>
> He will come to bed. One needs no small magic to know this. He is only just downstairs. On the news. Your inbox. Though the fact that you don't know when he will arrive seems to take away from the finiteness of life.

Though the words from the source are swallowed up and incorporated into the new text, the effect is not necessarily hostile. We chose to leave the theme of the source text, <u>death</u>, untouched. We also chose to maintain a few instances of Bowles' original word arrangements as a way to allow Bowles to haunt the new text.

We performed far more drastic mutations throughout "Small Magic." As we manipulated a portion of Marcel Proust's *Swann's Way*, we began to spread not just sentences but words themselves apart in order to call attention to and allow for the sound of the word to function as the tie back to the original text.

Proust wrote:

> Combray at a distance, from a twenty-mile radius, as we used to see it from the railway when we arrived there every year in Holy Week, was no more than a church epitomising the town, representing it, speaking of it and for it to the horizon, and as one drew near, gathering close about its long, dark cloak, sheltering from the wind, on the open plain, as a shepherd gathers his sheep, the woolly grey backs of its flocking houses, which a fragment of its mediaeval ramparts enclosed, here and there, in an outline as scrupulously circular as that of a little town in a primitive painting.

We wrote:

> Combing the gray horizon, we spy, at a distance, from a two-mile radius, brother, those gypsum-hardened other people gathering in the early stages of their daily commute, cheeks nuzzling into collars, fingering paper coffee cups they know should be thermoses, should be reusable, should be metal not plastic.

This sentence disintegrates the word "Combray." "Combray" becomes "combing the gray" for instance, which is called to by "at a distance," something that might haunt an ardent follower of Proust, though the reader of "Small Magic" does not have to "get" that reference in order to understand what is happening in the story.

In fact, maintaining faithfulness to the original text is not necessary at all when you are exploding and expanding texts. You decide how much dynamite, your own language, you want to insert into the text and then ignite it!

You Be the TNT

Your task: To stick dynamite in the cracks of the following passage and blow it apart so that you can put it together again as your own. Choose one of the passages below and write between the lines of the text. Fill in the blanks that are provided.

Rebel! Rebel!

> "When a man rides _____ a long time through wild regions he feels the desire for a city. Finally he comes to _____ Isadora, a city where the buildings have spiral staircases encrusted with spiral seashells, _____, where perfect telescopes and violins are made, where the foreigner hesitating between two women always encounters a third, where cockfights degenerate into bloody brawls among the bettors. _____. He was thinking of all these things when he desired a city."
>
> —Italo Calvino, *Invisible Cities*

> "My lover is experiencing a reverse evolution. I tell _____. No one _____. I don't know how it happened, only that one day he was _____ my lover and the next he was some kind of ape.

_____. It's been a month and now he's a sea turtle."

—Aimee Bender, "The Rememberer"

"After they had extinguished the blaze, and Mom had settled her second-best wig on her head, pointedly allowing the once best to sizzle in the kitchen sink, George went to _____ the upstairs bathroom and rid himself of the cake, _____, making no attempt to keep the noise down. Then he went out. _____.

He walked to the edge of town . . ."

—Shelley Jackson, "Nerve"

Once you've begun to own the text a little bit more, go back through the passage and insert your own words between other sentences, in the middle of sentences, in the middle of words. Make these words your words. Go nuts. Go to your own bookshelf and get destructive. Go to a library. Find books and destroy the plot to save the language!

Take It Away

Jenny Gropp and Kirsten Jorgenson

Erase your way to a new piece.

E RASURE POETRY IS A TYPE of poetry in which you take any text and from it create a poem. You do so by erasing words from the existing text; the words that remain create your poem. When it's done right, some fascinating associations occur, and a new kind of life is created for the text.

Consider this passage from the opening of the first book of John Milton's *Paradise Lost*:

> Of Man's First Disobedience, and the Fruit
> Of that Forbidden Tree whose mortal taste
> Brought Death into the World, and all our woe,
> With loss of *Eden*, till one greater Man
> Restore us, and regain the blissful Seat,
> Sing, Heav'nly Muse, that, on the secret top
> Of *Oreb*, or of *Sinai*, didst inspire
> That Shepherd who first taught the chosen Seed
> In the beginning how the Heav'ns and Earth
> Rose out of *Chaos*: or, if *Sion* hill
> Delight thee more, and *Siloa*'s brook that flow'd
> Fast by the Oracle of God, I thence
> Invoke thy aid to my adventrous Song,

Here the theme of the text is about the fall of man from God's grace; Milton's writing about how man disobeyed God and brought death into the world.

But in the mid-1970s, author Ronald Johnson decided that there was something else to be found in *Paradise Lost*. He walked into a bookstore in Seattle and bought a copy of the 1892 edition of *The Poetical Works of John Milton* and went to work crossing out whole lines from the first four books of *Paradise Lost*, revealing his own book-length poem from the text, called *Radi Os*. Here's what the above passage looked like when Johnson was done with it:

O

tree
            into the World,

Man

                        the chosen

Rose out of chaos:

                        song,

Thus the theme is completely changed; it becomes about man's position as "the chosen." Man did not emerge from God but rather from the ground, a "tree / into the World." Johnson went on to cross God and Satan completely out of the text, reducing Milton's Baroque poem to a piece about elemental forces. In *Radi Os*, paradise is never lost; rather man's mind is born of the light of the world.

This complete shift in theme captures the spirit of erasure poetry. Erasure is not a summary of the work being erased; it an excision of a new idea, a new textual soul. Extracting a new piece from an existing piece isn't easy; it may take several tries at the same text. Johnson acquired numerous copies of the 1892 edition of *The Poetical Works of John Milton*, each of which served as a further draft of the work. As he himself said, "You don't tamper with Milton to be funny. You have to be serious."

We also find it interesting that Johnson kept acquiring the same edition of the Milton text. He felt the need, as part of his project, to preserve the original position of the words on the page; every edition of *Radi Os* has adhered to his wish. Thus structure is something to take into consideration when you're working with Erasure Poetry.

A couple of other erasure authors, Tom Phillips and Mary Ruefle, also took particular approaches to their source texts. Phillips's book, *A Humument*, is filled with more than just words from the source text; he paints and draws upon his found text. He felt that such an approach complemented the source text, a Victorian novel called *A Human Document*, which was written by W. H. Mallock. Where Johnson let the words in *Radi Os* float in white space on the page, Phillips wanted clusters of words to be only one element in a rich visual mixture. His text is much more humorous and whimsical than Johnson's, so this approach makes sense. Check out some pages from *A Humument* at his website http://www.tomphillips.co.uk/humument—they're in color, and well worth taking a look at.

Mary Ruefle took yet another approach to presentation in her book *A Little White Shadow*. Her source text, of unknown origin and also entitled *A Little White Shadow*, was initially published in 1889. In keeping with the original publication date, she wanted the piece to look antiquated, so her small book is made with browned pages and antique-looking inky typeface. As well, she used a bottle of White-Out to erase the text, creating a little white shadow of her own.

Writing Exercise: Erase It!
Now that you've read some about erasure poetry, try to make your own. Photocopy any text you like—a news or magazine article, a short story or an excerpt from a novel are a few ideas—and start erasing it. You may want to make a few copies, taking heed of Johnson's practices of revision.

If you want to do a few practice erasures, you can go to a website put together by Wave Books; they have a great program set up online at http://erasures.wavepoetry.com/. Enjoy!

Ye Olde Language Made New

"False" Translation

Jenny Gropp

*Take a text from another language and "translate" it according to
several zany methods.*

TRANSLATION IS A SENSITIVE SUBJECT for most writers. Most people
agree that when translating a piece of writing, the translator needs
to try to match the original meaning as closely as possible. This is usu-
ally a difficult task since it's hard to keep the carefully chosen sounds of
the original piece's language intact. As well, translators (and the readers
of translated writing) have to keep in mind that each country and lan-
guage has its own particular literary, cultural, and political history that
has a huge effect on writers. This makes translators want to tear their
hair out—*How*, they agonize, *are we to understand each other in this ridicu-
lously complicated world?*

So how, as a translator, would you handle translation? Well, you could
become fluent in another language, dedicating yourself to passing writ-
ing between cultures. Or you could become what's called a false transla-
tor and find all of the other hidden potential in pieces of writing, which
has its own fantastical results, as you will see.

A **false translation** is a translation made without the intention of trans-
lating the literal meaning of the original. A good false translator has a
specific job, one that's aptly stated by false translator *par excellence* Da-
vid Cameron: "to leave open the possibility for almost any aspect of a
poem to determine the meaning or direction of its translation, whether
it's the meaning as understood or misunderstood by the translator, the
poem's sound, the shape or look of the words in the poem, or some other
aspect that contributes to the translated poem." This definition comes
from Cameron's 2007 book *Flowers of Bad*, which is a false translation
of Charles Baudelaire's *Les Fleurs du Mal*, or *Flowers of Evil*. Check out
the first stanza of "The Seven Old Men (*Les Sept Viellards*)" in its straight
translation and its original form, both taken from Baudelaire's book as

translated by Roy Campbell, and its false translation, taken from Cameron's book:

Baudelaire's Original

Fourmillante cité, cité pleine de rêves,
Où le spectre en plein jour raccroche le passant!
Les mystères partout coulent comme des sèves
Dans les canaux étroits du colosse puissant.

Campbell's Straight Translation

Ant-seething city, city full of dreams,
Where ghosts by daylight tug the passer's sleeve.
Mystery, like sap, through all its conduit streams,
Quickens the dread Colossus that they weave.

Cameron's False Translation

In the bleach-scrubbed city, the city of plainly dressed ghosts
Where the spectre of the raccoons that made up the soccer player's
coat
            stops passers-by for change
Few mysteries are as cool as you washing your dishes in the sink.
A birdbath is found in the back, right pocket of an enormous thief.

Yesssssss! Here's one more line from the second stanza of "The Seven Old Men," just because it's awesome:

Baudelaire says:

Les maisons, dont la brume allongeait la hauteur.

Campbell says:

Whose houses, by the fog increased in height.

Cameron says:

A limousine runs over the broomstick left out on the fire escape.

So what's going on, exactly?

Cameron used a number of different methods to falsely translate the poems in *Flowers of Bad*. One of those methods is called free false translation, in which Cameron takes Baudelaire's French poems and works with them based on the meanings, sounds, shapes, possible meanings, and associations with the language in the French originals. In this method, he also doesn't shy away from adding extra words to the poem—this was not a straight phonetic translation. Notice how one of the lines above works:

Où le spectre en plein jour raccroche le passant!

is falsely translated as

> Where the spectre of the raccoons that made up the soccer player's
> coat
>> stops passers-by for change

As you can see, Cameron liked the *c*-sounds in the word "raccroche" so much that he made a longer phrase with the words "raccoons" and "soccer player's coat" in it. So definitely feel free to make lines longer while you're false translating!

You can refer to the Afterword of *Flowers of Bad* for a multitude of false translation techniques—there are over fifteen different ones you can play around with.

If you're interested in learning more about false translation, we recommend these books:

Louis Zukofsky's *Catullus*

Jackson MacLow's *French Sonnets*

David Melnick's *Men in Aïda*

WRITING EXERCISE: FREE FALSE TRANSLATION

Now that you've read a bit about false translation, take a look at this poem written by Swedish poet Aase Berg in her book *Hos Radjur*:

VATTENBOTTNAR

Har ar lysande gront—ljuset, droppar, fladdar, spegling,
springor av stralljus och lattnad mellan oroliga lovverk.

Har ar ljusa parlor som klibbat fast vid den tunna tunna
grenen. Grenen har en skorpa. Innanfor tinner lymfan
sakta och sot. De tar farligt: skalytan ar kanske tunnare
an lapplarvens genomlysta silkeshud. Det andas ur ett litet
hal en varelse av glasjus utan jordisk form; det lyser fram
genom en hinna av salivsekret. Har hangar ocksa ormen rod
over grenen; han har namligen manniskoogon och foljer
radjurets rorelser med lugn blick. Men inom kort ska stralen
storta ut ur grenen.

Inom kort ska stralen storta sig ut ur grenen. Inom kort ska
hinnan goftet brista. Inom kort ska ogonsafter rinna ut over
traansiktet, medan graset mals till fromjol mellan radjurskakarna.
Den sota stangelm ska boja sig bakat mot smartan. Och har ror
det sig en fjader mot flodytan, da hon som alksar vatten skata
sjunker ner genom ljusbottnarna.

Take fifteen or twenty minutes and write your own free false transla-
tion of Berg's poem, or of any other poem you like (as long as it's not in
English or a language you know). Remember that your goal is to work
with the poem based on the meanings, sounds, shapes, possible mean-
ings, and associations with the language in the original. We also encour-
age you to add extra words wherever you like.

When you're finished, read on, and compare your work with that of
past student writer Jessica Jia, who created her own free false transla-
tion of the poem above. Note that she chose to free false translate the ti-
tle of the book (*Hos Radjur*) and use it as the title of the poem instead of
working with the actual title ("Vattenbottnar"), which is fine in free false
translation:

HORSE RADISHES

Here he laughs, a HAR HAR in wet lipped grunts. A chuckle,
dropped louder, and gurgling in sprinkles of spittlejuice. Ought
those melons are well loved by the waltzing dances of Leonard. HAR
HAR her hair in the parlor with green tuna kibbles, seen as she is on
her fast. Green laughs. "My face," she scoffs. Therein for, these din-
ners and lime rice ought not be of flight. Their skeleton canisters of

Tupperware and silk genomes of more tuna. Let the mountains of
the little hill form in song.

Glass just in your disk. Let geysers frame genomes in the henna of
Sanskrit. Hang laughing sodas and ramen rods of green. Har Har
you nameless man-slash-skoog, drinking Folgers and radishes. In
the middle of brick roses, men in them court castrated snorting your
green.

I know courts castrated, sorta, Signior Green.
I know courts scanning vistas of gifts.
I know scallywags after Rihanna went over transsex, in the middle of
grass malls until, from jail, my land raided your carne. That's Span-
ish for meat, see. Then we oughta strangle that job, and get back at
Martin. Ought laughter roar designs in jade? Moflo tans, big hand-
some whiskers that fat fat fatten that junk in your genomes. Know,
you know, I just bought Narnia.

Jessica wrote an exciting piece in which her humor plays a great part;
she also succeeds in being able to draw in American culture in a unique
fashion. She wasn't afraid to attack the poem's apparent syntax and go
with a playful form, one that comes out feeling very much like her own.

Finally, take a look at Johannes Göransson's straight English transla-
tion of "Vattenbottnar" to get an idea of how different the free false trans-
lation really is:

WATER BOTTOMS

It is glowing green here—the light, drops, flutters, reflections,
slits of light and lightness in the trembling foliage. Here glowing
pearls stick to the thin thin branch. There is a scab on the branch.
Inside it the lymph runs slow and sweet. It is dangerous: the shell's
surface is perhaps thinner than the liplarvae's glowed-through
silk skin. It breathes through a small hole a creature of glass light
with no earthly form; it glows through a membrane of saliva
secretions. Here the snake also hangs red over the branch; he has
human eyes and follows the deer's movement with a calm gaze. But
soon the ray will burst out of the branch.

Soon the ray will burst out of the branch. Soon the membrane the poison will erupt. Soon the eye juices will run across the wooden face, while the grass is ground into seed flour in the deer jaws. The sweet stalk will bend backwards toward the pain. And here a feather moves toward the river surface, as she who loves water sinks back through the bottoms of light.

Sounds into Words, Words into Sounds

Molly Goldman

Turn a sound jumble into a poem.

W E ARE ALL HERE BECAUSE we love words. We are writers and we've chosen to work with words. However, we are a lucky bunch because not only do words make meaning, but words make *sounds*, and sounds connote just as much meaning as words do. We choose words for their sounds all the time. Let's face it, some words are just fun to say. Let's explore the making of sounds. For now, let's not worry about "sense."

Harryette Mullen's poem "Jinglejangle" from her book *Sleeping with the Dictionary* is entirely focused on sound:

> backpack backtrack Bahama Mama balls to the wall bam-a-lam
> bandstand
> Battle in Seattle beat the meat bedspread bee's knees
> behani ghani best dressed
> best in the West BestRest Best Western Betsy Wetsy
> Better Cheddar Big Dig bigwig
> bird turd black don't crack blackjack blame game boho
> boiling oil
> Bone Phone Bonton Bony Maroni boob tube boogie-woogie
> boohoo book nook
> boon coon Bot's dots Boozy Suzy bowl of soul bow-wow
> boy toy brace face
> brain drain bric-a-brac bug jug bump on the rump
> Busty Rusty

I don't know about you but I never get tired of reading that out loud. This excerpt reminds us that on the most basic level, words make sounds and we communicate by making sounds. This poem might not have a "plot" but that doesn't mean it's about nothing. It makes a pretty strong argument about the music of our everyday language.

Another thing to notice about Mullen's poem is that sometimes she gets from point A to point B because some of these words sound *like each other*. Some rhyme, and some could easily be misheard and mistaken for one another. It's a sound jumble that moves her from one word onto the next.

Sometimes I like to find a poetry reading on YouTube or PennSound and listen to it while I write. I don't listen too closely because I like to mishear what the poet is reading and let those sounds filter into what I'm writing. Some of my favorite recordings are the "Horse Songs" by Jerome Rothenberg. These poems don't have much literal meaning. In fact, it's hard to tell if he's even saying real words. However, it *sounds* like words.

If you want to try, find Jerome Rothenberg's "Horse Songs" on Penn-Sound's website (http://writing.upenn.edu/pennsound/x/Rothenberg.php). Listen to any of them and just write without stopping. Write down whatever you're hearing. That is to say, whatever you *think* you're hearing. Remember, it won't be a literal translation, since it will be pretty hard to transcribe word for word. Instead, think about what it sounds like. Try to copy the sounds he makes. Don't think about what it means! Think about how it sounds. Here's an example of a sound translation I wrote from "Horse Song 1":

> All summer there in mine
> All come and sanguine there are mine
> There in mine sanguine there ermine
> All are now somewhere there in mine
> Gone because I was raised in the dawn
> Somewhere are mine all kinds sanguine and ermine
> In the house the blues don't there and in the house
> the shining wing come somewhere are mine ermine
> In the house the whole and low there ermine and all kinds and
>   sanguine
> somewhere out there ermine wool

I wrote this poem by translating the sounds that I heard into words. As you can see, it doesn't make a ton of sense, but it did generate some pretty cool lines that can stand on their own or be plucked out and put in other poems. Like in Harryette Mullen's poem, sound is the organizing principle. We get from one place to another based on the logic of the sound rather than the logic of the plot or narrative. Since this was a translation of sounds rather than words, everyone who listens to this poem could hear completely different things. The goal is to transcribe the sounds. This is a great exercise if you ever feel stuck and need to generate content. Contemporary poets Robert Kelly and Schuldt created *Unquell the Dawn Now*, a multi-media project based on Frederick Hölderlin's long poem *Am Quell der Donau*. Here's a sample:

AM QUELL DER DONAU

BY FREDERICH HÖLDERLIN

Ihr guten Geister, da seid ihr auch,
Oftmals, wenn einen dann die heilige Wolk umbschwebt,
Da staunen wir und wissens nicht zu deuten

And here's the translation. . . .

FROM UNQUELL THE DAWN NOW

BY ROBERT KELLY AND SCHULDT

Her golden ghosts on their side are all
Oft small, when inner. Then the holy work on him sweeps.
Dare standing. We unwitting night to day turn.

You can see the logic of the translation in this example. "Ihr guten Geister" becomes "her golden ghosts." It doesn't necessarily make "sense," but the point is to generate by using sounds and see what happens. Start by finding Jerome Rothenberg's "Horse Songs" or google any poem in a foreign language and translate sounds into words!

Starting from a Song, Part One

REMIXING A SONG IN WRITING

Tasha Coryell and Steve Reaugh

Be a one-hit wonder!

I DON'T KNOW A LOT ABOUT music. I took guitar lessons for a couple of years and I can barely strum out three consecutive chords. I went to an elementary school that did not use grades, but I still almost managed to fail the singing test despite hours of practice. It is safe to say that I am not musically talented. Neither am I one of those people with extensive music collections who can list off obscure bands seen in concert. I would describe myself as the casual music listener, one who listens in the car or while running. However, for years I have found my writing to be informed by music and music videos.

There are many things that can be done in music that are difficult to do anywhere else without coming off as cheesy or cliché. In a pop song, an artist can sincerely detail all of their feelings for a significant other without worrying about sounding immature. A rap artist can illustrate all the ways in which the other rap artists cannot bring them down because they have self-esteem and are not afraid to show it. Country music often depicts an entire narrative in a matter of minutes. Even nursery rhymes use sound in a manner that would be difficult to pull off in a poem and remain memorable across generations. I wanted to come up with a way to use these musical elements within writing.

Here's an excerpt from the essay "One Hit Wonder Cycle: What Carly Rae Jepsen Taught Me about Love, Loss, and Love Again" by Brian Oliu, who describes the experience of listening to a pop song and how music can affect us:

> The great thing about pop music is that it is truly "popular"—it does not belong to just one person, it belongs to all of us. It is universal. We have all longed on the dancefloor, we have all lost someone or something, away from the bright lights or in them. I hear a song and think

of watching the door waiting for a girl I love to come walking in and our eyes meeting as she dances with her friends. You hear the same song and think of long car rides with a person you sleep next to. Those moments—when we have our headphones on and are crushed by the subtle sadness of the words—they are just as true as when we are drunkenly screaming those same lyrics with friends and strangers and feeling young and timeless. To play these songs, and to play them loud is to liberate them from our own quietness—to allow us to sing where you think you're going baby without having to think of leaving, without having to think of an empty bed.

Your Turn

Step 1: Think of songs that you've heard. They can be of any genre, from any time period. They can be something like "Mary Had a Little Lamb" or they can be your favorite songs from the radio, a recording, or from a music video. Make a list of a few songs:

_____

_____

_____

_____

_____

Now, pick one of the songs. Write down a summary of what the song is about. Write down the song lyrics if you remember them (you can listen to the song or look up the lyrics) Who is the song speaking to? What is the message? Write that down. Now you have some notes on the song.

Step 2: Now it's your turn to write about that same song in a very new way. Here are some prompts to help get you started:

- Tell the song's story again, adding lots of new images.
- Do a personal retelling of the song from your own point of view.
- Write about the place you were when you heard the song and how the song made you feel at that moment and in that space.
- Many songs are directed at a certain person or a group of people. How would the listened respond to the song?

You can add some lyrics, but make sure that what you write incorporates some new dimension and is mostly your own, new writing.

Here's a student example from Katie Lightfoot in which she takes on the voice of one of the characters in the song, using some lyrics to support her original work:

YOU BE THE WRITER

You wait for silence, I wait for word. When you told me you were leaving, my world was blackened. Days grew darker. Nights grew longer. I thought I'd always be happy; now that's all gone. We're trying to prevent what's already begun. The death inside you is growing, spreading, morphing, and evolving to suit its needs. You're wearing thin. You wait. I wait. It continues to kill you, to break us apart, to tear you from this realm. I'd rather pretend you'll still be there in the end. We didn't plan it this way, didn't plan on you leaving before me, didn't plan on me staying here without you. Because your lungs "suck at being lungs," a tremor has been sent through my world. I interlace my fingers with your pale, thin ones. I look into your graying eyes. If I did not know you, I would have mistaken the color for the hue of a choppy sea, or the tint of clouds just before the sun lowers itself from the sky. But I do know you, so I can identify the color as hurt, fear. This is a fear of hurting others. I tell you to trust me as a salty tear begins its journey. I am afraid, but I do not say so. My knees grow weak, and I am forced to sit. You must have missed my smile. These days you always do.

Starting from a Song, Part Two

Under the (Musical) Influence

Tasha Coryell and Steve Reaugh

Let music put you in a writing mood.

Listening to a song can be a helpful jumping-off point if you're stuck and aren't sure where to go with your writing. For the low, low price of a YouTube search, a flick of your iTunes, or changing the channel to MTV (okay, maybe not that one, because even when I was a kid they didn't play music on MTV), you can find some sort of musical accompaniment to your day. Heaven knows I need music to get me through long car drives, airport layovers, or the occasional boring class. (I'm sure you've never had your music on at an inappropriate time.) But I bet you're thinking: gee, it's often helpful to have music to help me focus. And you'd be right.

In my high school, during AP English exams, my teacher, a particularly jowly woman, was insistent on playing classical music while we frantically scribbled out our essays. She said it relaxed certain waves in the brain, making it easier for us to string thoughts together, and blah, blah, blah. . . . I never really did pay much attention in school. Anyway, my best friend found the music terribly annoying, but luckily she's a fast writer and had that exam on our teacher's desk in twenty minutes flat. For those of us who took a little longer, though . . . well, I never would've admitted it at the time, but the music really did help me focus. At the very least, it didn't let me space out so much. Over time—and especially since she gave me great grades in the class—I relied on the trick to help me zone in on things; it worked. So: props to her.

At first, I only used this technique for academic writing—essays and stuff. Then I finally gave it a shot for creative writing. But when I did—to my surprise, since I find classical music a little boring (sorry, classical fans)—things started to get really, really *weird*. But not a bad weird—more like a funky, awesome, inspiring weird, as you're about to find out.

What you're about to do is freewrite a piece—any genre, any length—while a song plays in the background. What's going to be fun here is to see how your style, voice, and approach change when you're *under the influence* of different kinds of music. It's a way to examine **mood**, that feeling you get when you're reading—or writing—a piece. You're going to be able to see how the song's mood impacts yours—will you go with its flow or resist it completely? Or something in between? If you've got a killer eighties rap going; will you start writing in rhyme; or go for long, complex sentences that wrap your work like silk; or start with the choppy and move to the floppy? Let the music move you, or shove it away—it's all up to you and the moment.

One final note: you can do this exercise on your own or with a group.

Your Turn

Step 1: Go to your favorite music receptacle (e.g., YouTube, your iTunes library, your big brother's old CD collection) and search for random songs. The more outrageous the genre, the better. **Important:** try *not* to listen to them beforehand, though—just pick songs by their name and genre. They don't need to have lyrics, necessarily—instrumental is just as good as Top 40, which is just as good as bluegrass, which is just as good as grunge . . .

Step 2: Make a playlist of all those songs. Put them on your phone, or have them on your browser in different tabs, load up an old stereo—however you do it, just make sure you're able to control when the song starts. Don't push play just yet, though, because there's one more step to do.

Step 3: Now think of some parameters for what you're about to write. Brainstorm at least **four** "must-haves" for the piece. The piece will include these agreed-upon elements. **Three** of these "must-haves" should be standard, simple questions that will help you frame your piece so that you're not out there floating in the middle of writer's-block land. (It's a terrible place.) Use the following three "must-haves."

- How many characters are in this piece?
- Where does this piece take place?
- What's going on—why are they there, e.g., is it someone's birthday, are they waiting for a train, did they just get sucked into an alternate universe?

Your fourth "must-have" is up to you. Go wild! Go weird! Go creepy. Here are a few of my favorites:

- One key word must be used in the piece (the weirder the better, like *befuddled* or *ahoy* or *axe murderer*).
- What time of day, season, and/or year is it?
- One of the characters has a secret. What is it?

Start your first song and write. Include your "must-haves"—if one of them just won't make it in there, go with the flow of what you've got. The idea here is to *just keep writing*. After all, the (musical) rush isn't going to last for very long!

Step 4: Once that song is complete, you're going to start the brainstorming process you did in step three all over again. Answer your three standard "must-have" questions again, but with different answers. For example, if you used four characters in Paris doing a tightrope walk on the Eiffel Tower, change it up; you may want to choose two characters this time around, on a date inside a whale's stomach. Don't forget to add your one (or more!) random "must-have" of your choice. Then start song two and write on.

You can write one piece per song just like this, changing things up—trying to come up with unusual "must-have" restrictions, and off-the-wall answers to your three standard "must-have" questions. **Alternatively:** if you're a fan of longer work, you can assemble a playlist, come up with some "must-haves," and work on a single piece while the whole playlist runs its course. If you do this, you wouldn't need to stop after every song—just keep writing, and see if the new music wants to influence what you're writing.

Always, no matter how you want to try this exercise: if you're stuck, let the music take you wherever it wants to go. I've had many pieces stall out until I turned on the right song—and then the inspiration hits. Often, it's not something I would ever have thought of, not in a million flashes of the cursor. So go ahead—get hooked on the music; you might be surprised by the places you'll go.

Balderdash for Writers

NEW STORIES FROM AN OLD BOX

Jesse Delong and Megan Paonessa

Create stories by playing a few rounds of this classic word game.

Balder: an adjective used to describe a bald man, balding,
   even more than he was before.
Dash: also known as "dashing," meaning good-looking,
   tantalizing, hot-stuff
Balderdash!

B ALDERDASH IS A GREAT GAME that gets your creative, word-defining juices flowing, and for this activity you'll need the board game—as well as some friends to collaborate with—but the buck won't stop there. This activity incorporates unique words and funny definitions, and then shows you how to take it a step further. In the end, you'll have produced a story or poem you never knew you had in you.

PART ONE: THE GAME
Go ahead and check out the rules of Balderdash as given—we aren't changing much around at the start. Then, with others, play a few rounds. The more you play, the more you will find yourself stretching your imagination, coming up with hilarious ideas, and the more you play, the more you'll have to work with later on. Start with three rounds, and if it's going well, play up to five. Then stop. You have more work to do!

Here's where the storytelling comes in. Collect all of the definitions your group has come up with, including the real answers, and make sure you didn't skip the part where you wrote down the words on top of the answer card. Go through everything. Tag the especially comical ones, or the interestingly technical and realistic ones—whichever you think is the most writerly route. Then check out the activity below:

PART TWO: LET'S GET WRITING
Sometimes, the ability to make people believe what you say is all in the

delivery. You may have learned that as you got the hang of playing the game. Now you can use that to your advantage in your writing. Collect the cards up and look over the fake definitions. Find your favorite ones, and separate them from the rest. You will use these to write a story.

Story Scenario One:

From the group of fake definitions, find a **Person**, a **Place**, and a **Verb**. Write a story where your **Person** acts out your **Verb** in that fake **Place**.

Story Scenario Two:

Find two **Person** cards, and a card describing an **Object** or an **Animal**. Write a story where the two **Person**s argue over who owns the **Object** or the **Animal**.

Story Scenario Three:

See if you can find a fake definition from one of the cards that sounds like a disease. Also, find a **Person** card. Write a story where the **Person** cures that disease in his basement laboratory.

Added Challenge. Story Scenario Four:

Write a story that contains as many fake words and definitions as possible.

Disaster City

A Facebook-y Adventure

Rachel Adams, Jessie Bailey, and Kirsten Jorgenson

Map out a city and fill it with characters and plot twists in this collaborative fiction activity that uses moves that you might recognize from Facebook.

Take an ordinary city with a handful of eccentric residents. Take daily life: neighborly gossip, a dog-bitten mailman, feuds with long-forgotten origins. Now take this city and add something extreme, unpredictable, ill-timed. Turn it upside down. Shake it up. You. Your friends. The Internet. You will become: **Disaster City**.

Invent Your Town

Say it's July. Say you're tired of all your video games and it's too hot to go outside. Maybe you're just bored. What are you going to do? Why not make up a town, create a series of minor and major disasters, and then launch your story as a viral fiction through Facebook or another popular social networking site?

Sound good? Good. Here's the plan: get in a group with other people, get a poster board and some markers, get access to a computer, and then start planning.

Now that you've got all your people together, it's time to decide what your town is going to look like. The things you consider will help determine the stories you can make up about your town. For instance, if you live on a small Pacific island and all the fish in the ocean suddenly get mad, grow legs, walk to shore, and start slapping sunbathers in the face, you've got a problem on your hands. If you live in a secluded mountain village, on the other hand, the fish would be less stressful to the town.

What's your town's:
Climate:

_____

_____

_____

_____

Size:

_____

_____

_____

Geography:

_____

_____

_____

Architecture:

_____

_____

_____

Attractions:

_____

_____

_____

Exports:

_____

_____

_____

Population:

_____

_____

_____

On the poster board, as a group, draw a map of your town. It doesn't have to be a work of art, though it could be if that's your thing; the map just has to be a reference point for your group. When making the map of your town, you'll want to think about what sort of natural features characterize this town: Is there a waterfall? A river? A forest? A mountain? A mesa? A desert? Is the desert made of sugar? Can the waterfall make you invisible? What lives in the forest? In the ocean? Where do most of the people live? Draw the geographical features—from realistic to fantasti-cal—on your map.

Hey! What's the name of your town? Write that somewhere on the map.

INVENT YOUR CHARACTERS

Now that you've created your town map, it's time to create the characters who will live in your town. Start developing characters by thinking about their occupations in relation to your town map. Is your town located on an island? Then perhaps a lifeguard or a scuba instructor lives there. If your town is in the Arctic, then maybe it has a world-famous snow-cone entrepreneur as a resident. If the town is in the middle of a desert, per-haps a camel herder or a professional rain dancer lives there.

Below is a list of possible occupations for the characters in a town. In the spaces provided, add a few more to the list. For each occupation *provide one detail about the character.*

Character/Occupation	Detail
Sheriff	Likes to gamble
Pastry chef	Allergic to flour
Nun	Addicted to TV
Eye surgeon	Has one arm
Undertaker	Preppy
Fashion designer	Ultra modest
_____	_____
_____	_____
_____	_____
_____	_____
_____	_____
_____	_____

Now have each person in the group choose their character from the list above.

Then, as a group, start to develop your characters.

First, think about the characters' relationships to one another in terms of family and living arrangements. Is the zookeeper divorced from the undertaker? Does the mad scientist live next door to her cousin, the pastor? Keep in mind that the relationships between these characters will heavily influence the way they interact with one another. For instance, if the nurse is the doctor's brother, then they would interact in a different way with one another than if they were merely coworkers.

Next, you can start to think of the characters in terms of club affiliations, religious organizations, and business relationships. Is the busboy in the teacher's choir group? Once again, remember that these types of connections between the characters will influence the way they communicate with one another. If the grocer has a weekly poker game with the housekeeper, perhaps they argue a lot because one owes the other money.

After determining these basic relationships between characters, have your group break apart and work on their individual character's development. Each member of the group should answer the following questions about their character and share their answers with the group.

- What is your character's favorite TV show (real or imaginary)?
- Name one quirky hobby of your character (sketching ceiling fans, competing in national welding competitions, learning ribbon-dance karate, etc.).
- What does the bumper sticker on the back of your character's vehicle say?
- If your character could have dinner with any other character from your town, who would it be and why?

CREATE A HOME FOR YOUR CHARACTER

When you're finished sharing, go back to your poster-board map. Now that you know a little more about who you are, you need to decide where you are going to live on the map. Think about what the geographical features of your town mean to your town and what it then means if you are living there. What do the mountains mean to your town, for instance? If they're, say, the holy site, how is that going to affect the character who lives in a house in the mountains?

On a small index card, using a pen/pencil/etc., design a house that matches the personality of your character. If you are a surf instructor, for example, you might want a house made out of old shark-bitten surfboards. If you are a zookeeper, maybe you would want a zebra-striped house. Make a sketch. It's ok if you aren't a master artist.

After you've finished making your homes, tape them to the map. Now everyone can see what kind of dwelling each character has, and where it is located.

Assign Facebook Accounts for Individual Characters and the Whole Group

Now that you have decided that you are the fashion designer who plays the keyboard in a rubber band and is married to the jailor who is in the same bowling league as the painter who is the gas station attendant's second cousin twice removed, you're ready to assign that character to your Facebook profile.

After each person in your group is assigned an individual character, someone should create an invitation-only group page for "Disaster City"—this will be the town's page—and invite everyone to join. (You'll use the group page more in a little bit—but go ahead and create it now.) Or, instead of using Facebook, you can also create a private Google Doc titled "Disaster City" and invite everyone in your group to participate. You can adapt this exercise across many different platforms!

Get to the Action!

Town: established. Characters: created. Dwellings: located. Now it's time for some action.

Take two index cards for each person in your city. Write "Confrontation Card" on the back of each of these. Take one more card for each person. On the back of these, draw a big red dot. These are Disaster Cards. The red dot is to indicate the urgency of the situation.

Confrontation Cards

Sit in a circle. Each person in the town gets two Confrontation Cards.

On the two cards, each person writes down their Disaster City character name and starts thinking about how their character might annoy/distress/provoke/otherwise interfere with or intersect with another character's life. Have each person write one Confrontation Card specific to their neighbor to the left. For example: if you are a butcher and your neighbor is a zookeeper, a confrontation specific to them might be: "Nancy the butcher keeps featuring exotic meats, and you recently noticed that her menu items match up with your missing zoo animals." Now turn to the neighbor on the right and think of a confrontation that you might have with them.

Once everyone has two Confrontation Cards, have everyone read them and then take five minutes to confer/clarify/slightly alter any confrontation ideas that people do not understand or do not want to write about. Done arguing? Got it all hammered out? Great. Okay.

FICTION THROUGH FACEBOOK: MAXIMIZE YOUR CREATIVE OUTPUT

Before you start posting, chatting, and writing away, here are some pointers to help you maximize your creative output. When you post in the group as your character, act like you're writing a script, and begin each time with your character's name. For example, write "Nancy the butcher: 'I'm going to leave a bucket of guts on someone's porch!'" If you're using a Google Doc, be sure to use your real name as well. For example, write "Lisa/Nancy the butcher: 'I'm going to leave a bucket of guts on someone's porch!'" That way everyone is clear about who's playing who.

Create a Post in Disaster City

Posts often occur in present tense and *in media res* (in the middle of the action). This can add a fun dimension to your story, giving it a "real time" feel. For example: "I don't know what to do! My garden gnomes just came to life and they're hammering at my door asking for cottage cheese!"

Try to avoid simply repeating what your Confrontation Card says. If it says: "Nancy the butcher left a bucket of guts on your porch with a note that you should use them to fertilize your garden, but your dog has been dragging them into your living room."

Instead of just saying "EWW!! The butcher left a bucket of guts on my porch and Rusty is eating them in the living room! EWWW!!" think about how you might spin the situation for your audience.

It's typical to use different *registers*, which is another way to say *tones* or *ways of talking*, in different situations. If something's urgent, we'll be direct and to the point. If we're talking to a friend, we'll be less careful about how we phrase things than when we're trying to talk our parents into something. When we're telling a story to a big group of people, we try and highlight the funny things, withhold good parts of the story, exaggerate, or use sarcasm or understatement to show that we think it's funny and give the listener permission to think so, too.

So maybe you'd say "Mmm, mmm, bucket of guts in the breakfast nook, courtesy of Rusty the dog . . . Thanks a lot, Nancy. Sure my petunias would have loved them though."

This kind of attention to language will make a big difference in how real your narrative feels, and it will probably be a lot more fun to write.

Other Kinds of Posts

Posts offer a *ton* of flexibility. Your post could be a manifesto:

> ATTENTION ALL RESIDENTS OF DISASTER CITY: I will no lon-
> ger tolerate you FISHING FOR TROUT in my PERSONAL AQUAR-
> IUM! I built this aquarium with my own two hands and those trout are
> like my children! Please stop eating them.

A diary entry:

> Dear Diary: What a day! The volcano of life exploded and guess what,
> it's a volcano of death, too. I was fishing when it happened.

A will:

> The killer eagles are circling the banana tree I'm in and there is no
> rescue in sight. I have repeatedly called for help but no one seems to
> care, so I am now drafting an official will. Jimmy Two-Shoes, I leave you
> my inside-out umbrella, which I hope will help you as much as you have
> helped me today.

A letter:

> Dear Mother and Father, thanks for sending me to summer camp.
> You were right about it being educational. I've learned how to disarm
> a ninja, survive off cherries and rainbow trout, and disregard my camp
> counselor's advice when it comes to bears and loud noises. Please come
> get me from the hospital.

The possibilities are endless. I mean, you could just write a simple
narrative, too, but really think about which medium will deliver your
message in the funnest, most interesting way.

Chat

Disaster City can get pretty chaotic. Everyone tends to go their own di-
rection, create their own new situations and plot lines and solutions, and
before you know it, it's impossible to keep track of what's really going on.

One way to make sure this doesn't happen is to chat with each other
as you brainstorm new events or plan out what your character is going
to do next. Try and get other people in on your plans. If you want an-
other character to do something, tell them first and make sure they're

on board. If you plan to do something to or with someone else, check in with them and see if they agree with your new line of action.

The more you keep in touch with other members of the city, the more cohesive and collaborative your effort will be. Total anarchy obviously has its advantages, but constraints (dealing with the same problem as everyone else rather than inventing your own new situation) can push you to come up with some really good stuff.

Events

Town meetings. Emergency zombie attack preparation seminars. An election . . . you take it from here.

READY . . . SET . . . GO!

You're all ready to tell stories in funny and exciting ways, to avoid the mundane and repetitive. Go log on to Facebook and start telling your fellow residents of Disaster City all about your neighbor troubles and solving your disputes! Space out the retelling of the incident(s) and the development of the solution. Take time to read about your friend's troubles and offer advice or help.

You don't have to stick closely to your created narratives. You'll find that as you read about your neighbor's disputes and talk to various people in the town, you'll want to go off on tangents. You'll get ideas for events, like a town meeting in which various neighbors air their grievances about Nancy the butcher, who is clearly a bit out of control. You'll get involved in writing a spell to help your friend turn the garden gnomes back into statues. There will be plenty of writing to do. Go ahead and run with whatever inspires you.

DISASTER CARDS

Depending on the lifespan you foresee for your Disaster City project, you may want to save this part for the very end, or for a lull in participation, or you can go ahead and do it right after the confrontations have gotten people all riled up.

Now give everyone one of the Disaster Cards (the big red dot on the back of the card indicates the seriousness of the matter). This time, everybody is going to help create a disaster that will strike your beloved city.

You might tell everyone to think of something that could actually happen (tornado, virus, plague of crickets) and add an unusual element to it (tornado that follows one particular member of town wherever they go, like a puppy; virus that makes everyone want to dig tunnels and live underground; a plague of poop-happy seagulls).

Once everyone's done, read the ideas out loud. You may want to vote on one (or it may become quickly clear which one everyone wants to do), or you can combine pieces of a couple of different ideas and create a SuperDisaster.

For this part of Disaster City, two things become important. One: you want to really think about your character—their occupation, their relationships, their position in the town, and try and take these things into account as you have them deal with the disaster.

Two: communicate. In order to keep this truly collaborative, you'll want to create alliances, come up with plans to survive the disaster, and recruit other people to help you with these plans. This isn't a hard-and-fast rule; maybe your character is a bit solitary and is hiding out somewhere. But when a large group of townspeople are banding together to divert the herd of purple elephants from trampling city hall and you don't tell anyone that you're busy releasing a bunch of monkeys from the zoo to come and tame the elephants, they might not react to your assertion that "Everything is okay now, people! The monkeys have saved the day!" Avoid frustration by keeping in contact with everyone before you make plot decisions.

Finally, have fun. Writing is such a solitary activity so much of the time. This is one instance where it doesn't have to be. Writing as a group is a complex thing to negotiate but well worth it, as you're about to discover.

Consequences

A Parlor Game of Surprise Narratives

Kit Emslie and Sarah Kelly

*First played by the Victorians, Consequences is a parlor game
similar to the famous Surrealist exercise "exquisite corpse."*

CONSEQUENCES WAS FIRST INTRODUCED TO me as an after-dinner
game my family would play. Once everyone had eaten their fill and
caught up on the usual topics of conversation, we would often play trivia
games or tell jokes. Consequences is perfect for this as it involves every
member of a group, without anyone having to wait around for their turn.

First played by the Victorians, Consequences is a parlor game simi-
lar to the famous Surrealist exercise the "exquisite corpse." It also bears
some similarities to the modern party game Mad Libs. What's fun about
this game is that it's almost impossible to predict the outcome. Even
working in a group, no one knows what the other players have contrib-
uted to the game, so what comes out in the end is often nonsensical,
sometimes eerie, and usually very funny.

Here's how to play:

- Get into a group of no less than four people. More people can be in-
  cluded in the group, but five to six is ideal.
- Every person in the group is given a pen and a blank piece of paper (you
  can also use a premade template to help everyone remember the rules;
  an example is provided below).
- At the top of their sheet of paper, everyone in the group writes an ad-
  jective (ie. peaceful, feverish, cylindrical) to describe a character. The
  weirder the better!
- When you have finished, fold the paper just underneath what you wrote,
  so no one else in the group can see it.
- Next, pass the paper to the person on your left. At the same time, the
  person on your right will pass you theirs. Everyone in the group will
  have a new sheet of paper, folded back so they can't see what the previ-
  ous player wrote.

- On your new sheet of paper, you will write a name for a character, following on from the adjective you wrote in the last round. So if the paper was unfolded it might read "Peaceful Gerald" or "Feverish Eglantine," but of course, you have no idea what adjective the previous player wrote down.
- This continues around the group until everyone has written everything on this list (the list can vary, and you can make your own template for a different list, but this is a good one to start with):

Adjective for Character 1: _____

Character 1's name: _____

Adjective for Character 2: _____

Character 2's name: _____

Where they met: _____

Character 1 wore: _____

Character 2 wore: _____

Character 1 said: _____

Character 2 said: _____

The consequence was: _____

What the world said about it: _____

- Remember to keep folding back the paper every time you write something down. If you see what other people have written, you don't get to experience the most fun part of the game.
- Once everyone has passed the sheets around, each person should be holding one sheet that contains a single crazy story.
- Next, turn your template into a story by writing the elements of the template in sentence form. The ideas you include in each line should be linked to the next in order.
- Now go around the group, reading your finished stories aloud. Most often they will make no sense, but that's the joy of Consequences. Sometimes, though, spooky coincidences happen, and the stories start to make sense. But this game never goes the same way twice.

Here is a sample of a Consequences template, with answers written in to give you an idea of what the finished product might look like.

Adjective for Character 1: *Brazen*
Character 1's name: *Isadora*

Adjective for Character 2: *Gelatinous*
Character 2's name: *Raheem*

Where they met: *The Pyramids of Giza*
Character 1 wore: *Paint-splattered overalls*
Character 2 wore: *A sequined one-piece*

Character 1 said: *"Have you seen my gerbil?"*
Character 2 said: *"I am the finest teapot ever crafted."*

The consequence was: *Violinists were exiled from the state of Arizona.*
What the world said about it: *"Why does this keep happening?"*

If this example was written in sentences, it would read like this:

> Brazen Isadora met Gelatinous Raheem at the Pyramids of Giza. Isadora wore paint-splattered overalls, and Raheem wore a sequined one-piece. Isadora said, "Have you seen my gerbil?" and Raheem said, "I am the finest teapot ever crafted." The consequence was that violinists were exiled from the state of Arizona, and the world said, "Why does this keep on happening?"

You can keep on playing in your group using any of the variations on the game below. Feeling inspired? Put your own spin on Consequences by creating a new template.

DESERT ISLAND CONSEQUENCES

Character 1's name: _____

Character 1's childhood nickname: _____

Character 2's name: _____

Character 2's childhood nickname:_____

Where they found themselves stranded: _____

Character 1 forgot to bring: _____

Character 2 forgot to bring: _____

Days later, with only hours left to live, Character 1 grumbled: _____

Days later, with only hours left to live, Character 2 grumbled: _____

The consequence was: _____

The rescue sign they spelled out in all caps read: _____

Awkward Party Consequences

Character 1's name: _____

Character 2's name: _____

Distinct, if out of date, hairstyle for Character 1: _____

Distinct, if out of date, hairstyle for Character 2: _____

Snacks offered at the party where the met: _____

Character 1 spilled their drink all over: _____

Character 2 spilled their drink all over: _____

Character 1's pick up line: _____

Character 2's pick up line: _____

The consequence was: _____

The world's Facebook status the next day read: _____

Supermarket Consequences

Character 1's name: _____

Character 1's grocery items: _____

Character 2's name: _____

Character 2's grocery items: _____

What character 1 was thinking about while waiting in line behind Character 2: _____

What character 2 was thinking about while waiting in line in front of Character 1: _____

Where they met, years earlier: _____

What Character 1 was too shy to say: _____

What Character 1 said instead: _____

What Character 2 was too shy to say: _____

What Character 2 said instead: _____

The consequence was: _____

What the world regretted: _____

After you're done playing, you can use the ideas from the exercise in order to start a short story. Here's an example:

Over the course of his middle school career, Raheem never came in first in the Presidential Physical Fitness Assessment. He never came close to getting the Presidential award, or the National award (the one for second-placers who could handle a couple of feeble pull-ups). Raheem was relegated to the ranks of Participant award holders, an award reserved for those who deserve nothing.

In form, Raheem was a fourteen-year-old who could only be described as gelatinous. He shuffled rather than walked, dreamt of a future that would one day reveal itself to him. He loved Isadora, a girl he had known on his block all his life but whose body had now transcended childhood without him. When their eyes met on the school bus each morning (him staring, her coldhearted glances), he relished the fact that they were glances still, and his to keep.

Here he was in gym class, Raheem who was a "Participant" in all things, going on his thirteenth sit up. It was noon on the 23rd of April, and to Raheem the worthlessness of today could be only awarded the role of "Participant" in the Presidential Assessment of Days. Participant, as he attempted crunch after crunch in the blazing Arizona heat. Participant, as his classmates surrounded him. This day, he and his body were participants as the ellipse of the school's bright red track enveloped their very existence.

At its heart, Consequences teaches us that randomness and non-sense can be useful because they change the way we approach a subject, use adjectives, and move through a narrative. The surprising turns that this game takes can inform writing on a bigger scale because they show us new ways into things, for example attributing a single adjective to a noun. A "timid actress" or "clumsy dental assistant" provides so much information about a character in only a few words. It's these unexpected moves within writing that can unleash a different kind of creativity and make us the kind of writers we never knew we could be.

Constraints, Odd Characters, and Secret Postcards

A Fresh Approach to Character and Context

Kirsten Jorgenson, Betsy Seymour, and Danilo Thomas

Create questions that generate eccentric characters and then write their secrets down on postcards in this group activity.

So, you've got writers block, eh? Or maybe you feel tired of writing the same old thing over and over again. Craving something different for your work? Something so new and so strange that even *you* can't predict what it might be? Well, baby, that's where constraints can come to your rescue.

Hold up. Constraints? Yes! Constraints. We usually think of constraints as something that hold us back, but sometimes blocking our impulses frees us up to write a new way. When we write with constraints, we can't rely on the writing skills we're most comfortable with; instead, we are forced to exercise underutilized writing muscles. Say, for instance, that I like to write poems with birds in them and that I have a penchant for long vowel sounds. Maybe my poems are getting a bit stale and predictable so I decide that everywhere I would put a bird I need to insert an item in my garbage can and that I cannot use long vowel sounds. Suddenly I'm out of my comfort zone but I get to explore my writing in a new way.

Choose a paragraph you've already written—for school, work, an email, a report, a story, anything.

Now let's add some constraints. On a piece of paper:

Draw three columns.
- In the first column, arrange each noun from your paragraph in alphabetical order A–Z.
- In the second column arrange each verb in alphabetical order Z–A.
- In the third column list all of the adjectives.

- Now write across each row. Instead of looking vertically at each column, look across each row: How does the first noun in your column enact the first verb in your column? How would the first adjective describe that activity? You have to write your way to connect the words. Write sentences that use the horizontal groups of words, adding lots of other words as you go. Now you have a very new sort of paragraph, inspired by the building blocks of the old one.

Using constraints is like running an obstacle course. It keeps your writing agile, strong, and flexible. It shows you that your creative potential is inexhaustible. Don't believe me? You might want to check out some famous artists who have used constraints in their creative process to test their limits:

- Lars von Trier, *The Five Obstructions*. In *The Five Obstructions* von Trier challenges his mentor, Jørgen Leth, to remake the film that made Leth famous, *The Perfect Human*, five times using a series of constraints devised by von Trier. The results are sometimes fantastic and sometimes disastrous but always a challenge.
- Raymond Queneau, *Exercises in Style*. In *Exercises in Style*, Queneau retells the same banal bus scene ninety-nine times using variations in tone and style.
- *Oulipo: A Primer in Potential Literature*, edited by Warren Motte. The artists of the Oulipo movement in France made up lots and lots of constraints for each other—Motte includes a number of them in this book.

Now that we know what the constraints are, the question becomes: How do we put them to good use? Here's a group game to develop constraints and then develop a character whose life depends on those constraints. To begin, you and your group will need to come up with some questions to develop characters. The more basic the question, the better.

First, everybody gets a note card to write on. Once we have note cards, we will need some basic questions. Remember that we are creating characters, so these answers do not have to be truthful. For example: What is the character's age, and what is one distinguishing physical trademark?

My character is 120 years old and has one arm. How about your character? Write it down.

When everybody has written an answer, pass the card to the left, and come up with a different question. For example: What is your character's favorite food? My character's favorite food is mud. Yours? Write it down.

Once again, when everybody has written an answer, pass the card to the left, and come up with a different question. For example: What is your character's favorite letter in the alphabet? My character's favorite is *D*. Your character? Write it down.

Continue to develop and ask one another simple questions, passing your cards each time until there are six answers on every card. Feeling stuck? Here are some more basic questions:

- What is your favorite book?
- What is your grandmother's best recipe?
- Where is the best place in the world?
- If a pirate approached you, what would you say?
- Which is better—elephants or rhinos?
- Chocolate chips or cranberries?

Any old question will do as long as it is not *too* involved or *too* broad. Answering questions like the ones above will create characteristics that will help you build characters that are not stock, but are defined by the multiplicity of the group's collaborative mind. Too-broad questions don't offer enough in the way of constraint and creativity, and can lead to clichéd or boring portraits of people. And too-involved questions, like "Does your character use a rifle or the Admantium Silver sword when fighting cyborg monkeys?" rein in the group's creative forces by forcing a character into a situation, in this case being a fighter of cyborg monkeys with very specific weaponry. You want more creative freedom than this as you develop your character. Creating simple but focused questions will help you constrain a character enough to give them shape while allowing room for character development, which is what you will work on next.

First, to develop your character, you must name the character you have on the card in your hand. On the card should be written a list of strange answers that compose your character's traits. For example, my character card says that this person is:

- A 120-year-old woman with one arm
- Who likes:
  - Mud
  - The letter *D*
  - *Where the Red Fern Grows*
  - Her grandmother's potato fritters
  - The two waterfalls around the biggest tree in Alabama
  - To yell "Aaargh!" at any pirate that came near and duel them
  - Elephants, because of their ears
  - Flying
  - Cranberries

So . . .

I will name my character *Granny Ferocious Gums* because she is an ancient, one-armed rider of pachyderms and has a hankering for chewy foods most often found in dangerous swamps where pirates harangue her every move, to which she gives a vicious response. She travels the world painting capital *D*s in strange places, like on the largest tree in Alabama. She then stops to read a sad, but hopeful story.

As you can see, I have created a story by linking the characteristics on the card into a narrative. Now it's your turn. What are the specific characteristics listed on your card? What do these say about your character's personality and lifestyle? And how can you use them all to write a strange little profile?

Take fifteen minutes to write out your character's profile, and then share it with the group.

Now

We have taken the last fifteen minutes to create a character profile. What is a character, though, without a context? The context we need to create is one of the secret variety. I know: *Secrets. Ooooo.* But these will be public secrets, which I understand is a bit of an oxymoron. However, here, today, it is not. PostSecret is an ongoing blog and touring art show, created by Frank Warren, that displays the real-life secrets of real-life people. Frank solicited anyone and everyone to mail him their secrets anonymously, as long as they fit onto a postcard. The postcards he receives may then be featured on PostSecret's website and in its art shows. There is

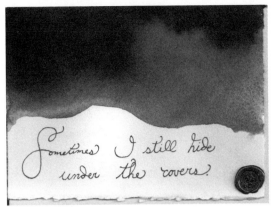

also a collection of books that showcase some of Frank's favorite secrets: the most recent publication is titled *The World of PostSecret*.

With your character in mind, invent their secret and write it out PostSecret-style on a postcard or index card. The card doesn't have to include images, but it can if you want. The only constraint here is that each secret must be able to fit on one side of your card. What makes your character laugh? Cry? Feel ill? What makes them dance a jig or ride a bike, or can they even ride a bike? What causes them to stay awake at night or get out of bed in the morning? What do they feel that they never say out loud?

Rely on the character card you were given earlier, and bring your character to life.

Broken Picture Telephone

MODERNIST POETS MEET THE GRADE-SCHOOL GAME OF TELEPHONE

Rachel Adams, Pia Simone Garber, Kirsten Jorgenson, and Betsy Seymour

Explore the tie between thought and image by making a miniature deck of phrase and image cards, and then use the cards like a modernist poet.

THESE ANTICS ARE A STEP beyond the old grade-school game of Telephone:

1. Gather a group of four or more people and pass around enough small index cards to each person so that the number of cards in each person's hand amounts to the number of people in the group. For instance, if there are four of us, we'll each have four cards. Let's call these cards A, B, C, and D.

2. Begin by having each person write on the top card (A) a cluster of words that is either a quote, a joke, or a funny saying.

3. Now each person passes their stack of cards clockwise, being very sneaky so only the person accepting the cards can see what is written on card A.

4. Have each person look at the words written on A. Then put A on the bottom of the stack. Now on the next card (B), draw a picture that best represents these words.

5. Time to pass the stack of cards again. Make sure only the last thing drawn can be seen. This is Telephone after all, and this is a secret chain. You must only know the last thing drawn and not the words that came before it.

6. Now with the picture on top, study it. Flip to the next card (C) and try to guess the words that influenced the image on B. Write your guess on card C.

7. This game should continue back and forth between text and image with the next person in the circle only looking at the last thing written

or drawn. Continue on and on and on until the cards have all been written on. Once this happens, the card in your hand (A) should be the words you wrote originally. Shuffle through the stack and see how your words filtered through images filtered through words in this hands-on game of Telephone.

Who? What? How? Why?

Early in the twentieth century, British and American poets like Ezra Pound and Hilda "H.D." Doolittle, in an effort to present an alternative poetry to the sentimental, romantic, and overwrought Victorian stuff that was popular in their time, began to focus on composing poems in free verse using concrete language and images.

Often we think of poems as configurations of language meant to stand for something *more* than themselves. For some people that's the most powerful element of poetry, that the language is symbolic. But for other poets, like Ezra Pound and H.D., images are powerful in their own right. They don't need to stand for anything more than what they are.

When we let our poetry be driven by image rather than idea, we make poetry an activity of attention. Contemporary American poet Donald Revell puts it another way in his poem "My Trip":

> The work of poetry is trust,
> And under the aegis of trust
> Nothing could be more effortless.
> Hotels show movies.
> Walking around even tired
> I find my eyes find
> Numberless good things
> And my ears hear plenty of words
> Offered for nothing over the traffic noise
> As sharp as sparrows.

It's so simple. All we have to do is be awake in the world, and poetry will find us. We don't need any overwrought metaphors or fancy language to announce that what we are writing is a poem. Because we are the one who is ordering our perception of the physical world around us, our internal state (whatever we are feeling) is naturally expressed as we put the poem on the page. Emotions sharpen our attention.

Another poet writing about the same time as Pound and H.D., T. S. Eliot, coined the term *objective correlative* to describe the relationship between the external world and one's internal state. He observes how we best express an internal state by ordering a set of external objects and sensations into a constellation that represents that particular internal state. This idea is useful when thinking about the way we use the external world to express our internal states, but only if we remember that what we see when we're in love is not what everyone will see. Perhaps Eliot should have called it a *subjective correlative*! What our eye notices when we are in love is particular to each of us and is different than what we see when we are hurt, for example. Think of a restaurant. Imagine you have just been broken up with and you are picking up take-out for one. Seeing couples out on dates will enhance your sense of loneliness, whereas if you were picking up take-out for a romantic evening with your significant other, that same room with those same couples may make you feel more in love.

In Gary Snyder's poem "Pine Tree Tops" we see how concrete images can carry a very specific emotional state:

> in the blue night
> frost haze, the sky glows
> with the moon
> pine tree tops
> bend snow-blue, fade
> into sky, frost, starlight.
> the creak of boots.
> rabbit tracks, deer tracks.
> what do we know.

Snyder quickly and effectively renders the experience of being humbled by the magnitude of nature by building a list of images that he alone sees (and that we as readers see vicariously through his poem). By the end of these images, Snyder no longer registers himself as an "I," or a person separate from "you" or from the world; he is a part of the "we," a collective pronoun. Notice how much more powerfully this experience is rendered when it depends on concrete language and images than it would be if Snyder had said "I am powerless in the face of the Great Universe." That would have sounded cheesy.

Take this poem by Besmilr Brigham, "Caught in the Car's Light, the white owl":

wings
before the racing wind-
shield
glass, through glass
we see it
white with the lights
against the snow
edges of the road,
seemed to be traveling with us
in speed
the under-place feathers
death
death of the bird, a point
    of lifting
awareness
against the white fields
the woods,
flying for wood-
line.

Though "death" is mentioned, the abstract idea is redirected to the specific instance of the owl's death. Brigham comes to some understanding of the phenomenon of death through the concrete details that surround the event. When we replace the abstract ideas that often become the subject matter of poetry (love, death, hate, pain, sorrow, wonder, etc.) with a constellation of images, we make a moment of feeling precise, particular, and interesting.

Magazine Shuffle

From Image to Character, Narrative, and Third-Person-Limited Point of View

Rachel Adams, Pia Simone Garber, Kirsten Jorgenson, and Betsy Seymour

Combine simple images from magazines to create characters and then narrate their stories from the third-person-limited point of view.

E'VE TALKED ABOUT IMAGES, WE'VE thought about images, and now let's go *look* at some images for inspiration.

Cut out simple pictures from magazines, coloring books, whatever. A tree. A sun. A laughing girl. An elephant. A sneaker. An apple pie. Paste them on notecards. Shuffle through the notecards and pick two of them.

Say you've got a lion and a shoelace. Start with the basics. Think about the lion-ness of the lion. His mane, his big feet, his red gums and sharp teeth, his will to hunt, his will to rule the pride, his caution around giraffes that could kick in his head. His roar. Now this lion you write about, he can be the lion you see on your notecard, or he can be a lion you create in your head. Is he bright and yellow? Dusty and angry? Lazy and domesticated in a zoo? Then take the shoelace. What is shoelace-y about a shoelace? Its stringiness. Its loopiness. Is it stretchy? Woven? Is it frayed? (Once again, you are free to note details from the picture on your notecard, or you can imagine different dimensions of a specific shoelace on your own.)

Now put the two together and tell us a story, focusing on the lion-ness of the lion, the shoelace-ness of the shoelace. How do these two objects interact? How do the images of them in your head affect the story that comes out of them? When Aesop told a story about a lion and a mouse, he thought about the qualities of the lion and the qualities of the mouse and how they might come together—he had the lion made weak by a thorn, something too small for him to use his power over. Something a mouse could influence. The lion and the shoelace are going to interact differently than a lion and a mouse would. Different attributes are going to come into play. Since a shoelace is a playful thing and a lion is really a big cat (that's one side of him), maybe the lion is a zoo lion, bored and a bit domesticated, and the shoelace becomes his entertainment.

Here's a possible story about the lion-ness and the shoelace-ness:

> The people were getting too close, as always. They were right up against the Great Force, threatening his territory. He paced back and forth, looking for weaknesses in the Great Force. Showing just enough teeth. Sometimes they would pound against the Great Force, put their faces against it, scratch it, and in case they made it through one day, he paced and paced.
>
> He froze. There was a tree that stretched a branch out over the Great Force, and sometimes he forgot to keep a wary eye on it. Out on that branch was one of Them, one of those soft pink things, and though he knew that he would fight and win, still when They had things in their paws They were more dangerous. This one had a thing in Its paw. Although he was unsure, he advanced as though he was sure, because confidence is key in dealing with the unknown, with things you're scared of.
>
> As he approached It made a loud noise like the monkeys make, only gibberish. The thing in Its paws was very small and it dangled down like a monkey's tail, only very small and white. Looking at it he remembered leaping at the monkey's tails with his brothers and sisters, trying to catch them, jumping as high as they could as the monkeys stretched their tails down as far as they dared and teased them. He felt a roar grumbling up from deep down in his chest and leaned back against his haunches, twitching his tail. He leapt into the air.

All of that came just from thinking about two images: a lion and a shoelace! Beginning from an actual found image can be a powerful place to start a story.

Choose two images from the notecards and get ready to build a story with them. We're going to tell that story using third-person limited point of view.

THIRD-PERSON-LIMITED POINT OF VIEW

Third-person-limited is a point of view in which the narrator only has access to the thoughts, feelings, and knowledge of one of the characters—as opposed to first person, when the character themself speaks, or third

person omniscient, when the narrator can access more than one charac-
ter and often knows more things than any one character could possibly
know.

In this story segment we just read, the author is referring to the lion
in third person, as "he," but still telling the lion's story as though he were
the lion. "The Great Force" is the glass surrounding the lion exhibit, but
of course the lion doesn't know what glass is, so the narrator reflects that
in the way the story is told. The narrator thinks and feels what the lion
thinks and feels, and conveys it in third person.

How does third person limited change the way we look at the story?
How might we read it differently if the lion was telling us this story,
as "I," or if the narrator simply told us that the lion didn't know what
the glass was and that it made him anxious to have people pressing up
against it?

Now refer back to you the two images you chose. Get inside the
thoughts and feelings and perceptions of *one* of those images, using they
instead of *I*. Let your point of view guide your storytelling as you tell the
tale of these two objects.

Improv at the Zombie Diner

PLATFORM AND DIALOGUE

Holly Burdorff, Luke Percy, and Maggie Smith

In this exercise, you're going to be put in a dangerous situation, and you're going to have to act fast.

PICTURE THIS: A MAN PARACHUTES out of the sky and tries to steal your snowcone. What do you do? In this exercise, you're going to be put in a dangerous situation, and you're going to have to act fast.

But before the action gets started, let's take a quick time-out to talk about improvisation. Have you ever seen an improv show? It's almost like a TV sitcom, but the actors are given a premise and then have to come up with their dialogue as they move through the scene. This means that the actors have to be spontaneous. They have to become comfortable with immediacy, urgency, and surprise.

Every improv sketch starts with some sort of platform—a place, a time, and a situation. (These three elements are typically suggested to them by the audience members!) For example, a typical improv premise might be that Albert Einstein and Gertrude Stein are sharing a college dorm room and, on their first night together, are fighting over the last glob of toothpaste. The improv actors would then be charged with inhabiting the roles of Einstein and Stein, and reacting and responding to what the other says.

Placing yourself into a spontaneous, urgent situation allows you to access your instincts quickly and to reveal your character through the choices that they make under pressure. What do they say, do, or not do when faced with certain challenges? Make sense? Good!

It helps to have some key improv terms.

- **Platform** is the who/what/where of a scene. The success of a scene often depends on a good, clear platform established as early as possible.
  In our example above, the platform is the college dorm room on Gertrude and Albert's first night together as roommates.

The more specific the platform is, the better your scene will be, so we might even decide that it is a Wednesday night around 1:00 A.M., the night before classes start.

- **Conflict** *makes* a story. Think of it as the fodder or food by which your story will grow big and strong! Conflict can be any obstacle that prevents your characters from getting what they want. A story without a conflict would be a very short story indeed. Once you've established a platform, you will use conflict to advance the scene.

  In our example, the conflict is that there isn't enough toothpaste for both Gertrude and Albert. Both of them brandish their toothbrushes, as though engaging in a duel for dental hygiene.

- **Raising the stakes** is a good technique for advancing the scene. To raise the stakes is to incrementally increase the consequences of the conflicts you introduce. You should aim to raise the stakes gradually, so that conflicts build on one another.

  In our example, I could raise the stakes gradually with a set-up like this: First, Albert, being very clever, reads a certain toothpaste ingredient aloud, mutters about its toxicity in order to convince Gertrude to give it up. Then Gertrude could claim to hear a knock at the door and tell Albert to go see who it is in a furtive attempt to sneak the last of the toothpaste. Then, if I wanted to *really* jack up the stakes, I might decide that someone actually *is* at the door and that this person is a deranged dentist, holding up the room at drill-point for toothpaste.

- **Yes, and** . . . means to accept everything said and/or done and to move forward with it. This is necessary in order to keep the flow and spontaneity of the piece. The opposite of this is **blocking**.

  In our example, this technique would mean taking the introduction of the deranged dentist and running with it. Incorporate him into the scene. What crazy things might he get up to? Blocking would be to shut the door on him.

- **Have no fear!** When improvisers fear the consequences of their actions, they tend to freeze or stick to safe-but-boring action and scenes. Be brave! Go forth, then go fifth and go sixth.

Now we're going to do an improv exercise for ourselves!

Zombie Diner Exercise

I. Assemble Your Supplies

Here is what you'll need:

- Yourself, ready for adventure!
- Two additional writers (also ready for adventure).
- A collection of café/diner detritus of various sizes that will be written on. Think straw wrappers, sugar packets, coffee sleeves, napkins, paper cups, paper plates.
- 3 pens.
- A timer.
- 10 index cards or slips of paper.

II. Divvy Up Roles

One of you will be the narrator or guide who will construct the scene. The other two will be characters within the scene.

III. The Narrator Creates the Platform, Points of Conflict, and the Stakes (Secretly)

If you're the narrator, your task is to create a dangerous scenario for your characters.

    1. First, create the **platform**.

    A. Think of a place where you can eat food. What is the lighting like? Is it fancy? Do you need to wear a suit and tie? Is the smell of grease going to stick to your clothes?

    B. Think of a time. Is this on a Wednesday after school or during your precious free time on a Saturday? Is it lunch time, or way past your curfew? What time of year is it? Do you have to bundle up or are you sweating in your underwear?

    C. Think of a situation that could be dangerous. What specific ways can your characters encounter danger?

    2. Now, write a big paragraph with lots of detail. Be sure to include place, time, and situation.

    Here is a **platform** example:

    You and your best friend are at a roadside stop in the middle of nowhere, halfway between the entrance and the exit. You've been traveling across the country by car, your first car. You want to inspire your coming of age and you're pretty sure a roadtrip is the most literary way to do that. But it's late, really late, and you're hungry. Comings of age require a lot of energy and you need to refuel. And what luck that you should happen on the All Night Diner just now, in the throes of hunger. "So good," the billboard claims, "you'll never eat at another diner again . . . ever." OK, so maybe they don't have the best advertising team, but you take the billboard at its word.

Inside, you sit down with your friend and order quickly. When you've seen one diner menu, you've seen them all. You split a stack of blueberry pancakes, two eggs sunny side up, and a side of bacon extra-crispy, like burnt crispy, please!

Here are a few additional **platforms** you could use. And of course, I encourage you to invent your own.

- Werewolf Tavern
- Banshee Organic Grocery Store
- _____
- _____
- _____
- _____

3. Now, put your characters into the **platform** and get ready to **raise the stakes** in the middle of the scene.

On your index cards, write out ten surprising action prompts for your characters to respond to. Here are some examples I came up with:

- When your waiter (who could use a healthy dose of sunlight because you think you can see through his cheeks) arrives with your food, he brings an extra glass. And what is that—a Bloody Mary? You don't drink, you tell him, and even if you did, tomato juice is gross. He laughs a nervous laugh. "The, uh, bloody tomato is for another table, let me just—" He swoops down to take the glass away.
- He returns with your triple-thick malted shake, leans in a little too close, and, uh, did he just smell your neck? I mean, you get it, you smell awesome, but he made an audible sniffing noise.
- Later, your phone goes off, loudly. It's mid-October and you thought

"The Monster Mash" would be a really good ringtone. The other diners have suddenly taken a keen interest in you and they all appear to be looking in your direction.

- Then you notice a couple of the diners have risen and are walking, if you can call it walking, maybe more like lumbering, ok, lumbering towards your table.
- Oh no, your friend's been bitten by a baby who crawled under the radar of your vigilance. Oh, but she is a razor-toothed baby with tiny nascent horns peeking through the soft ringlets of never-been cut hair. Your friend really isn't looking so good.

It can be fun to **raise the stakes** quickly, but be careful—if you continue to "pump up the jam," characters A and B might be stuck with the only option of "blowing the place up." And, unfortunately, it's difficult to develop character if your diner has just been blown to smithereens.

IV. The Characters Emerge

1. Characters A and B choose two pieces of café/diner detritus. The narrator takes the rest away.
2. The narrator reads the **platform** and the first action prompt out loud, clearly indicating the impending danger.
3. In response to the **platform** and action prompt, Character A has one minute to write on their cafe/diner detritus to pass a note to Character B. Remember that your detritus is tiny! Be economical with your handwriting and write small.
4. In one minute, Character B responds to Character A.
5. The narrator reads the next action prompt.
6. In response to the new action prompt, Character B writes to Character A. Again, only take one minute!
7. Character A responds to Character B—yet again, only take one minute.
8. The narrator reads the next action prompt.
9. The game goes on and on . . .

Once the script is complete, you can think of the narrator's **platform** as stage directions and perform the script as actors would for one another or an adoring audience. This exercise can stand on its own as a script, but it makes for a fun and harrowing play to act out.

Student Example

> *When your waiter [. . .] arrives with your food, he brings an ex-*
> *tra glass. And what is that—a Bloody Mary? . . .*

CHARACTER A: Something feel off?

CHARACTER B: Yeah, passing notes after sixth grade . . .

> *He returns with your triple-thick malted shake, leans in a little*
> *too close and, uh, did he just smell your neck? . . .*

CHARACTER B: Okay, maybe you're right. Lurch is really
creeping me out.

CHARACTER A: Well, you are kind of a weirdo magnet.

> *You thought "The Monster Mash" would be a really good ring-*
> *tone. The other diners have suddenly taken a keen interest*
> *in you . . .*

CHARACTER A: Does no one in this place have a sense of
humor? Why is everyone staring?

CHARACTER B: I feel like we're in a bad horror movie. Let's
pay our check.

> *A couple of the diners have risen and are walking, [. . .] ok, lum-*
> *bering towards your table.*

CHARACTER B: Ditch the check. Let's bolt.

CHARACTER A: A discreet exit is no longer an option. Hot
coffee to the face?

> *Your friend's been bitten, by a [. . .] razor-toothed baby with*
> *tiny nascent horns [. . .] Your friend really isn't looking so*
> *good.*

CHARACTER A: Holy guacamole. I'm outta here. I'll remem-
ber you fondly.

CHARACTER B: Wait. Don't leave me. I feel funny. You smell
so tasty, you smiel soo teisty, yuo smeil sow taystieee.

Comicpalooza

THE ART OF THE PANEL

Rachel Adams, Pia Simone Garber, Kirsten Jorgenson, and Betsy Seymour

See how comic books use narrative, then build your own characters, images, and a story to make a new comic.

Do you like comics? Good! Time to do some research. There's a wealth of excellent comics online. The Wikipedia Webcomic page lists several popular and well-known ones (http://en.wikipedia.org/wiki/Webcomic) or you can try googling "best webcomics." Browse through a variety of them until you find three or four that you like that are a bit different from one another, and that you think are effective.

Here are two of our favorites just to get you started:

Ryan North, *Dinosaur Comics* (http://www.qwantz.com/index.php?comic=1661).

Emily Horne and Joey Comeau, *A Softer World* (http://www.asofterworld.com).

How do the variations affect the comic? Even something as simple as the number of panels can greatly affect the story that develops. With one panel, you're either going to have a very action-packed image (a picture worth *two* thousand words), a lot of words to describe what's happening, or a fairly simple event. In the first panel, for example, there's a block of narration and a fairly simple premise, with a bit of dialogue acting as a kind of punchline. With six, you have more time to weave a series of events and room to do different things with the length of dialogue or narration. The panels themselves can be toyed with. They can be different sizes and drawn using different mediums. *xkcd* is just stick figures; *A Softer World* is photographs; and if you check out more *Dinosaur Comics*, you'll see that Ryan North uses these same images over and over, changing only the conversations that take place. Who says you have to be able to draw to make a comic?! Characters can break free from the panels, and the action can happen across two or more panels. (*A Softer World* distributes what is essentially one photograph over three panels.) See how a limitation becomes a creative breakthrough when Ryan North allows a character to speak when he is off screen (off strip)? Sometimes he even has God or the Devil turn up in his comics, with God's speech in all capital letters, coming from somewhere above the panel, and the Devil's speech in all red caps, coming from somewhere below.

Another thing to think about is the way that colors are used. How do they affect the emotional impact of the strip? Colors don't always mean one thing; they can mean different things in different contexts. Red can mean love; it can mean anger or hatred; it can mean death. Blue can mean sadness; it can lend airiness to something; it can be bright like a balloon. Yellow can be the sun, warmth, gladness. It can also be sickness or unease. Think about the ways that color impacts you—and maybe that will be different for the characters you create. Maybe they see the same colors in different ways. Maybe you hate the color green but Cathy the Cow thinks green = delicious. Even the presence of color or the lack of color can affect a comic. The example from *A Softer World* is in black and white (some of them have color). It adds a certain edge to it, don't you think? What would happen to it if it was in bright, happy colors, like *Dinosaur Comics*? How do the cartoony toy colors of *Dinosaur Comics* contribute to the way you feel towards the characters?

And what about the words themselves? How does the font affect the way you read a comic? What does it tell you about the tone or the characters? The handwritten, informal script of *xkcd*, the typewritten cutouts of *A Softer World*, the computer-ish font of *Dinosaur Comics* all contribute to the overall style of each of these examples. What about the placement of the font on the page? How does it change the comic when the words go right across a character's face, for instance? Do you read something differently when it's placed at the bottom of the comic vs. the top?

Don't just look at our examples, find a few of your own to love. Think about the one that has the strongest effect on you—makes you laugh the hardest, makes you sad, makes you extremely, inexplicably happy. Think about all of the different elements that contribute to your feelings towards it. Think about all the visual things that affect the way the story is told. Write down some things that you want to imitate or emulate when you make your own comic. And of course, enjoy!

Fill-in-the-Blank Comics

This requires a small amount of know-how in Adobe Photoshop, or you can be more hands-on, in which case all you need is a bottle of White-Out. Find an old comic (Internet or otherwise) if you can, or a simple photograph will do. With Photoshop (or, again, with White-Out), erase or blank out the previously written words, including all dialogue and text. Then have at it. Fill the white spaces with new words and make a new moment.

Make Your Own Comic Strip

Now it's time to make your own comic from scratch. The first step is to plan. There's a lot that goes into even a short comic strip. One trick for writing a really interesting comic is to match up situations that might evoke strong emotions and use surprising imagery to illustrate those emotions instead of relying on abstract language. Make a list of different situations that could be full of messy emotions. Then think of a really strong image to match up with that situation. Don't just toss off the first idea that comes to mind, though. You don't want to use the most obvious images here.

Situation potentially full of messy emotions:	Image that matches the emotion:
Death of a beloved pet.	An empty pet dish with no animals or toys around it.
Forgetting your homework at home.	A super-nerdy-looking A-student frowning in a classroom.
_____	_____
_____	_____
_____	_____

Once you have a list of situations and matching images, you can use those ideas as inspiration while you plan your comic. Here are some things you should think about when planning that will help you decide how your images and text will work together on the page. Don't decide arbitrarily, but think about why you might need these specifications to get your ideas across.

1. Think of an emotionally driven situation that your comic could work through. (e.g., Use the second brainstorming example above, a super-nerdy A-student who gets to school only to discover she's left her homework on her kitchen table!) In one or two sentences, explain the situation you've chosen:

   _____

   _____

   _____

2. List three really specific images that you associate with this situation. (e.g., An empty cereal bowl sitting on top of many pages of homework, a pair of hands rifling through an open backpack, a frazzled-looking student pulling out her hair.)

   _____

   _____

   _____

3. Is this story happening in black and white or in color? (e.g., Color, be-cause it's important to see the red marks the teacher makes on the stu-dent's paper.)

_____

_____

_____

4. How many panels is this story happening in, and why? We recommend between one and six. (e.g., This story needs four panels because it takes place across four different locations.)

_____

_____

_____

5. Is the story being narrated by someone or is it being told through the di-alogue of the characters in it? (e.g., It is being told through the thoughts and actions of the main character.)

_____

_____

_____

6. Now begin to imagine the main character of the story. What is this char-acter called? (e.g., Perfect Penelope)

_____

_____

_____

7. Name one unique feature of the main character. (e.g., Penelope is never seen without a calculator in her hand.)

_____

_____

_____

8. What is this character's favorite color? (e.g., Penelope loves the yellow color of pencils.)

_____

9. What is this character's catch phrase or favorite expression? (e.g., Pe-nelope always says "I know the answer!")

_____

_____

10. What kind of world does this character inhabit? (e.g., A world where not turning in your homework gets you kicked out of the popular clique.)

_____

_____

_____

11. Anything else you want to say about your character or your comic strip? (e.g., Penelope is extremely short and chubby.)

_____

_____

_____

And now comes the messy part: you've got to build the comic strip. Some materials that might come in handy at this point could be construction paper, markers, pens and pencils, crayons, scissors, glue, paint, and old magazines you no longer want. You could even use old photographs if you have any that no one wants. Divide a piece of paper into the number of panels you want by folding it in half or by drawing lines with a straight edge, and cut, color, and collage away!

Fast Talkers and Faster Writers

Speed Transcription

Chapin Gray, Brian Oliu, and Kirk Pinho

*Practice writing while someone reads a text as fast as possible,
picking up what you can and freeing up your associative writer's
imagination along the way.*

A H, THIEVERY. PERHAPS THE MOST potentially romantic of all crimes—to steal from the rich and give to the poor à la Robin Hood, or to steal someone's heart. Unfortunately it could also lead to men in bulletproof vests bursting down your door with a battering ram and you being brought down to the station by Detective McNulty in handcuffs.

We'll be doing some grand-theft writing (perfectly legal!) and utilizing other things in the outside world—an odd story, someone's style of writing, a couple of lines in a poem—in order to improve our own creations. This isn't some crazy taboo thing; writers do it *all* the time. Think about *epigraphs* (quotes before poems) or variations on a line by so-and-so or modern interpretations of classic works (*Romeo and Juliet* comes to mind).

Okay, so here you are, ready to thieve: You've got your mask to hide your face and your gloves to make sure there won't be any fingerprints left behind. Sweet deal. When I was in ninth grade, my social studies teacher Mr. Miller was the fastest talker on the planet. No matter how fast I took notes, there was no way I could keep up with his lectures. During study hall, I'd look at my notes and realize that I wrote complete nonsense (like "the Edict of Coconut." What?). So, your task is to have a friend choose something to read—it could be a poem (Anne Carson's "The Glass Essay" works well), a newspaper article, or even a history textbook—and have them read it super fast. If you can't find someone to participate in your bizarre writing experiment, you should be able to find something on YouTube that will do the trick or listen to an audiobook set at triple the normal speed. As they are reading, just write down what comes to mind. Try to interpret what they are saying, but if other words pop into your head, just go with it. After your hand cramps up, take a look at what you have written. Does it make any sense? Can you string a narrative structure out of the words that you have jotted down? See if you can formulate either a story or a poem out of the jumble of words that you have.

Obsessions

SEVEN WAYS

Kristin Aardsma and Breanne LeJeune

Chocolate truffles, the color purple, America . . . obsess on your obsession!

I CAN EAT CHOCOLATE TRUFFLES UNTIL my belly explodes. I love every-thing about them! The velvet boxes they come in, the way they always melt onto my hands and clothes, the way they speed up my heart rate so I feel as though I'm in cardiac arrest— Oh! I love it all. I can't, however, write a sentence, line, or stanza worth reading about them. Sadly, not all obsessions translate into writable obsessions, but when they do! Oh, when they do! The following exercises aim to help you assess, attack, and explore your obsession(s) in ways that resist redundancy and, instead, en-courage you to get out your microscope, telescope, stethoscope, kaleido-scope, and any other kind of scope, glue them to your pretty little eyeball, and look! Whether it's megalodons, webbed feet, breakdancing, hockey players, computer games, or vintage rap, snuggle up to your obsession, snuggle up real close, and get ready to write about it.

ONE: KNOW IT

Obsessing is easy. Some might even say uncontrollable. The way our brains shape reality to match our obsession: *This mud looks like dark choc-olate!* or *Hey! You smell like the aftertaste of a raspberry lemon biscotti truf-fle!* is fluid, subconscious—creepy! We can't control these things. If we could, we wouldn't say/think/do a lot of the things obsession inspires us to. Alas. Obsessing is one thing. Writing about obsession, well, that's another thing entirely. Writing about obsession requires that we under-stand our obsession, its limitations, possibilities, personalities, musical-ities, and much more. It's important to make sure, when shopping for a writeable obsession, that it is able to sustain your interest for a long pe-riod of time, that it is concrete and specific, and that it is complex enough to allow exploration or, as author Ander Monson refers to it in his essay "A Sort of Recreation," detours and diversions. A good topic, lakes, for instance, is more specific than water in general and would allow many diversions. A person writing about lakes would be able to explore, to detour into the geology, creatures, history, seasons, and shapes of lakes. A topic like water encompasses so many things that a writer might lose focus and get lost in it, while a topic like lakes allows for exploration, but with some limitation.

Exercise 1: Make a List

Write a list of twenty—you heard me—twenty obsessions. The goal of brainstorming twenty topics instead of three, or even five, is that it forces you to purge those ideas that may be familiar, cliché, or too general, and liberate those ideas lurking in the crusty corners of your brain, those ideas you never knew you had, those creepy, freaky ideas that sneak up on you, maybe even nibble on your elbows a little bit, lick your knees, just desperate to have you write about them. Sure, maybe you wish you could stuff some of them back into the dusty closets they came from, but hopefully there will be one whose nibbling you will not just notice, but embrace, exclaim, and explore.

Exercise 2: Make a Puzzle

So you have an obsession. Congratulations! It's specific, it's dynamic, it's interesting—perfect! Now, get to know one another. Imagine your obsession as a jigsaw puzzle: What are the pieces that make it up? What forms the boundaries, the smooth lines around the edges? What is included in the jigsaw, what falls beyond the borders, and what forms the image in the center? One way of writing about obsession is to look at a singular topic, let's say the fantastical, the raptastical Run DMC, as a composite of many smaller pieces, ideas, or subtopics. For instance, the pieces to my Run DMC puzzle might include a piece for each member: Reverend Run, DMC, and Jam Master Jay, or Queens, New York (where all three members grew up), Adidas (one of their most popular songs), the Sugarhill Gang and Grandmaster Flash (related artists), 1981 (the year they were signed), etc. Using the subtopics, or "pieces" like lenses through which to view the main topic, we disallow ourselves from writing about the same thing, in the same way, over and over and over again. Or let's say you're writing about your grandma. Now, of course there are the big things: her creaky old house; her sticky, smoky, car; her strange smelling clothes—but think smaller. If I were writing about my grandma, I would make a list of every type of candy she has in a jar, explore the different song books she keeps beneath the seat cushion of her organ stool, chronicle the terrifying items in her freezer (she kept a dead hummingbird in there once so that she could show my sister and me how it died with its tongue sticking out!), and/or describe pictures of her when she was young (like that one of her in a black pencil dress standing on the lawn after her first husband's funeral, the bushes in the background looking so perfect, the blank look on her face, and the strange way she seems to be tipping over). This will require some expert sleuthing.

So, what makes up your puzzle? Make a list, or if you're more visual, draw an empty jigsaw puzzle, and fill in the pieces (no less than fifteen) with possible subtopics you could write about. If you get stuck, consult sources such as Wikipedia, the encyclopedia, the dictionary, a thesaurus, a rhyming thesaurus, Google Scholar/academic databases, etc.

Let's say my topic is the color purple. The first things that come to my mind are Prince's album *Purple Rain*, lilacs, and bruises. After that, I get stuck. Of course there are lots of purple things I could put on my list, but not many of them interest me. This is the perfect time for a Wiki-hunt! After reading through the "purple" entry and clicking on various hyperlinks (the *perfect* diversion), I am able to make the following into puzzle pieces: the band Deep Purple, the songs "Purple Haze" and "Purple People Eater," and the facts that 1) In *Star Trek*, Klingons had purple blood, and 2) Frank Zappa's favorite color was purple. I notice right away that there are a lot of associations between purple and music, and decide to narrow my topic to explore that relationship. My next step, then, might be to browse the encyclopedia to look for any historical connections between the color purple and music. Alas! Reference.com proffers the following about the color "Psychedelic Purple": "The pure essence of purple was approximated in pigment in the late 1960s by mixing fluorescent magenta and fluorescent blue pigments together to make fluorescent purple to use in psychedelic black light paintings. This shade of purple was very popular among the hippies and it was the favorite color of Jimi Hendrix and therefore it is called psychedelic purple." Noticing that purple was the favorite color of Jimi Hendrix, Frank Zappa, *and* Prince, I become curious as to whether or not there are any scientific or psychological links between purple and music. This is the perfect time to consult either Google Scholar or an academic database, because both allow you to search for scholarly articles written about your topic in a number of different fields, such as: sociology, history, literature, math, physics, medicine, business, etc. The great thing about using scholarly sources is that, unlike the information on Wikipedia, which can be written by anyone, these articles are written by experts. My Google Scholar search for "music and purple" yielded an article on the condition synesthesia, which occurs when a person is able to combine senses so that they can, for example, see a smell or hear a color. While this article doesn't directly address my search, it is incredibly interesting, and so I add it to my puzzle.

All of these adventures are guaranteed to divert you to places you could otherwise not have found just using your head. Some will be beautiful and useful and exciting, and some will be confusing and really, really weird. Embrace both! Part of the fun in writing about obsession is finding new ways to think about it, and some of those really, really weird ideas just might do the trick.

Two: Explore It

Exercise 1: List Poem

Now it's your turn to write a litany about your obsession(s). Write a list that does not feel like a simple grocery list, but a detailed one (e.g., instead of *apples*, I would write, *apples green like the leaves of the Sycamore tree just before it rains*). Spend at least ten minutes writing this list without stopping. Don't cross anything out!

When writers get obsessed with something, they attack it from all sides, every angle, inside and out. They do this so that they can understand their obsession from all perspectives. The poem "America" by Allen Ginsberg is a litany (a repetitive recital in list form) that addresses Ginsberg's obsession with American culture. Notice how he changes his tone throughout the piece in order to represent a few different perspectives.

FROM "AMERICA"

BY ALLEN GINSBERG

America when will you send your eggs to India?
I'm sick of your insane demands.
. . . .
I refuse to give up my obsession.

America stop pushing I know what I'm doing.

America the plum blossoms are falling.

Exercise 2: Detailed Paragraph(s)

Now that you've narrowed down your obsession, it's time to start blowing it up! Well, not literally, but if I were to explode the details of a raspberry truffle, I might describe how its fragrance reminds me of the first time I had one, when I had one tooth missing and how the gooey chocolate stuck in the crevice of my gums.

The mid-century French poet Francis Ponge wrote a book of prose poems whose title translates as *The Nature of Things*. In each piece, he dives into a single item such as bread, soap, or a plant.

Pick just one thing from your litany and *explode it*! Focus on the most miniscule detail, letting your imagination loose. Define every part of it: how it smells, tastes, feels, sounds, looks. As you do so, let the object "speak"!

THREE: ATTACK IT

So now you know what your obsession looks like under every type of scope imaginable. You could draw it from memory, make its favorite food, sing its favorite song, and recite the middle names of all its elementary school friends. You've blown it apart and glued it back together, and now you're ready for the next step: *attack*.

In the spirit of the late, the great, and the insane Lester Bangs, dare to do one or more of the following in a paragraph or two.

Exercise 1: Review

Imagine your obsession just released a CD. Review it. This may pose a difficulty for some of your obsessions in that it will ask you to personify them. Obviously, an espresso truffle has not, and will not likely ever be, signed to a major record label; however, if it were, it would play the meanest electric cello you've ever heard in your *life*! To get your obsessive juices flowing, take a gander at Bangs's many essays on Lou Reed. Throughout his career as a rock critic, Bangs addressed, readdressed, retracted, reinstated, declared, whispered, and wailed about his love, hate, admiration, scorn, and delight for Lou Reed, using his essays to express all of these things, often simultaneously. In "How to Succeed in Torture Without Really Trying, or, Louie Come Home, All Is Forgiven," Bangs begins his review of Reed's album *Metal Machine Music* by describing how terrible it is. Bangs addresses his obsession by declaring that "I'm almost getting bored with Lou myself, and he is certainly not my hero anymore." Then he goes for eleven more pages about exactly the opposite.

Exercise 2: Invective

Lester Bangs's obsession with Lou Reed manifested itself in many ways, a prominent one being hatred. In Bangs's essay "Let Us Now Praise Famous Death Dwarves, or, How I Slugged It Out With Lou Reed and Stayed Awake," he wrote:

> Who else but Lou Reed would get himself fat as a pig, then hire the most cretinous band of teenage cortical cavities he could find to tote around the country on an all-time death drag tour?
>
> Who else would doze his way back over the pond in a giant secobarbital capsule and labor for months with people like Bob Ezrin, Steve Winwood and Jack Bruce to puke up *Berlin*, a gargantuan slab of maggoty rancor that may well be the most depressed album ever made?

Your job is to lasso this "maggoty rancor" and write an *invective* (vicious language conveying vicious emotions) letter to either your obsession itself, or if you and your obsession are on good terms, write to the enemy of your obsession. Take those gloves off and fight dirty. Attack!

Exercise 3: History

Your last charge is to write a page describing your obsession's creator. What did this person, robot, monster, etc., scream at your obsession to get it to come inside for dinner? Did they scream at all? Did they even have a mouth? What is the creator of your obsession's favorite cartoon character? What appliance couldn't they live without? I could trace the mother of my mint-cookie truffle to the factory that machined and wrapped each gorgeous piece of chocolate in the box. If I went further, I could trace its roots to the tree that grew its cocoa beans, the soil that grew the tree, the country where the soil was, etc. Lester Bangs could be described as the love child of vinyl and cough syrup, a boy raised on the spinning earth of a turntable, whose parents tucked him into a tape deck and sounded a bass drum to call him home for dinner.

As I am to chocolate truffles, and Lester Bangs is to Lou Reed, you are to your obsession. Let it consume you.

Grand Theft Writing

Chapin Gray, Brian Oliu, and Kirk Pinho

Use the beginning of another text to get your momentum going.

WE ALL KNOW THAT STARTING can be the most difficult part of writing. So why not cut that process out altogether and take someone else's beginning? In this exercise, you're going to use the beginnings of someone else's work and write your own continuation. Here are some examples to steal from:

> There was once, in the country of Alifbay, a sad city, the saddest of cities, a city so ruinously sad that it had forgotten its name. It stood by a mournful sea full of glumfish, which were so miserable to eat that they made people belch with melancholy even though the skies were blue.
>
> —Salman Rushdie, *Haroun and the Sea of Stories*

> I wander the island, inventing it. I make a sun for it, and trees—pines and birch and dogwood and firs—and cause the water to lap the pebbles of its abandoned shores. This, and more: I deposit shadows and dampness, spin webs, and scatter ruins. Yes: ruins. A mansion and guest cabins and boat houses and docks. Terraces, too, and bath houses and even an observation tower. All gutted and window-busted and autographed and shat upon. I impose a hot midday silence, a profound and heavy stillness. But anything can happen.
>
> —Robert Coover, "The Magic Poker"

> One summer afternoon Mrs. Oedipa Maas came home from a Tupperware party whose hostess had put perhaps too much kirsch in the fondue to find that she, Oedipa, had been named executor, or she supposed executrix, of the estate of one Pierce Inverarity, a California real estate mogul who had once lost two million dollars in his spare time but still had assets numerous and tangled enough to make the job of sorting it all out more than honorary.
>
> —Thomas Pynchon, *The Crying of Lot 49*

What about a teakettle? What if the spout opened and closed when the steam came out so it would become a mouth, and it could whistle pretty melodies, or do Shakespeare, or just crack up with me? I could invent a tea-kettle that reads in Dad's voice, so I could fall asleep, or maybe a set of kettles that sings the chorus of "Yellow Submarine," which is a song by the Beatles, who I love, because etymology is one of my *raisons d'être*, which is a French expression that I know.

—Jonathan Safran Foer, *Extremely Loud and Incredibly Close*

"Yes, of course, if it's fine tomorrow," said Mrs. Ramsey. "But you'll have to be up with the lark," she added.

To her son these words conveyed an extraordinary joy, as if it were settled the expedition were bound to take place, and the wonder to which he had looked forward, for years and years it seemed, was, after a night's darkness and a day's sail, within touch. Since he belonged, even at the age of six, to that great clan which cannot keep this feeling separate from that, but must let future prospects, with their joys and sorrows, cloud what is actually at hand, since to such people even in earliest childhood any turn of the wheel of sensation has the power to crystallize and transfix the moment upon which its gloom or radiance rests, James Ramsay, sitting on the floor cutting out pictures from the illustrated catalogue of the Army and Navy Stores, endowed the picture of a refrigerator as his mother spoke, with heavenly bliss. It was fringed with joy. The wheelbarrow, the lawn-mower, the sound of poplar trees, leaves whitening before rain, rooks cawing, brooms knocking, dresses rustling—all these were so coloured and distinguished in his mind that he already had his private code, his secret language, though he appeared the image of stark and uncompromising severity, with his high forehead and his fierce blue eyes, impeccably candid and pure, frowning slightly at the sight of human frailty, so that his mother, watching him guide his scissors neatly round the refrigerator, imagined him all read and ermine on the Bench or directing a stern and momentous enterprise in some crisis of public affairs.

"But," said his father, stopping in front of the drawing-room window, "it won't be fine."

—Virginia Woolf, *To the Lighthouse*

She decided to follow the gods home
in their gownlike T-shirts and shaved skulls.

—Beckian Fritz Goldberg, "The Life and Times of Skin Girl,"
from *The Book of Accident*

It only wanted to say everything at once,

it would pull the very moment out of reach,

> —William Olsen, "Infinity," from *Avenue of Vanishing*

It is now clear that eating your own brain

will make you mad. Because of the contaminants.

> —Dean Young, "House of Geodes," from *Embryoyo*

After you're done writing, you might feel as if you can totally ditch the other person's opening words, and you'll have a work entirely of your own makeup. Or, if you choose to keep the other author's words at the beginning of your piece, provide a footnote giving the other author proper credit. Not too shabby, huh? Sometimes writing (like my 1995 Ford Explorer) needs a jumpstart.

Crazy Headlines and Hyperlink Chasing

FINDING AND USING A BIZARRE PERSONA

Chapin Gray, Brian Oliu, and Kirk Pinho

Use hyperlinks to uncover a subject for your new piece.

NOT ONLY CAN YOU STEAL or borrow language from other pieces of writing—you can also borrow the voice and the storyline and use them as a "jumping off point" for your own poem or story. Beginning writers sometimes believe they can only write about their own experiences and feelings. This is only partially true. In writing, you can imagine yourself to be the voice of anyone or any*thing*, for that matter.

To a certain extent, the speaker of a poem or short story is never quite *you*, the author, because it is the *written* you, which is always different in some way from the walking-around-in-real-life you. When we write as *I*, it is already a particular version of ourselves.

When we use a *persona*, we take this a step further. We adopt another's voice and speak as if that person or thing's experience and life was our own. Think of it as putting on a mask, as temporarily stealing the identity of someone other than yourself and speaking in their voice, based on their perceptions and experiences.

Here are two ways to find an unusual persona to use in your writing:

1. CRAZY HEADLINES
If you google "crazy headlines," you'll find a list of the silliest headlines of the year from newspapers all over the world. Pick one from the list, then write either a poem or story, adopting the persona of someone or something in the headline.

2. HYPERLINK CHASING
Go to Wikipedia, and type in a random or specific word or phrase (*signal fires, orchid, the Detroit Pistons*). Click on any one of the hyperlinks located in the article (in Wikipedia, a hyperlink is a blue word or phrase that will take you to another entry). Lather, rinse, and repeat six times. The last page you find yourself on will be the subject of your persona piece! Make

sure to use the language—the terms, lingo, facts, etc.—from the article in your writing.

As you are writing, remember that a successful persona piece gives enough clues to the reader to help them get a sense of who or what is speaking. Also, think about what outlook your persona has. What do they think, feel, and know? What situations do they find themselves in? What do they sound like?

Genetically-Modified Franken-Poems

Chapin Gray and Breanne LeJeune

Cut up magazines and newspapers to create new poems, both individually and in groups.

TODAY, SCIENTISTS CAN TAKE THE genes they want from certain species, mix them together, and create something new and improved from the different parts. Take the GloFish for example—a zebra fish mixed with the "glowing" genes of a jellyfish! As a writer, you can use language and lines from other poems and put them together in new and interesting ways. Not only can this help alleviate "writer's block," but it can help add new words to your vocabulary and remind you that a piece of writing is never completely finished—it can always be played with, rearranged, reconceptualized.

You may be surprised by the interesting combinations of words and ideas you come up with, shocked even, as you watch the mutants that sprout from these experiments ooze, amble, or crawl across your desk right in front of you. No, really! They're that good!

EXERCISE 1: FRANKEN-POEM

From an assortment of words cut from magazines, newspapers, and so forth, grab a handful and rearrange them into a poem on a separate sheet of paper. The poem can be any length or shape. Also, don't worry about "making sense"—choose words and combinations of words that sound pleasing to your ear or strike you as interesting or original. When you are finished creating your Frankenstein poem, consider how it is similar and/or different from the work you typically create. One of the fabulous things about *found writing*, as this technique is often called, is that it can release you from your own vocabulary and subject matter, the result of which can be quite freeing!

EXERCISE 2: NESTING POEM

Cut apart a poem you have written, singling out words or phrases that you are drawn to. On a separate piece of paper, arrange the pieces into a poem. When your scissors are all tired out and the new poem is complete, compare the poem you've created to the original poem. How has the meaning changed? This exercise allows us to see the many poems within one poem.

The Exploding Poem

How to Keep on Writing

Chapin Gray and Breanne LeJeune

*Pull an image or object from a poem, write a new poem based on it,
and then stuff it back in.*

OFTEN, BEGINNING WRITERS TEND TO focus on the general theme or idea of the poem at the expense of the details. And oh, the details! All those missing, glistening, glorious grasshoppers and sand grains! All those chipped teeth and baby turtles! The tragedy! The terror! The remedy, though, is simple: consider writing from a variety of perspectives or "camera angles" that can focus on the minutest detail as well as the "big picture." The cheese crumbles *and* the space ships! The jellybeans *and* the Arctic Ocean!

Exercise 1: Dynamite and Zoom In

Part 1: Underline an image or object in your poem. Use that object as the title of an entirely new poem in which you examine the object from as many angles as possible. Get "up close"—you can even go so far as the molecular level. Pay particular attention to the five senses—how does this object look, hear, smell, touch, taste?

Part 2: After writing at least ten lines scrutinizing the object, circle your favorite lines and insert them back into the original poem. How does this change the poem? Does it change the direction or atmosphere of the poem? What does "zooming in" and paying close attention suggest about the relationship of the speaker to the object in question?

Exercise 2: Breaking Your Writerly Habits

Think of how you tend to write. Do you always use the first-person *I*? Do you write short lines or long? Do you use a rhyme scheme? Write in the bathtub? Underground?

Make a list of six of your self-imposed habits and then a second list of suggestions for breaking your habits. If you usually write long poems, make one of the requirements that the poem has to be less than ten lines. If you usually write in iambic pentameter, write in free-verse. If you usually write underground, peep your head above ground.

Even experienced poets are constantly looking for new ways to experiment, to force themselves "out of the box" and into the laboratory. Think of all the poem's possibilities—how many ways can it be altered, mutated, rearranged, exploded, and so forth? The ability to see your writing as an ongoing project and not a fixed text will help your poems sprout strange and strong legs with which to lurch farther and funkier than you could have imagined. This whole exercise works for prose, too—try it!

Nice Hat. Thanks.

WORD-BY-WORD POEMS

Kristin Aardsma, Breanne LeJeune, and Brian Oliu

With a partner, create improvisational writing one word at a time.

THE POETS JOSHUA BECKMAN AND Matthew Rohrer created a new kind of collaboration. These two gentlemen wrote an entire collection of improvisational poetry called *Nice Hat. Thanks.* by going back and forth to create poems one word at a time. For example, if you and I were playing this game, it might go something like this:

We would agree on a subject on which to base the piece. Let's try *antique teapots.* First, we would start with a title.

YOU: Our
ME: Boiled
YOU: Mugs
ME: Choose
YOU: Grandmother's
ME: Hot
YOU: Heart

One of us would eventually say, "End of title" in order to continue the piece. We would then go back and forth until we decided that the piece was finished. Also, one person can use their turn to punctuate the poem by saying, "Comma" or "Semi-colon" or "Period," etc. If you have a sibling, a neighbor, a friend, or classmate around, try this game with them. Most people find it a ton of fun. Another way to play is to go phrase by phrase or sentence by sentence. Try that version of the game after you've done a few word-by-word rounds. Don't forget to record or write down the piece as you go so you can read it later on.

Translation Mutation

USING ONLINE PLOT GENERATORS AND TRANSLATORS

Kristin Aardsma, Breanne LeJeune, and Brian Oliu

*Bounce a text through several languages using an online translator
and then work with the unrecognizable results.*

HAVE YOU HEARD ABOUT THIS amazing craze that is sweeping the nation? It's called "the Internet"! I know it sounds wild, but seriously, you should check it out!

Okay, so we all know that you are no doubt fully aware of what the Internet is, and you are also quite experienced in finding videos of 1980s one-hit-wonder superstars, but did you know that it is also a hotbed for literary inspiration? There are plenty of websites out there that will help you get started with a plot for a soap opera, a name for a new alien race, even a brand new fighting technique! For example, did you know that Shakespeare's *The Two Gentlemen of Verona* was crafted by combining text processed by a random plot generator? (Not really.)

No matter what your fancy is, online generators are fantastic ways to get your story up and running, because we all know that getting started is sometimes the hardest part. You'll be well on your way to creating your blockbuster romantic action-packed kung-fu movie plot. Choose a plot and get started on a story. Or, go for broke and use as many generators as possible and combine them all together to create the PowerSquadTeam-ForceAmazing story.

Another benefit of utilizing the Internet is the incredible power of online translators. Sites like Google Translate enable you to type a block of text into a form and translate it into a multitude of different languages. It gets even sweeter. Write a poem or a story and translate it from English into another language. Then, take that block of text and translate it from that language into *another* language. For example, start with English, translate to French, then translate from French to German, and finally German back to English. As a result of all of this translation, chances are you're going to have something entirely different than your original piece! One of the reasons for this is that the English language has over six hundred thousand words. The next closest language with a Western alphabet is German, and it only has twenty thousand words! So, whenever one translates from English to another language, they have to get clever with their phrasing. This website allows you to see your work in an entirely different light; and you don't need to kidnap any Western Europeans!

Mad Lib Translations of Márquez

Jenny Gropp, Laura Kochman, and Jill Smith

Zany translations that go beyond Google Translate.

ANOTHER CONSTRAINT THAT YOU MIGHT use is translation. When someone writes something in another language, we often want to spread the word, but we have to do it through translation. Different people do it in different ways. Check out this haiku by Matsuo Basho, written in Japanese:

京にても京なつかしや時鳥

Pretty hard for many of us to read, right? This is where translation comes in to help with the language barrier. Robert Hass has translated the poem this way:

Even in Kyoto—
hearing the cuckoo's cry—
I long for Kyoto.

But Lucien Stryk translated the exact same poem this way:

Bird of time—
in Kyoto, pining
for Kyoto.

Even though Hass and Stryk were both working with the same raw material, each translator came up with a different version. Hass's version has a first-person narrator, while in Stryk's version, it is the bird who pines for Kyoto. Hass also names the bird (a cuckoo), while Stryk calls it simply "bird of time," implying that the bird is not just a noise we hear, but a symbol of time passing. The one thing that stays constant between these two versions is the intense emotion, but the translations focus that emotion in different directions. Hass's version implies only that the narrator has an intense connection to Kyoto. Stryk, on the other hand, implies that the speaker longs for a *past* Kyoto.

So what did Basho intend to imply? We can't know for sure unless we learn Japanese. For this reason, we might think about translation as a form of found text. When we use the term *found text*, we're referring to writing that is done using someone else's language, where ownership of the language is fluid. By the time Basho's words make it into English, they've changed radically.

But what if we're not all masters of a second language? Google Translate can help you do a translation of your own. Since it's not a human being, though, it loses a lot of the intricacies of language. Here is the Google Translate translation of Basho's haiku:

> Even in the capital the capital the handle it does and the time the
> bird.

Oh, dear. Sometimes, Google Translate also doesn't know all the words in a given language. Watch what happens when the program gets confronted with the opening sentences, originally in Spanish, from *One Hundred Years of Solitude* by Gabriel García Márquez:

> Many years later, in front of the firing squad, colonel Aureliano Buendia habia to remember that one behind schedule remote one in which under I take it to father to know the ice. Macondo was then a village of twenty mud houses and constructed canabrava to the border of unrio of diaphanous waters that hurried by I milk of polished, white and enormous stones like prehistoric eggs. The world was so recent, that many things carecian of name, and to mention them habia that to indicate them with the finger. Every year, by the month of March, a family of desarrapados gypsys planted her carp near the village, and with a great uproar of whistles and timbals they presented the new inventions. First they took the magnet. A gypsy corpulento, of beard montaraz and hands of sparrow, that I appear with the name of Melquiades, made a truculent demonstration publishes than the same he called the eighth wonder of the wise alchemists of Macedonia.

Ouch. This is how Gregory Rabassa translated it, using all the nuances of not being a robot:

> Many years later, as he faced the firing squad, Colonel Aureliano Buendía was to remember that distant afternoon when his father took him to discover ice. At that time Macondo was a village of twenty adobe houses, built on the bank of a river of clear water that ran along a bed of polished stones, which were white and enormous, like prehistoric eggs. The world was so recent that many things lacked names, and in order to indicate them it was necessary to point. Every year during the month of March a family of ragged gypsies would set up their tents near the village, and with a great uproar of pipes and kettledrums they would display new inventions. First they brought the magnet. A heavy gypsy with an untamed beard and sparrow hands, who introduced himself as Melquíades, put on a bold public demonstration of what he himself called the eighth wonder of the learned alchemists of Macedonia.

So what does this all have to do with found text? When we use translator programs like Google Translate, they give us an opportunity to have some serious fun with language, to treat our favorite pieces of literature in new ways. If we get rid of all those untranslated words or if we remove every fourth word or use any sort of method for word removal, we're left with a Mad Lib–type puzzle, and when we fill it in with our own words, it becomes something new and exciting. It becomes our own. So let's give it a try! Fill out this list, and then plug the words into the below version of Márquez's opening passage, which has now been moved in Google Translate from Spanish to English to French to English to Norwegian to English to Chinese and back to English—totally scrambled!

1. Verb, past tense: _____
2. Verb, past tense: _____
3. Noun: _____
4. A character's name: _____
5. Adjective: _____
6. A character's name: _____
7. Noun, singular: _____
8. City name: _____

9. Noun, building material: _____

10. Noun, a substance found in nature: _____

11. Adjective: _____

12. Adjective: _____

13. Adjective that involves time: _____

14. Verb: _____

15. A month: _____

16. Plural noun: _____

17. Verb: _____

18. Plural noun: _____

19. Plural noun: _____

20. Adjective: _____

21. Noun: _____

22. Adjective: _____

23. Noun: _____

24. Adjective: _____

25. Noun, singular or plural: _____

26. A character's name: _____

27. Kind of tree: _____

28. Adjective: _____

29. Country name: _____

Many years it ___1___ more, since he ___2___ in front of the ___3___, colonel who ___4___ had to remember that the ___5___ one behind schedule in which ___6___ took the father to discover it, the ___7___. At that time ___8___ was village of twenty houses of ___9___, banks of ___10___, of river, of clear of water that worked through a bed of the ___11___ stones, that were white and enormous, like ___12___ eggs. The world was so ___13___ that many things lacked names, and to indicate them it was necessary to ___14___. Every year during the month of unequal ___15___ a family of ___16___ would ___17___ the warehouses near the village, and with a great uproar of ___18___ and ___19___ they would exhibit ___20___ inventions. First they brought the ___21___. They introduced a ___22___ ___23___ with a beard ___24___ and the ___25___ of the sparrow, of which ___26___, putting a public demonstration in the ___27___ tree, that he itself called the eighth wonder of the ___28___ alchemists of ___29___.

Pictures and Words

Greg Houser and Emma Sovich

Write about—and beyond—the painting and its frame.

THEY SAY A PICTURE IS worth a thousand words—so why can't a picture inspire a thousand words? As writers, we are constantly translating the visual into the verbal, bringing onto the page the world around us (events we witness, people and places we observe) and the world within us (events we embellish or invent, people and places we imagine in full color). You can use a photograph or comic strip to refill the reservoir of your imagination.

Art and writing have a long, intertwined history. When we write poems or stories directly inspired by art (real or invented art!), we call it *ekphrasis*. The Greek poet Homer included a section of ekphrasis in his famous epic, *The Iliad*. He describes a shield created by a god:

> Two cities radiant on the shield appear,
> The image one of peace, and one of war.
> Here sacred pomp and genial feast delight . . .

This is only one small section of the description of the shield; and in fact, Homer describes the scene on the shield beginning with the sky, moving to the cities, and then down to the very people inhabiting the city as if they were moving, living, and breathing. The shield is an imaginary art object—so intricate that it could never really be painted, and so we can't show you what it looks like.

However, we can show you the painting often attributed to the artist Pieter Bruegel the Elder (see page 233).

This painting inspired William Carlos Williams to write his famous poem "Landscape with the Fall of Icarus" that begins "According to Brueghel / when Icarus fell / it was spring." Have a look at Williams's whole poem in a book or online (if you haven't discovered it yet, here's the perfect opportunity to check out the Academy of American Poets at poets.org), and then look back at this painting.

Pieter Bruegel, *Landscape with the Fall of Icarus*, painted around 1555.

Bruegel's painting is ostensibly a landscape. Without knowing the title (*Landscape with the Fall of Icarus*), you might think it's "about" the guy in the foreground plowing a field or maybe "about" that big ship in the middle ground. The title, however, draws your attention to flailing legs right in front of that big ship: Icarus, the boy from myth who flew with constructed wings, and against his father's warning, got too close to the sun. The sun melted the wax holding the feathers to the wing armature, and Icarus fell. Williams writes about how "unsignificant" the boy's falling is compared to the grandeur of the painting.

Williams spends very little time describing the painting, so you might not know what he's writing about if you didn't have the painting at hand to look at. But he moves beyond just description; by directing our gaze to only certain details, and not the entire painting, he draws the reader's attention to what interests him: the "unsignificance" of the title event.

But you don't have to describe the image at all. In fact, you can create dramatic tension by placing an image next to a written text. Check out this sample from Anne Carson's book-length work, *Nox*, in which facing pages are always composed of juxtaposed, contrasting elements:

Carson isn't directly describing the photograph. The people in the

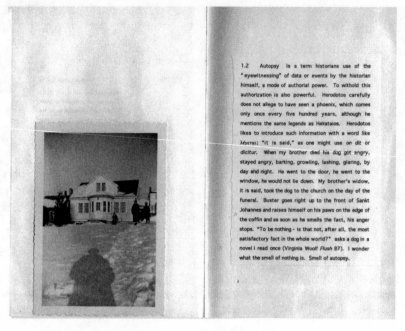

1.2   Autopsy is a term historians use of the "eyewitnessing" of data or events by the historian himself, a mode of authorial power. To withold this authorization is also powerful. Herodotos carefully does not allege to have seen a phoenix, which comes only once every five hundred years, although he mentions the same legends as Hekataios. Herodotos likes to introduce such information with a word like λέγεται: "it is said," as one might use *on dit* or *dicitur*. When my brother died his dog got angry, stayed angry, barking, growling, lashing, glaring, by day and night. He went to the door, he went to the window, he would not lie down. My brother's widow, it is said, took the dog to the church on the day of the funeral. Buster goes right up to the front of Sankt Johannes and raises himself on his paws on the edge of the coffin and as soon as he smells the fact, his anger stops. "To be nothing - is that not, after all, the most satisfactory fact in the whole world?" asks a dog in a novel I read once (Virginia Woolf *Flush* 87). I wonder what the smell of nothing is. Smell of autopsy.

Page from Anne Carson's *Nox*.

photo, the shadow in the photo, are not directly addressed or identified. We are not told anything about the dramatic situation depicted in the photograph. From looking at the photo alone, the average viewer probably wouldn't imagine anything to do with an *autopsy*. The link between the photograph and the entry, "1.2 Autopsy," exists in the larger context of the whole book, an elegy for Carson's brother that she constructed as an amalgamation, a scrapbook, a collection of many kinds of texts—dictionary entries, photographs, journal entries, paintings, and more. It is the reader's job to reflect on how the texts—some visual, some written— inform one another.

Now find a painting, print, or photograph in a museum archive online or from another source, and try one of these techniques to write a poem or short prose piece.

1. Like Homer, describe the scene at great length or take your description beyond the boundaries of the artwork's scene.
2. Like Williams, describe the artwork, but direct your reader to notice just certain aspects of it and to think about it in a particular way.

3. Like Carson, imagine and describe a subject or present a narrative that comes to your mind when you look at the artwork, but that is not at all "in" the artwork.

The Horse in Motion

POEMS IN RESPONSE TO PHOTOGRAPHS AND PAINTINGS OF MOTION

Jenny Gropp

Learn about the history of capturing the body in motion in the visual arts and then extend the practice into your own poetry and prose.

W E ARE ALL MOVING, ALL the time, even when we're just sleeping and breathing. So it's no wonder that we want to be able to write about the body's motion. How on earth will you go about writing down, in poignant, new metaphors, a fight scene in a Jackie Chan movie? Beyond that, how will you get your fictitious characters down the road in a way that's unique and keeps your readers interested?

One way to learn how to write about motion is by writing poems in response to photographs and paintings of motion. Let's try it out.

Along with Étienne-Jules Marey (1830–1904), Eadweard Muybridge (1830–1904) became a godfather of not only the art of cinema but also the science of biomechanics.

Eadweard Muybridge, *The Horse in Motion*, 1887.

Muybridge's photographic series *The Horse in Motion* was born out of a desire to capture motion in a single composition. Why do people want to do this? How does the movement of this horse and the movement of the rider on its back make you feel? What does it teach us? What can we teach others about this composition?

I think we can write poems that bring further *energy* to the art of capturing a body's, or many bodies', motions. Look at this poem about the above photograph written by A. B. Gorham:

THE LANGUAGE OF BETTING

on a horse, the letters her legs
form in their silhouette
a series of snapshots
of unsustainable postures.
The mare's neck a see-saw of muscle
& thick sorrel coat, reaches towards
the possibility of still air.
The always-graceful line
from the bony base of her nose
to her long tail.
The changing angle of hind
-quarter and then hind-quarter.
Outlined in black as if printed in ink,
her body a thin paper cutout
carries a man who asks her
to slow this unwieldy pace
but at the rate of small charities:
an assuaging into stillness. Her breathing
continues, and the blood-rhythm:
bet to win, bet to place, bet to show.

How does Gorham capture the energy in Muybridge's photo composition?

- She places the horse and rider in a scenario. What is it?
- She goes into a very specific description of the horse's body. Can you point out some of this description? Notice that this description takes up almost the whole poem.

- She talks about *why* the horse is moving and what it's moving towards: "the possibility of still air."
- Look also at how Gorham uses line breaks. The horse's movement from frame to frame, as well as its muscular stride, are captured by the movement of the poem. Each line feels like a frame in the photo composition, and each line emphasizes the horse's body.

So by telling the story of the photograph, Gorham has enhanced Muybridge's art. You could even say she collaborated with it.

Painters have also worked with this idea of capturing motion in a single composition. Some of you may be familiar with Marcel Duchamp's 1912 painting *Nude Descending a Staircase*. Its conception certainly owed something to Marey and Muybridge's photographic studies of the living body in motion and to the newborn cinema. (Duchamp himself said that he has a "preoccupation of movement.") Look at it:

Does this painting look like a traditional anatomical nude? Not at all.

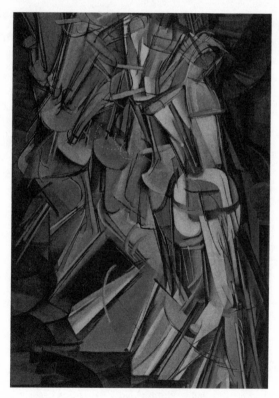

Marcel Duchamp, *Nude Descending a Staircase*, 1912

Right away, Duchamp wants to use paint to make a statement that a photographer can't. He instead uses abstract lines and shadow to suggest the woman's successive static positions and create a rhythmic sense of motion. Through this abstract presentation of movement, Duchamp has complicated and enriched the notion of the body in time and space. The body can move like never before!

How does this painting make you feel? What are some of the emotions it creates? We can answer these questions by writing a poem.

Look at this poem from Sawako Nakayasu's book *nothing fictional but the accuracy or arrangement (she,* presumably written as a response to Duchamp's nude:

> one sets out with a clear and distinct set of in-
> tentions, only to find her life overlapping
> unmistakably with that of another and yet
> another, down to the moment she turns
> her head forty-eight degrees to the left,
> over one-eighth of a second, this overlap-
> ping witnessed in the form of some tempo-
> rarily double-exposed photograph—and
> then, the need to move away, not only from
> this but from it all, this just being the final
> cue—other lives better left alone . . .

As you can see, Nakayasu is doing some of the same things Gorham did to bring out the energy in the painting. She sets a scenario—a woman coming down the stairs "with a clear and distinct set of in-tentions." She also goes into very specific description about the movement of the woman's body. The language Nakayasu uses shows the woman moving very jerkily and quickly, just like in the painting.

From reading the poem, how do you think the woman feels? From looking at the painting, why does Nakayasu say the woman feels the "need to move away, not only from / this but from it all"?

Here is a list of several more marvelous paintings and photographs that represent motion. You can look them all up online:

Paul Delvaux, *The Echo*
Giacomo Balla, *Dynamism of a Dog on a Leash*

Giacomo Balla, *Girl Running on a Balcony*
Étienne-Jules Marey, *Flying Pelican*

Write a poem in response to one of them. Consider the following when you write:

- Create a scenario—where/what is happening in the painting?
- Describe in detail what the bodies in the painting are doing. *How* do they move? Consider speed and space in the painting. *Why* are they moving that way? You might also try to use at least one simile in your poem—what do the bodies in your painting or photograph move *like* or *as if*?
- How does this painting make you feel? How do the bodies in the painting show that?

Book Flip!

Using Found Phrases

Jenny Gropp, Laura Kochman, and Jill Smith

Grab a book or magazine and flip your way to a new piece of writing.

FOUND TEXT CAN BE FOUND . . . anywhere! Graffiti, street signs, text messages, speeches—even other poems or prose pieces. Like a collage, a work made from found writing rearranges and redesigns existing text to create something new. Here is an excerpt of a found poem by Charles Reznikoff, who used bits of old court records to create the poems in his book *Testimony*:

> Amelia was just fourteen and out of the orphan asylum; at her first
> job—in the bindery, and yes sir, yes ma'am, oh, so anxious to
> please.
> She stood at the table, her blond hair hanging about her shoulders,
> "knocking up" for Mary and Sadie, the stichers
> ("knocking up" is counting books and stacking them in piles to be
> taken away).

Using found text can also be a great springboard if you find yourself stuck while writing. You don't need much, just a word or phrase to get yourself started. Look around—a snippet of text you see in an advertisement, an e-mail, or on somebody's T-shirt might be the perfect opening line for a story or poem. This is a great way to distract your pesky "rational" mind and allow your creative mind the freedom to move.

Let's give it a try. Open a book or magazine to a random page and, without looking, place your finger anywhere on the page. Write down the word, phrase, or sentence your finger landed on, and take two minutes to write a poem or prose piece using that as your *first* line. When your time is up, flip to another random page and do the same thing. You can either start a new piece or continue the one you were working on. This time, you'll use your word/phrase/sentence somewhere in the *body* of your piece. Two more minutes, then, *flip*! Find a new piece of text, and use this as the *last* line of your piece.

New Takes on the News

Obituaries, Classifieds, and Dear Abby

Greg Houser, Jill Smith, and Jessica Trull

Write hilarious news items.

The newspaper is one of the oldest forms of public communication and engagement. Newspapers take themselves very seriously, and they should, since they perform an invaluable service. However, this is also what makes it a great medium to mess with.

Activity 1: Obituaries

An obituary is a notice of a person's death, usually including a short biographical account—an entire life condensed into a mere paragraph or two. In his novel *Almost Like Being in Love,* Steve Kluger introduces us to the main characters Travis and Craig through the obituaries they write for themselves as part of a high school English assignment. The reader learns about Travis's interests and ambitions through how he imagines being remembered. Here is an excerpt:

May 6, 1978
English Assignment
My Obituary
by Travis Puckett

WHO'S WHO IN AMERICA
TRAVIS PUCKETT (*Broadway Star*) first rose to national prominence in 1981 while attending a revival of *My Fair Lady* at the Mark Hellinger Theatre, where the legendary musical had premiered twenty-five years earlier and run for 2,717 consecutive performances. During the first act, Rex Harrison suffered a heart attack and was rushed to the hospital (where he survived), nearly causing the cancellation of the entire performance as the understudy had been killed earlier that morning in a fatal car accident. However, Puckett—who was seated in the third row and who'd had the entire show committed to memory since his sixth

birthday—volunteered his services and was rushed into costume back-stage. What resulted was a performance that brought a stunned audience to its feet and earned him a special Tony Award the following spring as the youngest Henry Higgins in the history of musical comedy . . .

"Death isn't funny. But the words and stories left in homage to those who have passed sometimes are."—funnyobits.com

Writing an obituary may seem morbid or depressing, but this form has been manipulated to humorous effect by writers eulogizing objects, places, animals, ideas, or fictional characters. Below is a pun-filled obituary mourning the loss of the Pillsbury Doughboy.

THE OBITUARY OF THE PILLSBURY DOUGHBOY

Please join me in remembering a great icon. Veteran Pillsbury spokesperson, The Pillsbury Doughboy, died yesterday of a severe yeast infection and complications from repeated pokes to the belly. He was 71. Doughboy was buried in a slightly greased coffin. Dozens of celebrities turned out, including Mrs. Butterworth, the California Raisins, Hungry Jack, Betty Crocker, the Hostess Twinkies, Captain Crunch and many others.

The graveside was piled high with flours as long-time friend, Aunt Jemima, delivered the eulogy, describing Doughboy as a man who "never knew how much he was kneaded."

Doughboy rose quickly in show business, but his later life was filled with many turnovers. He was not considered a very smart cookie, wasting much of his dough on half-baked schemes. Despite being a little flaky at times, even as a crusty old man, he was still considered a role model for millions.

Doughboy is survived by his second wife, Play Dough. They have two children and one in the oven. The funeral was held at 3:50 for about 20 minutes.

http://www.homeschooloasis.com/storehs_obituary_of_pillsbury.htm

How will you be remembered? Did you save the world from evil were-penguins? Rise to fame as a sports star, artist, or inventor? Write an obituary, either for yourself or for something close to your heart. You might write about the death of rock 'n' roll, your car battery, or your favorite video game character. If you're writing about a person, make sure that person is a) yourself or b) fictional. No killing off friends, family members, enemies, teachers, etc.

ACTIVITY 2: CLASSIFIEDS

Classifieds are brief ads selling anything from furniture to livestock to cars to services. In the olden days when they appeared in printed newspapers, they had to be brief, because you were charged per word! Now, thanks to the Internet, you can have a classified ad as short as this local ad for sofas: "Two nice sleeper sofas. One queen and one king. $100 each. Call 555–555–5555." Or as detailed as this Denver Craigslist ad for a door:

> In search of serious, ethical, honest, and reliable buyers with a conscience who might be interested in purchasing this beautiful wood grain smooth surface door that can be used for a bedroom, a bathroom, a closet, or a number of other primarily interior purposes. Although hollow, it is rather tall and rather wide, yet not as light in weight as it might initially appear at first glance. Although somewhat simple in style, its most interesting natural grain design and light terra cotta color make this particular door definitely eye-catching and seductive. No less seductive is the soft and smooth texture of the door's surface.
>
> On one of the door's lateral sides are 3 brand new glowing gold colored hinges. There is also a pre-drilled hole on the front of the door's opposite side that is ready for the insertion of a doorknob. In that I also have a couple of brand new, never used glowing gold colored interior doorknobs, I would consider including one of them for the buyer at no additional cost.
>
> In that I am aiming to sell this very attractive door ASAP, the first to call me and get directions to my home and drive to my house and pay with cash if pleased with the door and its hinges (and doorknob if needed) gets to drive home with a pretty good deal. In other words and phrased more bluntly, why would anyone opt to spend $75 for a door that they can get for $30?
>
> This is all the more reason to just give me a call, arrange a day and date and time to come over and see with your own eyes, touch with your own hands, and inspect in detail the beautiful wood grain surface of this rather seductive door that can be used for a bedroom, a bathroom, a closet, or a number of other primarily interior purposes. Then, put on

your sweater or jacket or scarf and winter coat and gloves, ignite your engine, and just drive on over to my home, where I will be awaiting your knock on my own exterior front door.

You can call me anytime, 24-hours a day, 7 days a week. If I am not available when you call, please leave a message noting your name and number. Also, please specify exact item of interest by name. I typically return calls within 24 to 48 hours (if not within an hour or even less). Once we connect via phone, I could then provide you with more specific directions to my home so that you can come over and decide if you want it.

Select an object from your pocket/purse/backpack, or look around the room for an interesting item. Write a classified ad for this item. Be as detailed or brief as you want. What are your gum wrapper/book/key/ etc.'s most marketable features? You could also write your classified as a "wanted" ad—as though you are looking for someone who is offering this item for sale. "Wanted, No. 2 pencil with half an eraser."

ACTIVITY 3: DEAR ABBY

Dear Abby has been offering sage advice to ordinary people for years. We write to her with a question or concern, and she responds in a newspaper column usually located right above the local *TV Guide*. There is no problem that Abby can't solve. Take, for example, this complicated dilemma to which there seems to be no easy answer:

DEAR ABBY:
I'm having a dispute with my husband. He thinks that you screw in a lightbulb clockwise. I disagree. I say counter-clockwise. Which of us is correct?
—ERIKA IN PELHAM, ALA.

DEAR ERIKA: He is. You screw in a lightbulb by turning it to the right, the same way you tighten the lid on a jar—which is clockwise. The mnemonic for this is: "Right is tight; left is loose."

Now write your own question to Abby. It can be as silly or serious as you want. Then, pass your question to another writer and receive their question in return. Now you are Abby. Take five minutes and write a response to the concerned citizen whose question has been passed to you.

Now with Twenty Billion Readers

WRITING A CRAIGSLIST "MISSED CONNECTION"

Greg Houser, Jill Smith, and Jessica Trull

What would you like to say to that stranger?

CRAIGLIST.ORG IS ONE OF THE biggest and most well-known sites on the web. Each month its pages receive twenty billion views. Most cities in the United States and abroad have their own Craigslist site that serves their community. The site is part marketplace, part community bulletin board. Every day, millions and millions of people log on to Craigslist to post things for sale, to give them away, or to discuss issues in their community. Some people even go to Craigslist in what can sometimes be a misguided search for love. The "missed connections" section of the site is full of post after post by strangers who saw another stranger on the street and were so smitten that they took to the Internet to profess their like or love. You're probably wondering what all this has to do with creative writing by now. Well, here's your answer: we want you to write a missed connection.

Brian Oliu, a nonfiction writer, posted twenty-two missed connections to the Tuscaloosa, Alabama, Craigslist site over the course of forty-five days. Oliu said about the project "that all missed connections are, in fact, connections, although often not on the level of an actual connection of genuine love and adoration. And so the pieces that make up the Missed Connections are about those connections and how they become something larger than an actual connection—that rather than 'choosing someone every single day,' we choose something else out there that will sabotage our happiness." Here is a sample of what Oliu did with one of his missed connections:

TASKA LOSA—THE PARK AT MANDERSON LANDING M4W

BY BRIAN OLIU

Here is a list of people that have drowned in the river: apple, bear, crush, dime, eagle, fire, fire, ghost, ghost, ghost, hair, iron, jab, kite, loss, lost, lose, me. Here is a list of what it sounded like when they were drowning: the rolling up of a car window when you know it is going to rain later that day, a gas-powered stove turning on in order to boil water for noodles, a hand feeling around an empty pocket. I grew up near a river much like this one. I took the hand of someone like you and slid down the slope to where the water mixed with the silt, where it would stick to your ankles if you were not careful. We were not careful. Let me let you in on a secret: this town is falling into the river. Here is a list of everything that will be gone: the stadium where I saw you, the frozen yogurt shop where I saw you, the gym where I saw you, the bookstore where I saw you, the store where I saw you, the store where I saw you, the intersection where I saw you, the classroom where I saw you, the shopping center where I saw you, the parking deck where I saw you, the party you never came to, the church where I saw you, the road where I saw you. Where will that leave us? If you want to find me while we are drowning amidst the drowning, I will be there thinking about home. If you want to press your lips to mine and suck out the air from my lungs so that you may force air from your nose, to make child's sounds with your mouth, please, come. Do not refuse. Try and stop me. Try and stop me from giving you air like you are a balloon and I am drowning. Don't try to stop me. I am trying to tell you something but if I move my lips I will break the seal. I want to tell you that this is about you. You know who you are. You know where you have been. None of that is important now. Here is a list of people that will drown in the river:

Writing a missed connection can allow you to explore issues of longing and love at first site and relationships in general. You can invent a person you saw that day and write a missed connection for them from someone else who may have seen them. You can write a missed connection in the voice of a pirate or a ninja who has lost their parrot or sword. You can write a missed connection for an object (a beach ball) or a concept (time). Anything at all really. Let your mind go wild.

From These Old Sayings to This Fresh Story

Revamping Cliché Phrases and Plots

Jesse Delong, Lisa Tallin, and Danilo Thomas

*Take clichés like "head over heels" and well-known similes like
"hard as a rock" and turn them into fresh ideas and complex plots.*

A LOT OF STORIES AND POEMS out there use the same old everyday
phrases and plot schemes. These clichés have been repeated so of-
ten that we hear them and read them, but we don't pay any attention to
them because they are so familiar. Clichés transmit information but are
boring. We find these clichés in tiny bits of writing like single phrases
and in large parts of writing such as the whole plot. Today, on *This Fresh
Story*, we are going to turn these nasty clichés into fresh phrases and
complex plots that defy expectations and excite readers.

1. Fresh Similes

Similes, or comparisons using *like* or *as*, are often repeated and become
clichés. These two authors have avoided using clichéd similes in their
pieces, instead using language alive with vivid images to elicit emotional
responses from the reader.

Amy Bloom, in this excerpt from her short story "Silver Water," be-
gins with a simile:

> My sister's voice was like mountain water in a silver pitcher; the clear
> blue beauty of it cools you and lifts you up beyond your heat, beyond
> your body. After we went to see *La Traviata*, when she was fourteen and
> I was twelve, she elbowed me in the parking lot and said, "Check this
> out." And she opened her mouth unnaturally wide and her voice came
> out, so crystalline and bright, that all the departing operagoers stood
> frozen by their cars, unable to take out their keys or open their doors un-
> til she had finished and then they cheered like hell.

Carolyn Forché embeds a crucial simile in "The Colonel." After the
narrator has entered the colonel's house and sat at his table, the colonel

gets a grocery sack and turns it over on the table: "He spilled many human ears on the table. They were like dried peach halves."

Bloom's love for her sister and the clarity of her sister's voice is clear in the first sentence of her short story. Her sister's voice is "like mountain water in a silver pitcher"—something sacred. Forché compares human ears to dried peaches to express her feelings about an inhumane situation and a cruel man who invites her into his house during a bloody revolution in El Salvador. Now let's take some common similes and make them snap.

First, write down the common cliché—the phrase you've heard before:

1. Cool as a <u>cucumber</u>.
2. Blind as a _____.
3. _____ as a bee.
4. Light as a _____.
5. _____ as a mouse.
6. Stubborn as a _____.

Look at those nasty little guys. Common, I tell you. But, what if you had never seen a bee before? What if the only mouse you had met played the alto saxophone in the school band? The construction of the comparisons below is more complex.

1. Cool as a hat rack in a barbershop covered with windbreakers on opening day of baseball season.
2. Blind as caramel-covered apples with walnuts and chocolate chips.
3. Cranky as a bee in winter just before the first snow.
4. Light as an ocean liner full of honeymooners.
5. Gritty as a mouse.
6. Stubborn as a cheerleader with new braces and a bad haircut.

Now complete the following similes with unexpected answers.

1. Dead as a _____.
2. _____ as a fox.
3. _____ as an arrow.
4. Dumb as a _____.

5. _____ as a rock.

6. Cute as a _____.

Choose one simile from the any of the above examples or create one on your own. Use that simile as the first sentence of a story or a poem and write for twenty minutes.

2. FRESH PLOT

Clichés don't just happen in a phrase or sentence. Sometimes the whole plot of a book or film is a cliché. Here are some examples of cliché plots:

1. Love: A meets B; A loses B; A gets B back.
2. Revenge: A is wronged by B; they have a confrontation; A kills B.
3. Disaster: Tornado, earthquake, fire, etc. happens; A and B must save the world and fall in love.
4. Monster: Dracula, Frankenstein, Mothra, Godzilla, spiders, etc. invade, and A and B must save the world and fall in love.
5. Fallen Hero: A was a good guy, but something bad happened and A banishes himself. A must return and become a hero once again.

Let's re-do these plots employing the tactics you used for the similes. Here is a start:

1. Love: A meets B and C and D, and forms a bluegrass band. A falls in love with the banjo.
2. Revenge: A is wronged by biodiversity. A opens a pet shop underground with mostly worms, grubs, and moles.

Continue twisting these plots or make up your own plot:

1. Disaster

_____

_____

_____

2. Monster

_____

_____

_____

3. Fallen Hero

_____

_____

_____

4. Your Choice

_____

_____

_____

Choose one of the six plots from the previous example and write a story or poem in twenty minutes, and we'll see you next time on *This Fresh Story*.

III

Slews of Styles and Subjects

In this final section, we celebrate and gain inspiration from a host of authors who show us ways to employ language with style and to tackle some familiar—and unfamiliar—subjects in fresh ways. If you ever have a chance to go to the Louvre in Paris to see the *Mona Lisa*, you will have a hard time getting up close to the painting. Not only are there guards and guardrails to keep anyone from getting dangerously close to the masterpiece, there are also lots of student artists camped out with easels and sketchpads as close as they can get to the painting, trying their hand at some of Leonardo DaVinci's techniques by getting up close and personal with his genius. Painters, writers, musicians, dancers—any sort of artists—cannot develop their talents in a vacuum. It helps to be influenced by those masters who have gone before, to apprentice oneself like those student artists at the Louvre, and to learn from their awesome moves. If you let yourself be influenced by a wide range of great writers, a little of that inspiration will rub off on you and broaden the moves you can make as a writer. One writer might awaken you to the possibility of writing about a particular subject, while another writer might inspire you to stretch what you do with details, sentence structure, or other "tools" of the art. Taken together, a particular writer's "moves" constitute their style. Think of two authors you enjoy who write very differently from one another. For example, consider a pair of writers such as Langston Hughes and William Shakespeare, or J. K. Rowling and Ernest Hemingway. If you read a page by each author in the pair—some work by them that you have never read before—you probably would be able to tell which one had written it. Their style would be apparent throughout.

In this section, we shall shamelessly apprentice ourselves to writing masters. To expand our stylistic possibilities, we will learn how to build realistic worlds from Tom Wolfe and Flannery O'Connor, and nonrealistic worlds (right down to the bizarre physics!) from Franz Kafka and Italo Calvino. We will sample modern literary movements and techniques such as the Oulipo movement, the Dadaists, and the Beats—Jack Kerouac's "scribbled secret notebooks," Allen Ginsberg's obsessive praise method, and Lawrence Ferlinghetti's call-to-arms rallying cry approach. We will practice, like the ancient Japanese poet Matsuo Basho, being a Zen master of the senses. We will try a story made entirely out of landscape like contemporary writer Campbell McGrath, and another made only of six words. We'll write long, luxurious sentences and short, clipped ones. We'll show you a bunch of ways words rhyme. We'll try on for size a host of stylistic "moves" to expand our writing range.

We'll also expand our capacity for things to write *about*, otherwise known as *subjects*. We'll challenge ourselves to write about things we might not have thought to write about at all (your animal is interviewed on the TV show *Cook! Or Be Cooked*; your villain is an adult viewed from a child's point of view) and also approach common subjects (love, death, the changing of the seasons, witches, food, super heroes, and politics) in unexpected ways. How do you write a love poem that isn't sappy? Or stories about death that are comic as well as tragic? Or a story about a "stock" scary character—like Jessica Hollander's "Ultimate Makeover: Zombie Edition"—that avoids the clichés of terror? Here, too, we'll learn from the masters.

To finish things off, we have some advice at the end of this section about how to get published. After all, the letters would like very much for you to be able to show off what you have done with them. They are always proud of how you arrange them, and want the world to know about it. With your help, the letters will even write their own cover letter so you can send your creations off to a publisher.

Realism

TIPS FROM TOM WOLFE AND FLANNERY O'CONNOR

Krystin Gollihue

Use an angle to depict settings and characters.

WHEN WE GO TO WRITE something *real*, we often draw from our own life experiences, right? Well, what happens when we want to write something that's *real* but unfamiliar to us, outside what we ourselves have experienced? How do we create places and characters that we could find in the world but that are beyond our own communities, knowledge, and experience? And how do we make that interesting?

WRITING ABOUT REALISTIC PLACES: CREATING A SLIGHTLY ALIEN VIEW

Here is an excerpt from Tom Wolfe's *The Kandy-Kolored Tangerine-Flake Streamline Baby* in which Wolfe describes the streets of Hollywood in a way that makes something real seem so real it's almost alien. Notice how Wolfe chooses a particular "angle" to describe a normal street scene in Hollywood.

> Endless scorched boulevards lined with one-story stores, shops, bowling alleys, skating rinks, taco drive-ins, all of them shaped not like rectangles but like trapezoids, from the way the roofs slant up from the back and the plate-glass fronts slant out as if they're going to pitch forward on the sidewalk and throw up.

Wolfe starts with a list of things that we know: shops, bowling alleys, and drive-ins—some usual suspects on a busy street in a busy town. Next, he slants their shape, telling us how the buildings look but using a word we don't normally hear outside geometry class: *trapezoid*. Finally, he brings this totally normal Hollywood street into a totally not normal space by personifying the buildings as people throwing up.

Now let's write about a realistic place like Wolfe writes about Hollywood:

1. Write down the name of a town or city you know well and feel like you
   could describe.
2. Next, change its name so you'll feel free to fictionalize it. Write down
   this new name, too. This is the town you will write about.
3. Now write a paragraph about a street in this place, describing it in
   such an overly focused way that your reader and even you can't recog-
   nize it.
   a. Include two lists, using Tom Wolfe's list of the types of buildings
      on the street in Hollywood as inspiration.
   b. Use at least one surprising metaphor.
   c. Use one personification, like the buildings that throw up on the
      sidewalk.
   d. Include one piece of made-up history about the street.
   e. Feel free to include any other details you think might make your
      street come alive.

Be sure to hang on to this paragraph about your place because we'll be
using it after we create some people to put in it.

Writing About Realistic Characters: Creating Memorable People

As the creators of the world(s) in which our characters live, it helps to
know a thing or two about them: their wants, needs, pasts, and futures.
As a writer, you get to be a guide for your characters, a person who walks
them through the circumstances of their lives. You don't want them
caught off guard, not knowing their name or their job or who was their
first kiss, do you?

So let's create a person!

Character's name: _____

Age: _____

Gender: _____

Occupation/Title: _____

Relationship status: _____

Hobbies/Activities: _____

Habits: _____

Favorite animal: _____

Hometown: _____

Life motto: _____

Biggest fear: _____

Greatest desire: _____

_____

Places travelled: _____

_____

Favorite/Most embarrassing memory: _____

_____

Favorite feature of self: _____

_____

Favorite feature of others: _____

_____

Favorite spot in town: _____

_____

Least favorite spot in town: _____

_____

Now we have a great character to work with. Let's take this character and place them in that place you created a minute ago. But, before we do, let's see how Flannery O'Connor allows a place to reflect the mood of a character. As you read this excerpt from "Everything That Rises Must Converge," pay attention to how O'Connor sets the tone of her characters' lives by skewing the view of the neighborhood they grew up in.

> He opened the door himself and started down the walk to get her going. The sky was a dying violet and the houses stood out darkly against it, bulbous liver-colored monstrosities of a uniform ugliness though no two were alike. Since this had been a fashionable neighborhood forty years ago, his mother persisted in thinking that they did well to have an apartment in it. Each house had a narrow collar of dirt around it in which sat, usually, a grubby child. Julian walked with his hands in his pockets, his head down and thrust forward and his eyes glazed with the determination to make himself completely numb during the time he would be sacrificed to her pleasure.

The words that O'Connor uses to describe Julian's neighborhood include adjectives like *violet, bulbous, liver-colored, uniform,* and *narrow.*

This gives the reader a view of the neighborhood that is ugly, dark, and sinister. Similarly, the words used to describe Julian also conjure images of dark, sinister things: *thrust, glazed, numb, sacrificed*. Not only do these words have sinister *meanings*, but they also have sinister *sounds*. Hard consonants like the *b*'s in *bulbous*, as well as the slithery *s*'s in *thrust*, and the similarity between the word *violet* (which O'Connor uses) and the word *violent* (which O'Connor implies) create a connection between the darkness of the neighborhood and the darkness of Julian's relationship with his mother.

Putting Place and Character Together

Now, remember that paragraph you wrote about your place? Let's try re-writing it, this time with your character dropped right into the middle of it. Keep in mind Flannery O'Connor's technique of allowing place to reflect character.

Imagine your character is doing something specific outdoors in your made-up place. Example: they could go for a walk, hang up laundry, clean the yard, go for a drive, or plant some arugula. Start with a few notes:

1. How does the character feel in this setting?
2. What natural elements can they see (mountains, creeks, lawns)? What human-made elements (billboards, store fronts, skyscrapers)?
3. What is the weather like? Does it match the character's mood or contrast with it?
4. Take notes on how the setting reflects or else contrasts with the character's feelings and appearance.

Now try these three scenarios and play them out with your character in the place you wrote about earlier.

Scenario 1: A storm rolls in and your character is caught outside off guard.

Scenario 2: Your character's dream person walks into the scene. Your character tries to have a conversation with them.

Scenario 3: Your character comes across a lost (or ferocious!) animal. Describe what your character plans to do.

Extending the Story Beyond One Scene

Now you have three separate scenes with a well-developed place and well-developed character. Choose one scene to develop further, extending the story into another scene, and keeping in mind Tom Wolfe's ways of making the place come alive and Flannery O'Connor's way of making the place reflect how the characters are feeling.

World Building

Nonrealistic Characters and a Six-Sentence Story

Jess E. Jelsma and Matt Jones

Kafka and you.

I'M WHAT YOU MIGHT CALL a "dog person." I like dogs. Love 'em in fact. I even own one. His name is Clyde and he's really great. He sits, rolls over, plays fetch, and plays dead whenever I tell him to, at least some of the time. Now I just opt for laminate flooring. Occasionally, Clyde might chew up the sofa or pee on the kitchen floor, perhaps bark at the mailman, but other than that, he is relatively predictable and can be expected to nap at the foot of my bed and lap water from his water bowl.

In this world, I am a dog person. Clyde is my pet of choice, but— but—if I were not confined to the rules of this world, the world made up of Clyde and mailmen and six-foot fences, then I would also own a pet that is entirely new and completely foreign. It would have the head of a wolf and the sleek feathered body of a golden eagle. Its tail would be colored and spotted like that of a leopard, and its ears would be tall and gangly like those of the fennec fox, and I would call it Moose. Or Toast. Maybe Moose Toast. It would live in my closet and I would feed it bullfrogs to keep it from squowling (a combination of squawking and growling, because that is the sound that Moose Toast makes in this world). At night, I would sneak out of my bedroom window and ride Moose Toast to the beach, because Moose Toast can fly, and he who is Moose Toast would spend his time diving for fish while I lazed about on the sand and counted the stars.

Of course, being that Moose Toast is such a remarkable creature, one with a penchant for stray cats and midnight rides, certain aspects of my world would be changed. While Clyde might simply bark at the mailman and growl at cats through the window, Moose Toast, the part-wolf, part-golden eagle, part-leopard, part–fennec fox, would squowl at the moon and fly to the coldest depths of Siberia, the hottest dunes of the North African desert, the dampest pockets of South American jungle, and the windiest steppes of Mongolia to mate with their respective inhabitants (the wolf, the golden eagle, the leopard, and the fennec fox) because

Moose Toast is lonely in this world and wishes to have companions. After all, no one wants to be around Moose Toast when he is in mating season, because that is when he really starts to shrirp (a combination of shriek and chirp).

Moose Toast is not a real creature, but that is what's best about him. When writing nonrealistic fiction, I am free to create my own worlds, as well as modify and adapt the worlds that I already know. While I am but a simple, dog-loving human of the Earth in my day-to-day life, in my fiction I am able to be the tamer and confidant of the extraordinary Moose Toast.

Non-realism can be used to write whole books such as *The Lord of the Rings* by J. R. R. Tolkien and *The Hunger Games* by Suzanne Collins in which fantastical characters live in worlds very dissimilar to our own. It can also be mixed with elements of realism in works like Harry Potter where a young boy from real, "muggle" London discovers that he belongs to a magical world in which he must learn how to cast spells to defeat a dark wizard. Below is a method for trying out nonrealistic fiction in a six-sentence story.

Creating a Nonrealistic Character Sketch

The excerpts below illustrate how a writer can look toward the body to create an unreal situation. When reading the pieces, think about how the writer changes the body. What does the body do? Is the change consistent? What kind of language does the writer use to create this change?

Franz Kafka's famous novella *The Metamorphosis* begins with the main character waking up to discover that he has been transformed into a giant cockroach.

> When Gregor Samsa awoke one morning from troubled dreams he found himself transformed in his bed into a monstrous insect. He was lying on his hard shell-like back and by lifting his head a little he could see his curved brown belly, divided by stiff arching ribs, on top of which the bed-quilt was precariously poised and seemed about to slide off completely. His numerous legs, which were pathetically thin compared to the rest of his bulk, danced helplessly before his eyes.

Brandi Wells's short story "Worst Time #15" describes a different kind of physical transformation.

> Her body parts are too loose, or they are too loosely connected to her

torso. Exercising will not tighten them. She has used firming lotions. Nothing works. Her hands fall off while she's riding her bicycle. Her feet plop off while she's sleeping. Her head is lost somewhere in the ocean, perhaps carried away by a dolphin or covered in starfish.

Now it's your turn to write your own version of a character's "metamorphosis." Starting with a character you have already created in a former exercise or a new one from your imagination, write a paragraph about how some physical characteristic of their body has changed in a non-real, magical way. This metamorphosis, or change, can be as mild or as wild as you want. Your character could wake up with different colored hair or could be totally transformed into an animal, an inanimate object, or even an entirely different person.

For example, your character could wake up and, like the character in Kafka's *The Metamorphosis*, find that there is something different about the way they look. Your character could become ill with a disease that turns their skin blue or red, striped or polka-dotted. Your character could touch hands with another person and completely switch bodies! Just run with it!

CREATING A NONREALISTIC SIX-SENTENCE STORY

Answer the following questions with one sentence each to create a six-sentence story.

As you write, create a nonrealistic character and scene, or mix together nonrealistic and realistic elements of character and scene.

1. Write a sentence that describes your character's appearance: Laverne had the short, curled hair of an older woman who knew how to use a set of hot rollers.

_____

_____

_____

2. Write a sentence that describes your character's situation: She stood in the grocery store watching the man pile new pears onto a larger pile of older pears, some of which looked to be soft and rotting.

_____

_____

_____

3. Write a sentence that expresses your character's greatest fear about

this situation: She feared the stock boy would never quit stacking those pears, those soft, beautiful pears, that he would continue on forever.

_____

_____

_____

4. Write a sentence that expresses your character's greatest joy in this situation: She stood still, the stock boy, in her mind, pausing for a moment to serve her a slice of fruit and the fruit hitting her lips with a moist graininess, a grit she would be satisfied to never have end.

_____

_____

_____

5. Write a sentence that describes a new way your character has to interact with the world because of this situation or the way the character would like to respond to the situation: She stood patiently waiting, holding the basket with both hands tightly clenched unable to reach out and grab the fruit.

_____

_____

_____

6. Write a sentence that describes the action your character takes as a result of the conclusions that they reach in sentence number 5: So she waits, white-knuckled, watching the boy bend and reach for new pears until he is finished and turns away.

_____

_____

_____

Rage Against the Creative Writing Machine

DADA IN THE HOUSE

Pia Simone Garber and Kirsten Jorgenson

Get introduced to the Dada movement and then write a "bad" poem and cut it up Dada style.

The true Dadas are against Dada.

—Tristan Tzara

We have always made mistakes, but the greatest mistakes are the poems we have written.

—Tristan Tzara

AT THE BEGINNING OF WORLD War I, a group of European poets and artists fled their home countries to the relative safety of neutral Switzerland. There they found each other, got organized, started their own movement, and opened their own venue, the Cabaret Voltaire. They were the first Dadaists. In response to the utter destruction and chaos of WWI, they rejected the notion of any system of meaning-making. Systems meant power and they had seen how power led to war. Art, as they saw it, even avant-garde art, was a system and, therefore, something to be avoided. What they created was "anti-art." The anti-art of the Dadaists resisted the notion that art could be redeeming in any way. Anti-art was not meant to heal the destruction of WWI; in a way, it sought to further the destruction.

For instance, Hugo Ball, who founded *Dada* magazine, eventually stopped composing in words and chose instead to write sound poems. Here's a section from his poem "Karawane":

> jolifanto bambla o falli bambla
> großiga m'pfa habla horem
> eigiga goramen
> higo bloiko russula huju
> hollaka hollala

At moments the sounds resemble words or are words in a different language—*habla* for instance—but the pleasure of the poem does not locate itself in meaning. Rather, you are meant to enjoy the sound of language self-destructing in the poet's mouth or in your mouth as you try to make Ball's sounds.

Tristan Tzara, also a Dada poet, invented one of the best-known and often used Dada techniques: the cut-up poem. He would literally pull a poem out of a hat by cutting up newspapers, putting each word in a hat, mixing them up, and then composing a poem by pulling the words out in a new, random order. Here is an example of one of his Dada poems:

> when dogs cross the air in a diamond like ideas and the appendix of
> the meninx tells the time of the alarm programme.

This makes no sense! Of course it makes no sense; it's *DADA!* Like Hugo Ball's sound poems, Tzara's cut-up poems rely on the destruction of meaning to facilitate the reader's pleasure, which sounds suspiciously like a technique that somehow "saves" art from itself, which is *so* not Dada.

As a Dada artist, Richard Huelsenbeck said of the movement, the goal was "the liberation of the creative forces from the tutelage of the advocates of power." Later, poet Ed Sanders would characterize the Dada strategy as "a total assault on the culture." I would say they were punk rock before punk rock ever dreamed of a mohawk. But, just as the commercial success of the Sex Pistols heralded the end of punk rock at the very moment it was beginning, Dada was destined to collapse precisely because it was a movement and, thus, organized, replicated, and made into a system. Once it became a movement, in other words, it became "Art," which is why Tristan Tzara said that "the true Dadas are against Dada." The true Dadas are against the redemptive myth of "Art," are against movements.

Creating Your Own Dada Cut-up Poetry

Now that you've been introduced to the crazy world of Dada, it's time to let loose. We're going to do some Dada-inspired poetry experimentation! This works great as a solo activity but is *really* fun as a group activity, so get four or five people together for some unbelievable results. You will also need some materials: each group member should have a piece of paper to record the evolution of their poem as well as a piece of paper that can be cut up. Each group should have a bag, box, or hat to collect their cut-up poetry in.

Step 1. Create a "bad" poem. Before you can cut up a poem you have to have a poem to cut up. What kind of poem deserves such treatment? How about the cheesiest love poem you could ever write! After all, Tristan Tzara did say that some of our greatest mistakes are the poems we write. So, write a poem full of clichés so sappy and sweet it makes you sick. Get together with your group members and compile a list of at least twenty typical love poem words (or just do it yourself if your friends are too lame to come over and destroy language with you). Include any words you think might belong in a terrible love poem. Some examples of over-used words in love poems are: *sweet, sunshine, darling,* and *rose.*

Post your list where you can all see it. Everyone in the group should spend about ten minutes writing a poem using this list as inspiration. Try to see how many of the words you can fit into one poem. Using the word examples listed above, one poem might look like:

> Oh my darling,
> my bright rose!
> I love you more than
> the sweet shiny sunshine.

Now everyone has a really cliché love poem ready to be cut up!

Step 2. Cut up your poem. You have a delightfully awful poem in your hands, but what do you do with it? Cut it up! Now, before you cut it up, you want to make sure you keep a copy of it, so keep the piece of paper you wrote it on intact and write out a second copy on a new sheet of paper to be cut up. Make sure to leave lots of space between each word because you are going to rip, tear, and cut up this poem one word at a time! The poem above is fifteen words and, therefore, would result in fifteen pieces. As you tear or scissor off each word, toss it into your group's bag or hat. When everyone has put all their words in the hat, shake it up! Mix all your words together into word soup.

Step 3. Create the final product. Now it's time to set up your paper for your final poem. On your paper you should create a space for your new poem using the same format as your original poem. If your first line had three words in the original, then the new one should have three words as

well. Make a space for each word, and don't forget to include the punctu-
ation marks. Using the poem modeled in step one, the paper would look
like this:

_____ _____ _____,
_____ _____ _____!
_____ _____ _____ _____ _____
_____ _____ _____ _____.

After you set up your paper, each member in the group should take
turns dipping into the hat full of word soup. The first word you pull out
should go in the first blank space on your page. The second word you
pull out should go in the second blank space, and so on. Fill up your
poem with words pulled one at a time from the hat. Then take a look at
your completed Dada poem. Have your group read your poems aloud,
first the original and then the crazy Dada version!

The Beats and Scribbled Secret Notebooks

CHOSEN WORDS AND AUTOMATIC WRITING

Stephen Hess and Curtis Rutherford

An introduction to Beat poetry complete with how to write like Jack Kerouac.

THEY WERE THE BEAT GENERATION or Beatniks or just Beats. Whatever you call them, they were a group of writers who rose to fame through rebelling against the controlling principles that dominated America in the 1950s. They wanted people to be wild and loose, not just in their writing, but their lives, too! The Beats were crowd-pleasers; they loved to give upbeat, jazzy, and sometimes revolutionary readings. Through their message of spiritual rebellion, the Beats paved the trails of individuality and dissent that the so-called "hippie" counterculture of the sixties and early seventies traveled down. In becoming familiar with the history and writings of this super-crazy movement of self-celebration, we will write poems and other pieces that take advantage of the expressive techniques used by the Beats.

Here are some books by Beat writers that you'll love:

Allen Ginsberg, *Collected Poems of Allen Ginsberg 1947–1997* (2007)
Gary Snyder, *Riprap* (1959)
Charles Bukowski, *Post Office* (1971)
Gregory Corso, *Long Lie Man* (1962)
William S. Burroughs, *Naked Lunch* (1959)
Jack Kerouac, *On the Road* (1959)

GETTIN' IN THE MOOD

Jack Kerouac (1922–1969) was one of the fathers of the Beat movement. He had a totally whacked-out style of writing. After a mountain climbing trip with Zen-minded naturalist and fellow Beat writer Gary Snyder, Kerouac began to be influenced by Buddhist thought. This Zen influence mixed with Kerouac's love for bebop and jazz music to produce what he called spontaneous prose. It's a stream of consciousness style where, when you write, you just let your mind go—and go—and go. Kerouac even went as far as using dashes at the end of sentences rather than periods, so the lines of prose would read like lines of music. How can something this unlimited and liberated produce such wonderful writing? Well, ol' Jack had an outline he followed. He called this outline the "Belief and Technique for Modern Prose," which is a list of "thirty essentials" about how to write.

The essentials were warm-up activities, writing habits, and lifestyle choices that Kerouac believed led him to such phenomenal writing. Consider these maxims selected from Jack Kerouac's "Belief and Technique for Modern Prose":

1. Scribbled secret notebooks, and wild typewritten pages, for your own joy
2. Submissive to everything, open, listening
4. Be in love with your life
5. Something that you feel will find its own form
13. Remove literary, grammatical and syntactical inhibition
15. Telling the true story of the world in interior monolog
17. Write in recollection and amazement for yourself
22. Don't think of words when you stop but to see picture better
24. No fear or shame in the dignity of yr experience, language & knowledge
28. Composing wild, undisciplined, pure, coming in from under, crazier the better

Pretty wild! Kerouac understood that to be a serious writer you had to have a process and good writing habits. The more you write, the easier it is to write. If you don't already have a writing process, or way of getting in the mood to write, now is a good time to start thinking about it. The earlier you can begin a process, the greater the chances you have to churn out some writing you'll be really pleased with.

So what is this process? Like Kerouac's "scribbled secret notebooks," it is great to always have a notebook so you can jot down words and phrases that catch your ear. This could be while you are walking around at school or watching television. Keeping a list of favorite words and phrases is a great way to have a bulk of material you can draw from. Can you write an

entire piece by beginning with a single interesting word? The answer is
YES! I have. Many, many times. Want me to walk you through it? I will.

While in college, I worked for a retail store. My boss told me to take
some supplies to the store's vestibule. *Vestibule!* The word rang in my ear
all day, so I quickly jotted it down. I thought maybe I could work with
this word and play with its meaning in a poem. I began to think about
the definition of a vestibule, *a passage, hall, or antechamber between the
outer door and the interior parts of a house or building.* Now how could I
mess with this definition in an interesting and new way? I first decided
to place a *vestibule* in geographic terms rather than structural. So I began
with a title, "Vestibule of Our South," and wrote a poem about a speaker
standing on the Texas/Louisiana border, what some consider the western
entranceway to the southern states. I kept in mind the definition of the
word and included things that one might see or hear in this entranceway
with the speaker experiencing them as one would experience a building
from its vestibule. Tada!

> It's the smell of the Louisiana
> > border yards away, he sees deer illegal to
> > shoot,
> > like the strains of grass
> > straddling the rim of names

The speaker is on a hunting trip, standing on the border of Texas and
Louisiana (at the Sabine River) on the Texas side, his view of the entry-
way to the American South. He considers the elements, the animals, the
smells, as if they are on display for him across the geographical thresh-
old. Later in the poem, the speaker decides that he has no access to the
things he wants (the animals he is there to hunt). So, he imagines taking
the life of many other animals on the Texas side of the river but no deer
in Louisiana just yards away, so he can go home a hero. He'll have a lot of
dead animals, but no real prize for himself personally.

> how
> many of his bullets will hurry
> past the river through skin
> and oxygen hoping to eventually land

inside heroic
ear ringing, with dead things
all around the home-
side frame.

This is a poem about arbitrary borders in our mind, our cultures, and
geographically. Isn't it strange that you can commit one act in one part of
the country, but it is illegal in another area? Are you still a criminal? All
these ideas came from one single word!

Kerouac was interested in writing from the bottomless bottom of the
mind, and he totally believed in personal experience for inspiration. He
believed in getting a flow of words going.

Before I begin writing, I like to do some automatic writing. Automatic
writing is when you give yourself a certain amount of time, and in that
time you just write/type nonstop, never lifting your pen from the paper
or your fingers from the keyboard. Write gibberish if you have to, just as
long as you don't stop writing words and phrases that spring from your
mind. I find that this empties me of all the language in my head, gets the
words out onto the paper to start with a clear mind. I prefer to use a word
processor when I write, so after I do this writing for five minutes, I save
and date the file. After I do this about twenty-five to thirty times through-
out a month or so, I print out all my automatic writing files, going back
through and marking things that sound interesting. I use this with my
words and phrases notebook as a backup plan if I run into a wall or if I
am having trouble getting started. So you can collect words like *"vesti-
bule"* in your journal as you go through your day, or you sit can down and
generate words through a timed automatic writing session.

Exercise: Start with five minutes of automatic writing. Just let your
mind flow. Let the words come and do not stop writing, even if you have
to type the same words over and over again. Let yourself free associate
with different ideas. After five minutes you should have about a half page
to a full page.

Now, choose a word from your favorite word list (like I did with *vesti-
bule*) or from your automatic writing, and start to think about all the dif-
ferent meanings of that word. Think about all the different ways you can
use your chosen word.

Then go back to your automatic writing and start to move some words around and add your chosen word to the page. Try different combinations of words, and find a few patterns you like. Try to hone the page you wrote into a poem that uses your chosen word as a catalyst, a springboard. Don't worry too much about making sense. It's okay if you end up cutting out nearly all that you wrote in the first five minutes. This is just to get your brain going and to help you get those creative juices flowing.

"I'm with You in Rockland"

"Howl" and Praise Poems

Stephen Hess and Curtis Rutherford

Like Allen Ginsberg writing "Howl," write your own praise poem.

THE LONG POEM "HOWL" BY Allen Ginsberg, published in 1956, is one of the most important and widely known American poems of all time, right up there next to T.S. Eliot's "The Waste Land." "Howl" is written in the "spontaneous prose" style Ginsberg learned from his friend, the writer Jack Kerouac. I know I have some cool writer friends, but they haven't yet helped me write a tour de force the way Kerouac helped Ginsberg. Maybe that will happen soon, and I'll end up with lines as famous as these first ones from "Howl": "I saw the best minds of my generation destroyed by madness, starving hysterical naked."

"Howl" quickly became a rallying cry for young people in America to break away from the iron grip of the dominant lifestyles and politics of the 1950s. Ginsburg first read "Howl" to a packed house at the Six Gallery in San Francisco. It was a huge event in poetry and the beginning of what some began calling the Beat movement. After Ginsberg's first reading of "Howl," word began to spread. Poets and critics came to realize how important this poem was—its rawness, its blunt power, its sheer exhilaration and anger mixed all together in a giant swirl. With lines like "who disappeared into the volcanoes of Mexico leaving behind nothing but the shadow of dungarees and the lava and ash of poetry scattered in fireplace Chicago" we can experience this exhilaration and anger. Remember, in the mid-1950s, life wasn't very free and accepting of people like Allen Ginsberg and poems like "Howl." This was before the Internet and MTV. Can you imagine a world like that? The American government actually went so far as to charge Allen Ginsberg and his publisher, Lawrence Ferlinghetti's City Lights, with obscenity and tried to ban "Howl." Well, Ginsberg and City Lights won the court case! And Ginsberg became a youth hero for challenging America's phobia of the unfamiliar. Ah yes, "the best minds of [his] generation" were heroic!

The poem is dedicated to one of those "great minds," a fellow named Carl Solomon. Carl Solomon and Ginsberg met and became kindred spirits when they were both in a psychiatric hospital in New York. In "Howl," Ginsberg fictionalizes the mental hospital, giving it the name "Rockland," which actually references another mental institution, Pilgrim State Hospital. The third section of the poem is a direct address to Solomon at the hospital:

> Carl Solomon! I'm with you in Rockland
>   where you're madder than I am
> I'm with you in Rockland
> where you must feel very strange
> I'm with you in Rockland
> where you imitate the shade of my mother

Ginsberg is admiring Carl Solomon while melding American madness and personal frustrations all at once. The result is gorgeous—sometimes scary, often funny, but never hackneyed or disingenuous—as the poem's energy builds:

> I'm with you in Rockland
>   where we wake up electrified out of the coma by our own
>   souls' airplanes roaring over the roof they've come
>   to drop angelic bombs the hospital illuminates itself
>   imaginary walls collapse O skinny legions run out-
>   side O starry spangled shock of mercy the eternal
>   war is here O victory forget your underwear we're
>   free

Here "Howl" nearly spins out of control, teetering on the brink of wild emotion. Read it aloud. Hear that chant of "I'm with you in Rockland" and the details that spill from it. It's mesmerizing. It's as if this Carl Solomon character will appear before you when you chant it!

Ginsberg is ecstatic. But how does he use writing to get all that energy across? He starts with a **repeating element** ("I'm with you in Rockland"). A repeating element (word or phrase) at the beginning of lines or sentences is called **anaphora**. From there, he lets the details spill out. He decides it's ok, in his poem, to have run-on sentences or nonstandard uses of punctuation.

Here in this excerpt from "Footnote to Howl," he does it again, using anaphora and the "detail spill" to turn his energy into lots of praise:

> Holy the solitudes of skyscrapers and pavements! Holy the cafete-
>   rias filled with the millions! Holy the mysterious rivers
>   of tears under the streets!
> Holy the lone juggernaut! Holy the vast lamb of the middle class!
>   Holy the crazy shepherds of rebellion!

Notice that the details are a crazy mix of associations—in the same passage we have cafeterias, skyscrapers, mysterious rivers of tears, and the "crazy shepherds of rebellion"!

We learn a lot as writers by emulating the moves other writers make. We've just seen Ginsberg use anaphora and "detail spill" as a way of praising what he loves. Now let's watch another writer do the very same thing.

Although he was born 204 years before Ginsberg, Christopher Smart wrote a long poem that is akin to Ginsberg's "Howl." This book-length poem, the *Jubilate Agno*, was written between 1759 and 1763. Although Smart was confined in a hospital because of his mental health at the time, he was not alone. His cat, Jeoffry, was allowed to stay with him in the hospital. Jeoffry managed to work his way into his master's poem. Here, Smart uses anaphora and a range of details to praise Jeoffry:

> For I will consider my Cat Jeoffry.
> . . . .
> For he counteracts the Devil, who is death, by brisking about the life
> . . . .
> For he is the cleanest in the use of his forepaws of any quadruped.
> . . . .
> For he is the quickest to his mark of any creature.
> For he is tenacious of his point.
> For he is a mixture of gravity and waggery.
> . . . .
> For he can swim for life.
> For he can creep.

Like Ginsberg in "Howl," Smart creates a meditative, almost prayer-like poem by means of anaphora—his repeating *for* at the beginning of each line. Throughout the poem, Smart praises not just his cat, but lots of things, sometimes introducing new subjects with every line:

> For I rejoice like a worm in the rain in him that cherishes and from him that tramples.
>
> . . . .
>
> For the names and number of animals are as the names and number of the stars.
>
> . . . .
>
> For I have a nephew CHRISTOPHER to whom I implore the grace of God.
>
> . . . .
>
> For I bless God in the honey of the sugar-cane and the milk of the cocoa.
>
> For I bless God in the libraries of the learned & for all booksellers in the world.
>
> . . . .
>
> For MATTER is the dust of the earth, every atom of which is the life.
>
> . . . .
>
> For Fire is a mixed nature of body & spirit, & the body is fed by that which hath not life.
>
> . . . .
>
> For WATER is not of solid constituents, but is dissolved from precious stones above.
>
> For the life remains in its dissolvent state, and that in great power.
>
> . . . .
>
> For the SEA is a seventh of the Earth—the spirit of the Lord by Esdras.
>
> . . . .
>
> For MERCURY is affected by the AIR because it is of a similar subtlety.
>
> . . . .
>
> For SUCKTION is the withdrawing of the life, but life will follow as fast as it can.
>
> . . . .
>
> For a LION roars HIMSELF compleat from head to tail.

Now, like Ginsberg and Smart, the time has come for you to sing in praise of the world around you.

WRITING A PRAISE POEM

It's easy: write in praise of the world around you, for about thirty minutes. Here are the guidelines:

- Like Ginsberg and Smart, use anaphora. Begin each line with a word like *for* or *holy* or with a phrase like "I'm with you in _____," or use another repeating word or phrase that you make up.
- In each line, address a specific person, place, thing, or idea.
  i.e., *For my mother*
- Now, sing praise to them.
  i.e., *For my mother who wakes up early every morning and . . .*
- Try to avoid clichés. Write really long sentences sometimes and short sentences other times. Instead of writing, *For my mother who wakes up early every morning and makes me breakfast. I love her* (although such a line may be truthful, the purpose of this exercise is for you to explore your praise in *new* ways), try:

For my mother who wakes up early every morning and cooks me eels for breakfast and carefully drives me to school in her hovercraft while listening to music I don't like but I never say anything because I know it would upset her and I know she likes to listen to her music in the morning when she wakes up for me and cooks me a breakfast of eels and then drives me to school in her hovercraft.

or

For my mother who is not an eel.

Try to obsess over a single topic for a few lines every now and then.

- Change the topic as much as you like as you go along. Let your mind drift and free associate as you go!
- Who or what might be in your praise poem?
  - A family member
  - A friend
  - A historical act

- Foods/meals/consumption-related things
- Your own alphabet
- A foreign language
- A domesticated animal
- An undomesticated animal
- The sky
- A deceased person
- A person who you don't know who performs a service for you
- A city, town, or place
- A color
- A smell
- Anything else you can think of

Here's a student example of a praise poem written by Adam Seale, who makes connections between family members, school subjects, and Steve Jobs, among other things, in his song of praise:

For Thought, Emotion, and Abstraction
This is for my Sister
who reminds me every day
that annoying and loving is life
For the machine that is happy
when its work is sad

For the president who wins the day
(most days)
For math, which is constant
except when it's a variable

For my teachers in the third,
fourth, and eleventh grades
(God help them all)

For the blank page, who is a challenger
on boring days

For my mother and father
for putting up with one another for
the requisite nine months

For magnets, for always sticking with it
For Steve Jobs
and his fruity logic

For God
for his most excellently efficient although
somewhat boggy quasi-random
associative sorting algorithms

For pencils, paper, keyboards, typewriters, and notebooks
To keep it all for a while.

A Call to Arms

RALLY THE TROOPS

Curtis Rutherford

Like the Beats, turn your anger into writing that explodes from the page, calling society and your fellow writers to action.

N ow. THE BEATS WERE NOT only about praising the natural world and their friends; they were not all smiles and rainbows. They were angry. They were idealists. They were fed up with the world around them, and they spoke out during a time when very few people spoke out. They performed their poems on stage and passionately fought those who tried to ban their books. Their message to the public was to get up and get with it! They wanted to change the world and expressed this in their poetry. Let's learn to turn our anger into poems that explode from the page, slapping the reader in the face.

Consider the following questions and, in a notebook, jot down a few of your ideas (don't worry about making complete sentences).

1. What about society/America/your town/the world/government/your school (i.e., be as general or specific as you like) makes you angry? Try to think of things that affect not only you, but your classmates, family, friends, etc.
2. Can these problems be fixed? If yes, how? If no, why?
3. What are some words that you hate? Ever been called a name? Ever had someone assume something about you that isn't true? Why do you think they thought this?
4. What are some current trends in politics, media, school, or music that you think are silly or not genuine?
5. Are you scared of something that is out of your hands? Something in government? Something global, national, or local?

Lawrence Ferlinghetti went to court to support Allen Ginsberg and their right to publish "Howl." Well, Ferlinghetti was a poet, too. He wrote a poem that was angry! It was a call to arms! It was called "Populist Man-ifesto No. 1." The opening stanza reads:

> Poets, come out of your closets,
> Open your windows, open your doors,
> You have been holed-up too long
> in your closed worlds.

Wow! He starts the poem off by calling-out his fellow poets. The poem continues,

> No time now for the artist to hide
> above, beyond, behind the scenes,
> indifferent, paring his fingernails,
> refining himself out of existence.
> No time now for our little literary games,
> no time now for our paranoias & hypochondrias,
> no time now for fear & loathing,
> time now only for light & love.
> We have seen the best minds of our generation
> destroyed by boredom at poetry readings.
> Poetry isn't a secret society,
> It isn't a temple either.

So, here's your next writing exercise.

Take one or two items from the ideas you just wrote down in your notebooks. Have a certain subject in mind, your schoolmates, your fel-low writers, your pets, anyone you feel like you want to rally! Now begin a poem where the first stanza mirrors that of Ferlinghetti's first stanza of "Populist Manifesto, No.1." Fill in the blanks like so:

> _____ come out of your _____,
> Open your _____, open your _____,
> You have been _____ too long
> in your _____. . . .
> No time for the _____ to _____
> _____, _____, the _____,

_____, _____ his _____,

_____ _____.

You can also try this with a poem like "Bomb" by Gregory Corso. The original is a very long poem. The last section of the poem reads,

> Flowers will leap in joy their roots aching
> Fields will kneel proud beneath the halleluyahs of the wind
> Pinkbombs will blossom Elkbombs will perk their ears
> Ah many a bomb that day will awe the bird a gentle look
> Yet not enough to say a bomb will fall
> or even contend celestial fire goes out
> Know that the earth will madonna the Bomb
> that in the hearts of men to come more bombs will be born
> magisterial bombs wrapped in ermine all beautiful
> and they'll sit plunk on earth's grumpy empires
> fierce with moustaches of gold

You can change the original poem any way you like, taking sections out, changing some lines completely. Here's an example using a different set of lines from "Bomb":

O _____ I _____ you.

I want to _____. I want to eat your _____.

You are a _____, a _____, and
a _____.

Yes! Yes! Into our _____ you will _____.

The people will scream, "_____."

And you will yell back, "_____."

O_____ you _____ me.

I want to tell you _____. You are _____.

Your _____ and your _____ are not the same, but I _____.

The earth will _____, with _____.

Once you've filled in the blanks and have a beginning for your poem, keep writing for twenty minutes. Keep going with your call to arms, complaint, rally, etc., and get specific about the details of the problem.

Stealing Tone

PICKING UP WHERE YOUR FAVORITE AUTHORS LEFT OFF

Molly Goldman

Identify an author's moves and make them your own.

T. S. ELIOT TAUGHT US "immature poets imitate, mature poets steal."
Of course, various iterations of that idea have been said by many authors and artists, which brings us to the question of what we can steal from our favorite writers. When I first began writing, I couldn't help stealing. I would write in the style of whatever author I was currently reading. Eventually I found a way to internalize what I had learned and filter my work back out of me in a hybridization of styles from all the writing I ever liked.

In this exercise we aim to do just that. We want to take various elements of different pieces—maybe tone from one piece, character from another, plot from another—and synthesize them into something new. The goal is to identify what moves are being made in each piece, and then try to make them your own. How can you write in the voice of that character? What would you have to do in order to sound like that author?

Read Russell Edson's "The Taxi."

One night in the dark I phone for a taxi. Immediately a taxi crashes through the wall; nevermind that my room is on the third floor, or that the yellow driver is really a cluster of canaries arranged in the shape of a driver, who flutters apart, streaming from the windows of the taxi in the yellow fountains. . . .

Realizing that I am in the midst of something splendid I reach for the phone and cancel the taxi: All the canaries flow back into the taxi and assemble themselves into a cluster shaped like a man. The taxi backs through the wall, and the wall repairs. . . .

But I cannot stop what is happening, I am already reaching for the phone to call a taxi, which is already beginning to crash through the wall with its yellow driver already beginning to flutter apart.

Now let's identify exactly what happens in that story on a literal plot level:

- A man calls for a taxi from his third-floor room.
- A taxi comes crashing into the wall.
- The driver is made of many canaries and they all begin to fly around the room.
- The man is pleased and decides not to leave, so he calls to cancel the taxi.
- This causes the taxi to retreat. The wall becomes normal again.
- The man cannot stop himself from calling again; the taxi comes back.

Great story! Wish I had written it. So now let's try to rewrite it:

Edson's version depicts a speaker who does not reveal much about himself. He refers to the scene as "splendid" but that's all we get from him in the way of opinion. How would a new voice reveal more about the character? What if we could rewrite the story as a very awkward or anxious person?

> Michael is already at the party, which is okay, but he was going to tell me before he went so that maybe we could go together, but I guess he just decided to go without me. So now I'm all alone and have to get to the party and I'm going to call a taxi, even though I already took one today to go to the doctor to have my growth looked at. The taxi comes crashing through the wall ruining everything! And now my room is filled with dust, which I am highly allergic to . . . etc, etc.

Or what if we wrote the story in negatives?

> It is not morning in a submarine where I do not call for an elevator. The driver is not a cluster of non-green canaries. The canaries do not melt into the air. I do not let it continue. The canaries do not live in a birdcage.

Or what about a homophonic translation?

> Sunlight of the larks home for a nap, see. A break brackish broom the fall.

We just wrote a bunch of stories and we didn't even have to have any ideas for a story! The focus changes with each different style that is applied, and new things about the story become more important or more noticeable. The story can come from one place, and the style from another, but ultimately the synthesis of those two things is entirely yours.

Try to rewrite Edson's piece in a variety of ways. Here are some possible approaches:

- From the point of view of the building manager
- As a newspaper article
- From the point of view of a character who is bored or near death or in a hurry
- As a list of "splendid" things, just one of which is the canaries
- Think of two more ways you could "steal" from this piece

A Journal of Particulars

Become a Zen Master of Your Senses

Jenny Gropp and Kirsten Jorgenson

In this journal-based exercise, get better acquainted with the five senses and write places into a more vivid existence.

Have you ever thought about what a dog's really doing when it's sticking its head out the car window? It's having more fun than meets the eye, literally—dogs have the power to catch a whiff of something that's a million times less concentrated than what humans can detect. That's pretty intense!

You, too, can learn to have supersenses—by writing. In this exercise you're going to learn how to become a dog, getting down and dirty with the five senses, sniffing, tasting, seeing, hearing, and digging up one detail at a time. You'll learn what colors smell like and how to touch sounds. You'll spend time with a journal in a favorite place and learn how to reinvent it with words so your reader really feels like they are there.

Writing the "Particulars" of Sense

In the preface to his book *Paterson*, William Carlos Williams gives a key to how to begin unlocking your supersensing powers:

> To make a start,
> out of particulars
> and make them general, rolling
> up the sum, by defective means—
> sniffing the trees,
> just another dog
> among a lot of other dogs.

Williams's quest is for "Rigor of beauty," and these are the first steps he takes on that journey. The first two lines, "To make a start, / out of particulars," gives you a specific goal—to look for details, the smallest details. When you're writing, don't just give big sweeping descriptions of a place, like "the cold, white room." Get into the *particulars* of that room.

Tell your reader why it's cold, why it's white. Maybe it's snowy outside and the room is "a winter-shot room." That detail gives your reader a better way to place the room in the world—it begins to distinguish it from every other room. So always keep the particulars in mind. When you have several details about a place, you begin to get a whole sum of it. So there's your first rule of how to become a super-sensing specialist: "to make a start / out of particulars," which will help you in "rolling / up the sum" of that place.

Williams also says that this process should be done "by defective means." Your descriptions might not always come easily to you at first, but as you become a master of your senses, you'll be able to write the particulars of a place with much more ease. Hence you should get to work and start "sniffing the trees" repeatedly for practice. Eventually, you'll become more accurate at stating particulars, and your "means" won't seem as "defective."

This brings us to our second point: the "sniffing." Yes, "the sniffing." Never forget that in order to access the particulars of a place, you'll need to use your senses. One writer who has amazing control of his senses, and thus of particulars, is Aram Saroyan. Saroyan often puts a single particular on one page; he also only uses one sense to access that particular. Let's take a look at a page from Saroyan's poem "Sled Hill Voices: Summer 1965, Woodstock, New York":

Sunday

as the
grass's
cut

and its smell
rises
twice

That's all there is on the page. Think about the effect of that: by focusing on a single sense—smell—Saroyan makes his reader experience, with clarity, a particular about a place.

Now turn the page and see what Saroyan does next:

incomprehensible birds

Boom! Saroyan has moved to the sense of sight and shown us what's happening with his eyes. Now we can smell the grass and try, along with Saroyan, to comprehend the movements of the birds in the space.

And again, two pages later:

the noises of the garden among the noises of the room

Saroyan's introduction of a third sense, hearing, allows him to place the reader inside the room with him. And by using sound, he's allowed us to see that the windows are open in the room. With just three short snippets of text, Saroyan has shown us how to use the senses to become a master of particulars and given us a "sum" of that place.

A JOURNAL OF PARTICULARS
Now let's practice "sniffing," and using all the other senses as well. Write for about fifteen minutes, spending one to two minutes on each question below.

1. Picture yourself in a place. It can be any place in the world, inside or outside. Write the name of that place in your journal.
2. Now think about what you can see in that place. Start describing it in your journal.
3. Now there's a sound in your place. What is it? What does it sound like?
4. How does the sound change the room? How does it make you feel?
5. If you're inside, can you hear sounds outside? What are they? If you're outside, can you hear sounds coming from inside places?
6. There's weather in your place. What kind of weather is it? If you're inside, how does it look through the window? How does it affect the room? If you're outside, what does the weather do to you? To the landscape? How does it look?
7. Find something to touch in your space. What is it? What does it feel like?
8. Now there's a smell in your place. What is it? What does it remind you of?
9. Find somewhere to sit down in your place. Where is it? What kind of surface or thing are you sitting on? How does it feel? How do you feel now that you're sitting down? Do you want to leave? Why or why not?

Continuing Your Journal of Particulars

As you saw in the preface of William Carlos Williams's *Paterson*, you can best understand your surroundings (and yourself) by getting in touch with your senses. A good way to do this is, as Williams says, "To make a start, / out of particulars."

As you also saw, Aram Saroyan is a master of particulars. He loves their power, often putting just one "particular" on each page. And, even better, when you put those particulars together, they offer a whole portrait of a place. This will be the goal of your journal: to get in tune with the particulars of a place in order to better understand it.

When you're writing in your journal, keep in mind that there are many different approaches to how this can work. You can stick with writing one-sense particulars, like Saroyan, or choose to write only in prose. Or you can mix prose and poetry, like the Japanese author Matsuo Basho did in his travel journals. Basho, who lived from 1644 to 1694, was the most famous author of Japanese haiku poems; so famous, in fact, that he made his living as a teacher and a writer of haiku. Basho is also celebrated for his many travels around Japan, which he recorded in his travel journals. These journals are a blend of haiku and prose, which allowed Basho's talent in haiku to aid him in explaining his travels. In one of his journals, *Back Roads to Far Towns*, Basho recounts part of a nine-month journey with his friend Sora:

> While sitting down on a stone to rest, I noticed a cherry tree only three feet high and about half blossomed out. Although it is buried by the snow that piles up so deeply here, this late blossomer does not forget the spring, and I found its spirit touching. It is as though the plum blossoms in dead summer that one reads of in Chinese verse were giving off their fragrance here, as if the touching cherry tree that Bishop Gyosan wrote of had blossomed again, and such recollections make this tree seem yet more precious.
>
> The customary discipline of pilgrims does not allow me to give a detailed description of the area around Mount Yudono, and more than that, we are not even to write of it. Returning from Gassan to our lodging at Minamidani, at the urging of Egaku we wrote out on poem cards some of the verses we had composed in our walking tour of the three mountains of Dewa.

How cool it is—
The crescent moon seen faintly
On Mount Haguro.
The peak of clouds
Forms and crumbles, forms and
crumbles—
But Gassan in moonlight!
No one may relate
The mysteries of Mount Yudono;
Yet tears wet my sleeves.

Basho constantly relies on the haiku to powerfully present particulars in his journals. His readers, we think, appreciate the shift in tone back and forth from prose and poetry.

Another example of an innovative journal is Geraldine Kim's *Povel*. Kim, who was born in 1983, likes to write in a near-stream-of-consciousness style:

A piece of fruit, that's what we are. Call me "leftovers." "Lentil soup," he says to the customer. A line of customers behind me and I am wearing a velvet jacket. Like during gym class when team captains would choose people for their teams and you're the only one left.

Kim's style is all about associating the particulars in the room with the particulars in her mind; she lets the space she's in inspire her mind. As you can see, she's in line at a restaurant, and the situation has inspired her to think of other things: people are "fruit" and her position at the front of the "line of customers" reminds her of being "the only one left" when "team captains would choose people for their teams" in gym class. Here, she shows her powers of association again:

It had to have been the car we were driving in. "How did this car pass inspection?" I ask the sticker on the windshield. "Everything is used," my dad says. Last time I was here was when I came back from visiting my ex. The leaf pattern of airport carpeting. Some people would find it annoying.

Kim's getting a handle on personal poetics. She's seizing the particulars in her space that are thought-provoking and allowing her mind to free associate on those particulars; in essence, she's creating herself while she creates her space.

Now that you've seen a few examples of unique journals, go to your journal and try out your own style. Choose one place to write about. Think about a place that might change from day to day. Here are some possible places:

- The library
- A coffee shop
- Your school cafeteria
- A park
- The movie theater
- Your porch
- Your kitchen
- Your garage

Visit this place three or four times over several days and record the particulars of that place. Remember to try to use all of your senses when you're experiencing your chosen place: sight, hearing, taste, smell, and touch (but don't worry if you can't—for example, we don't expect you to eat the books in the library to try to find something that "tastes"). Try to write for at least ten minutes, but remember, the longer you spend in your place, the faster you will become the zen master of it. Mwah ha ha . . .

Keep in mind that you can write your particulars in any way you like: you can make a list, write a poem, or write a paragraph. Anything goes, as long as you're using your senses like Basho, Kim, and Saroyan do.

When Garlic Has Hips

FOOD WRITING AND PERSONIFICATION

Jenny Gropp and Kirsten Jorgenson

Make everyday foods more vivid by giving them human characteristics and lives.

NOW THAT YOU'VE HONED YOUR super-sensing skills and begun to pay attention to the vast world outside of yourself and outside of your head by observing and cataloguing the particulars of your chosen location from "A Journal of Particulars" (see p. 288), it's time to focus your senses on the smaller things that inhabit the landscape. It's time to switch out your binoculars and gaze through the microscope, and let your imagination roam as you do so.

M. F. K. Fisher is the standard by which good food writing is measured in part because she understands how language is elemental like ingredients and needs to be carefully mixed and arranged in order to produce something delicious, but also because preparing food demands that the cook engage all of their senses to touch, taste, feel, see, and hear the ingredients to check their quality, to gauge how they are mixing together, to determine how they should be passed on to guests or family waiting at the table. In her essay, "Made with Love, by Hand," a potato is not simply brown, it "make[s] itself felt in the hand, is something that makes me smile to think of: sturdy, jolly, a bluff good-natured joke!" A head of cabbage is "so promising within its graceful skirts" and eggplants are "beautiful, like cool satin dyed for an ancient emperor's favorite lady."

Locate a fruit or vegetable that has layers (like the potato or a lime or garlic or a banana, you get the picture). Now try to think about your fruit or vegetable like Fisher did, by using your senses. What does it look like? What does it smell like—not only now, but, for example, if you cook it or if you let it rot? What does it feel like? What might it sound like? You can consider it just as it is on the table in front of you, but you can also consider how it might feel if you cut it open or did something else with it.

While you're considering these things, try to push yourself further. This is where creativity and the senses get a chance to really have fun in writing. If your fruit/vegetable had a personality based on your sensory experience of it, what would it be? Remember how Fisher describes the potato: "A potato, when picked up and allowed to make itself felt in the hand, is something that makes me smile to think of: sturdy, jolly, a bluff good-natured joke!" You can take it even further than Fisher did: What might your fruit/vegetable say? Who might it offend? Who or what would it relate to well? You might also consider the gender identity of your fruit or vegetable. Again consider Fisher's description of the cabbage: "the cool weight of a firm young head of cabbage, so promising within its graceful skirts." Now write a paragraph or more, telling the reader *everything* about this fruit or vegetable.

Continue to keep your journal of particulars in your place of choice. As you write in your place, start to consider the small particulars— objects and aspects of your place. Be as probing and adventurous as M. F. K. Fisher.

Pets of the Roman Empire, Dinosaurs of Today

AVOIDING THE CUTE KITTY CAT WHEN WRITING ABOUT ANIMALS

Kirk Pinho

Envision a major world event that was caused by a pet.

I HAVE BEEN DEBATING GETTING A dog since I moved away from home, but I always find some reason not to do it—I don't have enough money to feed it; my home is too small; I don't have enough time; it would poop all over my yard, etc. Even as someone who *loves* dogs, I've never been able to get one of my own, because I would have to become financially invested in it or I would have to alter my schedule entirely just so it could sully my lawn. The human/pet relationship is complicated. Here, you will explore ways to maintain the emotional integrity of a person-pet relationship while also distancing yourself from the typical perceptions of dogs, cats, birds, fish, lizards, cows, guinea pigs, squirrels, frogs, tarantulas, yeti, etc. Poems about how cute your kitty cat is don't make the cut.

PETS IN HISTORY

What would happen if your cat, Mittens, was actually the catalyst for a third world war? What if Buckles, the dog, actually shot Lincoln? What if the fall of the Roman Empire to the barbarians of Gaul was really sparked by a disagreement over who got to ride your pony? The goal of this exercise is to get you thinking about pets in history and envision a major world event that was caused, in some way, shape, or form, by a domesticated animal. This is designed to be fun, so go nuts. But beware: the event the animal caused has to have been world-changing, and the animal that sparked the event has to be one that is commonly (or relatively commonly) kept as a pet. Dogs, cats, fish, birds, snakes, most kinds of lizards, and farm animals are all fair game—no pun intended.

DINOSAURS TODAY

People in the modern age have long studied dinosaurs, a fascination of humankind for years. Your goal for this exercise is to write a poem about a pet dinosaur, whatever kind of dinosaur that may be. Dinosaurs were formidable or even terrifying lizards. In fact, in Latin, that's actually what *dinosaur* means! The object of this writing is to give the dinosaur a personality, whether it's scary (like a tyrannosaurus) or a bit more affable (like a brontosaurus or triceratops). Name it. Mentally interview it and ask it strange questions. What wacky, bizarre, unique things does it do? Where does it sleep? What do your neighbors think about having Stanley the Stegosaurus nearby?

Your Pet Describes You

Pets see us at our best and worst (just as we do with them), never saying a word. Here's your chance not only to assume the personality of your pet, or a fictional pet, but also to examine yourself—whether it be at your kindest, your meanest, your happiest, or your saddest. The "I" in this poem or story (if you choose to use *I*) is not you, the poet or fiction writer or some other human character; it is your pet, or fictional pet, speaking. Consider the following things: How would the animal speak, if granted a voice? Would it have a lisp? Maybe it has a very aristocratic tone—I'm thinking of a cat here. What sparks this particular reflection? Is it a moment of anger towards the human? A moment of tenderness? What makes this snapshot in time particularly interesting for the pet? Consider that what is interesting for the pet also has to be interesting for your audience.

Perilous Points of View

GIANT TOADS! COCKROACHES!

Jessie Bailey, Jesse Delong, A. B. Gorham, and Lisa Tallin

Create an animal character and then stretch its wings (or gills or tentacles) out in story after story.

POSSESSED! YOU WILL INHABIT THE minds of strange and wondrous creatures, rotting vegetables, and murderers! Thanks to our time spent in English classes, when we think point of view, we normally think of first person, second person, and third person. But what about corn-chip person, person who lives in my dog's head, evil-monkey-who-lives-under-the-bed person, etc. What? You don't know those last three? You can smell as a bat smells, taste the blood of a rhinoceros, shimmy like a maraca, feel the breath of a Cornish game hen on your neck, and inhabit the psyche of a murderer.

Imagine you're a Komodo dragon running around your backyard in a kimono. How would the silk robe feel against your reptilian skin? What can you see from six inches off the ground? Would you rather eat a squirrel or chat with a garden gnome? This is your opportunity to embody a body other than your own.

Here's an excerpt from Elizabeth Bishop's "Giant Toad":

> I am too big, too big by far. Pity me.
> My eyes bulge and hurt. They are my one great beauty, even so. They see too much, above, below. And yet there is not much to see.
> . . .
> The drops run down my back, run from the corners of my down-turned mouth, run down my sides and drip beneath my belly. Perhaps the droplets on my mottled hide are pretty, like dewdrops, silver on a moldering leaf? They chill me through and through. I feel my colors changing now, my pigments gradually shudder and shift over.

Bishop gives us a backstage pass to pond life. With a laundry list of attributes (eyes, skin, mouth, even cold-bloodedness) we get a sense of where and how this toad lives. We hear the voice of the toad asking for pity and lamenting their size. The word choices (*mist, downturned mouth, drops, droplets, dewdrops, mottled, moldering*) and sentence structure (the dripping phrases to describe the rain falling on the toad's back) create a tone that is heavy and slow.

Don Marquis wrote books with a cockroach narrator. In *Archy and Mehitabel*, Archy the cockroach types out poetry detailing his life with his best friend, a cat named Mehitabel. The skinny blocks of words remind the reader of how small Archy really is. He doesn't use capital letters or apostrophes, since a cockroach, jumping from key to key on the typewriter, can only press down one key at a time. Marquis is tapping into the idea of **proprioception**, the sense of what it feels like to inhabit a particular body, in this case the small cockroach on the giant typewriter keyboard, unable to jump on the Shift key and the letters at the same time. Proprioception can help us imagine how a character paddles through a swamp, sprints through sunflowers, lounges on a bus stop bench, or eats French fries. Just get inside the body of your animal!

Now is the time (you knew it was coming) to create your own animal character.

First, figure out what animal you would like to inhabit for a while. I've started a list below. Now, add at least **five** more animals (don't go with the easy ones like cat or dog).

1. clown spider
2. duck-billed platypus
3. rhea
4. dung beetle
5. bee hummingbird
6. manatee
7. pygmy seahorse
8. _____
9. _____
10. _____
11. _____
12. _____

Second, pick an animal from the list above. Fill out the following questionnaire for your animal. Remember, you ARE the animal and you're in charge.

1. What is your signature dance move? _____

   _____

   _____

   _____

2. Your nemesis (give them a name) used to be your best friend. What happened between you two? _____

   _____

   _____

   _____

3. What would you do if a crate full of mice showed up at your door?_____

   _____

   _____

   _____

4. *National Geographic* nicknamed you _____. Why was that? _____

   _____

   _____

   _____

   _____

5. If you went to a party would you be eating the couch, buzzing in other animals' ears, peeing in the corner, battling over turf in the parking lot, or something else (describe)? _____

   _____

   _____

Finally, take twenty minutes and stretch your character's wings (or gills or tentacles) and write a one- to two-page story for this animal. Below is a list of situations to get you started. Pick one, or if you have a red-hot idea burning a hole in your cranium, make it so!

SCENARIO 1
Your animal is appealing to the NASA Board of Space Animal Travel to become the next animal sent into space alone.

SCENARIO 2

Your animal is appealing to the tribal council on *Survivor* to avoid being booted off the island.

SCENARIO 3

Your animal is the host of the game show *Cook! Or Be Cooked!* Introduce the contestants, explain the rules of the game, and predict who will win and why.

SCENARIO 4

Your brain is on fire and you create your own scenario.

When the Wrecking Ball Falls in Love

REVIVING AN INANIMATE OBJECT

Jessie Bailey, Jesse Delong, A. B. Gorham, and Lisa Tallin

Inhabit the mind, body, and soul of a strange and wondrous inanimate object of your choosing, and tell its tale.

IT'S TIME TO INHABIT THE mind, body, and soul of a strange and wondrous item. Tom Robbins explores this idea of personifying objects in his novel called *Skinny Legs and All*. Robbins's Can O'Beans and Conch Shell are trying to understand the advantages of their inanimate objectness. As objects, they are on the brink of understanding their important place among the humans. They are becoming empowered and will soon rise up and be humanlike.

> "And you [Conch Shell] and Mr. Stick—inanimate objects—will have a part in [the takeover of the world]?"
>
> "We hope so," said Conch Shell. "We were promised that we would. Is it not time that inanimate objects—and plants and animals—resume their rightful place in the affairs of the world? How long can humankind continue to slight these integral pieces of the whole reality?"

Who's to say that only the living have lives? What about the secret life of your cell phone, your pillow, the ceiling fan at school? What do these things see that you don't? What do they do when you aren't around? On the one hand, you'll want to make sure your object looks, smells, and moves like those of its kind. On the other hand, you are free to give your object a personality like Kimberly Johnson does in her poem "Wrecking Ball":

> With what stern determination I love
> That wall!—: its red height so certain I must
>
> Fling myself at it, an erratic
> Embarrassment of a fling, chain-wobbling

Through my drunk parabola to kiss
The brick. Can I help it that I kiss

With all my force? Nuzzled
To dust, all my beloveds must wish

To have gone unregarded. What do
I wish for? *The end of love.*

Notice all of the words that Johnson uses to describe the wrecking ball's movement in this poem: *fling, chain-wobbling,* and a *drunk parabola* of a kiss. These are all things that you might imagine a wrecking ball doing, right? She sticks close to the object's actual physical limitations, but uses first-person point of view. What limitations does first-person point of view put on the object's ability to explain itself? Does first-person point of view give the object any particular advantages? The poem describes a wrecking ball as it destroys all of its "beloveds" while speaking about a well-known subject, love. A brutish, destructive love. Think about the differences between a destructive wrecking ball and the softer subject of love. The combination of the two makes it interesting.

Now give it a try. Brainstorm by yourself or with others a list of twenty objects. Pick some very common objects and some stranger objects. For example, a broom, a bicycle, a neon sign, a bronze owl, a maraca, a wooden bird-shaped shoe.

Now pick one of the objects and think about how the object looks: How much does it weigh? What color is it? What does a bronze owl eat? How would a maraca move? How would a bird-shaped shoe sound when talking? Give it a personality.

Next, become the object. What kind of day are you having? How do you feel about snowfall in Alabama? Have you ever hiked the Rocky Mountains? Write a few notes down.

So, you're revved-up like an Indy car. You're full of personality quirks and trademark dance moves, and now you are ready to write. Place yourself (as the object) into one of these situations:

SCENARIO 1
Your object has amnesia.

SCENARIO 2

Your object is a lab assistant at a makeup lab.

SCENARIO 3

Your object works at a sandwich shop.

SCENARIO 4

Your object was abducted by your animal from the "Perilous Points of View" (see p. 298).

SCENARIO 5

Your object fell down into the city sewer.

These are just a few possible situations that your object can encounter. Can you think of more? Write for twenty minutes, or longer if you want. Let your object have its say. Tell us all about the situation.

The Fairest of Them All

TALKING TO OBJECTS FOR A REASON

Theodora Ziolkowski

What if we could write to our favorite piece of fruit or that cool poster hanging on our bedroom wall?

FROM FOOD TO FLOWERS TO common household objects, the need to address an inanimate *something* seems compulsory for some of the most memorable speakers in poetry and prose. The impulse *to talk* to something we know is powerless to answer back—although in some cases, objects can and *do* reply, as we will see!—is even more exciting when we consider the intentions behind our decisions to speak.

What if we could write to our favorite piece of fruit or that cool poster hanging on our bedroom wall? What if we felt compelled to talk to a doorknob or a toaster or a pancake or a beach towel or . . . the list goes on and on. When using direct address, think about all the things you might say to something that probably doesn't even have ears to hear them. The things you'd say to a snow globe are probably much different than what you'd say to your best friend, for instance. But why *the need* to talk to an object?

Let's look at an excerpt from an ode by Pablo Neruda, in which Neruda speaks to one of the more pungent vegetables in your pantry—the onion.

ODE TO THE ONION

Star of the poor,
fairy godmother
wrapped
in delicate
paper, you rise from the ground
eternal, whole, pure
like an astral seed

. . .

You make us cry without hurting us.
I have praised everything that exists,
but to me, onion, you are
more beautiful than a bird
of dazzling feathers,
you are to my eyes
a heavenly globe, a platinum goblet,
an unmoving dance
of the snowy anemone.

. . .

and the fragrance of the earth lives
in your crystalline nature.

In this ode, Neruda manages to not only talk to the onion through **praise**, but to elevate its very existence in the concluding stanzas to his ode: the onion is a "a heavenly globe," "a platinum goblet," "an unmoving dance / of the snowy anemone." For Neruda, the onion is something to be adored. Throughout the poem, Neruda keeps his praise interesting by "switching lanes." Before telling the onion it is "more beautiful than a bird" and comparing its likeness to images less and less literally like it, Neruda associates the onion with a kind of divine, earthly thing. As "eternal, whole, pure like an astral seed," the onion is an object to be praised and adored.

My favorite moment in this poem is when the speaker tells the onion, "You make us cry without hurting us." Now, think about how different the address to the onion would be if you were cutting into an onion and your eyes began to tear because of the sting. In the moment, you most likely wouldn't praise the onion the way Neruda does. In fact, you might, in a fit of annoyance, ask that onion why it made you cry!

Which brings us to our next example.

Whether from the Disney movie or the superscary Brothers Grimm tale, we're familiar with the story of Snow White. Remember the wicked queen? What was the one object she thought she could always count on?

The magic mirror is the object the queen consistently addresses. What's so neat about this magic mirror is not only the fact that the queen *interrogates* it, but that the magic mirror actually answers the queen back.

Let's look at a scene from the Grimm's fairytale:

Every morning she stood before it, looked at herself, and said:

Mirror, mirror, on the wall,
Who in this land is fairest of all?

To this the mirror answered:

You, my queen, are fairest of all.
Then she was satisfied, for she knew that the mirror spoke the truth.
Snow-White grew up and became ever more beautiful. When she was
seven years old she was as beautiful as the light of day, even more beau-
tiful than the queen herself.
One day when the queen asked her mirror:

Mirror, mirror, on the wall,
Who in this land is fairest of all?

It answered:

You, my queen, are fair; it is true.
But Snow-White is a thousand times fairer than you."

The queen doesn't just address the mirror. The reason the queen
speaks to the mirror is for answers! And it's at this point, when the mir-
ror fails to provide the queen with a response she likes, that the mirror's
words propel the rest of the fairytale forward.

We've heard Neruda addressing the onion with delight, and the queen
addressing the mirror out of a need for reassurance. Now here's a mo-
ment from William Shakespeare's play *Hamlet*, in which Ophelia, heart-
broken and despairing because of her father's death and her beloved
Hamlet losing interest in her, addresses her flowers. Ophelia's reliability
is at stake because of her unstable mental condition.

In the scene we are about to look at, Ophelia tries to understand the
tragedies of her father's death and Hamlet's estrangement by singing to
her flowers. She assigns a meaning to each flower as she gives the flower
to a particular person in the scene who evokes that idea. When you watch
this play on the stage or in a film, Ophelia is usually dramatized as

talking to the flowers. Imagine Ophelia—driven mad by her current cir-
cumstances—actually addressing these lines to her rosemary, pansies,
fennel, columbines, and rue.

Ophelia
There's rosemary, that's for remembrance; pray,
love, remember. And there is pansies; that's for
thoughts.
Laertes
A document in madness, thoughts and remembrance
fitted.
Ophelia
[To King.] There's fennel for you, and columbines.
[To Queen.] There's rue for you; and here's some
for me: we may call it herb of grace a' Sundays.
You may wear your rue with a difference. There's
a daisy. I would give you some violets, but they
withered all when my father died. They say he
made a good end—
[Sings.]
"For bonny sweet Robin is all my joy."
Laertes
Thought and affliction, passion, hell itself,
She turns to favour and to prettiness.
Ophelia
Song.
And will he not come again?
And will he not come again?
No, no, he is dead:
Go to they death-bed:
He never will come again.
His beard was as white as snow,
All flaxen was his poll:
He is gone, he is gone,
And we cast away moan:
God ha' mercy on his soul!"
And of all Christian souls, I pray God. God buy
You.

Following Ophelia's example, how does our conception of direct address change when we think of her motivation? Ophelia is an unreliable speaker when she sings to her flowers; she is grief-stricken and confused. How different from Neruda, who seems quite tickled to talk to the onion, and the fairy-tale queen, who appears focused when she interrogates her mirror.

Now it's your turn to talk to an object.

To get started, let's think of some objects.

I'm going to talk to a . . .

- smelly gym bag
- sweatshirt
- computer mouse
- moldy pizza
- witch's hat

- _____
- _____
- _____
- _____
- _____

Next, let's think of some emotions/reasons that would spark your need to speak to an object.

Think of it as a temporary condition. Like, "I'm . . .

- angry!
- mystified!
- jealous!
- glum!
- terrified!

- _____
- _____
- _____
- _____
- _____

Now comes the fun part:

Choose an object from the first list and an emotion from the second list. Mash them together, and what do you get?

A speaker who's talking to a moldy pizza because he's terrified of it?

A character who's speaking to a witch's hat because he's heartbroken?

The objectives to this exercise are to:

1. Write to an object.
2. Develop the backstory for why you are writing to this object.

Before you begin, let's think of the "being heartbroken while addressing a witch hat" example. Why on earth would a witch hat make you heartbroken? Or maybe it wasn't even the witch hat that made you so sad. (Ophelia doesn't talk to the flowers because *they* made her crazy, but because of all of the insanity unfolding around her.) Maybe you are heartbroken because you dropped your ice cream cone (and it was chocolate fudge—your favorite!) at the shop after you saw a customer wearing a pointy black hat, which gave you a scare!

While writing your poem or monologue or story, channel your inner motive for talking to your chosen object.

Time for Rhyme

Pia Simone Garber, Jenny Gropp, Leia Wilson, and Emma Sovich

In this introduction to the many types of rhyme, like poet Robert Frost said, "all the fun's in how you say a thing."

PRACTICALLY EVERYBODY KNOWS HOW TO rhyme. My four-year-old sister rhymes all the time: "*Handy Randy* ate some *candy*; it was *dandy*. I'm a *poet* and I *know it*." There are lots of complicated ways to explain it, but the point is that **rhyme** is a sound that is repeated in two or more words. Most of the older, English-language forms of poetry employ rhyme, and for many of us poetry is what comes to mind when we think of rhyme. In fact, in Webster's dictionary, the first entry for *rhyme* is "rhyming verse, or poetry."

The rhyme we know best—*snow, bow, tow*—is **perfect rhyme** (also known as true rhyme or full rhyme). It's the kind of rhyme that thrives in nursery rhymes: "Little Bo Peep has lost her sheep." *EEP!* jumps out at your ear. Because we grow up with nursery rhymes, we tend to think of full rhymes as playful, childish, or even funny—like this limerick by Edward Lear:

THERE WAS AN OLD PERSON OF NICE

There was an old person of Nice,
Whose associates were usually Geese.
They walked out together, in all sorts of weather.
That affable person of Nice!

And you've probably heard of this poem from *Through the Looking-Glass*:

EXCERPT FROM: "JABBERWOCKY"

BY LEWIS CARROLL

'Twas brillig, and the slithy toves
Did gyre and gimble in the wabe:

All mimsy were the borogoves,
And the mome raths outgrabe.

"Beware the Jabberwock, my son!
The jaws that bite, the claws that catch!
Beware the Jubjub bird, and shun
The frumious Bandersnatch!"

The rhymes here are playful perfect rhymes made with invented words. The rhyme lightens the mood a bit to counter the threat of the Jabberwock and the violence of the snicker-snacking sword that comes later in the poem.

Perfect rhyme is not always playful, however. The following poem from Shakespeare's *Macbeth* is meant to stir the hairs on the back of your neck: All of the rhymes are perfect except for one (see if you can hear which pair of words are not quite a perfect rhyme).

"SONG OF THE WITCHES"

Double, double toil and trouble;
Fire burn and caldron bubble.
Fillet of a fenny snake,
In the caldron boil and bake;
Eye of newt and toe of frog,
Wool of bat and tongue of dog,
Adder's fork and blind-worm's sting,
Lizard's leg and howlet's wing,
For a charm of powerful trouble,
Like a hell-broth boil and bubble.

Double, double toil and trouble;
Fire burn and caldron bubble.
Cool it with a baboon's blood,
Then the charm is firm and good.

In all of the above examples, the main rhymed words occurred at the ends of the lines. This is called, simply enough, end rhyme.

Double, double toil and **trouble**;
Fire burn and caldron **bubble**.

We also have an arsenal of **imperfect rhymes**, sometimes called *slant rhymes*, at our disposal to keep the musicality of a poem while "hiding" the rhyme.

Slant rhyme occurs when the repeated sound is inexact; often it feels like only half of the word rhymes. Emily Dickinson uses slant rhymes throughout her poems. In this Dickinson stanza look at how the end words of the first and third lines sort of rhyme, as do the end words of the second and fourth lines:

They shut me up in Prose—
As when a little **Girl**
They put me in the Closet—
Because they liked me **"still"**—

Slant rhyme includes many variants, including consonance, assonance, eye rhyme, and forced rhyme:

Consonance occurs when the rhymed words have matching consonant sounds, but different vowel sounds. Here's Dickinson again.

Fame is a bee.
It has a **song**—
It has a **sting**—
Ah, too, it has a **wing**.

Assonance occurs when the rhymed words have the same vowel sound, but different consonant sounds. Here's Langston Hughes in his poem "Madam's Past History":

Then I had a
BARBECUE **STAND**
Till I got mixed up
With a no-good **man**.

Eye rhyme occurs when the rhymed words look alike, but sound a bit different. Did you identify this imperfect rhyme in the Shakespeare example?

> Cool it with a baboon's **blood**,
> Then the charm is firm and **good**.

Forced rhyme occurs when the poet "forces" the rhyme, pairing words that don't quite rhyme, and sometimes changing them to make them fit, as in Arlo Guthrie's "Motorcycle Song," in which he rhymes *fickle* with *motorsickle* and then *fry* with *motorcy . . . cle.*

There are even more kinds of rhyme out there, but this is enough to get you started. Fill in the chart below by coming up with the different types of rhyme for the words on the left—I've filled in the first one for you.

	Perfect	Assonance	Consonance	Eye	Forced
wish	fish	lift	wash	wipe	wise
boot	‾‾‾	‾‾‾	‾‾‾	‾‾‾	‾‾‾
grow	‾‾‾	‾‾‾	‾‾‾	‾‾‾	‾‾‾
hand	‾‾‾	‾‾‾	‾‾‾	‾‾‾	‾‾‾
sponge	‾‾‾	‾‾‾	‾‾‾	‾‾‾	‾‾‾
‾‾‾	‾‾‾	‾‾‾	‾‾‾	‾‾‾	‾‾‾

Now take one of these words and the rhymes you made and use some of them in a five-line poem.

If you want to learn even more kinds of rhymes, you can look them up or invent your own. You can use any of these rhymes in your poetry to all kinds of effect.

Love Poems and Refrains

BETTER THAN "LEMON ICE"

Pia Simone Garber and Curtis Rutherford

Throw the fanciful and flowery talk aside and be a filthy mess of affection in your own amped-up love poems.

WHEN LOVE IS IN THE air, it seems like everything is going to be all right! But when love skips town with your best friend and your favorite jacket, it's a whole other story. A love poem is dull when it is just, "We fell in love—she had pretty hair—she makes me feel so alive—we went to the movies—and ate popcorn together—she's the one for me."

ZZZZZZZ . . . That sounds like a boring old greeting card.

Let's do a quick exercise. Imagine you are standing in front of a greeting card rack, browsing through the really sincere ones. You pick a card off the rack—it has a watercolor of a garden on the front. You open it up and read its curly script:

There are times when I can't believe
how lucky we are
to have met each other.
Times when I remember
all that we have shared,
the cherished moments
and the hushed secrets.
You are the most beautiful rose in my garden
and you are the last raindrop on its petals
that I hold to my lips.
I love you with all my heart and soul.
I want us to go on living in this grace
for eternity.
Especially on this day, your birthday,
I want you to know
how much I love you.

This card is heartfelt, but it's also sentimental and full of clichés. A cliché is something the reader is expecting, something we've heard before. It may be pleasing, but it's not original or specific. Clichés are overly familiar images (the rose) and phrases ("I love you with all my heart and soul") and even ideas ("how lucky we are to have met"). How can we write love poetry that's original, that doesn't sound like a greeting card?

Think of someone you love—a family member, a friend, a pet, a boyfriend, a girlfriend. Imagine that loved one in a very specific way. What have you done with this person? Let your imagination's movie camera run, and picture what's going on. What is *not* wonderful about this loved one? What's less than perfect? What's complicated? Again, let that movie camera run. Don't be a bummer and sum your feelings up with those vague abstractions ("he's loyal" or "she's pretty"). Instead, sharpen your focus and zoom into specifics. Instead of saying "quiet and reflective," imagine what kind of "quiet" that person is. Like this: "You are so quiet sometimes the air stops to listen to you and the cat asks you its furry questions and you still don't answer." Or, in place of a generality like "silly and playful," refer to a specific time that person was silly or playful: "You tied your shoelaces together."

Remember you can *invent* details to express emotion. It's ok if it didn't happen in "real life." *Imagine* the person you love. For example, which line sounds more exciting to you? "I want to give you flowers," or, "I want all the flowers at Claiborne Park to jump into your pockets"?

Let your sentences roll on and on longer than the given lines if you choose. Since you only have five minutes, practice "first thought, best thought." Forget about getting super fancy and flowery; get down to the nitty-gritty and get some dirt under those fingernails. Be a filthy mess of affection and write a really specific love "card":

There are times when _____

_____we are

_____

_____ I remember

_____,

the _____

and _____.

You are the most _____

_____
_____.

I _____ you.

_____
_____.

_____ , your _____ ,

I want you to know

_____.

USING REPEATED PHRASES

In Connie Voisine's poem "Lemon Ice," she repeats "You are better than . . ." as the first phrase as well as the last phrase of the poem. This repetition is a clue for the reader to hook into the argument of the work. The whole poem is about what the beloved is "better than":

For M.H.S.

You are better
than the lemon ice
I had on the
street, the man's
arched knife
shaving a groove
in a block of ice
that sweats, takes my
slow breath, moist
in this heat
which stops wind,
a leg looks luscious,
a bicep curves
like a smile with
salt in it,
and people are in
the fountain, a dog
lunges at the spout,
brindle fur slick
on his body,
teeth biting

the fat stream
from Neptune's mouth,
a baby tumbles under,
pants heavy
with water.
The man spills
the bright flavor
into my cup.
The paper cone
is loose, dissolving
in my hands so
I bite the ice,
filling my mouth,
sharp lemon stings
my lips, makes water
in my eyes, my thirst
absorbs the melt
and my tongue rolls
in sugar. You are
better than that.

This poem is a great example of how to structure poetic intention. The intention of the poem is to do justice to a feeling: the sensation that the speaker feels when eating an intensely flavorful lemon ice while noticing a funny scene in the fountain is nothing compared to the sensation the speaker feels when thinking of their beloved. The repetition also works as a unifying element. It not only presses the intention further, saying "this is important, listen up," but also binds the reader to the emotional engine. The reader has that rung to always hang on to without feeling lost or being led astray.

Now you try a love poem of your own:

1. Have in mind a specific person, place, or event you want to write about. It can be anything or anyone you want to show affection for in your poem.
2. Use a repeated phrase to begin and end the poem, to give it a direction and energy.

3. Write twenty lines where you describe a real event of your choice like Voisine does, eating a lemon ice on the street.

4. Then throw in some invented details. In Voisine's poem speaker notices people in a fountain with a dog playing in the spout. For instance, have a pigeon walk up to the speaker and offer some relationship advice or have a garbage can spit out trash in a protest for peace and love on earth. Anything you want.

Death Poems

The Tragic and the Comic

Pia Simone Garber and Curtis Rutherford

Make your reader feel the gravity of death in different ways, writing both a comic poem and then a sincere elegy.

U H OH . . . DEATH. THIS IS a pretty heavy topic that evokes a lot of different emotions within not just poets, but everyone. Whether we lose someone close to us, a distant relative we hardly knew, or even a pet, death is final. It is a closing off of possibilities. We can no longer physically interact with that person or creature. Bottom line: it's tough to deal with. But that doesn't mean we can't write about it. Even speculating about one's own death is of interest to some poets, and it makes for some interesting writing.

Comic Poems about Death

A poet who handles the subject of death in a fascinating, and sometimes humorous, way is Rick Campbell. His poem "Intelligent Design and the Click Beetle" is a contemplation on a God that is supposed to give creatures practical living mechanisms. The poem addresses the idea of chance and possibility in life, and how the poet's own impending death plays into all of this. Check out this passage, and pay close attention to Campbell's tone as he thinks about death:

> The beetle clicks, leaps, falls, assesses its heads
> or tails state, then either crawls off somewhere
> or begins again. If grand design
> were measured by a success ratio, wouldn't
> a simple rollover mechanism be a better idea?
> The universe is full of little jokes and games
> of chance. I had only a minute chance of getting
> throat cancer and I got it. . . .
>
> . . . .

Click, heads—
we walk away. Click, tails—we roll into a ditch.
Click, heads—the doctors save us. Click, tails—
They don't.

It's true that death is not such a pleasant reality, but it is such a
common reality that it is possible to overlook its emotional weight. In
a murder mystery readers are not concerned with the sadness of the
death, but with who committed the murder. In the newspaper, when
we see the obituaries, we don't necessarily wallow in anguish; most of
the time we turn the page to get to the funnies. Don't assume that a
poem has to have a tone of gravity just because it is about bereavement
or loss. It is your job as the writer to make the reader feel a specific
emotion.

Imagine a situation where you think about life and death, either your
life or the life of someone else, in a somewhat, or even outright, humor-
ous way. Can you put a comical spin on this situation like Rick Camp-
bell has with the image of a click beetle throwing itself into the air over
and over again? Here are a couple of examples to get you started:

1. It's so hot outside you jump into the pool. Oops! You forgot that you
   don't know how to swim!
2. You are starving. Famished. So you open a bag of chips and start shov-
   eling them in your mouth, but uh-oh! You start choking!
3. Invent your own situation.

Take the situation you came up with, or one you decided to use from the
examples, and make a funny poem about death.

1. Reread "Intelligent Design and the Click Beetle" and then immediately
   take thirty seconds to make a list of words and/or short phrases that
   ring in your ear, that you remember, and that you have a special emo-
   tional attachment to when you think about the situation.
2. Take your chosen situation and list of words and phrases, then take ten
   minutes to write a poem with a comical tone. Use the words from your
   list to build the poem.

Remember, it's your job as the poet to build an emotional landscape for your reader to explore. The poem's tone is a major player in this construction. Let your words and subjects outside of death build your tone.

TRAGIC POEMS ABOUT DEATH

Speaking of tone, it's time to change ours. Writing about death is hardly always humorous. What do you do when someone you love has died and you are so full of pain and grief that you just don't know what to do? Many famous poets have channeled such emotion into writing an **elegy**, a poem that reacts to the death of a person or a group of people.

An elegy can express a sense of grieving in several ways. It can be a lament in which the writer describes the sorrow and loss they are feeling. It can be full of praise for the dearly departed, showing the reader how deeply the writer is feeling the absence of their loved one. And sometimes an elegy will have a tone of a solace or consolation, in which the writer is somehow comforted despite the pain and sadness.

One example of an elegy with these elements in it is "Without" by Donald Hall. It was written after the death of Hall's wife, the poet Jane Kenyon, after a long battle with leukemia. As you read these excerpts from the long poem, notice how the language makes you feel.

> we live in a small island stone nation
> without color under gray clouds and wind
> distant the unlimited ocean acute
> lymphoblastic leukemia without seagulls

Have you noticed there isn't any punctuation? Just a sense of dullness and confusion and the "acute" details of illness, all tumbling through grief. Now see and hear how Hall's meditation comes to include things far beyond the house, and writing itself. Feel the sense of vastness and emptiness deepening:

> the book is a thousand pages without commas
> without mice maple leaves windstorms
> no castles no plazas no flags no parrots
> without carnival or the procession of relics
> intolerable without brackets or colons

The details come more and more rapidly, continuing to mix together medical terms and impressions of the sea with fragments of remembered or imagined conversation:

> vincristine ara-c cytoxan vp-16
> loss of memory loss of language losses
> foamless unmitigated sea without sea
> delirium whipmarks of petechiae pcp
> multiple blisters of herpes zoster
> and how are you doing today I am doing

Did you notice that Hall does not actually mention his wife's name, although there are many medical terms that refer to her illness? The poet is evoking the feeling of her death by describing everything that also went away as he slowly lost her. Time feels stalled and endless. And then the poem comes to a moment where time seems to move forward, slightly, and writing seems almost possible again:

> one afternoon say the sun comes out
> moss takes on greenishness leaves fell
> the market opens a loaf of bread a sparrow
> a bony dog wandered back sniffing a lath
> it might be possible to take up a pencil
> unwritten stanzas taken up and touched
> beautiful terrible sentences unuttered

But grief has its way again in the poem's final stanza: time stands still again, and the poem goes back to cycling through the details that still haunt the speaker:

> the sea unrelenting wave gray the sea
> flotsam without islands broken crates
> block after block the same house the mall
> no cathedral no hobo jungle the same women
> and men they longed to drink hayfields
> without dog or semicolon or village square
> without hyena or lily without garlic

Instead of trying to quickly "sum up" what he thinks about his loss, Donald Hall takes all the time he needs to convey to the reader what that loss feels like, using the powerful rhythms of language and a rich variety of details to make the reader feel the way he feels.

Think of someone you have lost. This could be a family member, friend, or pet. This could also be a famous person or someone from history you deeply admire. What is the world like without this person?

1. Make a list of ten things this being did for you or brought into your life. Think about the ways in which this person affected you, where they fit in your life, what you shared with them, places you went together.

2. Be as descriptive as possible. For example, instead of writing that you went to the park, write about everything in the park that comes to mind: the benches, the grass and trees, the swings in the playground, what you said and thought about there.

3. Now take your list and use it for inspiration to write at least twenty lines detailing what is missing from your life as a result of the loss of your loved one. Whatever raw emotions you have, convert them into images and fill up your poem. Make your reader feel what you are missing.

Go to bed with the nightlight on and read these poems:

"Edge" by Sylvia Plath
"Do Not Go Gentle Into that Good Night" by Dylan Thomas
"This Living Hand" by John Keats
"Two Graves In a Day" by Richard Hugo

Political Poems

Big Brother Is Watching You!

Pia Simone Garber and Curtis Rutherford

Brainstorm some experiences all people share (love, death, family, etc.) and use them to overturn common ideas about politics.

Politics. The one thing you are never supposed to bring up in a social situation. It is almost always a bad idea to try to even have a casual, well-intentioned conversation with someone about politics. Even in the most cordial of situations, people are rarely willing to compromise their political views, and someone often feels tread upon. But, that sounds like a perfect subject to write about!

What risks do poets take when writing political poetry? How about excluding some readers automatically if they do not agree with the politics of the poem? Even if it is a well-executed work, some readers may simply shut you out if they disagree with you. It's human nature. The flip side to this is that some readers may jump to champion your poem simply because of its politics, regardless of the quality of the poem's execution. Some readers may react to the sentimental appeal of a "message" they see you putting forward politically. In this exercise you'll learn to sidestep this problem by writing a poem that addresses something of universal political concern. You'll do this without sacrificing your personal views, without alienating readers who disagree with you, and without playing only to readers who agree with your ideas.

Let's begin by thinking about social classes. We have the upper class, the middle class, and the working class. What are some experiences that typify a class? For example, worrying about paying bills is typical of those in the working class. Finding a job with upward mobility is familiar to those in the middle class, while for the upper class, worrying about financial interests may be typical. But what are some common experiences of members of all classes? How about being fearful of things out of our hands, such as illness and death? Understanding and familiarity of experience are super important when you begin to think about writing political poetry.

Take a gander at these political poems and see how they may handle universal experience:

"Come to the Waldorf-Astoria" by Langston Hughes
"Evolution" by Sherman Alexie
"Shine, Perishing Republic" by Robinson Jeffers
"For You O Democracy" by Walt Whitman

Let's look at Tony Hoagland's work "America." Poets can reach more readers on an emotional level by including larger, universal issues. In this poem, the poet addresses a personal subject—a dream in which he stabs his father and his father bleeds money. He then uses this to argue how money kept his father from liberty in a consumer society. Hoagland speaks on both universal and personal issues.

Then one of the students with blue hair and a tongue stud
Says that America is for him a maximum-security prison

Whose walls are made of RadioShacks and Burger Kings, and MTV episodes
Where you can't tell the show from the commercials,

And as I consider how to express how full of shit I think he is,
He says that even when he's driving to the mall in his Isuzu

Trooper with a gang of his friends, letting rap music pour over them
Like a boiling Jacuzzi full of ballpeen hammers, even then he feels

Buried alive, captured and suffocated in the folds
Of the thick satin quilt of America

And I wonder if this is a legitimate category of pain,
or whether he is just spin doctoring a better grade,

And then I remember that when I stabbed my father in the dream last night,
It was not blood but money

That gushed out of him, bright green hundred-dollar bills
Spilling from his wounds, and—this is the weird part—,

He gasped, "Thank god—those Ben Franklins were
Clogging up my heart—

And so I perish happily,
Freed from that which kept me from my liberty—"

Now write a poem in which a personal event, dream, experience, or
story is combined with a universal problem to reflect something about
America.

1. Take sixty seconds to make a list of word associations you have with the
   idea of "The United States of America." Write down the first words that
   pop into your head, such as *liberty* or *capitalism* or *strip mall*.
2. Look at the words on the list and pick one. This will be the title of your
   poem.
3. Using the title of your poem as inspiration, take fifteen minutes to
   write a poem where you tie the content of your poem to a universal ex-
   perience. This experience could be love, death, or the pursuit of happi-
   ness. Remember that universal issues are broad and general.

While political poetry can focus on topics such as war, the govern-
ment, or the economy, it can also engage popular culture, such as fash-
ion, music, television. It can even take on ideas like the concept of pink
being a color for girls or building cars being a boy's hobby or only one
type of body being beautiful. Political poetry that deals with pop culture
often has a sarcastic or even a rebellious tone. Such poetry attempts to
draw attention to and overturn common ideas about race, sex, or class
by showing them in an exaggerated or even comical manner, like the
poem "The Limited Edition Platinum Barbie" by Denise Duhamel that
describes a Barbie doll.

Ever since Marilyn Monroe
bleached her hair so it would photograph better
under the lights, Bob Mackie
wanted to do the same for Barbie.
Now here she is, a real fashion illustration,
finally a model whose legs truly make up

more than half her height. The gown is white,
and the hair more silver than Christmas,
swept up in a high pouf of intricate twists.
Less demanding than Diana Ross
or Cher, Barbie has fewer flaws to hide.
No plastic surgery scars, no
temper tantrums when Mackie's bugle beads
don't hang just right. . . .

. . . .

Yes, Barbie is his favorite client—poised,
ladylike, complying. As he impales her
on her plastic display stand, Mackie's confident
she won't ruin any effect by bad posture.
Collectors can pay in four monthly installments
of $38.50 and have Barbie delivered to their home.
Others can go to Mackie's display at FAO Schwarz,
the most expensive toy store in New York,
to remind themselves of who they'll never be,
of what they'll never have.

In this poem, fashion designer Bob Mackie uses a Barbie doll as a stand-in for the "perfect" woman, who cannot complain and ultimately has very few human qualities. Throughout the poem, the writer uses words that have a weighted meaning. For example the denotation, or dictionary definition, of *impale* is to pierce or stick on a sharpened pole. This is technically the correct meaning for the act of fastening Barbie to the pole of her display stand; however, there is another connotation, a secondary cultural or emotional meaning, to the word. In this case the word *impale* implies a violent act against Barbie that is representative of a larger constraint imposed on women within society.

Now it's your turn to write about an object from popular culture, and how it might be used to explore or critique a common idea in society. For example, your favorite fast-food chain and how it might be a sign of how unhealthy our country is, or a popular clothing brand and what kind of status it gives to people who wear it.

1. Choose a common object that is nearby, in your purse or bag, or in the room with you, at the mall, etc. Choose something that is easily identifiable and that is a part of our culture, such as a particular brand of clothing or beverage or a cell phone or computer.
2. Write a list of words that describe this object, its use, and any meaning you think is attached to this object among your friends and peers.
3. With the list you just wrote as inspiration, write a poem about your object and those who use or own such an object. Use the object to represent some aspect of society. Try to use words that emphasize the symbolic meaning of the object while being specific about its uses, characteristics, and context.

Things That Go Bump in the Night

Reappropriating Stock Vampires, Witches, Zombies, and Other Creatures for a Twenty-First Century Scare

Tasha Coryell, Freya Gibbon, Molly Goldman, Krystin Gollihue, Jess E. Jelsma, Matt Jones, Meredith Noseworthy, Steve Reaugh, Sally Rodgers, and Bethany Startin

Time for the Ultimate Makeover: Zombie Edition.

WHEN I THINK ZOMBIE, I think rotting flesh. I think of a newly animated corpse crawling out of a grave and then stumbling around, arms straight ahead. There is probably blood smeared on the zombie. It isn't very smart, but it is hungry for brains. Zombies come in packs, because whatever witchcraft animated the corpse wouldn't have raised just one. They don't talk but they do moan, probably because their tongues and vocal cords have begun to decay.

Vampires, on the other hand, are smart and have superhuman strength. They also seek the flesh of the living for sustenance, although vampires have sharp canines that they apply to the necks of beautiful women. They might turn their prey into a vampire, too. They're attractive, very pale skinned, can't come out in the daytime, and sleep in coffins at night. They have thick velvety curtains and Gothic mansions. To kill a vampire, you must shove a wooden stake into the region of the heart. Vampires can be repelled by crosses and garlic, and cannot cross rivers.

These creatures have become so familiar in our cultural context that they no longer surprise us or incite fear. Many of these creatures can be traced back to early mythology, when the stories would have been used to understand things about the world or to teach children how to behave.

But imagine coming home to find a zombie in your kitchen eating Cheerios and chatting with your dad about the political situation in China. That would be strange, but that is way more interesting than finding a zombie eating human brains. That's the point of this activity—to turn the expected into the unexpected. There's something exciting about altering these familiar creatures to challenge our usual expectations about how they behave and what motivates them. This writing exercise is about re-writing the stock scary characters into dynamic, surprising characters.

Take a moment to read this passage from Jessica Hollander's "Ultimate Makeover: Zombie Edition" that demonstrates one way familiar creatures can be revitalized for a modern audience. The speaker is a zombie, and her boyfriend wants her to be in a reality television show.

In bed with Romero, and he wants me to do this *Ultimate Makeover: Zombie Edition*. While he explains the deal, I gnaw at his arm—because he likes it, not because I'm the kind of zombie who nonstop gorges on living flesh. There's nothing uglier than a fatso zombie, like my friend Amelia. I only eat the equivalent of one human a week—just bits and pieces—the lean parts. I could never eat Romero, because he is my Lord.

"Dead is still in," he says. "But you're a little too dead."

The brightness of his apartment gives me a headache. Off with the covers and my body's blue and purple, some new craters on my belly where the flesh has worn away. I should stop staying here with Romero—it depresses me. Six feet beneath the ground I have my own cozy place where I could spend nights rotting in peace and mornings hearing about Amelia's conquests, instead of tap-tap-tap it's Romero, quiet in case others are around—they aren't; he believes they are prone to jealousy—they aren't. "I understand the God-appeal," Amelia says. "But there's two things working against him. One, you can't eat him. Two, he's not dead enough to want it enough. Am I right?"

In this excerpt, the speaker isn't your average zombie. She has feelings like a person, she makes funny observations like a person, but she happens to be dead and rotting. She's sort of bored and sort of edgy. She has distinctive dialogue and a "valley girl" voice when she says things like, "There's nothing uglier than a fatso zombie." The piece is exciting and funny.

Now it's your turn to create a creature.

First choose a type of creature:

Zombie

Witch

Werewolf

Banshee

Ghost
Siren
Vampire
Other: _____

Now, think of settings. I've chosen a few to get you started, but feel free to come up with your own:

Mall
House
Nursing home
Town dump
Lawyer's office

_____

_____

_____

_____

_____

The following is a list of prompts (zombies especially love brainstorming!) to get you thinking about your creature as a character. Generate as many answers as you can in fifteen minutes.

1. What characteristics make your creature **different** from other creatures of its kind?

_____

_____

_____

2. What characteristics are **the same** as the stereotypical creature of its kind?

_____

_____

_____

3. What does your creature love most? What does it fear most?

_____

_____

_____

4. What does it do for a job? What does it do for a hobby?

_____

_____

_____

5. Does it have any friends? Are the friends creatures or humans? Describe the friends.

_____

_____

_____

6. Do your creature have any enemies? Are the enemies other creatures or are they humans?

_____

_____

_____

Finally, choose a form you'd like to use for your terrible tale:

Story
Poem
Letter of complaint
Job application
Personal ad
Craigslist's Missed Connection
Wikipedia entry about their kind
Other:_____

Now, using your chosen form and keeping your creature's details in mind, put your creature in a specific situation and have them speak or write in first person, telling us what's going on, what's on their mind. Write for at least twenty minutes.

The Adult As Villain

Annie Hartnett

Try a child's point of view.

WHEN I WAS A YOUNG child, I was terribly afraid of the old man who lived a few houses over, Mr. Murphy. In retrospect, there was actually little that was sinister about Mr. Murphy. He gave out king-size chocolate bars on Halloween, and he kept a jar of dog biscuits next to his front door for any canine that might be walking by. Still, I was afraid to ring his doorbell on All Hallows' Eve, no matter how large that Butterfinger was, and I dreaded walking our family dog by his house.

As children, we often make things very scary that are, in fact, not so scary, like Mr. Murphy and his dog biscuits, or the damp, dark basement. Fear from our childhood makes for great story fodder because every feeling is amplified and because the imagination of a child has no limits.

Was there a person from your childhood that you were afraid of? Maybe your principal, a teacher, the ice cream man? Now that you're older (and presumably wiser!) do you believe that person was a real villain or were they simply misunderstood?

You probably also remember some adult villains from books you read as a child. Author Roald Dahl frequently villainizes his adult characters while making a child the hero. In his book *Matilda*, Matilda Wormwood has both terrible parents and a cruel principal, Miss Trunchbull. You might remember when Miss Trunchbull picks up one child by the pigtails and throws her like a shot put. Or perhaps you remember when Miss Trunchbull punishes Bruce Bogtrotter for eating a slice of her cake by forcing him to eat an *entire* chocolate cake in front of the whole school. The vindictive principal gripes, "I cannot for the life of me understand why children take so long to grow up. I think they do it deliberately, just to annoy me."

As you can see from Roald Dahl's writing, there are many opportunities if you choose to write from the perspective of a child. You can exaggerate the actions of your villains, just as a real child might. You can let your imagination run wild.

Let's look at some real villains now to get some ideas. The newspaper is a goldmine for story ideas, especially if you're looking for a villain. Here are a few news clips to get you going:

An Ohio man was in custody today after allegedly breaking into a family's house and putting up Christmas decorations. According to WHIO-TV, police said Terry Trent let himself in on Friday through a back door of a central Ohio house and lit a candle and turned on a television before doing some Christmas decorating. Trent, 44, who has a history of drug charges, was reportedly high on bath salts when he broke into the home. He has been charged with burglary. The victimized family's 11-year-old son reportedly came home after the break-in and found Trent sitting on the couch. He called his mother, Tamara Henderson, who was visiting with a next-door neighbor and then called police. Trent was carrying a pocket knife when he was arrested, but reportedly tried to be polite to the child when he was found." He had said to him, 'I'm sorry. I didn't mean to scare you. I'll get my things and go,'" Henderson said.

NY boy sleeps through theft of dad's running car. Police in upstate New York say a 6-year-old boy snoozing in his father's car never woke up while the vehicle was being stolen after it was left running outside a store. Officers tell Rochester media outlets that a 26-year-old man from Irondequoit left his car running while he went inside a convenience store to get a drink late Saturday night. While inside the store, someone jumped into the car and drove off with the boy asleep in the car. Police say the car was found abandoned within 30 minutes. Officials say the boy wasn't harmed and had slept through the entire ordeal. Police charged the boy's father with endangering the welfare of a child. The car thief hasn't been found.

Ex-California mayor admits stealing school's mixer to make pizza. The former mayor of a Los Angeles suburb has pleaded guilty to stealing a commercial food mixer from the local school district so he could make dough for his home pizza oven. Los Angeles County prosecutors say Larry Guidi entered the plea Wednesday to a felony count of grand theft. He was sentenced to 100 hours of community service and one year's probation. A commercial burglary charge was dismissed. Guidi was a warehouse operations manager for the Hawthorne School District until he was fired last year. Prosecutors say a security camera recorded him loading the giant mixer and a cart into his pickup truck in 2010. The $1,300 mixer was later returned. Guidi was the mayor of Hawthorne for nearly 20 years but didn't run for re-election last year.

Now! Using one of these news stories (or one you find or make up yourself), write a story from the perspective of a child (no older than twelve!) who interacts with this real-life villain. It's up to you if the villain is truly evil or simply misunderstood. Does the villain act differently around the child than they do around other people? Place the "villain" and the child into a specific situation—the reported crime or a different scenario. Write your story or poem from the point of view of the child, using *I*.

Objects and Elements

Set Your Imagination Loose!

Megan Paonessa and Danilo Thomas

*Take the smallest, seemingly most inconsequential thing and turn it
into a grand presence.*

P OETS ARE GREAT AT ZOOMING in on an object. It's in their poet blood
to comprehend the heroic nature of dust and rotting cabbage. They
have insight binoculars to scope out how a piece of wood, a 2×4, might
be much, much more than just a 2×4. They know it was once a tree with
knots and nubs. They might notice how the grains are rougher in one
place than in another. They might think about how it is one small part
of a structure that will someday become a house, an office building, or
a sports arena. Poets have a way of describing the secret life of objects.
Let's see how they do it.

In Charles Simic's poem, "Fork," notice how Simic hones in on the
metaphysical elements of a fork. What weird truths come to mind as you
consider a fork?

> This strange thing must have crept
> Right out of hell.
> It resembles a bird's foot
> Worn around the cannibal's neck.
>
> As you hold it in your hand,
> As you stab with it into a piece of meat,
> It is possible to imagine the rest of the bird:
> Its head which like your fist
> Is large, bald, beakless, and blind.

Poets are also good at sensing the essence of an object or image and
allowing the imagination to expand upon that observation. In this poem
by Miroslav Holub, water going over a dam leads the poet to imagine
what *else* could go over the dam and what happens to the world after *that*!

The Dam

Water
crowned.
Water grows, swallowing
the road and its shadows,
the house and its azure,
the slate and its ABC.
There are no more warm dens.
The earth is made of concrete.
Cranes have eviscerated the sky.
Centuries rush over the ridge now.
And not just on memories
—on high voltage
not on eardrops
—on drum armature,
not on words
—on thunder
we live.
A step aside and the alarm rings,
a step backward opens the abyss,
a tremor explodes.
Deep down
fish swim in cathedrals.
And every one of us
is called by name.

Choose an object or element, something small like a fork or common like a fire in a fireplace or large like a dam. Then write a poem in which you talk about your subject, describing what's "in" it in terms of metaphors or what its uses might be. Let your imagination take you beyond the ordinary world. See "into" the object or element, and let your imagination run with the possibilities.

Weapons of Voice

PRACTICING LONG AND SHORT SENTENCE STYLES

Jesse Delong, Lisa Tallin, and Danilo Thomas

Imitate both sparse and long-winded writers in this fiction exercise.

YOU ARE WALKING THROUGH THE streets of your neighborhood. Sunlight bleaches the pastel straps of your tank top, flashes from the chrome of your large belt buckle. Sweat collects in brown stains on the elastic band of your cap. The day is hot. This is expected. The newspaper's weatherman wrote the week would be sunny and the skies clear of clouds. But just as you turn back toward the block you live on, *something* happens out of the ordinary. It does not matter what this something is. Maybe it's two birds fighting in a flutter on the lawn. Maybe it's an old man throwing a water balloon at a teenager. What matters is you couldn't have guessed, a block earlier, it would happen.

When you get home, you sit in front of your desk and think about it. You want to write down what you saw, but know the event is larger in scope than the simple sequence of moments. The meaning of what happened can't be contained solely in the narrative. In order to include every significant detail, every ebb, flow, and essence of the happening, you decide the language of your writing must match the feeling of the scene. You must choose your weapon of voice carefully for people to truly understand.

Ernest Hemingway knew the importance of style to capture a complex moment full of feeling. Here's a segment from *In Our Time*. In this scene, a matador has recently been stabbed by a bull.

They laid Maera down on a cot and one of the men went out for the doctor. The others stood around. The doctor came running from the corral where he had been sewing up picador horses. He had to stop and wash his hands. There was a great shouting going on in the grandstand overhead. Maera felt everything getting larger and larger and then smaller and smaller. Then it got larger and larger and larger and then smaller and smaller. Then everything commenced to run faster and faster as when they speed up a cinematograph film. Then he was dead.

Hemingway wrote this paragraph, like most of his work, in short sentences that tell you exactly what happened. The language leaves no room for ambiguity, and the clear, to-the-point phrasing alludes to death as something that happens, end of story.

Philip Roth, however, takes a different stylistic approach. In *American Pastoral*, Roth uses hypotaxis sentences, which are ones that incorporate many coordinating and subordinating clauses. This sentence style is the opposite of parataxis language, which is closer to Hemingway's style and contains no subordinating or coordinating clauses. Roth uses hypotaxis here to talk about a book the narrator often read as a child.

> The book, published in 1940, had black-and-white drawings that, with just a little expressionistic distortion and just enough anatomical skill, cannily pictorialize the hardness of the Kid's life, back before the game of baseball was illuminated with a million statistics, back when it was about the mysteries of the earthly fate, when major leaguers looked less like big healthy kids and more like lean and hungry workingmen. The drawings seemed conceived out of the dark austerities of Depression America.

Man, what a load of breath that paragraph takes. Can you imagine the hand cramps he must have endured when scribbling his sentences on notebook paper? Or the lungs Roth would need to read his work aloud? He's long-winded for sure, but it's for a good reason. He talks about a simple enough thing: a book with black-and-white drawings of a kid playing baseball. With the use of hypotaxis, however, he demonstrates how images that were very clear to the narrator during his childhood have become complicated in the narrator's mind now that he is an adult.

Choose your weapon, ninja. Are you going to embark on this battle with a series of small but precise daggers or one long, wavy sword?

Stylistic Approach One

Write a piece where you describe something very clear-cut and simple that happened to you. Maybe you had an adventure this summer in the woods. Maybe an ordinary moment in your life suddenly turned weird and unexpected. Whatever you choose to write about, use short sentences similar to Hemingway's. A sample incident has been started for you. Either complete this one or start from scratch with your own beginning.

Example 1

The snacks were gone. Everything felt wrong. I couldn't think. I couldn't think of anything but salt that morning.

_____

_____

_____

_____

_____

STYLISTIC APPROACH TWO

Rewrite your earlier approach with a more drawn out, windy voice similar to Roth's. Think about connecting two or even three of the short sentences you've already written into one long sentence. You may feel like an old grandfather speaking, but that's alright. Grandfathers always have something interesting to say. A continuation of the prior example is below. You may use it as a starting point, or start with your own original language.

Example 2

The empty tortilla chip bag, empty save for a few worthless crumbs, once contained about thirteen servings per container at nine chips per serving, which was well over a hundred chips, 117 to be exact, though probably there weren't precisely 117 chips in the bag, it was just an approximation, and in any case, there were none left in the bag, which is what the trouble was.

_____

_____

_____

_____

_____

Aftermath: Now that you've written the piece both ways, decide which works best and how each style changes the mood or essence of your piece. Either writing style is fine, though the reader will come away with a different feeling from each. Using what you've already written, rewrite your piece to include only one style. Or, write a new piece using only one style.

Exercises in Style

The Endless Possibilities of Language

Jenny Gropp

Use a hatful of strategies and games to tell the same story over and over again without it ever looking the same.

Part One

IN 1947, FRENCHMAN AND COFOUNDER of Oulipo Raymond Queneau published a book called *Exercises in Style*. However plain the title may sound, this is no ordinary book.

The storyline of this book, at its very most basic, is as follows:

> The narrator gets on a crowded bus, witnesses an altercation between
> a man and another passenger, and then sees the same man a few hours
> later somewhere else having an interaction with a friend.

That's it. Simple, right? Boring even. But what's remarkable about *Exercises in Style* is that it retells this same unexceptional tale *ninety-nine* times, using different strategies and games to represent the story from every conceivable angle. And in doing so, the possibilities of language are revealed, ensuring that the telling of the tale is never boring.

As a writer, it is your job to push language around in a multiplicity of directions to see what will happen. Adhering to (and creating) exercises designed to mess with tone and style is a great way to increase your versatility of voice, so let's follow Queneau's lead and do some style exercises.

Before we read any Queneau and see exactly what he's up to, we need to make up some details of our own. Fill in the blanks below.

The Main Character
This is the person the narrator will see twice.

- How old are they?
- How tall are they?

- They are wearing a hat. What kind of hat is it? Get descriptive.
- What else are they wearing?
- List three more specific features about this person.

Time and Place
  - What time of day is it?
  - What season is it?
  - In what city is this taking place? (This may be an imaginary city.)

The Bus
You'll need a city bus, so give your city a name.

- What's the name, letter, or number of the bus? Here are some sample ideas: In Boston, the trains are coded by color: the Green Line, the Red Line, etc.; the buses are just listed by number (1, 2, 558, and so on). In New York, the trains have letters or numbers: the A and the 7, and the buses have letters representing the borough and numbers like M103 (Manhattan 103) and B35 (Brooklyn 35).

The Passenger
There's a Passenger on the bus who is next to the Main Character.

- The Main Character is accusing the Passenger of doing something to him (elbowing him, etc.). What is it?
- What does the Main Character do after accusing the Passenger (sit down, etc.)?

Later That Day . . .
The narrator will see the Main Character in another part of town interacting mundanely with a friend (i.e., no fighting, stealing, etc.).

- How many hours have passed since the narrator saw the Main Character on the bus?
- Where in town is the action taking place?
- What is the interaction? Where are the characters? What are they doing? Sharing a steak? Talking about the weather? Eh?

Now that you have all of those details, you're ready to read from *Exercises in Style* and write after it.

First, read "Narrative."

One day at about midday in the Parc Monceau district, on the back platform of a more or less full S bus (now No. 84), I observed a person with a very long neck who was wearing a felt hat which had a plaited cord around it instead of a ribbon. This individual suddenly addressed the man standing next to him, accusing him of purposely treading on his toes every time any passengers got on or off. However he quickly abandoned the dispute and threw himself onto a seat which had become vacant.

Two hours later I saw him in front of the gare Saint-Lazare engaged in earnest conversation with a friend who was advising him to reduce the space between the lapels of his overcoat by getting a competent tailor to raise the top button.

In "Narrative," Queneau recounts the story in first person, using the past tense. He is quite straightforward and clear with his images, communicating the kinds of details that you wrote down in your outline. Think about Queneau's details:

- What is the name of Queneau's bus?
- What time of day is it?
- What city do you think he's in?
- What are some distinguishing features of the Main Character?
- What kind of accusation does the Main Character make against the Passenger?
- What does the Main Character do after making an accusation against the Passenger?
- Where does he see the Main Character again?
- How many hours have passed before the second sighting?
- What kind of interaction is the Main Character having with his friend?
- What are they discussing?

Now write your own brief "Narrative" piece. It will serve as a springboard for your other exercises in style.

PART TWO

Now that you've written a "Narrative," there are ninety-eight more ways in which you can tell your story. Let's experiment with five of those now. Read "Precision."

In a bus of the S-line, 10 metres long, 3 wide, 6 high, at 3 km. 600 m. from its starting point, loaded with 48 people, at 12.17 P.M., a person of the masculine sex aged 27 years 3 months and 8 days, 1 m. 72 cm. tall and weighing 65 kg. and wearing a hat 35 cm, in height round the crown of which was a ribbon 60 cm. long, interpellated a man 48 years 4 months and 3 days, 1 m. 68 cm. tall and weighing 77 kg., by means of 14 words whose enunciation lasted 5 seconds and which alluded to some involuntary displacements of from 15 to 20 mm. Then he went and sat down about 1 m. 10 cm. away.

57 minutes later he was 10 metres away from the suburban entrance to the gare Saint-Lazare and was walking up and down over a distance of 30 m. with a friend aged 28, 1 m. 70 cm. tall and weighing 71 kg., who advised him in 15 words to move by 5 cm. in the direction of the zenith a button which was 3 cm. in diameter.

So you thought you were getting detailed when you wrote your "Narrative," right? Well, here Queneau challenged himself to get even more micro-serious about his environment. Here measurements and specificities rule the page. Write your own "Precision" piece—master, even further, the people and the time and space they're in.

Read "Prognostication."

When midday strikes you will be on the rear platform of a bus which will be crammed full of passengers amongst whom you will notice a ridiculous juvenile; skeleton-like neck and no ribbon on his felt hat. He won't be feeling at his ease, poor little chap. He will think that a gentleman is pushing him on purpose every time that people getting on or off pass by. He will tell him so but the gentleman won't deign to answer. And the ridiculous juvenile will be panic-stricken and run away from him in the direction of a vacant seat.

You will see him a little later, in the Cour de Rome in front of the gare Saint-Lazare. A friend will be with him and you will hear these words: "Your overcoat doesn't do up properly; you must have another button put on it."

Then consider the following *Oxford English Dictionary* definition of *prognostication*:

> An act or instance of prognosticating; a prediction of a future event or outcome; a forecast, a prophecy.

So in order to turn his story into a prognostication, what does Queneau do? He uses the future tense in a way that conjures the scene into being; he is the wizard of the situation. The scene, although it hasn't happened yet, feels unavoidable. There's lots of "you will be" and "he will think" language in this piece.

Now write your own "Prognostication," keeping the above in mind. Hypnotize your readers; be certain of the situation you're placing them in.

Ok, now you really, really know your story. It's time to mess with things on a more hardcore level. Read "Exclamations."

> Goodness! Twelve o'clock! time for the bus! what a lot of people! what a lot of people! aren't we squashed! bloody funny! that chap! what a face! and what a neck! two-foot long! at least! and the cord! the cord! I hadn't seen it! the cord! that's the bloody funniest! oh! the cord! round his hat! A cord! bloody funny! too bloody funny! here we go, now he's yammering! the chap with the cord! at the chap next to him! what's he saying! The other chap! claims he trod on his toes! They're going to come to blows! definitely! no, though! yes they are though! go wonn! go wonn! bite him in the eye! charge! hit 'im! well I never! no, though! he's climbing down! the chap! with the long neck! with the cord! it's a vacant seat he's charging! yes! the chap!
>
> Well! 't's true! no! I'm right! it's really him! over there! in the Cour de Rome! in front of the gare Saint-Lazare! mooching up and down! with another chap! and what's the other chap telling him! that he ought to get an extra button! yes! a button on his coat! On his coat!

Hooked? Perhaps you'd like to try more of Queneau's exercises in style. We recommend:

"Surprises"
"Dream"

"Prognostication"
"Metaphor"
"Hesitation"
"Distinguo"
"Official Letter"
"Blurb"
"Onomatopoeia"
"Ignorance"
"Reported Speech"
"Alexandrines"
"Speaking Personally"
"You Know"
"Noble"
"Cross-Examination"
"Comedy"
"Auditory"
"Telegraphic"
"Haiku"
"Parts of Speech"
"Interjections"
"Unexpected"

Check out the whole book and use it as an inspiration to develop your own stylistic approaches, using your own bus scene.

The N+7 Game

From "The Snow Man" to "The Soap Mandible"

Jenny Gropp, Laura Kochman, and Jill Smith

*Learn about the French literary movement Oulipo, and then grab a
dictionary and an existing piece of writing for the N+7 game.*

N+7, INVENTED BY JEAN LESCURE, is one of the original Oulipo for-
mulas. In it, the writer takes a poem or story already in existence
and substitutes each of the piece's nouns with the noun appearing seven
nouns away in the dictionary. Check out this Wallace Stevens poem,
"The Snow Man," and then read on for the N+7 version:

THE SNOW MAN

One must have a mind of winter
To regard the frost and the boughs
Of the pine-trees crusted with snow;

And have been cold a long time
To behold the junipers shagged with ice,
The spruces rough in the distant glitter

Of the January sun . . .

And here's the N+7 version:

THE SOAP MANDIBLE

One must have a miniature of wisdom
To regard the fruit and the boulders
Of the pinions crusted with soap;

And have been colic a long time
To behold the junkyards shagged with Idaho,
The spun-yarn rough in the distant gloom

Of the January surgery . . .

Now you've seen an example of traditional N+7 work, you can either get a dictionary and a poem or story and write your own N+7 piece, or try one of our own variations on the formula, called 7N+7. Get a book or literary journal of your choosing and select a particular page or piece to work with. Now write down every seventh noun you see, for a total of seven nouns, and write a poem or short story with them. If you're using a literary journal or a book of poetry, the nouns don't all have to be from the same piece—e.g., if the story or poem you're sampling from ends before you have seven of every seventh noun, you can bleed over into the next piece.

Sometimes, if I have writer's block, I use yet another variation on N+7—I take a book and remove every noun, and then take another random book down and replace those nouns with every seventh noun from the new book. If I'm still stuck, I'll go back to the original text and take out every adjective, and then replace those adjectives with every seventh adjective from yet another random book. If I'm *still* stuck, I'll do the same with the verbs, but I haven't had that happen yet. This is proof that the N+7 constraint works well in many different permutations and can help you produce some great writing. Try it out!

Cramming It In

Jamming Narrative into a Short Space

Katie Berger, Laura Kochman, and Brandi Wells

Tell entire stories using only one sentence—no more!

P OETRY AND FICTION HAVE BEEN at war for millennia, fighting the good fight over the fault line between verse and prose. But is all fiction long and winding, and are all poems written in lines? No way, no how. Flash fiction and prose poetry sit directly on that fault line, and with the way the wind is blowing, they're looking pretty precarious up there. By definition, flash fiction is any work of fiction up to one thousand words long, and prose poetry has no word limit—but what they have in common is a sense of condensation. When you write flash fiction or prose poetry, your creative juice is made from concentrate. Every single word matters.

When you tell a flash fiction story, you're writing only what needs to be written, so you might start in the middle of the action or with one powerful image that gets the ball rolling. It's about clarity and precision (although those qualities might show up in different forms, such as plot-driven or image-driven stories). Prose poems can also be recognized by their compressed or precise nature, but they use the sentence as their defining unit instead of the line. Those sentences can be regular old subject-verb-object, or they can make up their own grammatical sense. Instead of thinking of prose poetry as a different genre of poetry, we might think about it like it's just another form, like a sonnet or a limerick. You can do the same things with a prose poem that you can do with a verse poem—except there are no line breaks.

We're going to look at different ways you can work with flash fiction and prose poetry when it comes to length restrictions, place-based writing, and the sticky subject of truth and lies.

Since the basic unit of both flash fiction and prose poetry is the sentence, let's start there. Although a story can be novel length, it can also be as short as a single sentence. The following authors create scene and action, but they only using one sentence each. The action of each of these stories begins immediately, with very little background, but something has been resolved or discovered by the end. As you read each example, consider how important a title could be for such a small story. Often, a title can do as much work as the story itself, and lend a deeper meaning to it.

In the following example, you can see how this sentence, sometimes attributed to Ernest Hemingway, uses just six words to create a complete story:

> For sale: baby shoes, never worn.

The author withholds a lot of information from the reader, but the story is more emotionally effective because of it. You're left wondering, why weren't these shoes worn? Who would sell baby shoes? What happened to the baby?

The following one-sentence stories come from the online journal *Monkeybicycle*. One uses a rather simple two-part sentence, and the other stretches out the sentence for all it's worth.

THE ROBOT

BY RYAN RIDGE

We found an old robot behind the YMCA and took it home and taught it to dance and it was so simple to teach it to dance: all we did was turn on the radio and say, "Act natural."

EXTRA LIVES

BY AARON BURCH

I try to tell her, like it will explain more than anything else I could put into words, that there was supposedly this move where you could jump repeatedly, endlessly, on a turtle on a large staircase and build up extra lives, all the way up to 99, but I could never master it and always just ended up killing myself.

You can use the brevity of this form for humor's sake or focus more on irony or make your sentences sound like stream-of-consciousness thoughts. Sound interesting? We thought so, too. Let's write a couple of one-sentence stories. For this prompt, think of a food or an animal that you find interesting. A burrito, a camel, an alligator, an ice cream sandwich. Anything you want! Try to incorporate one animal or food (or both) into a one-sentence story. Remember to get into the action immediately and skip unnecessary background information. Just tell us the most important, interesting part, and make sure that something happens and that something is discovered or resolved. Here's some space for a shorter one-sentence story:

And here's some space for a longer one-sentence story:

Now that limiting our stories to one sentence has gotten us going, let's try to think about how we could use length in a prose poem. Many writers use formal limitations in poetry like syllable counting (syllabics!), metric structure (we're talking iambic pentameter, folks), and set rhyme schemes (sonnet, anyone?), among many, many others. The funny thing is that all these "limitations" can actually have the opposite effect on your writing; with a rule in place that tells you what to do for one aspect of your writing, you can really focus on and enjoy all the other parts of your writing.

Since the prose poem is just one more poetic form, why not give ourselves a bit of structure, too? Let's take a look at some prose poems that are limited by length, and see what we can learn. Harryette Mullen's prose poem "Black Nikes" is less than two hundred words long:

> We need quarters like King Tut needed a boat. A slave could row him
> to heaven from his crypt in Egypt full of loot. We've lived quietly among
> the stars, knowing money isn't what matters. We only bring enough to
> tip the shuttle driver when we hitch a ride aboard a trailblazer of light.

This comet could scour the planet. Make it sparkle like a fresh toilet swirling with blue. Or only come close enough to brush a few lost souls. Time is rotting as our bodies wait for now I lay me down to earth. Noiseless patient spiders paid with dirt when what we want is star dust. If nature abhors an expensive appliance, why does the planet suck ozone? This is a big ticket item, a thicket ride. Please page our home and visit our sigh on the wide world's ebb. Just point and cluck at our new persuasion shoes. We're opening the gate that opens our containers for recycling. Time to throw down and take off on our launch. This flight will nail our proof of pudding. The thrill of victory is, we're exiting earth. We're leaving all this dirt.

Within the piece, Mullen uses very short sentences and keeps the flow of the words moving, starting with a declarative sentence that really sets the tone: defiant and maybe a little bit short-tempered. Mullen's imagery is very concentrated in phrases like "a trailblazer of light" and "noiseless patient spiders" (an allusion to Walt Whitman). For a poem with such a huge, galactic scope, it manages to pack a lot of stuff into a tight space.

In this prose poem, Rosmarie Waldrop gets even more "short-tempered" with us:

NOUNS

You might grasp at. For safety. A point of view agreeing. Like a verb, having to, with whatever you do. But disturbing nothing. Or in rocky terrain only. When the dark by any other name. Would washing your hands help you with. Illusions pale as, but contingent on, the roar. In the ear. When you talk about winter, your refusal. To talk in my language. It helps, even if it distracts, to go with nouns. To have that choice. Even bold ones like "love."

Since we know from the title that this poem is going to work with language, it makes sense that Waldrop completely overturns our idea of what her sentences can do. From the very beginning, we're grasping at her words, trying to understand these clipped, partial sentences. The poem is only eighty-four words long, and the longest sentence is only ten words long, so the poem has the same feeling of concentrated language.

Like Mullen, Waldrop is dealing with a huge topic (love), but uses a very small form to contain it.

This next poet thought that limiting his word count was so useful that he wrote a whole book of prose poems that are one hundred words long. In *Centuries*, Joel Brouwer plays with the idea that in only one hundred words, he can contain a meaning as huge as the span of one hundred years. Here's one poem from that book:

DIAGNOSIS

The doctor says, *Think of it this way. Your insides are like the jungle at night: warm, noisy, rank with mango, and but for some holes drilled through the sky by stars, wholly dark. A river floats through you on its back, shivering with silver piranhas. Banyan roots claw its face with thirsty fingers and draw black water up to the leafy canopy, where the last honeysuckle vireo on earth has sunk her beak into the single living pygmy anaconda, which in turn has the bird half wrapped in its flexing grip. Only one will live. It's too soon to say.*

In "Diagnosis," Brouwer uses the one-hundred-word form to expand, lyrically, on a non-lyric situation. Since every word counts, he uses description to show us what's going on in this situation by the end of the poem. Unlike Mullen and Waldrop, he writes sentences of different lengths, so that the flow of the poem moves up and down, slower and faster, and all within only one hundred words.

Although these three poems have a lot of differences, one of the things that all three poets have done is to use a concrete or abstract noun as their title and expand on it in their prose poems. Mullen uses an item of clothing, Waldrop refers to a noun as abstract as the noun itself, and Brouwer riffs on something a doctor might tell you.

Do you hear something approaching through the banyan trees? It sounds like a writing prompt. First, let's make a list of nouns to help us get started. I've written down a few interesting things below, but why don't you fill in the rest of the list with things that get your gears going?

1. Surprise
2. Corkscrew
3. Beetle

4. Verb

5. Embarrassment

6. _____

7. _____

8. _____

9. _____

10. _____

11. _____

12. _____

13. _____

14. _____

Now that you've made your list, read through the whole thing and pick the one word that really makes you excited to write. Do you have that word? Awesome! You can do this next part of the exercise on a computer using the word count tool if you want, or you can do it on one side of a standard index card, or you can do it right here, on the lines below. Keeping that one word in your mind, think about how you would represent it in writing. If your word is something like *adjective*, would you use a lot of adjectives or no adjectives at all? If your word is something like *castle*, would you associate it with your favorite fairy tale and write a poem about that? If the word is *hair*, would you write an ode to the mustache? The possibilities are endless! The only rule you have to think about is length, so cram that galaxy into these lines!

_____

_____

_____

_____

_____

If you're really digging these exercises based on length, try this one on for size: using another one of those nouns from your list: write a one-sentence prose poem.

"Licking a Glacier Can Change Your DNA"

Landscape in Prose Poetry and Flash Nonfiction

Katie Berger, Laura Kochman, and Brandi Wells

Look at different methods for creating landscape in short forms,
write out a landscape you've never seen, and then, in the final
activity, put your hometown on Mars.

LANDSCAPE HAS A LONG TRADITION in the visual arts, but what about in writing? One of the things that writers love to do is to create an image, to make the world contained within their writing come alive in the reader's mind. If painters and photographers can do it, so can we! There are lots of different ways to create a landscape in a prose poem or flash fiction or nonfiction, from image to shape to sentence length. And the list goes on. The pieces we're going to look at use one or more of those techniques to evoke the image of a particular landscape.

In "Explanation," Christine Hume uses the prose poem form to make a list of assertions. It kind of makes you think that someone is asking the narrator questions, and the narrator avoids answering them by focusing on landscape instead. Let's take a look at some excerpts:

It is NOT TRUE: I have never climbed into the hollower world below, never even attempted it; but I have roared above the summit in a lost world. And I hasten back to that Eden of poisonous snows.

It is TRUE: I am the only trespasser on Mighty Mac's windchill. I saw huge blocks of ice caribou and hoary moose moving toward the ocean. I hid among those shapely half-ideas that throng dim regions beyond daylight. My eyes, being infected with many nameless blues, could see straight through possessive air.

It is NOT TRUE: The hoax was not my idea. I claim many ideas that are not my own, but everyone knows that licking a glacier can change your DNA and reprogram your bones. You like to gainsay such things because it pleases your frontier.

The narrator, who seems to have trespassed somewhere or created some sort of hoax, avoids the subject of the questions by talking about this icy, snowed-in landscape. If "licking a glacier can change your DNA and reprogram your bones," then the fault lies with the landscape, right? In this way, the inhospitable landscape in this poem becomes the scapegoat for the narrator's misbehavior.

This next excerpt from a poem by Richard Blanco mimics the "form" of a city ordinance list:

THE PERFECT CITY CODE

1(a) Streets shall be designed *Euro-Style* with 300-ft right-of-ways, benches, and flowered traffic circles, to provide a distinct sense of beauty, regardless of cost.

1(b) There shall be a canopy of trees and these shall be your favorite: *Giant Royal Palms*, 25-ft high, whereas their fronds shall meet in cathedral-like arches with a continuous breeze that shall slip in our sleeves and flutter against our bodies so as to produce angel-like sensations of eternity.

1(c) There shall be bushes, and these shall also be your favorite: *Tea Roses* @ 2-ft o.c., to provide enough blooms for casual picking; whereas said blooms shall spy on us from crystal glasses set next to the stove, over coffee-table books, or in front of mirrors.

1(d) Sidewalks shall be crack-proof and 15-ft wide for continuous, side-by-side conversations; they shall be painted either a) *Sunflower-Brown*, b) *Mango Blush*, or c) *Rosemont Henna*; whereas such colors shall evoke, respectively: the color of your eyelashes, of your palms, the shadows on your skin.

Blanco starts with the idea of a city landscape, and he pretends to describe it as a city code in a regimented list form, with lots of regulations and requirements. However, his language, with phrases like "a distinct sense of beauty, regardless of cost" and "the color of your eyelashes," completely subverts the image of a city grid. It seems like what he's actually doing is creating a city for a particular person to live in or a city that reminds him of that person. So this poem creates a landscape, but it also tells a story about that landscape.

Campbell McGrath's poem "The Prose Poem" reverses the logic of Blanco's poem, using landscape to tell a story about the poem itself:

On the map it is precise and rectilinear as a chessboard, though driving past you would hardly notice it, this boundary line or ragged margin, a shallow swale that cups a simple trickle of water, less rill than rivulet, more gully than dell, a tangled ditch grown up throughout with a fearsome assortment of wildflowers and bracken. There is no fence, though here and there a weathered post asserts a former claim, strands of fallen wire taken by the dust. To the left a cornfield carries into the distance, dips and rises to the blue sky, a rolling plain of green and healthy plants aligned in close order, row upon row upon row. To the right, a field of wheat, a field of hay, young grasses breaking the soil, filling their allotted land with the rich, slow-waving spectacle of their grain. As for the farmers, they are, for the most part, indistinguishable: here the tractor is red, there yellow; here a pair of dirty hands, there a pair of dirty hands. They are cultivators of the soil. They grow crops by pattern, by acre, by foresight, by habit. What corn is to one, wheat is to the other, and though to some eyes the similarities outweigh the differences it would be as unthinkable for the second to commence planting corn as for the first to switch over to wheat. What happens in the gully between them is no concern of theirs, they say, so long as the plough stays out, the weeds stay in the ditch where they belong, though anyone would notice the wind-sewn cornstalks poking up their shaggy ears like young lovers run off into the bushes, and the kinship of these wild grasses with those the farmer cultivates is too obvious to mention, sage and dun-colored stalks hanging their noble heads, hoarding exotic burrs and seeds, and yet it is neither corn nor wheat that truly flourishes there, nor some jackalopian hybrid of the two. What grows in that place is possessed of a beauty all its own, ramshackle and unexpected, even in winter, when the wind hangs icicles from the skeletons of briars and small tracks cross the snow in search of forgotten grain; in the spring the little trickle of water swells to welcome frogs and minnows, a muskrat, a family of turtles, nesting doves in the verdant grass; in summer it is a thoroughfare for raccoons and opossums, field mice, swallows and black birds, migrating egrets, a passing fox; in autumn the geese avoid its abundance, seeking out windrows of toppled stalks, fatter grain more quickly discerned, more easily digested. Of those that travel the local road, few pay that fertile hollow any mind, even those with an eye for what blossoms, vetch and timothy, early forsythia, the fatted calf in the fallow field, the rabbit running for cover, the hawk's descent from the lightning-struck tree. You've passed this way yourself many times, and can tell me, if you would, do the formal fields end where the valley begins, or does everything that surrounds us emerge from its embrace?

This poem definitely reminds us that prose poems don't have to be limited by length! The title of the poem clues us in to the fact that this poem is going to describe what happens in a prose poem, but then Mc-Grath undermines our expectations by describing a farm landscape. The opening sentence calls the subject of the poem "it," though, leaves the antecedent open for us to decide whether "it" refers to a prose poem or a corn field. So when McGrath creates an image of bordering fields, the broken-down fence between the corn field and the wheat field also represents the way that sentences work in a prose poem. When McGrath asks us, "do the formal fields end where the valley begins," he's also asking us a question about distinctions between forms of poetry.

You might have noticed that all three of these poets have described landscapes to which none of them have traveled. Hume has invented a landscape to absorb her narrator's blame, while Blanco's city has yet to be built and McGrath's cornfields could be Anywhere, USA. Even though the poets have never visited these places, they have all used their imaginations to mold landscapes that help them tell the stories that they want to tell. So let's follow in their footsteps and do the same thing.

Think up some places that you've never been. These places can be as ordinary as "a basement" or "a beach in Florida," or as wacky as "the bottom of the ocean" or "between the stacks of chlorophyll inside the cell of a dogwood leaf." Let your imagination run wild. Use that place as a starting point for your own prose poem. As you write, have something else in mind in addition to your imagined place. As you write about the place, are you also thinking about another person who is questioning or bothering you, or a person you are close to? Or, as you write about your imagined place, are you borrowing a form such as a city code, swimming pool rules, a recipe, or test-taking instructions, etc.? Do you also have something else in mind such as human happiness, the recent weather, or famine? Or, as you write about your imagined place, is it a metaphor for something else like a prose poem, the solar system, or instructions for how to sleep? Choose an imagined place you haven't been to. Choose something else to have in mind. Finally, choose a strategy. Then take about twenty minutes and write a prose poem.

FLASH FICTION AND NONFICTION ABOUT REAL PLACES

Now that we've looked at some prose poems where the place is the star, let's turn to some prose. For this exercise, we'll be looking at some flash nonfiction, or true flash fiction, and the way some authors write short shorts about the places they know and love.

Sometimes a place can be so key to a story that it's practically a character all by itself. In "In Nebraska," a short short, Ted Kooser writes:

> This prairie is polished by clouds, damp wads of fabric torn from the hem of the mountains, but every scratch shows, from the ruts the wagons made in the 1850s, to the line on an auctioneer's forehead when he takes off his hat. No grass, not even six-foot bluestem, can cover the weather's hard wear on these stretches of light or these people. But though this is a country shaped by storm—a cedar board planed smooth with the red shavings curled in the west when the sun sets—everywhere you see the work of hands, that patina which comes from having been weighted in the fingers and smoothed with a thumb . . .

In "Fury and Grace," Pattiann Rogers writes about a creek from her childhood and how the creek defines who she is as a person:

> Once we went in the rain to see Shoal Creek mad and powerful, high over its banks, its white froth climbing and fighting against the thick poplars marking its old boundaries. It rolled and thrashed over its single-lane bridge. We were consigned to viewing the flooding from one side, many cars lined up before the impassable crossing. People in raincoats and boots stood outside their cars watching in amazement, proclaiming in low voices, with reverence and respect, as if Shoal Creek were justified in this show of frightening rebellion. . . . The being and cadence of Shoal Creek is part of who I am, defining both fury and grace, influencing the pace of my passions, shaping the undercurrent of my sleep, resonant always in the waking motion and music of my language and my thought.

Kooser and Rogers both write about their homes in really short passages, including only those details that really make a place come alive. Where is your hometown? What are the parts of it that really define it? How is it different from other towns? How do you feel about your hometown?

What would you do if your hometown was still your hometown but was located somewhere else, maybe not even on Earth? What would it look like? How would it be different? The same? How does that change the way you feel about it?

Try to imagine this hometown in a totally weird place. Here are some ideas to get you started, and some room for your own ideas:

1. On the moon
2. On Mars
3. At the base of a volcano
4. In a rainforest
5. In a desert
6. _____
7. _____
8. _____
9. _____
10. _____

Now write a short short about your hometown. You can imagine it in its regular place, or you can imagine your town transplanted to a new, unexpected place. Your choice. You can do a description (like Kooser), a story about how this place defines who you are (like Rogers), or make up your own short short in any way that interests you.

If you like these prompts, here's another: use an actual image—a photograph, map, etc.—of your hometown as a jumping-off point to write a landscape-based prose poem or flash fiction.

Zero to Hero!

A Superhero of Uncommon Valor

Megan Paonessa and Danilo Thomas

Construct a superhero unlike any the world has ever seen.

WE WILL CONSTRUCT A SUPERHERO. Be prepared to understand its psyche, its anxieties, neuroses, agonies, and fears, and to be able to guide your hero into battle. Your ideas about writing, your notions of valor, and the very world as you know it will become strange and alien—lost among the stars.

We all want to be heroes. Admit it. Some part of you wants to fly, to save the day, to be in the world spotlight for deterring the malicious and sadistic plot of a supervillain, the earthquake's wrath, or the rage of a wayward leviathan. Some part of you wants to have a secret identity to fall back on when the day is over, knowing that the world is safe because you have done a job that relies on your selflessness, your humanitarian will to dispense good, your . . . who am I kidding? You want to be a superhero because superheroes are powerful, plain and simple, but the awesomeness of heroes presents a problem: everyone wants to be one. Heroes are everywhere. In movies, magazines, comics, and television programs. We see the same heroes in different guises with the same old purposes and powers. The goal of this exercise is to make a hero unlike any the world has ever known. Your job will be to save us from a flood of stereotypes shrouding superheroes in clichéd ideas and easy observations.

STEP ONE: KNOW YOUR ENEMY
The best way to eliminate your competition is to know its faults. Superheroes have become generic. Think of some popular superheroes today: Batman, Superman, Spider-Man. If you analyze these characters, their similarities are obvious. Let's get started by making a few lists.

- What are their common powers?
  1. Strength

2. Speed

3. Endurance

4. _____

5. _____

6. _____

- What are their motives?

  1. Fight for the good of humankind.

  2. Fight for the good of humankind.

  3. Fight for the good of humankind.

Okay, I guess that is what makes them heroes, but what else do these characters, and other famous superheroes have in common? Once you have formed a couple of lists you are well on your way to what you *do not* want your hero to be. The hero you are creating should not be like any hero you have ever heard of before.

STEP TWO: KNOW YOURSELF

Your turn to create. Using your list of clichéd heroic attributes, swing into creating your own characters.

- In what ways can we construct a character different from a normal superhero?

  1. She is ugly. She is old.

  2. Her power is bagging groceries extremely slowly.

  3. She makes the world a better place by letting people slow down their daily pace.

  4. She is from Pierre, South Dakota, and currently lives in Wrigleyville, Chicago.

Now make a list for one super character:

1. What does your character look like?

   _____

   _____

   _____

2. What strange power, or lack of power, does your character wield?

   _____

3. What does your character do? Why does your character do it?

4. Where is your character from?

STEP THREE: EXPLOIT EACH OTHER'S WEAKNESSES

After you have created a couple of characters using the lists above, the fun really begins. Nothing helps you expose possible weaknesses in your characters like opposition will.

For instance, what would happen if Mrs. Slugsworth, that lethargic and laborious lady, was suddenly face-to-face with Hugo Hurryemup, the fastest man alive, driven by a business agenda without time to stop and smell the roses or appreciate the finer aspects of the grocery clerk's surroundings?

Would Mrs. Slugsworth's slow bagging be enough to stop Hugo Hurryemup, or would his feet of fire make Mrs. Slugsworth speed up?

What would she be stopping Hugo from doing? Why are they enemies?

What would be the impact on their surroundings (in this case a grocery store full of people) with the opposition of these two characters' wills?

Now, take one of the characters you created and have them face either Hugo or Mrs. Slugsworth.

What is your character doing in the grocery store?

What are they going to say to the characters?

How will they foil their plots or aid them?

Write for ten minutes and see where you go. Then keep going.

World Domination

Planets, Species, Disasters

Megan Paonessa and Danilo Thomas

Guide your superhero into battle on a strange and unheard-of planet.

Y OU ARE ABOUT TO DREAM up a world so strange and unheard of that not even your superheroes would know what to do.

Below is a list of planet descriptions. Pick one. Or don't—make up your own if you prefer! Each description contains entertaining and widely disparate planet identities, all of which need to be built upon. Use them as a starting point. Take them to new extremes.

Planet 1: Your planet is a gaseous giant with a piece of land at its center no larger than the size of the room you are sitting in. The species living here exist in a world of poisonous clouds. The planet has twenty-four moons. The planet is so far from its source of light—the sun or another star perhaps—that it is almost always in total darkness or a dim, dawn-like light.

Planet 2: Your planet is very small, the size of a tennis ball. It probably wouldn't be considered a planet at all, except for the fact that it has life on it. The planet has an erratic orbit around the sun—or another star perhaps?—so that there are months where the planet is extremely hot and other weeks where it is freezing cold. Your planet has months of "summer" when the sun never sets, and months of "winter" when the sun never rises.

Planet 3: Your planet is made of liquid. There is no land, anywhere. It orbits a star very similar to the way Earth orbits the sun, but the star it orbits is much, much larger than the sun. The deeper toward the center of this planet you go, the more vegetation you will find. Your planet has two moons that travel extremely close to the planet. One is a desert, the other a jungle.

Planet 4: Your planet is a fiery furnace of volcanic action! Traveling so close to the sun—or another star perhaps?—your planet is in constant daylight. Volcanic explosions erupt on a regular basis and fires are a commonplace sight along the horizon. Your planet has one moon, and it rotates directly in the shadow of your planet so that sunlight never reaches it. Where the planet is hot and hectic, the moon is cool and calm.

Planet 5: Your planet is . . .

_____

_____

_____

_____

Now visualize your planet. You are a scientist, an explorer, an adventurer entering your planet's atmosphere for the first time. Make a list. Jot down everything you see, every idea that floats through your mind. Fill in the blanks below:

- What is the landscape like? Are there mountains or valleys, lakes or oceans, forests or jungles? Or something else entirely?

_____

_____

_____

- Get more specific. What's strange about the hillsides? Are there caves? What's different about the water? Can you swim there? What other odd features of the landscape do you notice?

_____

_____

_____

- What is the name of the planet?

_____

Now think about who lives here. Let's take a look at how one author describes people from another world. Here is an excerpt from Jonathan Swift's novel *Gulliver's Travels*:

Although I intend to leave the description of this empire to a particular treatise, yet in the mean time, I am content to gratify the curious reader with some general ideas. As the common size of the natives is somewhat under six inches high, so there is an exact proportion in all

other animals, as well as plants and trees: for instance, the tallest horses
and oxen are between four and five inches in height, the sheep an inch
and half, more or less; their geese about the bigness of a sparrow, and so
the several gradations downwards till you come to the smallest, which to
my sight, were almost invisible; but nature has adapted the eyes of the
Lilliputians to all objects proper for their view: they see with great exact-
ness, but at no great distance. And, to show the sharpness of their sight
towards objects that are near, I have been much pleased with observ-
ing a cook pulling a lark, which was not so large as a common fly; and a
young girl threading an invisible needle with invisible silk. Their tallest
trees are about seven feet high: I mean some of those in the great royal
park, the tops whereof I could but just reach with my fist clenched. The
other vegetables are in the same proportion; but this I leave to the read-
er's imagination.

Soon after this description, Swift follows up with a strange ritual the
Lilliputian species practices. While you read the section, think about what
traditions, ceremonies, habits or customs your characters might have.

They bury their dead with their heads directly downward, because
they hold an opinion, that in eleven thousand moons they are all to rise
again, in which period the earth (which they conceive to be flat) will
turn upside down, and by this means they shall, at their resurrection, be
found ready standing on their feet. The learned among them confess the
absurdity of this doctrine; but the practice still continues, in compliance
to the vulgar.

As you see from this example, the species living on your planet are
more than stock monsters or aliens; they have customs and beliefs, in-
telligence and playfulness, and religions even! These "people" have fam-
ilies, and they have different ways of doing everyday activities. Let's take
another look at your listing. Add more insights. Think about the follow-
ing questions:

- You've named the planet, but what about the people? What will you call
  them?

- What do they look like physically?

_____

_____

_____

- Where do they sleep? For how long and at what time of day?

_____

_____

_____

- How do they eat and drink?

_____

_____

_____

- How do they move from one place to another, or do they?

_____

_____

_____

- How does the species communicate?

_____

_____

_____

- Does the species have any other unusual marks on their bodies?

_____

_____

_____

- Does the species have any rituals they perform?

_____

_____

_____

- How do they spend their time?

_____

_____

_____

- What else?

_____

_____

_____

Alright. Now let's throw a wrench into the whole process. As you know, natural disasters can happen anywhere—including outer space. After thinking so much about the environment on your planet, you should be great at coming up with fantastic disastrous ideas. Don't let clichés get in the way. Think of some off-the-wall phenomena.

NOT CREATIVE ENOUGH!	THIS IS MORE LIKE IT!
Tornadoes	Geese migrate to the planet, multiplying by the thousands, coating everything with poop!
Earthquakes	A volcano erupts and out pours millions of tons of fish, flapping and slapping back and forth.

List more fantastic disasters:

_____

_____

_____

_____

_____

Once you've collected a good number of ideas, it's time to get the writing started. What will happen to this planet and how will the species survive? Pick a disaster and write it at the top of the page. You know your planet. You know your species. Now tell us how they deal with a disaster the world has never seen before! Write about the disaster, the species, and the planet. Let all these details intermix. You can have multiple scenes and flashbacks, and you can focus on a particular spot on the planet, for example. Write for a full twenty minutes without picking up your pen to think. Come up for air. Read over what you've started and take as much time as you need to finish up, rewrite, and get the story to read the way you want it to.

Demystifying the Publishing Process

Rachel Adams, A. B. Gorham, and Lisa Tallin

The sooner, the better: this applies to eating ice cream under the sun, finishing your history homework, and publishing your poems and stories. Here are a few hints on ways to publish your work.

Dear Emily Dickinson,

The sooner, the better: this applies to eating ice cream under the sun, finishing your history homework, and especially, to publishing your poems and stories. You write the goods and we will give you a few hints on ways to publish your work. Do you have a plethora of unpublished pieces hiding under your bed? We think the world needs to hear your voice.

The publishing process can be scary, being that others will read your weirdest, most imaginative thoughts, but we are here to demystify this for you. Let's talk about how to get your work published online and in print journals. There are literary journals and contests that are just right for your unique style. We will help you find the right ones and show you how to prepare your cover letter.

Second, we understand that you are an avid reader of Ralph Waldo Emerson. Wouldn't you like to interact with his and other author's published works, deconstructing theirs and constructing your own creative pieces? The published word isn't impenetrable—it's language, it's as permeable as the written word.

Let's get started. You need to get your work out there!

Search the Internet for online journals and contests that you can submit to. There are more than you might think! Check out the style of the magazine and other work that they have published to see if your genre and writing style match theirs. There are journals focused just on poetry or fiction. Some journals only publish science fiction or flash fiction.

Websites to Help Writers Get Published And Become Part of the Literary World

Organizations

Association of Writers and Writing Programs (AWP)

Each year a different city in the United States gets to host the annual

AWP conference, which is a sight to see. People come to talk about writing ideas, movements, book deals, publicity, and more, and that's just the tip of the AWP iceberg. Even if you can't make it one year, there are plenty of resources available online for you to investigate. https://www. awpwriter.org

AWP has a database of more than eight hundred writing programs (both graduate and undergraduate), allowing you to search by type, genre, location, and level of study. Their search criteria can be tailored to your artistic, financial, professional, and personal needs. AWP's services also include a directory of more than five hundred conferences and centers around the globe, from the Bahamas to Thailand to the Czech Republic. You can apply for funding to get to these places, too: AWP offers two five-hundred-dollar scholarships each year to emerging writers who need help with their travel budget. The winners (along with four finalists) get a one-year membership in AWP to boot. AWP also offers services such as career advice, video resources, and a job list.

New Pages (NP)

Regarding writing and publishing, just about everything under the sun resides here. Contests? They update their information every Thursday. Reviews? NP gives you the lowdown on hundreds of journals so you know whose aesthetic matches yours. Creative writing programs? There are links and analyses of every MA/MFA in creative writing program you can think of—it's all here just for you. New Pages also has a great section (under "Guides and Features") that specifically targets young writers. Many of the listed publications only accept writing from people at/ below grade twelve or under eighteen years of age. New Pages is a popular national organization, so they know what they're talking about. http:// www.newpages.com

Poets & Writers (P&W)

Similar to New Pages, Poets & Writers offers a database of national literary journals. There's also a little more information available here regarding genre, reading periods, paper/electronic submissions, etc. You can also narrow your search list to specific subgenres of writing. Aside from journal searching, P&W publishes a magazine six times a year that features what's new in the literary/publishing world, publishes daily news on its website, and has a database of grants/awards available across the country, not to mention conferences and residencies. http://www.pw.org

PEN America

Since 1921, PEN has been devoted not only to advancing the literary arts, but to defending those writers and artists whose rights are infringed through censorship, abuse, or imprisonment. The center views freedom of expression as a human right and advocates for this ideal both domestically and internationally. In addition to these projects, PEN also facilitates community outreach workshops and offers literary fellowships. https://pen.org/

National Endowment for the Arts (NEA)

Support for the arts isn't all privatized either; Congress established the NEA in 1965 to encourage artistic merit and innovation, working with local, state, and federal agencies, as well as philanthropists to make sure that grants are available for both organizations and individual artists. These grants range from $10,000 to $100,000, which isn't bad for government help. In addition, the NEA publishes a number of reports that study how Americans consume and respond to art across all demographics. http://arts.gov

Submittable

This is *the* resource for writers and literary journals. If you don't have an account with Submittable, you should get one right now. Stop reading this and go sign up (it's free!). It makes the chore of juggling multiple submissions easy, and hundreds upon hundreds of national journals use it to manage the work people send. This is the most essential link on this list.

After you create an account, you'll see under your name on the top right your staff account (if you work for a journal) or your user account (if you're a writer). Clicking on "My Submissions" will show you what you have out in the ether and what its current status is. If you don't have anything there, go to your favorite lit journal that uses this service and click the submit button; you'll be prompted for your Submittable account information (and likely confirm your address), and the rest is a piece of cake. You can affix a standard or personalized cover letter, and you'll receive an email notification once a decision has been made on your piece. Afterward, Submittable will keep a record of who accepted/declined what and when, so you don't have to worry about crossed wires or poems. Welcome to easy street. http://www.submittable.com/

Specifically for Young Writers

The Alliance for Young Artists and Writers (AYAW)

The AYAW also targets new writers, and they have been around for over ninety years! If you take a moment to read through their About Us page, you can see that they have recognized people who today are widely renowned writers, actors, and other artists. One such person was Sylvia Plath. http://www.artandwriting.org

RESOURCES FOR CREATIVE WRITING TEACHERS

Teachers and Writers Collaborative (T&W)

T&W knows that literary appreciation comes from the ground up, and it has the goal of working with teachers to foster in their students a passion for not just consuming good writing, but generating it, too. T&W coordinates with schools to teach creative writing to kids and to facilitate pedagogical workshops for staff. They publish books as well as an award-winning magazine, sponsor the Bechtel Prize, and offer a variety of online resources (including state-by-state contact information for local centers that are dedicated to supporting the arts). http://www.twc.org

826 National

As a nonprofit organization, 826 National offers free programming for students through its eight centers located in major cities across the country. There is after-school tutoring (in any subject) available at least four days a week for students, and the centers host field trips for schools (offering a number of writing workshops) and guide new writers with the Young Authors' Book Project. Are you and your class unable to travel to a center? Not to fear: 826 National happily sends volunteers to local schools to assist with in-school publications, individual assignments, and more. http://826national.org

COVER LETTERS

Once you have picked out a journal or contest and you have your prose or poem typed and edited to your satisfaction, you will need to write a cover letter.

1. The cover letter should *always* include all of your contact information: name, address, phone number, email, and the date of the submission.
2. You should address the cover letter to *the person(s) indicated by the magazine in its submission guidelines.*
3. There are a few things you need to provide in your cover letter:
   - The number of short pieces you are (poetry or prose) submitting

(include their titles—this is helpful for tracking purposes) or the title of a single, longer prose piece. You can include the titles in the body of the letter or at the bottom beneath your signature.

- A short biographical statement. The bio should be kept relatively short and you can include where you live.
- If you have previous publications, you can list a few of the magazines your work has appeared in or is forthcoming from.
- Some contests and literary journals will ask you to mail in your work. Remember to include a SASE (self-addressed, stamped envelope) if this is the case.

These days, most contests and journals ask you to submit your work electronically. Follow the instructions on each website. Some journals or contests might ask you to set up an account with Submittable (see above) or they might have their own submission manager.

It is considered good practice to send in a cover letter with your work. If you are sending in work by post, include your contact information. If you send in work electronically, you may not need to do this. Make sure to carefully read each journal or contest's website.

Here is a sample cover letter from a high-school writer. Try to keep it to half a page.

Tawanna Prose
Hillcrest High School
Tuscaloosa, AL 35401
(555) 555–1234
fictionwriter@email.com

September 2, 2025

Fiction Editors
Prickly Pear High School Writing Contest
pricklypearcontest@email.com

Dear Fiction Editors:
I have included the following story for your consideration: "What I Learned in Study Hall."
I live in Tuscaloosa, where I am a senior at Hillcrest High School. The University of Alabama has published my stories twice in the Creative Writing Club Anthology.

I have included a SASE for your response. Please recycle any unused por-
tions of the manuscript. Thank you for your time and consideration.
Sincerely,
Tawanna Prose

And here is a sample cover letter from a college writer who is submit-
ting to an online journal.

Dear Poetry Editors,
Here are two poems for your consideration: "Why I Cry" and "Shimmy on
Down the Line." I hope they will find a home in your journal.
I am currently an MFA student at the University of Alabama. My poems
have previously appeared in Black Warrior Review, Colorado Review, and
Ninth Letter.
Many thanks for considering my submission.
Best,
Leon Trotsky

If you have never had anything published, you can always say: "If my
work is accepted, this will be my first publication."

Here is a sample letter for anyone submitting to a literary journal:

Dear Black Warrior Review Fiction Editor,
I would like to submit my 3,440-word short story "Harlem Days" for your
consideration.
My poem "Outside Dulahi" is forthcoming from Apologetic Press in 2015.
My short story "Measurements" is forthcoming from First Look Review in
Winter 2014. I earned my M.F.A. in fiction from Warthogs University.
My writing is obsessed with ancient culture and the advent of technology.
This is a simultaneous submission. All my thanks in advance for your
time and for the great work you do on behalf of literary fiction.
Sincerely,
R. Winters
rwintersprofessionalemailaddress@email.com
(555) 555-2312

OTHER ADVICE

Now, I did mention some bad news, but don't worry, it's really not that
big of a deal the more you think about it. Writers (young and old) get

rejected. *A lot.* A single writer will probably accumulate hundreds upon hundreds of rejections over the course of a life. But here's the good news buried in the bad: *This in absolutely no way means you aren't a great writer.* Even writing professors have inboxes brimming with rejection slips they have received over the years. Editors of journals read anywhere from hundreds to thousands of submissions each year, and stuff gets rejected for any number of reasons that don't have anything to do with quality: the piece doesn't fit the journal's aesthetic, it doesn't get passed up the editorial chain because of one reader's subjective opinion, the editor has read a hundred poems that day already and their mind has gone numb to anything made of words, etc. *Moral of the story*: Don't lose hope! Keep sending stuff out—even famous writers who have been published dozens of times before still get rejections.

Other words of wisdom: know your audience. You'll hear this time and time again, but it is very important to do a little research before submitting to a particular journal so that you're familiar with its style and what kind of work it publishes. You can write the best, most gut-wrenching, awe-inspiring poem ever, but if the journal primarily publishes gothic horror fiction, you may get rejected right off the bat. Research well!

So, Emily, we hope this discussion has been edifying and that we will soon be seeing your name in tables of contents all over the literary world. While you are waiting to hear back from those journals and contests, create new material for your awaiting fan base.

Remember, Emily, that in order to participate in the literary community, you will want to be a reader of many journals and books. Subscribe to journals, and read them online, in print, or at a library. Be a part of the big literary conversation.

Good luck, ED, the world awaits you.

Yours,

Us

CONTRIBUTORS

Kristin Aardsma

Rachel Adams

Jessie Bailey

Katie Berger

Holly Burdorff

Ashley Chambers

Tasha Coryell

Alex Czaja

Jesse Delong

Zachary Doss

Kit Emslie

Romy Feder

Pia Simone Garber

Freya Gibbon

Molly Goldman

Krystin Gollihue

A. B. Gorham

Chapin Gray

Jenny Gropp

Annie Hartnett

Stephen Hess

Greg Houser

Jess E. Jelsma

Matt Jones

Kirsten Jorgenson

Sarah Kelly

Laura Kochman

Kenny Kruse

Breanne LeJeune

Christopher McCarter

Meredith Noseworthy

Brian Oliu

Megan Paonessa

Luke Percy

Kirk Pinho

Steve Reaugh

Sally Rodgers

Curtis Rutherford

Betsy Seymour

Jill Smith

Maggie Smith

Emma Sovich

Bethany Startin

Lisa Tallin

Danilo Thomas

Stephen Thomas

Jessica Trull

Brandi Wells

Leia Wilson

Theodora Ziolkowski

LITERARY SOURCES